HOUNDING THE MOON

Irene Radford

Writing as

P.R. Frost

Book View Café
304 S. Jones Blvd. Ste #2906
Las Vegas, Nevada 89107

Table of Contents

Raves for *Hounding the Moon:*

"Readers who crave the fantasy equivalent of a summer movie will welcome Frost's debut, which introduces Tess Noncoiré."—*Publishers Weekly.*

"Frost's fantasy debut series introduces a charming protagonist, both strong and vulnerable, and her cheeky companion. An intriguing plot and a well-developed warrior sisterhood make this a good choice for fans of the urban fantasy of Tanya Huff, Jim Butcher, and Charles deLint."—*Library Journal.*

"Featuring a courageous, witty, and downright endearing female protagonist reminiscent of Laurel1 K. Hamilton's Anita Blake and Charlaine Harris's Sookie Stackhouse, this is a fast-paced supernatural-powered thriller that blends Native American mythology, paranormal romance, and dark fantasy with the oftentimes wildly eccentric culture of science fiction/fantasy fandom."—*The Barnes & Noble Review.*

"This is a fun, fannish romp full of sarcastic quips and supernatural action."—*Locus*

Copyrights & Credits

Book View Café
304 S. Jones Blvd. Ste #2906
Las Vegas, Nevada 89107

Dedication

*To my agent
Carol McCleary of the Wilshire Literary Agency,
and to my editor
Sheila Gilbert of DAW Books,
both of whom I cherish.*

Acknowledgments

Many thanks to Maya Kaathryn Bohnhoff and Jeff Bohnhoff for their awesome music and hilarious filk. They have inspired many wonderful images and gracefully gave permission to use *There's a Bimbo on the Cover of my Book* in the final scene.

My thanks also to Lea Day, Deborah Dixon, Bob Brown, and Maya Bohnhoff for their patient reading and wonderful suggestions as well as pointing out my flaws to make this a better book. Appreciation also to the joysofresearch@yahoogroups.com and SF-FFWs@yahoogroups.com for keeping me going when I stalled. Any errors are mine not theirs.

Prologue

"What yous think yous doin' here, imp?" the head Kajiri Sasquatch demanded. Three of his comrades bore down on me with fangs bared and paws clenched to hammer me back into my own dimension. Two brown and one red. All of them ugly as a twenty-year drought and twice as mean.

"Just passing through," I quipped, keeping my eyes on those sledgehammer fists. Rapid transit for imps requires popping into the guarded chat room, the entryway to all the portals to all the dimensions.

I edged around the vast expanse of whiteness, keeping my back to the barriers and the myriad doors that opened up from here. Each door led to another dimension. All of them warmer and more comfortable than my own. But I had other reasons for trying to escape my home. First I had to get by the Sasquatch—dedicated and loyal, they made excellent sentries.

You'd think I could pick a better day when something smaller and less excitable than a Sasquatch had guard duty. And Kajiri are the worst of any species: half-breeds out to prove themselves better than both species that spawned them.

The lead guard had more smarts than his three cohorts combined. He (very obviously and blatantly male) turned his big black body to keep me in sight. He couldn't swivel his neck, so he had to move his entire skeleton. His buddies, one of them female with pendulous breasts covered in matted red fur, took a few seconds, that felt like minutes, to figure out that I had moved.

I fluttered my little wings as if I expected them to support me in flight. Fat chance of that. My wings are as stunted as the rest of me. My bat-wing ears might do a better job, come to think of it.

Big Black lunged for me. I hopped to the left. He sprawled on the stone floor with a roar.

The three dimwits finally turned in the right direction. I feinted into a fairyland filled with inviting floral perfumes and pretty little beings who giggled a lot.

Big Red reached for me with a fist the size of a turkey platter. She was faster than I expected. My tail crimped in her grip.

"Yeaow! That hurts, lady," I protested, trying to yank my appendage free.

"No imps in fairyland," Big Black said.

Red hauled me out of the fairyland doorway and flung me against the portal back to impland. The freezing temperature of home nearly burned my belly and my nose when I thumped against the doorway. Mum had firmly closed it against me.

Blood oozed out of my nose and from scrapes on my tail. I groaned. If my wings had been big enough to support me, I could have eased my landing. Not a proper imp at all. Not even any warts to make me cute.

"Need some help opening the door, imp?" Big Black lumbered over.

"Jus aw 'ittle," I said, trying to breathe through my mouth and talk at the same time.

"You talk funny for an imp," Big Red said, arms akimbo.

"Ya' boke my nothse."

"Well, that's what you get for trying to sneak out of your home dimension, imp. No trespassing. That's what we're here for, to keep unauthorized personnel from moving between dimensions." Big Black pronounced each word carefully as if he'd memorized his mission statement.

"I can see that."

"When we've served enough guard time, we'll get twenty hours' home time in the dimension of our choice."

"And if you believe that, I've got some sunshine in the rain clouds of Oregonia I can sell you." Duping demons into doing guard duty is the primary entertainment of the powers that be in most dimensions. Fulfilling the promised free time never happens. Can't have demons roaming freely. Have to keep them in their ghettos so they don't contaminate the rest of the universe.

No being in their right mind would let a bloodthirsty demon run free. We keep them in the worst corners of the bleakest dimension for a reason. Like maybe they'll die off.

Big Black bent down to pull aside the leather flap that marked the portal to impland.

I darted between his legs and slid through the nearest doorway, right into Earth, the land of humans. This time I kept my tail tucked between my legs so Red couldn't grab it.

I just hoped they wouldn't track the trail of blood I left behind. Or, worse, let Mum know where I'd gone.

My day had begun just as weird as it ended.

"Out!" Mum had screamed at me for the umpteenth time that day. That week. That decade. "Look at you. Fully two hundred years old and no bigger than a twenty-year-old. You're just a scrap of an imp and will never amount to anything."

Hence my name. Scrap. She'd named me something else at birth, but no one remembered what it was. Likely she'd recycled the name to one of my one hundred two siblings. Most of them still lived, much to my torment and dismay.

Her tirade went on for a few hours as she swatted me with her broom. She only uses her broom to discipline her multitude of offspring, never to clean anything. Not my mum. She's a proper imp who likes living in a refuse heap.

I hopped ahead of her from couch to corner to dining table. But finally she managed to herd me out the door. All the while my siblings laughed hilariously at me.

Of course, if I'd had enough of a wingspan to properly fly, I might have eluded her. But then, if I had a proper wingspan, she wouldn't be kicking me out of the old garbage dump—I mean homestead. The fact that it was a dimensional garbage dump piled high with the detritus of a dozen different realms doesn't mean I need to insult Mum's cozy home.

I kind of liked growing up playing amid broken refrigerators, some skeletons dragons had discarded, and a few hidden demon artifacts. I spent many happy hours every day arranging them in some kind of order. Only my sibs took equal delight in messing things up again.

Most imps can't abide tidiness.

"We only have respectable imps in my family. All a proper size, of course! Fit warrior companions by their first century," dear old Mum called after me. Her angry skin, nicely blotched with warts, shifted

from normal gray green to an ominous vermilion. In a minute she'd transform into something ugly.

Uh-oh, I was in real trouble now. I tried to hide by going transparent. But I can't do that in my own dimension, and Mum can always find one of her one hundred three offspring, no matter what color or shape they are. Just so long as they live, she can find them.

So that left me out in the cold and having to make my own way across the dimensions. When I say cold, I mean cold. When-hell-freezes-over cold. Nothing-ever-decays-here-so-let's-dump-anything-that-might-prove-useful-later cold. Hence impland is also the garbage dump of the universe.

We got stuck there because the same internal combustion engine that allows us to change color at will also generates heat.

We can generate enough body heat to cultivate vast quantities of mold in our otherwise cold and damp home. Mum cultivates it. I eat it, cleaning her walls on a regular basis. Mold is quite a delicacy. My family eats it because they have to. Fuel for their bodies, you know. Not a lot of energy left over to go out across the dimensions and find ourselves a warrior to meld with. So a lot of us get kind of trapped there.

Not me. Free from Mum's tyranny so I didn't have to obey the rule that says you have to be at least four feet tall and have a wingspan twice as wide before you can survive a portal transfer, I took off for parts unknown.

That's when I first saw Tess. Teresa Noncoiré to those who haven't met her. She's absolutely gorgeous, and strong, and intelligent, and all the things a heroine is supposed to be.

But that's now. And she still doesn't know this about herself.

She was dissolving into a puddle of tears, forty pounds overweight, and wearing her emotions on her sleeve the first time I saw her. In the Pacific Northwest where they grow great mold.

And I couldn't do anything to help her. She hadn't been infected with the imp virus yet. I wasn't big enough to transmit the disease to her.

But I knew in that first moment, as she walked away from her husband's wake, held in a rustic bar in a timber town on a mountain, that I loved her. I knew in that instant that she was going to make a formidable Warrior of the Celestial Blade. She was going to kick some demon ass and knock the uppity Sisterhoods on their ignoble butts.

But that's a long story. Let's cut to the chase. She managed to stumble into the infection, survived it, and emerged . . . well, she and I both emerged.

Outcasts.

Not exactly ready to confront anything the dimensions could throw at us. But we were stuck together like glue.

That's when life started to get interesting.

Chapter 1

Bats do not tangle in people's hair; if they can locate a mosquito to eat in a dark night, they can certainly avoid human heads.

"I miss you so much, Dilly, my teeth ache," I cried. "I miss you so much I can't believe in anything but my memories of you."

I traced the letters on the tombstone.

DILLWYN BAILEY COOPER
REST IN PEACE
BELOVED SON AND FRIEND

And the dates of his life, cut short two years ago.

He had been so much more than just a friend to me. I choked back a sob. Dill's parents, two more D. B. Coopers, hadn't allowed me to put the precious word "Husband" on the grave marker. We hadn't been married long enough for that, they said.

When I had control of my voice again, I said aloud, "Dill, I'm sorry I couldn't visit you sooner. I got sort of lost. You are probably the only person I know who would believe my tale. It's more unbelievable than the stuff I write. I got very sick. Then a Sisterhood adopted me and nursed me back to health—not a convent as we know it, more a sorority of warriors. We battle . . .

"Come to think of it, maybe you wouldn't believe my story." The fantasy fiction in my novels was more believable.

Out of the corner of my eye I spotted movement. An adolescent girl with the dark hair and copper skin of a Native American stooped to pick some flowers on the verge of the cemetery. Queen Anne's lace, chicory, and dandelion blooms filled her hands. One by one she scattered them around the graves.

I smiled at the image of innocence. My grief had no place in her young life. I should have outgrown it by now. But then I *had* gotten sidetracked and never found an opportunity to visit Dill's grave until now. I was still having trouble letting go of the man I loved so intensely.

The girl looked up and smiled back. Then she ambled over and offered me one of the white filigree blooms. "Here. You didn't bring any flowers. You look like you need one."

"Thank you," I choked out. After a moment, when I'd regained control over my voice, I added, "Do you have someone special here?" I couldn't say the word "dead," or "buried." That would make the wound of Dillwyn's absence from my life too raw. Again.

"Not here. Back home on the Colville reservation." She turned and looked wistfully to the north. "I can't give them flowers, so I spread them here, on graves that look lonely."

A moment of comfortable silence passed between us.

"Thank you again for the flower. I'm Tess." I held out my hand to the girl.

She shook my hand with all of the solemnity of an almost adult. "Cynthia. Cynthia Stalking Moon."

"Hey, Cindy!" a boy called from the nearby skate park. "Come show us that twisty thing you do."

"Gotta go." Cynthia waved and ran off to join her friends. She scattered her flowers randomly as she ran.

Nice kid, Scrap said. He reclined against Dill's headstone, a translucent pudgy shape without much definition. Except for his stinking cigar, a black cherry cheroot. He remained his usual tranquil gray.

My imp companion didn't truly live in this dimension. I sometimes wondered if I did. His ubiquitous cigar appeared all too real and noxious. But then tobacco comes from here and now.

Other than Scrap, I had this Alder Hill, Oregon, pioneer cemetery to myself once more. The traffic roaring up Highway 26 toward Mount Hood gave me the sense of privacy and isolation I craved while I mourned Dill.

I heard an indelicate snort from Scrap near my left shoulder, but I ignored it. Scrap liked to perch there. He was so insubstantial I couldn't feel his weight. But I always "sensed" him there.

"Even your weird sense of humor, Dill, can't explain Scrap." I laid the long-stemmed flower at the base of the tombstone. "He's an imp from another dimension. A scrap of an imp. Not fully grown and not fully functional yet. We're supposed to grow together as we work our way up through the ranks of the Sisterhood of the Celestial Blade Warriors. You'd like Scrap. The two of you could trade sarcastic and irreverent comments on life and compete for the most outrageous puns."

Dill had embodied everything I enjoyed in life. He was my hero, cut down in the prime of his life. He had saved my life at the cost of his own.

I chuckled through another closing of my throat. "I told your favorite joke at your funeral, Dill. Your folks disapproved, of course. Afterward, they went back to the house for a formal reception."

I looked up toward the white house with gray stone facing and gray trim that squatted on the hill above the cemetery. No signs of life there. Dill's parents were probably at work in the family furniture store in Gresham, the closest city to Alder Hill.

I continued to tell Dill about his final send-off. "Your friends and I, the ones who truly knew you, retired to a bar after the service. We all lifted a glass in your honor and then we sang all of your favorite filk songs, you know, the parodies full of puns, and recounted every hideous joke you ever told, over and over. We laughed until we cried. That's the only kind of tears you approved of. We left your wake with many fond memories of you. Just the way you wanted us to."

Would I ever be happy again without Dillwyn Bailey Cooper?

One lonely tear dripped down my cheek. I swallowed and swallowed again, trying to force the useless emotion back into its dungeon behind my heart.

"Jokes won't dull the pain and loneliness, Dill."

A whiff of cigar smoke and an itching tingle along my spine jolted me back into reality. Scrap.

Can the waterworks, Tess, dahling. We have work to do.

"Scrap, you know you are not supposed to smoke those foul things where someone might smell them," I snapped at my companion. Bad enough that the gaseous emissions from his lactose intolerance brought dogs sniffing at my heels from miles around. I didn't need the reek of tobacco clinging to my clothes and hair as well.

The imp pulled my hair and jumped off my shoulder. His chubby body with bandy legs, pot belly, vestigial wings, bat-wing ears, (ugh, I hate bats, but that's the only description that fits his huge, jagged ears), and snub nose became almost visible to my sharpened eyesight. His spike tail beat an arrhythmical tattoo against Dill's tombstone. Pale pink replaced his gray skin. He wasn't totally pissed at me.

Trouble is brewing, babe, Scrap informed me in an accent that was part flamboyant interior decorator, part leering cabbie, and all obnoxious sarcasm.

"What kind of trouble? I don't have a lot of time," I replied, checking my watch. "I need most of an hour just to drive the twenty-five miles between here and the city." With air-conditioning in the rental car, thank God . . . or Goddess . . . whoever might be listening.

If anyone listened at all to my prayers.

They hadn't when Dill died.

Later. Scrap jumped back up onto my shoulder.

I heaved myself off the ground, scanning the vicinity for what had alarmed Scrap. All I could hear over the roar of traffic was Cynthia and her friends with their boards at the skate park behind the cemetery.

We've got trouble. Now. Scrap started to turn vermilion. Waves of heat radiated out from him.

I began to sweat through my goose bumps.

This had never happened to us before. I'd almost begun to believe the lost year of my life was just that, lost in a fever dream.

"What and where?" I asked in alarm. The base of my spine tingled in warning. Just like Sister Serena said it would.

The noise from the skate park grew a little louder. The thumps and bangs became shrill screams of fear. I jogged across the cemetery, zigzagging around tombstones.

Right direction, dahling. Wrong speed. Scrap puffed on his cigar like an old steam engine.

I lengthened my stride to a ground-covering lope, hurdling tombstones and other obstacles. Scrap had to tangle his claws in my frizzy hair to stay on board.

He grumbled something that I couldn't quite understand.

The normal squeals of adolescents burning off energy turned to terrified screams.

"Hang on, Scrap." I ran full out, defying three cars to hit me as I crossed the back street at a gallop.

No one seemed to notice the frightened commotion close by.

I skidded onto the green space between a ski rental shop, closed for the season, and an abandoned church, painted white with a steeple and a red front door. Dill had attended Sunday School there as a child. The park sloped steeply downward to a creek. A half-pipe wooden ramp took advantage of the landscape. But no kids flew down the polished wood and up the other side on their boards. They were all huddled beneath the support struts.

Not quite all. Two boys lay sprawled facedown upon the grass. Their arms and legs were twisted at unnatural, broken angles. Blood pooled from mouths and gaping wounds in backs and throats. A third boy tried to crawl toward the protective illusion of the shade beneath the ramp. He collapsed at every third movement. His left arm was a mangled mass of raw meat, torn tendons, and protruding bone.

So much blood! I gagged. The smell brought back memories of the night Dill died. I wanted to run away from here. As far and fast as I could. With or without Scrap.

Cynthia stood in the middle of the carnage. Her screams split the air like nails on a chalkboard. A huge, ugly dog, with jaws big enough to engulf the girl's head, enclosed the fleshy part of her upper arm and tugged.

I could not abandon Cynthia or her friends.

She'd given me a flower because I was as lonely as Dill's grave.

My heart beat double time and my focus narrowed to the dog. The rest of the world seemed to still around me. My assignment, my quest, justified this fight.

No time to call for help. I yanked my cell phone out of my belt pouch and tossed it toward the huddled kids.

"Call 911," I shouted. Then I snapped my fingers. "Scrap, I need a weapon."

Instantly he jumped into my extended palm, elongated, thinned, became more solid. Between one eye blink and the next I grasped a . . .

"A soup ladle!" I screamed. "How am I supposed to fight off that dog with a *soup ladle?*"

I threw away the useless tool and grabbed an abandoned skateboard. With all of the strength in my upper arms I swung at the dog's flank.

I smacked his brindled, fur-covered body with a satisfying whomp and crack of the skateboard.

Dog yelped and released my thoughtful friend.

He turned on me with bared yellow fangs as long as my fingers. His massive head was nearly level with my shoulder. He growled and drooled long ropes of greenish slime.

"At least I got your attention," I said to Dog, gulping back my fear. I had trained for situations like this. But facing the real thing was different in the field than on the training ground.

Sorry. Scrap's face appeared in the metal bowl of the ladle, cigar still clamped in his wide mouth. He stretched again, darkened, became heavier and sharper.

I grabbed the fireplace poker he had become. "Better," I sighed.

The dog, bigger than a wolfhound, meaner than a pit bull, and uglier than a mastiff, bunched his powerful haunches for a lunge.

I met him with a sharp thwap across the nose. I heard something crunch.

He kept on coming.

I let my momentum carry me full circle and out of his direct path as I shifted my grip on the poker.

The dog twisted in midair and landed beside me, grabbing my forearm. His teeth did not break my skin. Insistent but not vicious.

An uppercut to his snout from my poker. Then I brought the weapon down hard on the dog's spine. He yelped and released me.

We stared at each other for several long moments; judging, assessing.

Scrap hissed at the dog from the crosspiece at the tip of the poker.

I blinked.

Scrap blinked.

The dog ran off, downhill into the tangled undergrowth. I heard him splash into the creek.

Then I heard the sirens. One of the kids must have gotten through to 911.

I sank to the ground and stared dumbly at four puncture wounds on my forearm. Top and bottom. Blood and green slime oozed out of them.

I retched. Long painful spasms tried to turn my stomach inside out.

My head threatened to disconnect from my neck. Darkness encroached on my vision.

"I thought you were only a legend. But you are real," a gentle masculine voice with a slight British accent whispered in my ear. His finger traced the crescent scar on my face that ran from left temple to jaw. A scar that Scrap had promised me was not visible in this dimension to anyone other than the Sisterhood of the Celestial Blade Warriors.

Crap!

Who was this guy? He really wasn't supposed to see the scar unless he'd had a touch of the imp flu.

Wish I knew how to research him.

I'm too tired. Transformation takes energy. A quick trip back to my own dimension would restore me. If I survived the trip through the portal. The Sasquatch that guard the portals around here are pretty mean, undisciplined teenagers, all of them. They make Mum look nice.

Maybe a good shot of mold. I wonder if Tess' coffee cup in the car has had time to decay yet.

But Tess is going to need help to see this situation through.

What to do? What to do?

Maybe a cigar will help.

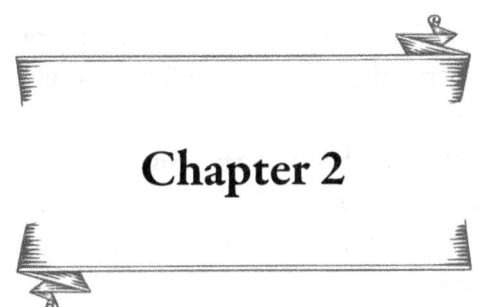

Chapter 2

Adrenaline shot through me. I bounced to my feet, away from the stranger's touch and his all-too-keen gaze. A glance told me that he was gangly, skinny, very blond. He peered at me curiously. His glasses slid down his nose.

I could not allow this stranger to penetrate my secrets.

Every nerve ending in my body came alive in warning.

Then I was off, keeping my back to him.

I had to check on Cynthia. I had to stay away from this stranger.

A paramedic who'd come with the emergency response team sprayed something on Cynthia's upper arm. I did not see any blood.

Between us and the skateboard ramp, two more paramedics worked on the boy with the mangled arm. The scent of blood and vomit and fear drove me away from the primary victims, toward Cynthia.

Two uniformed policemen stood with notebooks open, trying to make sense of what the kids under the ramp said. Their voices still shrilled with hysteria. One of them ran over to return my phone rather than have to find the right words to relate what happened.

Two more cops thrashed through the blackberries toward the creek with weapons drawn. I knew the dog was long gone. The itching tingle at the base of my spine had vanished.

But the stranger hovered. I could *feel* him staring at me. I almost heard his questions. Questions I dared not answer.

Another contingent of uniforms directed traffic around the park entrance. They did their best to keep curiosity seekers at bay.

I knelt beside Cynthia, murmuring soothing phrases that meant nothing. I wrapped an arm about her thin shoulders, clinging to her for my own comfort as well as hers. I had no idea what had become of Scrap. He probably had his own recovery ritual after transforming. He'd never had to become a weapon for me before.

"I don't understand it." The paramedic shook his head. "The dog's teeth didn't penetrate the skin." He rubbed a damp pad over the girl's arm, cleaning off some of the green drool. His fingers quested from the edge of her red-and-white-striped tank top to her wrist.

I spotted two red dimples that might have been canine tooth marks. Other than a slight irritation, her skin was unbroken.

"Unlike you." The paramedic grabbed my arm and began cleaning it. "I recommend rabies shots for you if we don't find the beast." He paused and stared as my wound began to close as soon as he cleaned it.

"He . . . he was almost gentle with me. Like he was protecting me from the rest of you," Cynthia sobbed. She hiccuped, and turned her huge brown eyes toward me, imploring me to agree with her.

"From my observation, I agree with the girl," the stranger with the clipped accent and drooping glasses said.

Tension built in my nape, rippling downward. Different from the presence of monsters and demons from other dimensions, but still alert to danger. If I'd had a tail as bony and as sharply barbed as Scrap's, I'd beat it against the ground.

I gave him another brief scan. Squarish jaw, limp blond hair, not bad looking, with a nerd's, or a scholar's (there's a difference?) pasty skin. His navy polo shirt and crisply pressed khaki slacks seemed almost a uniform. He scrunched his nose in an attempt to keep his tinted glasses from sliding off. I almost wished he had let them go so I could see his eyes better, read his emotions, maybe even figure out how he could see my scar.

A new man, in shirtsleeves with his tie half undone and a summer-weight sports jacket slung over one shoulder skidded down the embankment.

"And you would be . . . ?" he asked both me and the stranger with the clipped accent. He flipped out a notebook and licked the end of a stubby pencil. I pegged him as a police detective. A reporter would have sponged the coffee stain off the front of his shirt.

The nerdy stranger towered over him by half a head, but probably weighed less. He was downright skinny. I like a little more beef and less length on men.

I tried to melt into the background. How could I explain Scrap? How could I explain the fact that the previously gaping wounds in my arm were already almost closed? The virus that had caused the scar on my face had left enough antibodies in my system to combat anything this world, and several others, could dish out.

That dog had not been a natural creature. Neither was my infection. The itch in and around the puncture wounds told me I wouldn't get away from the encounter totally clean.

Police and paramedics did not like paranormal explanations.

The nerd gave a long name. Guilford van der Hoyden-Smythe. Ph.D. No one gave children such pretentious names. It sounded made up to match the academic degree.

I did my best to fade into the background while giving Cynthia as much support as I could.

If I stopped long enough to give a statement, I'd miss my appointment in Portland. Less than two hours until I needed to be downtown for a book signing at Simpson's, the largest bookstore on the West Coast.

Autumn was at least three weeks behind schedule. It was way too hot for September. The heat beat down on my back and shoulders. Sweat trickled between my breasts and around the waistband of my shorts. A tank top, shorts, and a sports bra seemed almost too many clothes for the climate.

I needed to leave, but I would not abandon Cynthia. We'd connected back in the cemetery. Her flower had lightened my loneliness for just a moment.

An ambulance, a separate company from the first responders roared up, sirens cutting through the rising noise of too many voices, too many questions, not enough answers. Attendants spilled out, grabbed a gurney on collapsible legs, and slid down the steep hill, nearly on their butts. They worked efficiently and gently to lift the injured boy onto the mobile bed. An inflatable cast contraption hid the strips of raw meat, bone, and blood on the arm that might never work properly again. The paramedics had already started an IV drip and fixed an oxygen mask to his face.

That dog had a lot to answer for.

Up on the street a woman wailed in recognition. One of the traffic cops kept her from pelting down the hill.

My heart wrenched in sympathy.

I avoided watching the turbulent emotions by turning my attention back to Cynthia. I ignored the detective. The bespectacled stranger occupied most of his attention anyway. The paramedic pumped up a blood pressure cuff on Cynthia's thin arm and frowned. He signaled a second ambulance crew to join him.

"I don't want to go to the hospital. I just want to go home," Cynthia said. She looked imploringly into my eyes, as if I could order the world for her. She tried hard to keep her voice firm, but tears already streaked her face.

"Your blood pressure is really low, honey," the paramedic said quietly. "You are going into shock. It's only natural. We need a doctor to check you out."

"Are your parents up on the hill?" I asked her. "They will go with you." I smoothed her long dark hair where it escaped her tight braids. She leaned into my caress a moment, then straightened. I wished I could accompany her, keep her safe.

"My folks are dead. My foster parents won't bother coming to the hospital. That might cost them money. They'll just expect Social Services to deal with the bills and the doctors. I wish I could go home." She began crying openly now. Her breathing became shallow and her coppery skin looked gray.

The paramedic eased her back until she lay upon the trampled grass. He checked her blood pressure and pulse again and frowned.

"Why can't you go back to the Colville reservation?" I asked, trying to calm the girl. I wished I could take her there, where she would be safe from the a hell hound from another dimension as well as the monstrous people who called themselves her foster parents.

The girl's voice and eyes brightened a little. "My parents lived here before they died, and Children's Services won't let me cross state lines to go home. No blood relations close enough to me, they say. I want to go home. The tribe will care for me. They are my people. There are no orphans among us."

I wrapped my arms around her, not knowing what else to do.

I wanted to go home, too—home to my husband. But he was dead, and no one could replace him.

The ambulance crew arrived with another collapsible gurney. I eased out of their way. The paramedic was occupied with Cynthia.

The detective seemed occupied with the tall stranger. Medical people handled the wounded. Someone else supervised putting two bodies into heavy black bags.

Two adolescent boys, cut down by a monster before they even had a chance to grow. Something twisted inside me.

"I'll do what I can to get you home, Cynthia. I promise," I bent and whispered to her.

Then the paramedics pushed me aside.

Psst, Blondie, Scrap hissed in my ear. *You're gonna be late, babe.* The imp completed his statement with a passing of gas.

I had to bite my cheeks and scrunch my nose to keep from coughing. The people around me subtly shifted position and looked away.

"Thanks, buddy," I said, not at all certain what I was thanking him for. Still, I grabbed the chance of diverted attention to sidle toward the tree line behind the church. With that little bit of cover, I made my way back up to the street and the crowd of gawkers, wailing parents, and frantic authorities.

The too-observant stranger seemed to be giving a complete statement to the police. Better than I could. I had been too busy fighting Dog to notice much else. No one needed me here anymore. Not even Dillwyn Bailey Cooper.

Except maybe one lost and lonely little girl. As lost and alone as I was.

I slumped my posture, gaped my mouth, and made my eyes a little vacant. A little twitch of the tank top made it bag and hang awkwardly. "Scrap can you fade the colors a bit? I'm too bright and noticeable."

Sure, babe, he whispered.

I blinked my eyes and felt Scrap slide across my back. A quick glance over my shoulder confirmed that my hot pink tank top had faded to a hideous yellow-green and my lavender shorts to a bluer green. The two did not complement each other.

I sagged my jaw and let my eyes cross a little.

Again, the crowd shifted away from me. People did not know how to deal with those they perceived as deficient.

A quick dodge around the cemetery and I dove into my rental car on the side street. The white compact from Detroit looked like every other compact rental car in the country and was stifling hot inside. I turned on the ignition so I could open the electronic windows. The ninety-degree summer heat felt comfortable in comparison.

As I sat there, waiting for the air-conditioning to blast out some of the hot air, I became aware that I stank. Heat, exertion, fear, all contributed to the damp, sourness of my skin. And the wound itched so badly it burned. My nose wiggled trying to avoid my own body odor.

You, dahling, are more rank than I am.

Scrap appeared on the dashboard, directly in front of me. He looked gray again, but too pale and not quite healthy, like he'd been working too hard.

Got any mold I can munch on? He looked in my half empty coffee cup with hope. *Shifting into your weapons is hard work.*

"No food this trip, Scrap. I'll get you beer and OJ as soon as I can. Hang on, we've got to get out of here. And you didn't really shift into a weapon. A soup ladle, for Goddess' sake!" I spotted a uniformed cop prowling around the parked cars, looking into each one, occupied or not.

I shifted into gear and peeled out.

Turn right, right, right, right here! Scrap screeched loud enough to slice an eardrum.

"That's away from town," I objected and kept on driving straight. No left turn presented itself behind the Safeway, only the high school athletic field where a Med-Evac helicopter descended in a typhoon of dust.

Trust me, Tess. Turn right at the next intersection. Scrap shifted his black cherry cheroot from one side of his mouth to the other. Fortunately, he hadn't lit it.

"Why should I trust you?" I stopped at the big red sign that said I must.

A black-and-white police car turned onto my street.

Without waiting for an answer from Scrap, I yanked the wheel right and stepped on the gas. At the next street, a broad one, but free of traffic, I turned left. I didn't see the police car in my rearview mirror.

Good move, dahling. Now just follow this road for six point five miles.

Scrap jumped down onto the passenger seat and pulled a map out of nowhere. He could do that when he wanted to be helpful and not just a pain in the ass.

"Six point five miles! How far out of our way is this?" I knew Dill's hometown was removed from the city. How far removed I had not appreciated until I needed to be back in Portland in a hurry.

The road twisted and burst into a straight stretch. It hung on the edge of a bluff. Off to my right stood Mount Hood in all its towering splendor. The grand old man of the Cascade Mountains was a little bare of snow in mid-September, but still sported a few glaciers to take my breath away. At the bottom of the bluff spilled a long river valley full of green. Green trees, green meadows, green crops.

I wanted to linger and stare in awe at the wonder of it all. Words began to form in my head. I had to describe this scene, use it somehow. Where? Where in my book could I plant this landscape?

Wake up, Tessie, and drive. Dirty rotten copper on our tail. He doesn't like the way you weave across lanes while you gawk. Scrap bit down on his cigar. Then he reached for my coffee cup.

"Paws off my coffee!" I screeched. But I kept both hands on the wheel and my eyes on the road. "There's a ton of heavy cream in it and you are lactose intolerant, Scrap."

Not even any good mold in it yet. I hate book tours. You never stay in one place long enough for mold to grow, and I have to pick up after you before the hotel maids come to clean.

Scrap turned bright red. Steam blew out his ears.

"Stop sulking, Imp, and prove your worth. I need clothes, something respectable. I need my professional face and persona."

One best-selling fantasy author coming up.

Scrap faded to passionate pink. When he had a job to do, he could stop thinking about his malfunctioning digestive system and perform fashion miracles.

The obnoxious scrap of an imp would rather play dress up with me than fight demons any day.

So would I.

Whoopee! Time to play.

A quick slide through the car's air conditioner for another restorative bite of mold and off I go. Imps can go anywhere from the chat room. Other beings are usually limited to one or two dimensions. Humans even fewer, unless they are unusually persistent—for that, read stupid.

Time is just another dimension, if you know how to use it. So I decided to take a moment for a quick visit to Mum. Just to see how she was doing. I hadn't been home in a while—like since she threw me out. Maybe she'd finally accept my diminutive stature now that I'd melded with a warrior companion. After all, being small made me low maintenance compared to my siblings.

"Hi, Mum, what's you up to?" I asked as I dropped in from nowhere. Nowhere being the portal.

"Out, out, out." She swished her broom at me. "I banished you yesterday and here you are back again."

Crap. There's that time thingy again. I'd been gone nearly three years human time, barely a day by Mum's. I'd had time to grow one whole wart on my bum, but she didn't bother noticing the beauty mark.

"But, Mum, I've m . . ."

She swung the broom again.

"The least you could do is sweep up some of the dirt with that thing!" I dove beneath a pile of interdimensional garbage. I skidded, scraping my nicely rounded belly on some flash-frozen watermelon rind. Good thing my wings are dwarfed, otherwise they might have snapped off

when I bumped against a cast-off 286 cpu. Goddess, there were a ton of those—literally—in our backyard alone.

Someone tossed the cpu aside. I rolled, expecting a swat from Mum's broom, but it was just a gamer treasure hunting. Did I tell you that to get out of the chat room through a portal humans have to be incredibly persistent? That's gamers for you.

I came up short with my nose on top of a pretty hair comb with only one broken metal tooth. The curved back of it was decorated with all kinds of semiprecious stones and filigree gold knotwork.

"Oooooh, Tess will love this!" I snatched it up, broke off a bit that might look like a stylized bat, and flitted back through the portal to her hotel room where I snagged some clothes and other niceties. The magic glamour of the comb shone like a pulsar in my dimension; in the mortal realm it faded to a soft patina of antiquity.

Chapter 3

Fruit bats have been known to cut and shape leaves into tents for roosting.

Fifteen minutes later Scrap popped back onto the passenger seat carrying my favorite tote bag. A friend had machine embroidered the fabric with magicians and dragons and castles.

"Did you remember my bookmarks and autograph copy stickers? What about my favorite pen?"

Better than that, babe.

Scrap glowed green with pride.

I brought a wet washrag, lightly soaped, and moist towelettes. And perfume. I'll have you smelling like a rose in no time.

"Can you do something with the dog bite first? It burns. I'm afraid of infection."

Ooooh, that is a nasty one. Nothing like imp spit to fix you up.

"Scrap, no!"

He went ahead and licked the wound anyway. I had visions of all kinds of otherworldly bacteria having a feast on my flesh. The wound cooled instantly. Then he wiped it with the soapy washrag.

Don't even need a bandage now.

"Uh, Scrap, what did you do?" I twisted my arm, trying to look while keeping both hands on the wheel.

No need to bother looking. Imp spit is a natural antibiotic to our warriors. To anyone else, though, it's a lethal toxin.

He giggled wickedly.

I didn't like the sound of that.

Then he began scrubbing the tension out of my neck with his washrag. I sighed in relief. Just that little bit of moisture and coolness made me a lot less anxious.

The road stopped winding and widened as we neared civilization. I'd seen enough nurseries and Christmas tree farms to last me the year. A gas station, a lumberyard, and a feed store looked positively civilized.

"Time?" I asked. The digital clock in the rental was positioned wrong for the angle of sunlight coming in through the windshield.

We've got forty-five minutes, Scrap replied, moving the washcloth down my arms.

I lifted my elbow so he could reach the pit.

"Time enough to get to Simpson's, not enough time to change clothes," I grumbled despite the relief of the impromptu bath.

Trust me, dahling. I brought clothes.

Strangely, I did trust the imp. When it came to clothes and makeup, he had better sense than I did.

We came to a red light beside a tractor dealership. I stared in awe at the size of the farm implements. The wheels were taller than I. More fodder for my fertile imagination. A scene began to form in my mind.

Half a mile down the road, with the entrance to Highway 26 in sight, Scrap gave me new directions. *Take a right here,* he said from somewhere around my left foot. He'd slipped off one of my pink tennies and bathed my bare foot.

I sighed in near bliss and turned away from the road I knew would take me to the freeway.

Next thing I knew Scrap had slipped a high-heeled, white sandal onto my left foot. He was working on un-tying my right shoe. At the next stoplight, three miles downhill and approaching a community college, I braked with my left foot and he worked on my right. By the time we reached the freeway at the base of the hill, I had proper shoes on clean feet.

"What about the rest of me?" I rummaged with one hand in the tote bag.

Scrap slapped my wrist. I felt only a swish of air.

Two hands on the wheel, babe. I don't fancy having to transport you into another dimension to free you from a car wreck.

The miracle of freeway speeds brought me through the junction with I 5 and up to the City Center exit faster than I thought. I even had enough time to throw on the denim wraparound skirt and a white blouse with blue and lavender sprigs—the long sleeves covered the still angry-red dog bite on my arm. Instant color coordination with the tank top. I threw the pink belt pouch into the tote, refreshed my lipstick, layered new makeup on the scar—the stranger had seen it, maybe someone else would, too, and ask questions.

"I'm as ready as I can get, given the circumstances."

A surge of delightful adrenaline sprang through me, lightening my step. I supposed I should get used to battling demons and rescuing damsels in distress in my spare time.

What spare time?

Your hair, sweetums! Scrap called from inside the tote. He handed me a wide decorative comb. *Your dishwater-blond curls are a tangled mess.*

"Dill used to say I had sandy-blond hair. This is new. Where'd it come from?"

Don't ask.

"Ill-gotten gains?" I hesitated. Even after two years together I had no idea if Scrap considered theft illegal or immoral. The comb looked expensive. *Very* expensive, and although lovely, not something I would indulge in for myself.

Trust me, dahling, the comb is legally and morally yours.

"But my hair is so short, I'm not sure it will hold the comb." If I didn't keep my hair cropped short, the curls became so tight the only way I could comb or brush them was if they were soaking wet. But I'd been on tour and attending science fiction conventions for close to three months with few breaks, while promoting the new book. No time for a haircut. I could probably put the comb to good use now.

Would you rather I turned myself into a hat for you?

I winced at the thought. I didn't need the imp wrapped around my head all day. I was close enough to a headache without him.

I scooped the mass of curls into a twist and anchored as much of it as possible with the comb. As I walked the two blocks to Simpson's—a former warehouse turned into the biggest bookstore on the West Coast—I grabbed my cell phone out of the pouch. Two buttons connected me with Sylvia Watson, my agent. Miracle of all miracles, she answered the phone.

"Tess Noncoiré, where are you? Simpson's expected you half an hour ago," she barked into the phone.

"They can expect me forty-five minutes prior, but I don't have to show up until the scheduled time," I barked back. Then I relented "I'm sorry. I did some sightseeing and ran into a monster of a traffic jam. Listen, Syl, I don't have a lot of time and I have an important job for you."

"It's Saturday, my day off."

"You are in the office. You answered your business line, not your private one. Just listen and do. Please. This is important. I need you to find me the best lawyer my money can buy." My heart beat faster and my concentration narrowed on the cell phone, just like I did before a fight. This was right. I lost all hesitancy.

"What kind of trouble are you in, Tess?" She sounded instantly alert. I could almost see her flicking through the pages of her computerized address book.

"Not me, Syl. There's a little girl, Native American, twelve or thirteen, Colville tribe, Cynthia Stalking Moon. She's been in foster care in Alder Hill, Oregon. About now, she's being admitted to the nearest hospital. Probably in Gresham. Dog attack. She wants to go back to her tribe, but officious officials won't let her because the reservation is in a different state. I agree with the girl; she should go home to her people."

My arm began to shake while holding the phone. That dog bite had affected me worse than I thought.

How was I supposed to sign dozens of books with this injury?

"Uh, Tess, this doesn't sound like something you want to get involved in."

"I promised, Syl. It's important. Trust me, please." I owed the girl.

"Are you sure, kiddo? Why this child? Why Now?"

"Because she gave me a flower to put on Dill's grave. I haven't allowed myself to care about anyone since . . . well, since Dill died."

"I know, I know. If you don't care about them, they can't hurt you when they leave."

Sylvia was silent a moment. "Okay. Good publicity for you, championing the cause of an underdog."

I winced at the canine reference. "Sic the press on the case but keep my name out of it. I don't want anyone to know I was in Alder Hill this morning."

She tried to talk me into a press conference.

"No. Just let me know the moment Cynthia is safe in the hands of either her tribe or a relative. And I mean safe."

We made small talk. I disconnected as I approached the bookstore.

I swept into the nirvana of Simpson's. Four stories of books, books, and more books. And today, a couple hundred copies had been written by me.

Mold! Scrap crowed. He popped out of my tote and disappeared into whatever part of the old building was the dampest. He'd feast, hopefully on something that had nothing to do with milk and leave me alone for a while.

The staff treated me like royalty. Before I could hint at the need for the restroom, they directed me. Mostly I needed to check myself in the mirror. Wow, the comb worked wonders on my frizzy mop, even if it did leave a few tendrils dangling.

When I returned to the reading/signing/lounge area, the staff had a large double latte, two sugars, waiting. I'd move to the Pacific Northwest just for their coffee, but home was elsewhere. The coffee hadn't been enough to keep Dill here. I sipped at the nectar of life and took my seat behind a fortress of books. The line of readers waiting for my signature stretched through two departments.

I smiled and poised my pen to sign the first book. I pushed aside my morning adventures and settled into the fun part of my job.

For two hours I talked to the people who made my work worthwhile. I answered the same questions over and over again. I even forgot the burning ache in my arm.

"Where did you get the idea for the warrior Sisterhood serving a Goddess manifested in the stars?"

I directed them to the cover artist for my book and a painting he'd done years ago. Each time I answered this question I caressed the cover art.

I traced the curve of a crescent moon that defined *Kynthia's* cheek much as I had traced the lettering on Dill's tombstone. The slash of light reminded me of the hidden scar on my own cheek. Clusters of stars revealed the

Goddess' eyes and mouth, smiling in gentle beneficence. The Milky Way streamed away from her face like hair blowing in a celestial wind.

As I looked at the cover, I realized that the Indian girl Cynthia's face was a younger, reversed image of the Goddess. Dark hair and eyes in opposition to Kynthia's star-bright features. Cynthia's coppery skin was alight and alive; the Goddess' face was defined by night and darkness.

"Is there really an order of Sisters who battle demons?" Usually asked by an adolescent girl or an awkward teenage boy in serious lust.

"The book takes place in the far future, after a devastating apocalypse. It's fiction," I replied. Sometimes I added, "Why don't you start your own order?"

No way could I tell the truth.

"How do I get my book published?"

I hated that one.

"When is the next book coming out?"

When I have the time to finish the damn thing. But I couldn't say that in public, so I smiled and told everyone it was scheduled for June of next year. Actually, book two was done, awaiting revisions from my editor. Book three was barely more than outline, but the publisher wanted book three done before releasing number two.

"I have some of your earlier, out-of-print works. Will you sign those, too?"

I loved that person.

Questions about where I had been for the last two and a half years, since my last book hit the stands, I avoided completely.

Scrap came back once to check on me. He bored easily and returned to his orgy of mold in a subbasement near the river that had been neglected for years. I worried then that the damp could not be good for the books, the treasure trove of Simpson's. An employee pointed out a state-of-the-art heat pump and dehumidifying system. I sighed in relief.

At long last the line of people waiting for me to autograph their copies dwindled to a trickle and finally stopped.

I was free to wander through the temple of books. By this time the comb was beginning to pull and strain my scalp, so I released my hair and dropped the lovely piece into the tote.

First stop, the rare book room, properly escorted by two employees. One of them screamed "Security" in his posture, attitude, and super-short haircut. I'd be willing to bet my next advance that he was a former Marine.

First editions and one-of-a-kind antiques did not cover the subjects that interested me. I left the Holy of Holies with a smile to the clerk and the guard, breathing a little easier in the less rarefied air of the main store.

My feet took me to the myth and folklore section. Simpson's had a wonderful collection of used books stacked cheek by jowl with newer works.

I found an obscure and dusty tome translated by G.V.H. Smythe in the thirties from an even more obscure Italian scroll dating to the 1540s. It listed and described a myriad of demons. Most of them quite accurately. This should have been in with the rare books but wasn't in the best of condition.

The original had been written during the heart of the Reformation when Catholics accused Protestants of consorting with demons and monsters, and the Protestants accused Catholics of being the tools of the Devil Pope. They both had it wrong. The book was a true treasure nevertheless. I thumbed through it greedily.

"If you are looking for references to your monster dog, you won't find it in that book," a man with a clipped accent said from about a foot above me.

"How . . . how did you find me?" I looked up anxiously at the nerdy stranger from the skate park this morning.

"Would you sign my copy of your book? I'm afraid it's a little dog-eared. I've read it three times. The picture of you on the back does not do you justice. It makes your hair look nondescript, but it really has a wonderful golden translucence." He held *Imps Alive* open to the title page and produced a pen from his shirt pocket.

"I'm Guilford Van der Hoyden-Smythe, by the way, but my friends call me Gollum. The author of the book you are holding is my great-grandfather. I'm named after him."

His slacks still had a sharp crease and the collar of his navy shirt lay flat and neat. He smelled faintly of a spicy and exotic aftershave. I wondered how he'd managed to remain neat, tidy, and clean after the chaos of this morning.

But then, he hadn't fought a demon in the shape of a dog. I had.

The reminder brought back the burning intensity of the bite on my arm. Not as bad as before, but still uncomfortable.

"Only once have I heard a reference to your Sisterhood, Ms. Noncoiré. Perhaps you could enlighten me on their origins." He looked over the top of his tinted, wire-rimmed spectacles at me. "Is your imp around? I would dearly love to examine him, or is it a her?"

Chapter 4

The common brown bat can eat up to six hundred mosquitoes in an hour, including disease-carrying insects, and thus are necessary in controlling the spread of insect-borne viruses like West Nile.

"Excuse me, what are you talking about? Do you see an imp on my shoulder?" I blinked up at the tall meddler in wide-eyed innocence. His broad, long-fingered hands still clutched my book with an odd intensity.

Inside, I quaked with fear that he really could see Scrap sitting on my left shoulder.

Maybe he was just an obsessive fan. I'd run into them before, borderline stalkers.

He'd seen my scar.

"Your assistant?"

"Who are you, and why am I talking to you?" I made to move around the all-too-perceptive man before he saw more of my secrets.

What kind of powers did he have? Did I need to go into attack mode?

Nice evasion, Tessie-babe, Scrap snorted in my ear.

His gray skin had a faint pink tinge. He wasn't happy, but he wasn't about to transform. The base of my spine remained tingle free.

And yet this stranger knew about him. He'd seen my *scar!*

Scrap's cigar smoke wafted in front of my nose. I resisted the urge to fan it away. A sneeze began building. I had to bite my cheeks to hold it back. I wanted to wiggle my nose, but that would be a dead giveaway to my stranger that something was amiss. Or that he had touched upon the truth with his observations.

"Sorry." The man actually blushed! "Guilford Van der Hoyden-Smythe. Ph.D. Professor of Anthropology and... and from a long line of students of the weird and supernatural."

I stared at his proffered hand as if it were contaminated.

"Good day, Mr. Van der Hoyden-Smythe." I clutched the treasured book to my breast and once more tried to pass him. He shifted slightly to block my path.

"The book does not mention the monster dog that was in the park this morning," he said. "My friends call me Gollum." He repeated and he held out his hand again.

"Gollum, as in the Tolkien character?"

"Gollum as in . . . Gollum." He shrugged and looked uncomfortable.

"Have you read this book?" I held it up between us. Then the translator's name jumped out at me upon the cover. "G.D.H Smythe."

"My great-grandfather. So, of course, I have studied the book extensively. He inspired me to get my first Ph.D. in cultural anthropology. The book covers only European myth and folklore. The dog's attention to the Native American girl leads me to believe he derives from a more local tradition." Van der Hoyden-Smythe paused for breath. But before I could reply, he plunged on. "Interesting that your imp did not assume the Celestial Blade configuration while you battled the beast."

"I think you need to consult medical help for your imaginings. You seem to have lost touch with reality." I tossed him the book. While he grappled with it, I ducked beneath his arms and away from him. I'd come back later to buy the book if it was still there. If not, I'd find it online.

"With my luck, Guilford Van der Hoyden-Smythe deals in rare and antique books and has locked up every copy of that tome," I muttered as I wended my way through the crowds of Saturday afternoon shoppers.

Hey, chickie-babe, you need a disguise? A greenish Scrap tweaked one of my stray curls, all the while puffing like a steam engine on his cigar. The smell nearly gagged me. I had to get out of the confines of Simpson's.

When had I ever hastened *out* of a bookstore? Nearest thing to blasphemy I'd ever committed. Blasphemy is a state of mind. I didn't believe in anything anymore; therefore, I could not commit that sin.

"Just lose the cigar. Maybe that meddling stranger will follow the smell rather than me." I dodged through the security detectors at a side door. Nothing in my tote set them off. A minor miracle. They usually reacted to the metal in my lipstick case, or something in the tampon packaging. Sometimes they just did not like Scrap. I'd gladly have left the imp behind if the things had blared out their warning of theft.

I walked as fast as I could, without drawing undue attention. As I ducked into the driver's seat of my anonymous rental, I spotted Van der Hoyden-Smythe's tall figure hastening toward me with long and determined strides. Some perverse inspiration made me honk my horn and wave at him as I merged into traffic. I turned two corners at the first opportunity and lost sight of him running behind me.

His offhand compliment lingered, though. I checked myself in the rearview mirror.

"Golden translucence, my ass," I scoffed. Same old dishwater-blond curls packed into a tight mass. Though they did look a little lighter than usual in the evening light.

Now where, Tessie? Scrap eyed my cold coffee cup longingly. He'd gone back to his normal peckish gray.

I grabbed the tempting cream-laden coffee away from him and dumped the dregs out the window. "Back to the hotel and some downtime. I need to work. What's on the schedule for tomorrow?"

The imp grabbed my phone out of my purse and opened the calendar app. He handed it to me rather than fight the electronics any further. He hadn't quite mastered the art of scrolling screens or accessing the internet with his talons. I dreaded the day he figured it out and moved on to my laptop. All I needed was his acerbic insertions into my novels.

Actually, I wondered, not for the first time, how he could manipulate physical objects in this dimension and yet weigh nothing on my shoulder and appear to have no mass. Another mystery for another day. Scrap didn't talk about himself or his abilities often. He just did things.

"Nothing on for tomorrow but a flight home." I glanced at the schedule page while driving one-handed up Broadway. "How did that happen?"

Remember how you bitched at the publicist that you had to have a week to work on your book?

Scrap levitated to the dashboard and pointed excitedly at a cigar shop. He turned royal blue in anticipation of a new blend of tobacco.

I was mightily sick of black cherry cheroots. I ignored his wild gestures and salivating, though.

"I remember bitching. I don't remember getting any time off from this interminable publicity tour."

You compromised on four days. Monday through Thursday. Sunday, tomorrow, is travel day. Thursday morning we head out to the next convention.

Scrap shifted his concentration to a department store with a display of perky autumn hats for ladies. He remained a happy blue, but not as intense a hue as when he wanted a new cigar.

"Then I presume I have airline tickets home tomorrow," I commented absently. My concentration centered upon finding the shadowed driveway into the hotel's underground parking garage.

Please, Tess, can we go back to the hat place?

Scrap looked positively innocent sitting on the dashboard with his paws clasped neatly in front of him and his bat-wing ears folded downward. He'd taken on a lovely shade of lavender, one I hadn't noticed before. His pleading color? Two years and he'd never pleaded with me before.

"What? No sarcasm? No demands? This must be important to you, Scrap." I glanced away from the street for half a heartbeat and missed the driveway. *Damn.* Now I had to go around the block again.

My skin turned clammy and my spine crawled as if big ugly bugs skittered up and down my back. I squirmed and twisted.

What? Scrap demanded. He scrambled around and around, turning deeper and deeper red. His big eyes moved back and forth and his ears twitched.

"Just a weird feeling." I flipped on the blinker and turned right.

Park, babe. We got work to do.

"Now what?" I sighed. A car in front of a parking meter signaled his intent to merge into traffic. I let him, then twisted the wheel and claimed the spot.

The driver behind me yelled something obscene out his window and leaned on his horn.

I resisted flipping him the finger. No sense in aggravating him more.

Still sitting in the air-conditioned coolness, I unfastened the wraparound skirt and shed the overblouse. The moment the light changed and traffic eased around me, I was out of the car clad in shorts and tank top. I barely remembered to pocket the keys after locking the vehicle.

"Think you can manage the Celestial Blade this time?" I asked Scrap as I jogged back toward the underground parking lot.

Scrap did not say a word. He became so insubstantial and colorless on my shoulder I had to look to see if he had remained in this dimension.

"I can't do this without you," I said quietly, mindful of the crowds on the sidewalk.

Still no answer.

I stopped short just shy of the shadowed entrance to the underground hotel parking lot. My skin twitched all over my body. My heart rate sped up and my focus narrowed to a dark recess just beyond the last visible car parked against the right-hand wall. A cream-colored BMW, I thought. Maybe one of the Detroit-made luxury cars that tried to imitate a Beemer in styling. Definitely not a Mercedes.

"Stand by, Scrap," I whispered. Slowly, I edged into the structure, keeping to the shadows at the left of the door. From there, I could keep an eye on the sleek car and not be noticed. Hopefully.

The sudden relief from the relentless sunshine brought goose bumps to my arms and thighs. I did not know if I should welcome the coolness or heed it as an additional warning.

My eyes adjusted gradually to the dim lighting. I watched a tall man, silver streaking his dark hair at his temples, emerge from the luxury sedan. Long legs, nicely tailored dark slacks, and an equally dark knit shirt. For a moment I thought it might be Van der Hoyden-Smythe, but this man had broader shoulders and wore only sunglasses, not the thick spectacles of my stalker.

My senses continued to hum. A part of me knew that the sun neared the horizon. Twilight descended.

A tiny winged shape materialized out of nowhere in the dark corner above the cream-colored Beemer.

"Yeep!" A tiny sound of huge fear escaped my lips. It overrode the humming need to confront the menace in the garage.

I dropped into a quivering crouch, my head between my knees and arms covering as much of my head as possible.

A bat! All I could think of was the animal tangling its claws in my hair and yanking it out by the handful. Or worse, nesting in there.

The logical adult part of my brain called me an idiot.

The childish nightmare fears knew better. My newly attuned warrior senses had warned me there was a bat in here.

Up, Tess. Get up. We need to do something! Scrap implored.

I peeked through my crossed arms to see what had become of my imp. Surely he'd transformed into my Celestial Blade in the face of the evil vampire bat.

I hated my stupid phobia. But every time I caught a glimpse of the winged mammals, even on TV, my skin crawled and I grew short of breath. Panic overrode logic.

It's just a little brown bat, and it's gone, Scrap said. Did he whisper out of mutual fear?

Then out of the corner of my eye I saw the man turn around and face me. His eyes seemed to seek mine. He removed his sunglasses. Our gazes locked. He smiled at me.

All my fears dropped away like water flowing over a deep fall, leaving me almost light-headed and giddy with relief.

The bat was gone. "Stupid, stupid, stupid," I muttered to myself. "Grow up, bats can't hurt you."

At the moment I truly, I mean *truly* believed that.

I registered that the man's smooth skin showed no signs of a five o'clock shadow on his prominent jaw. A deep dimple appeared in his left cheek as his smile increased. My heart went pitter-pat in excitement.

All memory of the bat and my phobia disappeared.

He took two steps toward me.

I remembered that I had spent the morning at Dill's grave site and backed out into the evening. No man could replace Dill. I did not want any man in my life again, not even a casual flirtation.

Whoa, Tess. Scrap pulled my hair with both paws as if yanking on reins. *Why are we running from a fight?*

"Hungry yet, Scrap?" I asked rather than face my own fears. Which was greater, the atavistic fear of bats? Or the fear of finding another man attractive?

"I think we'll explore Chinatown. You need a good dose of MSG to counteract the lactose intolerance." Don't ask me why the food additive negated his noisome gas, but it did.

Can we stop at the hat place? my imp asked eagerly. *There was that rust-colored one with the long feather. It would look spectacular with your new winter suit.* He salivated into my hair. *And maybe the cigar store?*

Thank heavens he did not truly exist in this dimension and did not soak me with lavender slime.

"If you insist. I also want to go to the Chinese Gate and gardens. They are supposed to be spectacular, real landmarks. We should sightsee a little bit tonight before we pack to go home. Stay away from the hotel," and this bat-filled garage, "for a while."

If you say so, Tessie-dahling. I was born to serve.

He produced a new cigar, already lit, and proceeded to blow smoke rings across my face.

"I'll believe that when I see it," I snarled at him as I pulled the car into traffic and sped away from my hotel and my phobias.

But did you stop to think long enough to wonder why your demon-sense started tingling before you knew there was a bat inside? You normally don't react to bats until you see one.

Interlude

Imp lore will tell you that what drew me to the Timber Town Bar and Grill in Alder Hill, Oregon, that slushy day in early February two years ago was the potential warrior setting herself up to contract The Fever. I'd been drifting aimlessly around the Pacific Northwest for a few weeks gorging on mold, replenishing my energy reserves after using all my wits and a good deal of my strength battling the Sasquatch who guarded the portal out of my home dimension. They might be undisciplined teenagers, but once engaged in the "game" of guard duty, they remained intensely focused on the task.

I think it was all of the outrageous puns passed in a circle with each new round of beer that pulled me into the dim tavern that smelled of smoke, stale beer, peanut shells ground into the floor planks, and, of course, a wealth of mold. What better place to find mold than in the damp foothills of Mount Hood in February?

"Have you heard this one?" called a man with a black beard and mustache that compensated for a balding head. "I swear it's true; read it in the paper the other day."

"What now, Bob?" A collective groan went through the crowd in anticipation.

"Some guy was arrested for throwing rocks at seagulls. But the judge let him off 'cause he took a vow to leave no tern unstoned!"

More groans and slurping of beer.

"Moldy oldy, Bob."

"I got a better one," Tess said. She slurred her words just a little and her eyes were rimmed with red from all the tears she had shed. I could tell she was hurting inside from the way her in-laws (or are they outlaws in this culture?) had cut her out of their grief. She needed to

share her emotions. This crowd of her husband's friends from science fiction conventions and colleagues from the local community college where he taught geology gave her the best outlet.

"We're going to have to change all of the breakfast menus in this country. The restaurants are calling them 'Pope's Eggs' rather than 'Eggs Benedict' now."

"Boooooo! A decade out of date. We have a new Pope now!"

Someone threw peanut shells at Tess.

She ducked, laughing and crying at the same time.

"Dill told me that one just as we were going to sleep that last night. Before the fire broke out," she said quietly.

I think I might have liked this guy Dill.

The room sobered instantly.

The Bob person began singing in a gravelly baritone, "There's a bimbo on the cover of my book," to the tune of "Coming 'Round The Mountain."

"Come on, Tess, sing it, sing the greatest filk song ever written!"

Color drained from Tess' face. More so than what her prim little black dress robbed her of. She looked terrible in black, and I hoped she never had to wear it again.

"I can't sing," she choked and took a long draught of beer.

I think that was the beginning of the fever.

Anyway, the party broke up soon after. By this time Tess had me hooked. I had to follow her. She left the party with only one lingering look at the substantial house on the hill behind the white church with the red door. All of her hurt and anger and guilt for living when the love of her life had died so tragically saving her was caught up in the gaze.

Then she got into her mid-sized sedan and started driving. East at first, then north over the mountain in rotten weather on tires that were in no condition to handle mountain pass snows the first week of February.

I gritted my teeth and held on as she took the curves too fast. A death wish in the making.

She couldn't see me yet, of course. The fever hadn't taken her and changed her brain enough for that. But I like to think I had a little influence on her. She slowed down and made it over the mountain, in the dark.

Somewhere along the line she stopped for food and checked into a motel. The next day she headed north with grim determination along a chain of mineral lakes in Washington, just east of the Cascade Mountain Range. She was headed back to the scene of her husband's untimely death. I know now that she was looking for answers. Answers that might not exist. But she had to look.

By the end of the second day she was within a few miles of her destination. By that time the fever had overwhelmed her. Only she knows what nightmares she endured in the grip of the virus. She doesn't talk about it. Not even to the Sisters who shared her infection and survived.

It took all of my willpower to keep her on the road that day. Six times she nearly drove into one of those mineral lakes when the fever slowed her reaction time and skewed her perceptions.

I sat in her lap and yanked the steering wheel in the right direction. When we came to the dirt track that most people don't notice, I *steered us along it. I even managed to avoid most of the potholes that would rip out the undercarriage of a high-crop tractor.*

Finally, we stopped dead outside the citadel. The one place in the world I knew she would be safe, and I knew she would wake up and claim me as her own precious imp, companion, and Celestial Blade.

I WALKED HUNCHED OVER, a little wary of the surgical incision beneath my belly button and the one that ran along the right side of my face from temple to jaw. Sister Serena, the only doctor in the citadel, had to cut the infection from my face and abdomen to save my life.

Spring sunshine softened the austere landscape within the citadel of the Sisterhood of the Celestial Blade. Stout stone walls made of reddish rock from the local area defined at least ten acres of land and buildings. All around me, my Sisters worked. All of them had visible scars on their faces like the one on mine. Some hoed and planted a huge vegetable garden. They tended to be the older women, middle-aged mostly. I didn't see any truly old women here. Some of the more vigorous women repaired storm damage to the roof of the refectory where we took our meals. Still others stripped down to red sports bras and shorts to practice various martial arts in a sandy area set aside solely for that purpose.

I paused about every third step to watch the bustle and to rest. I'd spent at least two months in the infirmary and still hadn't regained my strength from the wasting fever.

Sister Serena walked beside me, as she did every day I ventured outside. She stood straight and tall, mid-forties I guessed. Her muscles flowed easily beneath her bright purple scrubs. All of the Sisters wore bright colors in celebration of life. Not a sign of a uniform among them—except for the sports bras and shorts—those always seemed to be blood red.

"Don't walk too far. Even if you feel better, it is too easy to overdo," Sister Serena said. Her voice, like the rest of her, oozed soft contentment. In two months of rather intimate contact, I'd never seen anything upset her mental or emotional equilibrium. Though once I'd seen her slip on some spilled gelatin and nearly lose her balance. She let her frustration flow out her clenching fingers.

"I need fresh air," I panted. Sure, I'd walked too far already, but I wasn't about to let Sister S put me back to bed in the closed and stale atmosphere of the infirmary. Not yet at least.

A bevy of children, all girls by the look of them, erupted from a small building in the corner. I stared at them in puzzlement. Only one of the girls, the eldest by the size of her and the maturity of her face and figure, had a scar.

"Future Sisters in training," Sister S explained.

"Do you kidnap children?"

"No." Sister S laughed long and loud. I noticed she laughed a lot. "The fever that marks us does not render us infertile. Nor do our vows to the Sisterhood make us celibate. We raise our daughters to fill our ranks."

"What if you have sons?" I sank down onto a conveniently placed bench in the middle of a flower garden that caught the sunshine. A small fountain burbled beside me as it irrigated the soil.

Sister S stilled in thought. "I don't think any of us have had sons, at least not in living memory. I wonder if we are even capable of having boys?"

"So not all of you come from the outside world like I did." I felt the rough skin along my face. The infection had ruptured before Sister S could lance it clean and straight.

"Very few of us have come from the outside. You are the first in living memory. You have a lot to learn before you can hope to truly be one of us." She looked puzzled, as if she wasn't sure what to do with me.

I didn't know what to do with me either. I'd managed one cell phone call to my dad to make sure my house and finances were taken care of. That was the only outside contact they allowed me. By that time the phone had a dead battery, and there was no electricity here to recharge it.

"And if the fever doesn't take one of your daughters? What becomes of her?"

"All of us go to high school and college on the outside. How do you think I became a doctor?" She raised perfectly arched black eyebrows at me. I'd give my eyeteeth to look that beautiful even on a good day.

"We board with the families of girls who were born here but elected to remain outside, marry, and have children. Usually the few women who come to us from the outside come from those families."

Again, she shook her head and looked puzzled.

"So why me?" I asked the question that had burned inside me since I fell into a fever of grief and wound up here.

"The fever finds those who need to become one of us. We never ask why. We welcome anyone the fever chooses." But she pursed her lips in disapproval.

Sister S settled beside me. Her gaze lit fondly upon the oldest of the girls—the one who already had a fever scar. It looked fairly fresh and raw.

"How old are they when the fever selects them?" I waved vaguely at the girls. At twenty-six, I thought myself a little on the old side.

"Usually in their mid-twenties, when they've had a chance to taste life outside and know if this is where they belong or not."

"Am I trapped here for the rest of my life?" That didn't sound so bad. Without Dill, I didn't have a lot left behind. Mom would take over my house, as she took over everything in her orbit. Dill's life insurance—double indemnity for accidental death—and the mortgage insurance would ensure that she could afford the place. I had completed my contracts with my publisher. Nothing drew me back to reality outside these walls.

Except the burning question of "Why?" Why had the fire started in the crummy motel where Dill and I stayed while he grubbed about looking for specific geological examples. He was due to start teaching at the community college in Cape Cod near our new home in spring quarter. He wanted special samples to take with him.

"No, dear." Sister S laughed again. "None of us are trapped. We can come and go as we choose. Mostly, we choose to stay here, where our work is, where we are needed."

"What, exactly, is your work?" My gaze kept straying to the Sisters working out with quarterstaffs and wrestling. Two of them donned boxing gloves and engaged in something akin to Tae Bo.

"The same work you started when the fever took you."

"Huh?" All I remembered about that was a long and involved fever dream of fighting demons.

"Exactly," Sister S replied.

"Exactly what?"

"Think about it."

Chapter 5

Bats are not blind. Their eyes are adapted to see in the dark and some species can see in light as well as humans.

A huge bat loomed over me screeching in my sister's voice, "I'm going to drink all your blood!"

I screamed and covered my head with my arms, crouching down to make myself as small as possible.

And then the monstrous bat began pulling my hair. Great clumps of the tight curls tangled in claws as long as fingers.

I screamed again in abject terror.

The sound of my own voice croaking woke me up. The sterile hotel room with my half-packed clothes strewn about offered me little comfort. My scalp still hurt from . . . from . . . from wearing the comb. Not from a bat that had really been my older sister Cecilia dressed up for Halloween.

Funny. All these years and I'd never remembered the incident that had triggered my bat phobia.

I looked over at the clock. Not quite ten on the West Coast. I'd been asleep maybe a half hour. Nearly one at home. Would Mom be awake?

Probably. She didn't sleep much since she and Dad divorced fourteen years ago. "Call Mom," I told my phone. The programming remembered the numbers for Sylvia, my agent, and my editor. I'd never deleted Dill's cell phone from my standard set up. Somehow doing that would be a symbolic erasure of our brief marriage.

"Hi, Mom. My plane lands in Providence at three. I should be home in time for dinner," I greeted her before she could monopolize the conversation.

"That's fine, dear. I'll fix a nice pot roast. I found it on sale at WelSave this morning. We'll eat early and go to evening Mass together."

Not on your life, Mom. I hadn't been to Mass in years, and I had no intention of starting now. She knew that. But she never acknowledged it. Mom and reality sometimes had only a passing acquaintance.

She rambled on with more domestic details in her Québécois accent. It sounded rather thick tonight. Like it did when she'd been alone too much and thought in the French dialect of her childhood.

Her parents had left Quebec when she was seven and never spoke French again. Somewhere in her twisted mind she had created a need for her Québécois roots and pieced together half memories of baby talk in French and called it the pure language.

Her need for the linguistic security blanket increased after Dad left. He'd brought me up nearly bilingual with a Canadian accent. I'd taken Parisian French in high school and college and tried to correct Mom once. After having my ears boxed for corrupting the language, I never tried it again.

Somewhere along the line, I figured out that Mom understood real French. She just refused to speak it. While I mourned Dill, I began to understand her need. She grieved for people and things lost in her life, her grandparents in Quebec City and her husband, much as I grieved for my lost husband.

"Mom, do you remember an incident about a bat when I was small?"

"Oh, yes. Your sister was quite naughty. But she so loved that Halloween costume I made her. She wore it for months and months every time you three children played dress up or make-believe. Why do you ask? It's been years. I thought you were too young at the time to remember. Barely three."

"I had a nightmare about it." If I was three, then Cecilia had been a very grown-up and authoritative seven. Our brother Steph, between us in age, had defended me when he could. But Cecilia always won our sibling battles. "What triggered it, Mom? Cecilia isn't one to like creepy animals."

"Oh, we'd all taken a road trip with Chuck that summer." She never referred to my dad as the father of her children. She barely acknowledged his existence after the divorce and church annulment. "We toured the Grand Canyon while Chuck audited a client's branch office. When we got home, we found a dead bat plastered to the radiator grille. It was quite mummified from the heat of the engine I think. Just a little thing but it fascinated Cecilia. Nothing would do but she had to be a bat for Halloween, *la petite*

garnement." Little scamp, I translated the term, almost an endearment. Mom
rambled on a bit more with memories from that wonderful summer trip that
I could not remember.

Eventually sleep tugged a yawn from me, and I said my good-byes with
assurances that I would indeed be home the next day.

"You okay, baby?" Mom finally asked.

"Yeah, Mom. I am." And I was. The dream had faded from the reality of
nightmare to just another annoyance about my sister.

But the phobia? That was still something I didn't want to push.

"I'll press a dress for you to wear to Mass," Mom concluded just as I
clicked off.

Mumble grumble. I settled back into sleep, satisfied that my nightmare
hadn't been real.

I felt a disturbance on the mattress beside me. Dill often came to bed late
after reading and studying for the next day's fossil hunt.

"Dilly," I murmured only half awake.

"Move over, love," he whispered. His smooth tenor voice caressed my
mind and senses.

As I had longed to do, every night for two and a half years, I scooted
to the edge of the bed. Dill lay down behind me and wrapped a light arm
around me. I snuggled in, cherishing the feel of him, the smell of him, the
weight . . .

He had no weight. No substance. No warmth. Only a preternatural chill.

I jerked awake. "Dillwyn Bailey Cooper!" More a plea than a question.

"Tess," he whispered. "Don't ask questions. Don't object. Just be here for
me. Let me feel you."

"Talk to me, Dill," I said warily. I turned onto my back and pushed
myself into something resembling a sitting position. Light creeping around
the hotel room drapes and under the door showed only the dimmest outline
of a man sitting cross-legged on the other side of the bed.

I ran my fingers through my tangled mop of hair. For half a moment I
considered confining it in the lovely comb Scrap had given me. But it was
across the room in my tote bag.

Where was the imp anyway?

Dill brushed his hand lightly around my head without touching me. My scalp tingled where the hairs stood on end.

"This is what I miss most about you, Tess," he breathed. "The sight of you all sleep tousled and adorable. Lovable."

A soft draft passed my ear. I shivered from the temperature change. The room was now colder than the air conditioner could make it.

"Don't shy away from me, lovey. You said you missed me so much your teeth ached."

Lovey, his pet name for me. Much better than *lumpy,* which the kids had called me in school.

"I do miss you, Dill. There's a gaping hole inside me that only you can fill." I reached a tentative hand out to him, not quite daring to touch in case this was only a dream. I couldn't bear to lose him again.

"Then let me fill the gap. Let me watch for you. Get rid of the imp. Keep me by your side instead." He smiled at me, as he used to.

My resistance to his ghostly presence dissolved. No man had touched me in a very long time. I ached for more than just his presence. I wanted his body. Next to me, inside me.

Bad plan, Tessie. Suddenly Scrap on the night table was more substantial than Dill at my side, in my bed. Scrap also glowed pink in warning.

"Dill, why did you have to die?"

"I told you not to ask questions." His voice rose in anger. "I can't answer questions."

He faded.

I needed to see his eyes, to look deep inside their hazel depths to understand what he was thinking and feeling.

"Dill, don't go. I need you. Stay with me."

The phone rang with my five AM wake-up call.

The mattress creaked.

The room warmed.

I fumbled for the lamp. Light flooded the room and dazzled my eyes.

The room was empty. Even Scrap had deserted me.

The ache in my gut doubled from loneliness.

"It was all a dream. I visited Dill's grave yesterday, so of course I dreamed about him." The sound of my own words in my ears convinced me that the conversation had not happened.

I was still alone and more lonely than ever.

What's up with this spook? Where did he come from? Why is he here? Imp lore tells us nothing about ghosts. When we die, we die. We do not come back as ghosts or reincarnations or anything. Our bones burrow through the dimensions to take root in the great garbage heap of the universe.

So we live a long, long time and cling to life like a hamster gnawing on a finger.

Nothing can break the bond between a Warrior of the Celestial Blade and her imp. So why is this ghost trying to oust me?

I need answers this dimension cannot give.

Do I have time to seek? And while I'm at it, I should make some inquiries into Guilford Van der Hoyden-Smythe, the scholar who sees too much.

COOKIES! Scrap chortled at the smell of charred flour, sugar, and fat that greeted us upon opening the kitchen door of my rambling home on Cape Cod.

A hint of movement in the oak tree at the front of the house made my heart skip a beat. A blacker-than-black shadow. A bat?

I had to sit in the car a moment to catch my breath before I had the courage to dash for the kitchen door.

Even though I now knew it was too early in the day for bats, and why I feared the creatures, I couldn't banish the phobia overnight. If anything, it might be worse. I couldn't get the dream image of the huge bat out of my mind, twice as big as me, threatening to drink my blood and rip out my hair. My scalp hurt just thinking about it.

"Teresa!" Mother rushed to greet me at my own kitchen door with a fierce hug. She squeezed the breath out of me, as if she hadn't done the same thing ten days ago. "Come in, child, come in." She took the lightest of my carry-on luggage from me, leaving me with two heavy suitcases and my laptop case. Each one was loaded with books—research and my own personal reading.

"Mother." I acknowledged Scrap's delight with a sinking heart. My plans for a long bubble bath, a quiet snack, and then a good workout at the fencing *salle* vanished.

I'd tried martial arts when I first left the Citadel, but all the philosophy, meditation, and breathing exercises bored me. I needed to move.

Sport fencing fit me better.

I lugged the bags into my kitchen and dumped them in the middle of the floor. The previous owner of the house had run a bed and breakfast. The oversized kitchen and casual eating area gleamed with modern colonial-style furniture and lighting.

"You really should stay home more, Teresa. You haven't come to family game night in ages. You *will* be there tonight," Mom prattled. After being away for a while I noticed her French accent more than usual.

Great, another excuse to spend "quality" time with my harpy, control-freak sister Cecilia, bachelor Uncle George who couldn't tell the truth if you paid him, Mom who talked endlessly about everything and nothing whether someone listened or not, deaf and forgetful Grandma Maria, and Auntie Em . . . er, MoonFeather, as she preferred. She was from Dad's side of the family and thus not named for a saint. In fact, MoonFeather was a card-carrying member of Wicca (if they have cards and membership and such) and the only relative I could describe as close to normal. We played Trivial Pursuit* for about four hours every Sunday so we wouldn't have to talk or have to feel guilty for totally ignoring each other the rest of the week.

Dad and his much younger partner Bill, tennis pro at the local country club, had a life and therefore avoided family game night. Their invitation was a holdover from before the divorce, and Grandma Maria asked after them every week. She knew her acceptance of the men as a married couple irritated Mom and Cecilia to no end.

Why had Dill and I decided to settle on Cape Cod and not in the Pacific Northwest? We'd given up wonderful coffeehouses on every other corner for this?

We'd traded his eccentric family of D. B. Coopers for my dysfunctional family. Every one of his clan, parents and siblings, were named some variation of D. B. Cooper.

I'd often wondered if his parents were related to the infamous D. B. Cooper, the first successful airplane hijacker who had disappeared with his ill-gotten gains into the Cascade wilderness back in the seventies and become a local folk hero. In the decade when baby boomers sought new and unique ways to defy authority, D. B. Cooper had bested them all at the game.

Dill had liquidated his trust fund for the down payment on the huge old house. He'd offered to sell his share of the family furniture store, too, if we'd needed it to put three thousand miles between us and his family.

My brother Stephen had been smart enough to move to Indiana as soon as he graduated from college. He'd finished his master's in organic chemistry and worked for a pharmaceutical company. Last Christmas he'd announced plans to begin work on a Ph.D. I talked to him regularly, but I don't think he called Mom or Dad more than twice a year.

"I need a nap and some exercise, Mom." I dove for the oversized steel fridge, looking for a cold drink. I grabbed the last bottle of beer. Either Mom had really cleaned house or she'd thrown a party in my absence. More likely, Uncle George had pilfered five bottles.

Mom is the only person I know who can clean more thoroughly than Scrap.

"You have time for a nap before we gather at eight. You can go for a walk tomorrow. All that fencing nonsense isn't good for you. It isn't ladylike." Mom stood in front of the center island, between me and the bottle opener in the drawer.

Fortunately, her back was to the racks of cooling cookies. Scrap scarfed up three of them. Then he disappeared—probably into the cellar.

"I have to work tomorrow." I pushed her aside to open the drawer for the church key. Where the bottle opener should be, it wasn't. I rummaged deeper, thrusting aside a myriad of cooking utensils I couldn't name and rarely used.

"Mom, you rearranged *my* kitchen!" I wailed.

"Well, if you'd stay home more often, you could clean your own house and keep it more efficiently arranged." She stood with hands on hips in affronted outrage. "I don't see why you travel so much. You never traveled this much before you met that Dillwyn person."

"Dill was my husband," I ground out for the umpteenth time.

"Humph," Mom snorted. "A quickie ceremony in Reno with no family or friends when you'd known him less than a week? I don't call that a wedding. Then three months later he takes off, just disappears. That's what you get for hooking up with a man you met at one of those weird conventions. I don't see why you can't write something normal, like romances, or histories."

"Mother, Dill died. He was horribly burned in a motel fire. I barely escaped alive. He was burned to death. TO DEATH, Mom."

"So you say. It's easier to tell people that he died rather than admit to being a grass widow like me. And he left you with this huge mortgage and tremendous debts, so you have to work too hard and can't spend time with your family."

Back to family game night.

"Dill and I bought this house together. His life insurance paid off the mortgage." Double indemnity for accidental death on the life insurance, plus mortgage insurance. I had money left over to live off until I finished writing *Imps Alive* and started earning money of my own. "No mortgage means I can afford to let you live in the guest cottage rent free. Mom, I'm tired of this argument."

Tired of the memories. Tired of taking care of Mom. Tired of remembering how Dill and I had planned to fill this rambling old house with children.

I worked too hard to avoid remembering.

I ran miles every day and worked out at the *salle* so I'd sleep without dreaming.

This old house had ghosts aplenty, so far none of them Dill. Would he haunt me now that I had been to his grave?

I almost hoped he would.

She cleaned with bleach! Scrap screamed in my ear.

He flickered from deep orange to red and back again.

I don't need bleach to clean. She dumped all of the mold I was cultivating. The whole house reeks of bleach—even the cellar, he wailed.

"Then eat cookies," I snarled back at him. "No one else will."

Then a new thought struck me. *Did Mom get into the armory?* Only I had the key to the secret room in the cellar filled with all kinds of weapons, most of them very sharp, pointy, and lethal. One hundred fifty years ago it had hidden runaway slaves as part of the Underground Railroad.

I didn't check. Scrap popped out again.

"Mom, I'm going to take a bath. Lock the door behind you."

Without looking to see if she actually left, I made my way through the butler's pantry to the dining room, then into the oldest part of the house to the steep stairs up to the suite of rooms I kept above. This was part of the original five-room New England saltbox that dated to the pre-Revolutionary era. I loved this part of the house; three rooms downstairs and two up, all clustered around a central chimney.

"Oh, and, Teresa," Mom called after me.

I froze halfway up the stairs, the part where I had to duck to keep from banging my head on the support beam. That tone of voice never boded well for me. On top of that, the base of my spine itched and my heart beat at double time.

"You might want to watch the news in a few minutes. Your face is all over the media about a strange incident in Oregon yesterday. Something about you rescuing an Indian girl from a rabid dog."

"Shit!"

Mom exited out the front door at the base of the stairs without another word.

I scrambled up the remaining steps, practically on all fours, to keep from knocking myself out on the beam. The attack of the monster dog wasn't the first item on the news. That belonged to the latest drive-by shooting in Providence. But the dog and I were second. The local anchor showed a composite sketch of the dog that looked more like the mastiff from the *Hound of the Baskervilles* than the brindled mutt that was taller than a wolfhound and broader than a rottweiler.

Then they showed my publicity photo, since no one had captured any shots of me in action. Someone in the crowd—probably that snoopy Guilford van der Hoyden-Smythe—had recognized me. At least they only talked about how I had subdued the beast with a skateboard, not how my invisible imp had become a fireplace poker.

The newscast went on to say that a similar attack had taken place near Puyallup, Washington, three days before. An adolescent Native American girl had also been the object of the dog's attention and had not been hurt.

At last, the news went on to say that the Colville tribe had filed suit for custody of Cynthia. The Stalking Moon clan claimed her even though the closest blood relation was a second cousin of her father's.

Chills ran all over my body. The name was just too much of a coincidence for me to not take heed.

Cynthia: Greek for moon. *Kynthia:* the name of the Moon Goddess in my books, based upon the Sisterhood of the Celestial Blade Warriors. My Sisterhood. The women who had rescued me from a raging infection and uncontrollable grief.

Stalking Moon: her clan. My Sisterhood worshiped a Goddess who manifested in the stars defined by a crescent moon, the stalking moon.

The base of my spine tingled and itched. I forgot my need for a bath. Leaving the TV on, I prowled through the sitting room of my suite and the long addition over the dining room for reference texts on Native American folklore.

Nothing. All of my work so far had been based upon European myth and legend. The American tribes had never interested me before.

Time for an Internet search and probably a hefty order from some rare book dealer.

Chapter 6

"Tess, are you awake? We brought game night to you," my sister Cecilia called as she tapped on the door to the sitting room, one of the two small rooms in my suite at the top house. Soft Celtic ballads sung by a friend of mine from the science fiction/fantasy conventions played on the stereo system.

I stifled a groan. I'd decided to deal with game night by ignoring it. I was curled up with a book on the overstuffed sofa in front of the fireplace. A fire crackled and lent a lovely golden light to the shadowy room. The comfortable presence of Maggie, one of the resident ghosts, dissolved, leaving me cold and alone with my family.

"Chicken," I muttered under my breath to the ghost.

"Really, Cecilia, I am too tired," I added, slamming my book down on the end table. This was my house, damn it! Why couldn't my family respect that?

"Maybe you just need to get laid," Cecilia chirped. "Then you wouldn't be so snippy."

"A lot easier to just buy a vibrator and rent some porn."

"*Merde*, we did you a favor bringing game night to you." Cecilia stomped down the stairs, ducking carefully to avoid the beam.

Don't you just wish you could ignore them, babe? No such luck tonight, dahling.

Scrap chortled from his perch on the spider—the wrought-iron swinging arm in the fireplace designed to hang pots over the flames for cooking. He always sought a heat source. I'd often wondered if his home dimension was hotter than hell and ours too cold for him.

Reluctantly I followed her. If I didn't, the rest of the family would make a constant parade up to my rooms to "check" on me.

"Sorry," MoonFeather, Dad's sister, mouthed as she bustled in behind Cecilia. She headed into the dining room—one of the first additions to the original saltbox.

I rolled out of the armchair and stretched my back until it cracked. I wasn't going to get out of this easily, and burying my nose in the book wouldn't work. I'd tried that before.

"Where's the beer?" Uncle George demanded, heading directly for the kitchen, inconveniently at the other end of the house.

"Mom, I told you I couldn't make game night. I'm too tired," I protested.

Mom flitted her hands in dismissal as she placed the game box on the long table that could seat twelve comfortably.

"Someone close the door. It's cold in here." Grandma Maria shivered in the open doorway. Stepping out of the way and closing it herself seemed beyond her faculties tonight.

But I'd almost be willing to bet my new hair comb that she'd trounce the lot of us in the game. The space in her brain she used to store vast amounts of trivia must crowd out the room she needed for short-term memory.

Since no one else seemed to think it prudent to close the door, I performed the chore myself. Fluttering shadows from the old oak tree out front sent deep chills through me and robbed me of breath. I had to make sure they were just leaf shadows and not bats.

Uncle George returned with a beer in one hand and a bag of chips in the other. He took the place of honor in the captain's chair at the head of the table with his back to the fireplace and looked around as if startled that the rest of us hadn't set everything up in his absence. My sister Cecilia began laying a fire without permission.

"I'll make coffee." I escaped to the kitchen.

"Make it decaf, dear. It's evening and we don't want the caffeine to interfere with our sleep," Mom called after me.

"Unleaded, my foot," I grumbled and started making a full pot of the real thing.

While the filtered spring water from my own well dripped through freshly ground gourmet beans, I rummaged through the luggage I hadn't taken upstairs or unpacked yet.

In the mesh bag, wrapped in your dirty underwear, Scrap said, reading my mind again.

I wasn't sure I liked this new ability of his. He appeared inside the big suitcase, clawing the drawstring of the mesh bag open with his talons.

"Thanks, buddy." I retrieved the antique comb from deep inside the protective wrapping.

An argument between Uncle George and Grandma Maria erupted over possession of the captain's chair and its placement closest to the fire. I took the time to rinse the comb in cold water and let the moisture ease its way through my tight mop of curls rather than intervene in the argument.

I kind of liked the glamour of elegance the new hairdo gave me.

Then I switched the carafe of coffee for my favorite heavy ceramic cup shaped like Earth with a blue dragon circling the center while it still dripped from the coffee maker. One sip and the room seemed brighter, warmer, and friendlier.

A tap on the glass half of the back door interrupted my savoring of the second sip.

"Dad!" I opened the door and hugged him tight. He'd kept much of his rugged blond handsomeness as he approached sixty; even if Chuck Noncoiré was a serious-minded accountant who peered at the world over half glasses. Living with a tennis pro kept him lean and fit.

"MoonFeather warned me of your mother's plans. Want me to chase them off?" He stepped into the breakfast nook alone. A rare occurrence.

"Nah. They'll only gang up on me worse next time I'm home on a Sunday night. Where's Bill?"

I peered through the glass top half of the back door for signs of Dad's partner. I didn't mind Dad being gay and had accepted Bill Ikito as a member of the family long ago. But Mom had never forgiven Dad for preferring a male tennis pro—younger than herself by fifteen years—to her. I couldn't remember her being in the same room with Dad except for an occasional Thanksgiving dinner at my house since I was twelve and the scandal erupted all over Cape Cod.

"Bill's coming down with a cold. I tucked him into bed with a cup of lemon and honey tea and a romance novel. I'm serious, I'll send them all home if you aren't up to company. You've been on the road a lot this year." He placed a thick hand on my shoulder, squeezing with gentle affection.

"If I get too tired, I'll call Maggie to chase them off." I grinned at him.

"Tess, I don't mind that you let your overactive imagination take off in your books, but believing in ghosts is pushing the limits of true sanity." His blue eyes looked tense behind the magnification of his glasses.

"Don't worry about me, Dad. It's all a family joke," I hedged. If I ever mentioned Scrap and everything his existence entailed, Dad just might find a way to commit me.

"Besides, what am I supposed to do? When Dill and I bought this house, the earnest money agreement specifically left possession of three ghosts in the house along with the appliances and the dining table with twelve chairs." The table had come into the house through an open picture window during remodeling and was too big to get out any other way.

"I guess it is only significant that your mother believes in the ghosts. Go ahead and sic Maggie on her early. I'll call you tomorrow. We'll have lunch at the club before you take off on your next junket." He kissed my cheek and went back to his loving partner.

I was left with my . . . possessive, obsessive, wacky and . . . and yes, loving family.

We exchanged a few comments about me attacking rabid dogs. Mom muttered that should include her ex and his partner.

"Hey, Tess, I heard there was a bigfoot sighting out in Oregon. Same newscast as that dog fight. We wondered if the monster had kidnapped you," Uncle George said. He pronounced it ore-ee-gone rather than orygun. I didn't correct him. He wouldn't have listened.

He wasn't lying that the family worried I'd been kidnapped. Uncle George couldn't tell the truth if it hit him in the face. But right now I knew he spoke it. I knew it in my heart and my head.

How?

"Bigfoot might be preferable to you lot," I quipped.

They call themselves Sasquatch, Scrap hissed in my ear.

"And the proper name is Sasquatch," I added. "How many points do I get for that?"

"That isn't one of the questions, dear," Grandma Maria said, patting my hand. "We haven't started yet. We were waiting for you. Have you done something to your hair? It looks lighter, blonder." She cocked her petite head like a little bird, her soft curls looking like a halo. I'd inherited her hair and hoped mine became as soft and silky when I was her age.

"No, Grandma. I just changed the style a bit. I might let it grow out."

"That would be nice. Long hair is more ladylike." Mom patted her own coil of medium brown hair atop her head.

Bill, I might add, kept his straight black hair buzzed so short it looked like a dirty shadow on his skull.

"I'm worried about that Sachey-foot guy," Uncle George grumbled as he grabbed the dice to begin the game. "You're going to California next weekend where they had that sighting. You watch your step and don't get caught by one of them monsters."

"I agree," MoonFeather added. Her keen gray eyes pinned me with otherworldly knowledge. "I've seen in the stars grave portents on your horizon."

I don't like that word grave, Scrap added.

Interlude

You know the difference between Chimpanzee art and Michelangelo's Pieta?

Well that's a similar difference between Moonfeather's dabblings in astrology and the way the Warriors of the Celestial Blade, male and female, study the stars. It is their faith, their sole purpose in life, and the reason they gather together into cloistered armies, centers on a single configuration in the sky. When the Goddess reveals her face in the skies, then Her warriors will be blessed with victory over demons and the world will be safe for another space of time.

Far be it from me to scoff. Imps have their own Gods and sacred rituals that mean everything to us. The warriors' Goddess might not do much for me, but then garbage dumps in cold storage don't do much for humans.

I've seen the face of the Goddess and so has Tess. We've seen the aftermath of a demon battle.

The first new quarter moon after Tess was up and about in the citadel, Sister S invited her to watch—not participate, just watch—as the Sisterhood gathered to pay homage to their Goddess.

A lot of cultures watch the stars, and a lot of cultures worship at the full moon, or the dark of the moon. I hadn't run into any other that worships at the new quarter moon.

As darkness fell, the Sisters drifted away from their dinner, their study, their exercise into the central courtyard. Each of them carried a lighted taper with a hand cupped around the flame to shield it from view as well as the wind. If one of those tapers ever snuffed on its own before the ceremony ended, ill winds blew for the entire Sisterhood. Each Sister had an adult imp on her shoulder to help protect the candles. They talked and joked softly among themselves, cheerful; family going to church on Sunday morning. Except this was a Tuesday night.

Tess shuffled out of the infirmary wing on the arm of her doctor, Sister Serena. She stood a little straighter today. Sister S had taken the stitches out of her belly incision the day before. Tess also took slightly firmer steps than yesterday. But only I could discern the difference because I watched her so closely, so lovingly.

A swarm of older Sisters stood three deep in a crescent facing east, at the point where the moon would rise. The honored dozen of the leadership of the order assumed seemingly random spots within the arms of that crescent. All of the youngsters and the bulk of the warriors took their places across the top of the formation, assuming east as the top, in a scattered wash. Imp wings kind of made the entire formation look fuzzy and bigger to my eyes. Sort of like looking through an out-of-focus telescope.

Tess stood apart, on the top step of the infirmary building. Of all those present, we alone could see the pattern of lighted tapers and compare them to the miracle that was about to rise in the sky.

This courtyard, though protected by high walls—ten, twelve feet, what do I know of exact measures?—was slightly elevated and gave a clear view of the eastern horizon.

The Sisters all got real quiet, all at once.

The quality of light changed as the moon thrust one curved arm into view. One day, soon I hoped, I'd become Tess' Celestial Blade, in a good imitation of that waxing quarter moon. Sister S, standing among the leadership, began a soft hymn of praise. I didn't understand the language. I don't think Tess did either. An ancient hymn preserved through countless generations of Sisters pledged in the eternal fight to keep this dimension safe from interlopers known as demons. The others joined her song, swelling the courtyard with music that raised goose bumps on Tess' arms and made me spread my ears to gather maximum sound.

The hymns continued, all in the haunting language that lingered in the back of the mind, almost understood, not quite discernible. Like a racial memory or an atavistic need.

The moon rose higher. The night grew darker. Overhead, the Milky Way spangled the heavens with a river of light.

And then the top of the moon touched the Milky Way. A few stars below the elliptic plane of the galaxy burst into view.

The Sisters raised their tapers high and continued singing.

"THE FACE OF THE GODDESS," I gasped in wonder as the constellations and moon came together in the sky. For one breath I felt a part of something bigger, something greater and more important than my solo life, the pain in my scars, and my grief.

The Sisters stood in imitation of the miracle I saw reflected in the sky. I needed to be part of that homage.

"Hush," a Sister in the courtyard below me hissed. "The Goddess has not yet appeared. Your place is to watch, not to comment."

"But . . ."

"Hush."

Of course they couldn't see Her. Kynthia. The Goddess of the Warriors of the Celestial Blade. They had their candles above their heads, blinding them to the wonders in the night sky. A kind of mist covered the lot of them.

Dimwits. They should extinguish their candles, or hold them below their faces, so the flames didn't blind them to the miracle above.

The image lasted only a moment. Clouds gathered. A breeze came up.

Spielberg couldn't have staged it better.

"There," someone shouted as her candle blew out.

Other candles extinguished. Other Sisters gasped at the fading magnificence in the sky.

"To arms, Sisters, to arms! The demons march this night."

"Inside. Stay low, stay safe. Whatever you hear, whatever you think you might want to do, do not emerge from your room," Sister Serena commanded, suddenly appearing at my side. She shoved me into the infirmary and firmly locked my door behind me.

I pounded on the door, suddenly afraid of the darkness and the way the base of my spine tingled. Energy coursed through my blood as it never had before, demanding I take action.

No one answered my demands.

Over the course of the next several hours, I heard the clash of blades, a strange ululating battle cry, and screams of pain.

"Let me out, I can help," I pleaded over and over again.

But my Sisters had other concerns that night.

After a while, the cacophony of chaos gave way to bumps and thuds within the infirmary. Women gave orders, equipment moved. Lights showed beneath my door.

In the morning I learned a small contingent of furred demons, perhaps two dozen of them, had broken through the portal the citadel guarded. Three Sisters, including Sister Serena, had received serious wounds. A fourth had died.

But they had beaten the monsters back.

"That doesn't sound right," I said when I sat beside Sister Serena's bed the next day. "I write sword and sorcery stuff. It doesn't make sense for them to send only a small contingent against the full Sisterhood. Of what? Two hundred fifty, maybe three hundred, trained warriors?" I held a glass of water with a bent straw to the doctor's mouth and let her sip.

"Unless the demon population is way down and they are desperate to breed with humans. Otherwise, why didn't they send more to secure the portal?"

"You know nothing of demons," Sister Gert, the leader of this citadel, snarled from the doorway. "We were triumphant and suffered only minor losses."

"Sounds more like a diversion to me," I muttered. "What else were the demons up to last night?"

"You know nothing! Your place is to watch and learn, not to question." Sister Gert turned on her heel and left before even inquiring about the health of their doctor.

"She is right," Sister S said quietly. "We of the Sisterhood do not ask questions. We follow tradition and do our job. 'Tis the only way to keep the demons subdued. You were not raised here. You have never fought a true demon."

Oh, yeah? What about the demon of grief? What about the demons in my fever dreams? No questions, my ass, I thought, but kept my mouth shut.

This time.

Chapter 7

The smallest bat, the bumblebee bat, weighs less than a penny. Its forearms measure barely twenty-five millimeters. The largest bats, the Old World Flying Foxes, have a wingspan of two meters and can weigh seven hundred fifty grams.

"You know what I love about my job, Scrap?" I asked the next weekend. I threw open the French doors of my room at the Double Lion Hotel in San Jose, California. The balconied room looked out over the pool rather than the parking lot or the freeway. Such luxury! "Now that I'm really making money, I get to go to West Coast conventions as well as those closer to home."

I drew in a deep lungful of dry air scented with some desert plant I couldn't name. A touch of salt on the edge of my taste buds told me that rain would come in from the Pacific Ocean tonight.

Scrap just slithered into the air conditioner looking for mold. The little glutton.

"Time to go to work, Scrap. I'm going down to the green room to register and get my schedule." I'd also nosh on the goodies spread out for the visiting pros. Airplane food had become nonexistent in the latest economic crisis. "I'll buy you a beer later, Scrap." He still didn't answer, too absorbed in his feeding frenzy.

I'd started attending conventions—or cons—in college with friends who had grown up in the culture of fandom. They soon became an addiction. Any weekend of the year, somewhere in the US, there is an SF convention. Three or four days, depending on the weekend, of costumes, books, writers, readers, gamers, filk—the folk music of science fiction and fantasy—nonsense, and fun.

Just because I hadn't been able to sing since Dill died didn't mean I couldn't listen to the filk concerts. But I didn't go to the filk circles and open sings anymore.

Oh, and did I say books? Book dealers, new and used, classic and potboiler, abound at cons. They tend to stock up on books by visiting writers so the fans can get them autographed. I loved the atmosphere as much as I loved the people who dashed up to me wanting an autograph or those who came and sat in rapt attention when I did a reading or spoke on a panel discussion.

During the lean years, when my writing barely put food on the table, and I had to work as a substitute teacher in Providence to keep a grubby little apartment, I had to limit my cons to New England. If I could conveniently drive there and crash with friends, I attended, had a great time, and promoted my books as much as I could.

Then there was High Desert Con in Tri-Cities, Washington. My oldest friend from college, Bob Brown, the man who had first introduced me to cons, ran programming on that convention. I always scrimped and saved or went into debt to attend his con.

I was just beginning to make more from writing than teaching when I met Dill at High Desert Con and everything changed.

I hadn't been back since.

I'd be guest of honor, or GOH, there in a few weeks with my expenses paid by the con. I wanted to see my old friend again, but . . . I just wasn't sure how I felt about going back to the place where I'd met Dill.

Would he haunt me there as he had in Portland? I almost hoped so. I desperately needed to see his smile again, feel the special warmth his love gave me.

I also dreaded the pressure he had put on me to discard Scrap.

Bright and friendly smiles greeted me in the green room. Three volunteers jumped to answer my questions, provide me with maps of the sprawling hotel, introduce me to everybody and anybody. I glad-handed my way around the room, basking in their welcome. Then I smelled the cake. Chocolate. Rich double devil's food chocolate.

I barged into the connecting room, the lounge, of the suite and made a beeline for the luscious treat. My feet came to a skidding halt and backpedaled.

The cake had come from a bat-shaped pan, Halloween orange-and-black candy sprinkle bats littered the dark frosting. It was the weekend that bridged September and October. Appropriate decorations for the season.

I lost my appetite.

What's the matter, babe, afraid of a little bat candy? Scrap goaded me.

"I am not afraid. Just turned off."

"Tess, I may call you Tess, might I? I'm Dee Dee Richardson, head of costuming." A short, blowsy, bleached-blonde held out her hand as she zoomed in on me from the registration area. "I'm sorry to impose on you and your busy schedule, but one of my judges for the masquerade just canceled out. Emergency appendectomy. Is there any way I could impose upon you to take her place? Having a celebrity like you on the panel of judges would be such an honor," she said all in one breath.

Gratefully, I turned my back on the bat cake and led her back to registration. "Of course, you can impose. I love costuming. I used to do quite a bit of sewing myself and consider myself quite competent to judge workmanship as well as creativity."

The heady aroma of ranch-flavored chips and dip began to blot out the now nauseating smell of chocolate.

"Did you know that I knit and crochet as well? My Grandmother Maria taught me *la frivolité,* 'tatting' you call it. I love textiles," I blathered on.

"Yes, I noticed how your details about clothing and textile textures add so much richness to your books."

That settled, I went to find some dinner so I could enjoy the rest of the con.

I met up with some old friends from the costuming guild in the hotel garden café. I sometimes wonder if this same café teleports around the country for each and every con. It looked the same in every hotel. We had a marvelous discussion about how the development of scissors had changed clothing construction.

A few people dining near us sported *Star Trek* and *Star Wars* costumes. A few others were more creative and elaborate. I saw everything from elegant and historically accurate Regency and early Georgian wear on both men and women, to green-painted ogres wearing horns and wispy rags. I noted a lot of women and children had commercially made fairy wings stuck on the back of their outfits. Chiffon drifted and floated nicely out from a wire framework. I almost wished I had brought some of my own garb.

The best costumes would come out tomorrow night for the masquerade. I wiggled with happy anticipation at being allowed to judge them.

Then a large family group with three small children filed into the café. They all wore black leather with brown fur hoods. When they raised their arms, black leather bat wings connected them from wrist to knee. A tall man, their seeming leader, threw back his fur hood revealing a thick black braid going halfway down his back. His hair was going gray at the temples, like silver wings.

Where had I seen him before? Some con probably.

Not a con, Scrap whispered to me. *The underground garage where you cowered because a bat dared fly past you on its way to dinner.*

I shuddered in memory of my own stupid fears. But I had questions too. How big a coincidence was it that I'd first spotted him in Oregon only a week ago? My curiosity over rode me phobia. I took half a step toward him...

The man smiled, and the entire room seemed to go quiet, more relaxed. He raised his hand to smooth back that magnificent head of hair. His bat wings flowed out from his costume.

Breathing became difficult. I couldn't think, couldn't move. My heart beat overtime and cold sweat broke out on my brow and back.

Then the three-year-old began running around making squeaky noises. My companions all "Ahhed" at how cute she was.

I lost my appetite and pushed away the remnants of my otherwise excellent salmon Caesar salad.

My room seemed the best respite from the bats at the con. I scuttled away and turned on the evening news, something I never do at a con. Reality had no place here. But right now, I needed a heady dose of reality.

While the local anchor prattled on about bank robberies, gang violence, and road rage, I yanked the antique comb out of my hair and began brushing my curls, now long enough to cover my neck. And . . . and definitely lighter in color. I seriously contemplated cutting it. But I really liked wearing that comb.

A particularly tight tangle broke off in my hand as I worked the brush through. As I stared at the near transparent gold strands, a word on the TV caught my attention.

"Another in a series of dog attacks that have plagued the Pacific Northwest..."

"What?"

The screen flashed briefly with a picture of the hind end of a big dog—it could have been any big dog—and then the face of the scholar with the clipped accent who had followed me from Alder Hill to the book signing at Simpson's.

The station went to a commercial.

Five agonizing minutes later, the news came back with a thirty-second story including one sound bite from Guilford Van der Hoyden-Smythe. "This dog seems to be on a mission," he said.

Time up. Old news now. New story.

The news readers reported a Sasquatch sighting in the wilds of the high desert plateau east of the Cascade Mountains. They both had to bite their cheeks to keep from laughing out loud.

The base of my spine tingled. I wanted—no—needed, to rent a car and drive up to Pendleton, Oregon, near the Oregon and Washington border and quite close to Tri-Cities, Washington. Also part of the high desert plateau east of the Cascades. Once there, I could check out the latest dog attack upon a Native American adolescent girl. Too far to go during the con. Monday would be too late.

And what was Guilford Van der Hoyden-Smythe doing there?

Needing to *do* something, I called my agent, Sylvia Watson. "What have you heard about Cynthia Stalking Moon?"

"Who?" She sounded distracted. I gulped an apology for calling so late. I'd forgotten the time difference.

"The Indian girl I wanted to help get back to her tribe."

"Oh, yeah, Cynthia Stalking Moon. Last I heard, the tribal lawyers were working on it. They'd found a second cousin willing to take her. Middle-aged man with grown children. Empty nest syndrome if you ask me."

"Is it done yet?"

"Don't know."

"Oh." The dog was still out there, and I didn't know for sure if Cynthia was safe.

Damn. No wonder my spine itched.

I gave Sylvia a brief progress report on the new book and disconnected.

I cursed and bit my nails. "Is this my fight, Scrap?" I asked.

He shrugged and dove back into the air conditioner like a ghostly cartoon.

Curiouser and curiouser. There are no coincidences in imp lore. Nor are there any references to four-eyed scholars stalking a monster that should be stalked by my warrior. I need an imp version of the Internet to do some research. Lacking that, I just might have to figure out how to use Tess' laptop.

I SPENT THE NEXT DAY jumping at shadows and avoiding bat wings. Those bat costumes creeped me out. Finally, after dinner—a sandwich grabbed at a nearby restaurant filled with con goers but no bats—I retreated to my room to change for the masquerade.

Dahling, don't tell me you're going to wear that *to judge the masquerade.*

Scrap folded his stubby arms and looked offended. He took on a bilious yellowish-green color that made me feel sick just looking at him.

"What's wrong with this?" I twirled in front of him showing off my little black dress—which is really midnight blue since I hate wearing that much black—that I never travel without.

The skirt is too long. It cuts off in the middle of your calves and makes them look fat, Scrap sneered.

Fat calves! Before the imp flu I'd been fat all over, but I was particularly sensitive about my cancles—where my calves made a straight line to my heels. Never again, I was not going to put back the near fifty pounds I'd lost.

Scrap fluttered around me, sniffing and wrinkling his nose as if I smelled bad.

"Don't do that. I just had a shower."

Take it off, he insisted, tugging at the demure elbow-length sleeve that hid the lingering twin red marks left by the monster dog's teeth. They still itched but showed no sign of infection.

"No. I like this dress."

Why, pray tell?

"It's . . . it's practical."

It's ugly!

He was right. I looked ten years older and . . . heaven forbid, was returning to my former *lumpiness.*

"Oh, all right." I unzipped the soft crepe and flung it onto the bed. "What do you suggest I wear?"

Go play with your computer for ten minutes.

"I can't go out in just my black slip and I didn't bring another dress."

Hmm, that is a nice slip. Silk?

"You know it is. You picked it out." And the garment dripped lace.

I plunked down into the desk chair and awakened the laptop. I didn't dare get embroiled in my work in case I forgot to leave for the masquerade on time. So I played three hands of solitaire.

Hey, Blondie, I fixed your dress.

I groaned, dreading the result. Scrap had been known to crop dresses so short they showed my butt. While playing cards on the computer, I'd decided to wear my black slacks with the red silk blouse and black sandals with two-inch heels.

"Wow!" What else could I say. Scrap had sculpted the dress, slitting the side seam almost to my butt, removing the sleeves and plunging the neckline. I slipped into it and surveyed the result in the inadequate mirror.

"I look almost sexy. But I need makeup to cover that dog bite."

What do you mean, "almost"?

"I've got cleavage!"

And legs and a teeny, tiny waist. Every man in the room will be looking at you, babe, and not the costumes.

I turned side to side, surveying the transformation. "It needs a necklace."

Just that hematite pendant. Scrap dropped the gleaming black necklace in my hand.

Two minutes later I strolled (strutted) down the corridor to the staging area beside the main ballroom. A couple of Trekkers whistled. A pirate and his minion kissed my hand.

I tossed my loose curls and smiled.

Until I saw the bat troupe mingling with the crowd. They sported big blue ribbon rosettes—awards for hall costumes. Thankfully, that took them out of competition for the masquerade. I wouldn't have to touch their costumes to judge workmanship. The younger members had gone from furred hoods to full fur masks. I walked around them quite warily.

The tall man with the wings of silver hair paused to stare at me. He lifted his hand to smooth his braid with a wonderfully long-fingered hand (a habitual gesture?), showing the full breadth of his bat wings. He smiled.

I froze. Our gazes locked. I couldn't look away, couldn't move, totally entranced by the chocolate depths of his eyes.

That flash of teeth and the steadiness of his brown eyes reminded me of Dill.

Then he looked away.

I shivered and entered the private area as quickly as possible. Those bats could take all the fun out of this con for me.

SUNDAY MORNING, THE last day of the con, when half the members walked around in zombie trances of fatigue, I slipped into a filk concert performed by a couple of acquaintances. I'd picked up their latest CD in the dealers' room and was anxious to hear them.

Scrap bounced and twitched in time to the music.

We don't have anything this good back home.

"And where is your home?" I whispered.

Elsewhere.

He never said anything more than that.

We were deep into a rousing version of a movie parody sung to a familiar tune when I felt a sharp tug on my hair. I jerked my head around. One of the bat children grinned at me. She had on black lipstick and kohl around her eyes. I glared at her and slapped her hand, with its unnaturally long fingers, away from my head.

Watch your left, babe, Scrap hissed at me. *She's just a diversion.* He bared his teeth and morphed to hot pink bordering on red.

Then I noticed a bat brother crawling up beside me, one hand (also with extra long fingers) reaching into my tote bag. I pulled it into my lap and hugged it close. What was in there to entice them, other than the challenge? Some bookmarks, autograph copy stickers, book covers minus the books, my con schedule, some aspirin, and a hairbrush. And the antique comb. I'd pulled it out of my hair an hour ago. The tines were beginning to irritate my scalp, and I noticed more very pale gold hairs breaking off every time I took it off.

Nothing of value. My wallet and room key were in a belt pack.

The children retreated.

I tried to enjoy the concert after that. But my mind kept returning to the black-clad brats. What did they want from my tote bag?

Gratefully, I flew home that night. That was the first con I hadn't thoroughly enjoyed in ten years.

Chapter 8

Two weeks later, I had exhausted my creativity on the Internet with no luck in finding a reference to the monster dog. I spent hours looking through sixteen new research books on Native American religion and mythology. In the process I'd found a lot of material for my next book. Somehow, I'd also added four chapters to the current work in progress.

Still, I had nothing referring to a big ugly dog attacking adolescent Native American girls. Two more attacks had made the news, one in western Idaho, another near Spokane, Washington.

Sylvia Watson had not called with news that Cynthia Stalking Moon had returned to her clan. I worried about her as much as I worried about that damn dog.

Each report of a dog attack was accompanied by yet another Sasquatch sighting. An intrepid hiker had even managed some hazy footage of the beast on his cell phone. Those few frames could have been of a big hairy dog or a kid in a gorilla suit. No way to tell without fewer shadows, less shrubbery in the way, and much better light.

No one seemed to make a connection between the dog attacks and the Sasquatch sightings. Most news readers passed the craziness off as symptoms of increased stress due to a downturn in the economy.

In order to stop the dog, I needed a cultural anthropologist who specialized in Native American lore of the Pacific Northwest. No one but me had the skills and determination to take it out. My instincts told me that. So did Scrap. He claimed that I had permission from the Sisterhood of the Celestial Blade to pursue the dog. As if I needed their permission for anything.

They'd kicked me out because I didn't conform to their ideals. I'd left their hidebound sanctuary gladly.

Hey, Blondie, Scrap called to me from his perch on the wrought iron spider hanging inside the fireplace of my office. He swung back and forth on the hook. His barbed tail twitched dangerously near the flames. It glowed red.

He jumped to his feet on the hearth and slapped his tail against the bricks. A few sparks fell harmlessly back into the fire as he blew on the burn.

I scooted my chair back to peer at him from my desk in the back parlor. This room stretched the width of the house and contained an original, still-working fireplace big enough to walk into. The two smaller original rooms also had working fireplaces in the same chimney. I used the little rooms as a library and a private sitting room where I could entertain special guests or read.

"You are disrupting my concentration as usual," I replied, not all that upset.

You are turning into a computer potato, Tessie dahling. Time for a workout. Scrap had turned a pale orange all over to match his still hot tail.

Then I realized my muscles ached from inactivity. "What day is it?" I searched for the icon to open my calendar file.

Tuesday.

He came up with the information at the same moment I did.

"I'm going to the *salle*. You coming with me?" I closed down the computer and stretched my back, still seated.

You'd do better working out with the Celestial Blade in the basement. I'll coach you.

"Tomorrow, Scrap. I need confrontation with people to hone my reflexes. I also need to socialize. I'm turning into a grouchy hermit."

Surprisingly, Scrap agreed.

Before I could weave a path through piles of books and papers filed upon the floor, Scrap disappeared, then popped back with a whoosh of displaced air carrying my gym bag with two foils, an epee, and a saber sheathed and attached to the side with a special strap.

Clean jacket, knickers, mask, and glove inside, he told me. *You'll have to find your own shoes and socks.*

I looked down at my fuzzy green slippers in the shape of dragons and sighed. "Any idea where I left them?"

Your mother put them away.

I rolled my eyes upward. Who knew what interesting nook or cranny Mom had found to stow them in. Her idea of organization and mine were entirely different. At least she didn't dare clean up after me when I was home. Only when I left town for more than twenty-four hours did she ferret out all of the half empty coffee cups, dirty dishes, and laundry wherever I dumped them. Scrap cleaned, but at least he left things where I could find them!

"Okay, Coach will have to put up with my dirty running shoes and mismatched socks." Those I found on the first step. I had intended to take them up to my bedroom with me next trip. That had been last Thursday.

Twenty minutes later I walked into the *salle,* a good-sized storefront in an old strip mall. Coach had marked three lanes on the floor with duct tape. Two of the lanes were equipped with electronic equipment for competition fencers. I staked out the third lane. I didn't compete. I came here to hone my skills and reactions should I ever have to confront a demon with my Celestial Blade.

If Scrap could ever transform properly.

I had that funny feeling at the base of my spine. Something told me that I was headed for another confrontation with the monster dog.

No sooner had I stretched out and warmed up than someone tapped me on my shoulder.

A tall man with long dark hair pulled back into a tight braid, dressed in a European styled padded jacket, faced me. He smiled and showed brilliant white teeth against his bronzely tanned face. His teeth were brighter than the silver wings of hair at his temples.

Something familiar . . .

"May I have this bout, miss?" No discernible accent.

"I haven't seen you here before." I had seen him somewhere else.

He shrugged. "I am visiting from . . . the West Coast."

"You look familiar."

He flashed those brilliant teeth at me once more.

My heart threw an extra beat. Soda bubbles danced through my veins.

"You signed a book for me in Portland a few weeks ago."

"Of course." I returned his smile and picked up my foil, whipping it back and forth a couple of times to test its balance. A stalling technique.

I'd have remembered him if he had stood in line at Simpson's. He'd stand out in any crowd, especially that one, which had been filled to overflowing with teenagers and young con goers, with only a sprinkling of people his age.

What was his age? His smooth face, without a trace of five o'clock shadow, and sparkling brown eyes placed him at early thirties. The silver in his hair pushed that guess up a decade or two.

I had seen him in Portland, though; driving a cream-colored BMW. He'd smiled and my fear of the little brown bat had vanished.

Then I'd seen him at the con in San Jose wearing a bat costume himself.

Something akin to warning flared at the base of my spine. But . . .

He smiled.

We moved onto the strip, four meters apart. Two more fencers took up positions on either side of the center line. My opponent and I saluted each other with upraised blades that we snapped downward with an appropriate whoosh through the air. We saluted our officials and then put on our protective masks.

The blade seemed to come alive in my grip, eager for me to use it. Niki, the assistant coach, had tweaked the alignment last time I'd been in. She did excellent work.

Gareth on my left called, *"En garde."*

I assumed the position, right foot pointed forward, left foot ten inches back pointed outward at a right angle, both knees bent, weight to my center, foil held level, wrist straight, palm up, left arm behind my shoulder, hand up.

My opponent mimicked me. But he centered his weight over his front leg. An aggressive fencer. I watched him for other tells.

He used an Italian foil with a pistol grip that required the fencer to slip two fingers through rings. Impossible to knock the blade from his hand. Which is good if you are fighting a duel to the death. Those grips had been known to break fingers. That can ruin your day in sport fencing and knock you out of a competition.

"Fencers ready?" Gareth asked. His teenaged voice carried through the suddenly quiet *salle*.

I could hear my heart beat inside the enclosed mask.

"Ready," I replied, as did my opponent.

"Fence."

I crept forward, watching my opponent's blade and his eyes, what I could see of them through the black metal screens of our masks. He kept his head up, assessing, planning. He circled the tip of his blade, testing my reaction. I beat my blade against his once, knocking his blade aside and slid in, aiming for his *quarte,* the upper inside of his chest—the side opposite his weapon hand.

Lightning fast, he parried my attack and riposted to my exposed *sixte,* the upper outside—the side of my weapon hand. I parried that attack and withdrew one step. He followed, pressing me, rapid thrust after thrust. I gave ground, seeking a weakness, an opening.

Then before I could find a way beneath his longer reach he caught me with a *doublé.*

Did I say he was tall? Make that very tall with long arms and longer legs. He struck me at a distance that would require me to do a double advance and a full lunge. He only did a half lunge.

My heart raced. Heat flooded my face. I could learn from this man.

His broad shoulders and lean waist enticed me to explore more than his fencing technique.

"Halt," Gareth called. He recounted the last action and called the point good.

We backed apart, putting the full four meters between us. A long four meters. This time when Gareth called "Fence," I leaped forward and lunged beneath my opponent's attack while he was still planning.

My blade bent with the force of my thrust. I was close enough to smell the musky undertones of his sweat. My nose twitched and my body tightened with desire.

The score was one to one. Sometimes a surprise attack works against the most highly trained and skilled opponents. I'd have to remember that.

He countered my next lunge with one of his own. We met in the center, masks and bodies so close I could feel his heat and see his smile behind the mesh.

The bell guards of our foils clanged.

My senses sang.

"Halt. *Corps á corps!*" Gareth called. "If you two are close enough to kiss, you're too close to fence. Yellow card to both of you."

We backed apart. I had to bite my cheeks to keep a feral grin at bay.

For many long moments we battled, back and forth. My face and back dripped with sweat. The terry cloth band inside my mask caught most of it. But the occasional salty drop stung my eyes.

Every time I changed tactics, he met my attack and countered, always leading with a strong point and incredible flexibility.

If this bout were a duel to the death, I didn't know if I'd have the stamina to win through. Even with the added advantage of my Celestial Blade.

Told you, dahling, you need more work with a true weapon, Scrap whispered into the back of my mind. But he stayed away. I couldn't sense him near my left shoulder, his favorite perch.

The next clash of blades brought us *corps á corps* again, which gained us each a point but did nothing to dampen the heated sensuality of the match.

Finally, my opponent caught me with a wicked flick. He took the bout with a score of five to four.

We removed our masks and saluted, then moved together to shake hands—left-handed without gloves. Our gazes locked. His long fingers wrapped around my hand with something more than respect for a bout well fought.

We nearly exchanged promises with our eyes.

"Good bout," I said sincerely, trying not to pant.

His hand remained folded around mine. Little thrills of electricity raced up my arm to my heart. I forgot where and when I was.

"Sloppy, Tess," Coach Peterson said. He stood, hands on hips and with a deep frown of disapproval on his face. All the while his eyes twinkled with mischief and fire for good fencing.

Embarrassment burned my ears, and I finally dropped the stranger's hand. Then I pointedly stepped off the strip, clearing it for the next pair.

"You can't let a pretty face distract you, Tess. Your grip was too tight and your balance too far back," Coach continued his lecture. "Slowed you down."

"And as for you, my friend." He slapped the stranger on the back. "You overreached yourself the first three times she scored. You left your lower *octet* open and vulnerable. She caught you there on two of her points. Tess, let me formally introduce you to my old friend, Donovan Estevez. We trained together in Colorado Springs umpteen million years ago. He'd have made a good fencer if he wasn't so busy making millions in gaming software."

"Tess Noncoiré." I shook hands with him again, right-handed without gloves, needing to feel the warmth of his hand in mine. By this time we'd both opened the neck flaps of our jackets to dissipate body heat.

It didn't help.

"I know who you are. I've read all of your books—even the ones you wrote under a different name. The last one was worth the wait." Estevez smiled again, nearly blinding me with those teeth.

I slipped my hand free of his and dropped my eyes. I did not discuss the long years between my fifth book and my sixth, the most recent one.

No one knew about the year after Dill's death when I'd made myself sick with grief and locked myself away from reality in the Citadel of the Sisterhood. When I finally emerged, scarred, trained in many weapons, and accompanied by Scrap, I'd needed another half year to finish writing the book and sell it, then another nine months until it saw print.

"Enough mooning about. You can flirt over coffee after class," Coach intruded. "Drills, Tess. You need drills and concentration." He practically shoved me toward the back corner where Morgan, a twelve-year-old girl, awaited me. "Parry/riposte, until your arms threaten to drop off," Coach called after me.

I knew the girl; she'd make the Olympic team if she didn't get distracted by boys and high school in the next couple of years. No insult to drill with her. We stood nearly eye to eye.

I looked over my shoulder to see coach setting up a bout between Estevez and Gareth, the young man who had officiated for us. Gareth was quick and strong but lacked discipline and point control.

By the end of the evening, I'd fought seven bouts, winning all but that first one. I even managed a win against Niki, the assistant coach, in saber. She was the only one who defeated Donovan Estevez that night.

I dripped sweat, and was on an exercise high by the time the clock clicked over to nine. I needed coffee and carbs to replenish my body and calm my mind.

For those long two hours I had totally forgotten Scrap. But I could not forget Donovan Estevez. My eyes strayed to his whenever we had a moment to breathe between bouts.

We spent far too much time just staring at each other.

Coach gathered Estevez and me, along with three other adult students. We all headed toward the diner across the street that served the best pie on Cape Cod.

A decidedly yellow Scrap appeared out of nowhere and jumped into my gym bag, strangely subdued. He remained in the bag when I tossed it into the back seat of my car on the way to the diner. But he poked his head up long enough to hiss at me.

Watch yourself, Tess. He smells wrong.

Then I looked around the parking lot for Donovan Estevez. Scrap could only mean the newcomer.

Estevez dropped his gym bag into the trunk of a cream-colored BMW sedan.

My sense of danger flared at the base of my spine. At the same time, his dazzling smile threatened to swamp my common sense and willpower to resist him, or any man who was not Dill.

Oh, Tess, my love, what have we gotten into this time?

I cannot come close to this man. I dare not let you get close to him. What does he smell like? Certainly not human. But not demon either. Something almost familiar. Like leather and sage and a dry musk, not acrid but not sweet either.

I need to make a quick circuit through the dimensions to trace that scent. I dare not leave my babe. Yet I cannot get close to her while that man holds her enthralled.

I wish she could find a nice, normal man to love. One who loves her as deeply as I do. One who has the right smell about him and won't be intimidated by her warrior calling. For it is a calling. A vocation. A way of life she can never give up.

Until she dies. And then I will die, too. For my life is tied to hers more completely than in a marriage or a mortal love.

For the first time since leaving the Citadel, I am truly afraid, for myself and for Tess.

Chapter 9

I went into the diner cautious and withdrawn. By midnight, Donovan and I sat alone, coffee cups empty, pie eaten, and totally fascinated with each other. At least he held my fascination. I presumed he was equally entranced by the way he held my gaze and looked longingly into my eyes.

He held my hand across the table. Little thrills invaded my sense of calm and rationality.

He admitted that fairly equal mixtures of Coleville Indian, Irish, Spanish, and Russian blood flowed through his veins. I confessed to my parents' French Canadian heritage, but not that Dad and his thirty-something male tennis instructor partner lived a few miles away from me, to Mom's total embarrassment.

We discussed politics, art, the state of the school system, the weather, and fencing. Often back to fencing and other blade weapons, fighting strategy, and the place of rules and honor in a battle.

The diner staff sat bleary-eyed and resentful in a corner booth, having already cleaned up and cashed out.

Scrap never made an appearance though he loved the old diner for its damp cellar.

Every time I paused to think about this oddity, Donovan smiled and I forgot to be worried.

When my yawns punctuated my sentences too heavily, Donovan paid the bill and escorted me back to my car.

"Nice car," I said when the conversation stalled, needing to become more personal or be abandoned. I didn't know which.

"It's a rental. I travel enough to reserve the same model I own. I don't want to have to think about where the windshield wiper switch is while driving strange roads." He grinned again and I forgot to breathe.

Dill had had the same effect upon me.

"May I follow you home?" he asked a bit wistfully.

"I can defend myself . . ." I replied, thinking only of the chivalrous meaning behind his words.

My body tightened with longing. Heat flashed from my breasts to my ears and downward. Could I? Dared I?

Would Dill haunt me in the middle of sex with another man?

"Oh, I'm sorry, not tonight. I have a lot of work to do before I leave town again Thursday morning." But, oh, I wanted him to take me in his arms and kiss me, lingering long, holding me tight, as we learned each other's bodies.

Some tiny part of Scrap's warning nagged at me.

"Where are you headed this time, Tess?"

"Tri-Cities, Washington. I'm GOH at High Desert Con."

"I have clients in Pascoe, Washington. Perhaps I can arrange to be there . . ."

I lifted my face, expecting his lips to meet mine.

He paused.

We looked at each other with longing.

His lips brushed my cheek.

Disappointed—and relieved—I got into my little hybrid car and started the engine before he could add any more persuasion to his request.

The moment I cleared the parking lot, Scrap popped onto the dashboard, pale red and puffing away at his smelly cigar. He snarled between clouds of acrid smoke.

About time you showed up, babe.

I opened the window and let some chill night air in and some of the smoke out. Along with some of his noisome gas.

You want to do an Internet search on that guy, Tessie. He smells wrong. He smells so badly I can't get near him.

"And you smell rotten from mold and cigars. Not to mention your lactose intolerance. You've been into the heavy cream again. Tonight, I want to sleep in my own bed, not bent over the keyboard of the computer."

Maybe you should teach me to use the computer . . .

"Not on your life."

What if it means your life?

He grinned around the cigar, showing his dagger-sharp teeth. His color paled, took on the greenish tinge of teasing.

I couldn't take him seriously when he showed his teeth and flapped his ears. He looked too much like a cartoon.

"Tonight I sleep. Tomorrow we search."

Monday, after the con, we go look at that motel. Maybe Dillwyn's death wasn't senseless. Maybe he was saving you from something worse than the fire.

"Like what?" I demanded, suddenly angry. I couldn't go back to that little place in Half Moon Lake, Washington. I just couldn't.

Though I'd thought about it after that dream of Dill in my bed back in Portland.

The tiny resort town built around a mineral lake was only a two hour drive north of Tri-Cities. I could rent a car, drive up after lunch, and be back at the con for a late dinner.

Like that guy that you left in the dust back there. Hooking up with him might be worse than burning at the stake.

Scrap disappeared into that other dimension where I could not follow.

"DONOVAN ESTEVEZ IS CEO and founder of Halfling Gaming Co., Inc.," I said as I swept a wooden replica of the Celestial Blade through the air of my basement, testing the weight and balance. Each end of the quarterstaff curved into a sickle blade, one waxing and one waning. A dozen fine spikes extruded from the outside curve of the blades. Symbolically, I fought with the twin faces of the Moon Goddess Kynthia with the Milky Way flowing behind her like tresses blown in the solar wind.

I'd actually seen her face in the sky once. A considerable blessing according to my Sister warriors.

And only once. Most people never got the opportunity even if they knew what to look for.

The moment of peace, serenity, and connectedness to the universe I'd experienced in that instant of viewing the Goddess spurred me on to finish my training. Despite the tension and disagreements that grew steadily between me and the Sisterhood. All in hopes of catching another glimpse of the elusive star configuration and regaining that moment when I knew my place in the universe and why I existed.

I was still striving for that.

So you found out his company is legit. What about him?

Scrap unfurled his wings. They'd grown a little since I first met him, and now supported him for short flights and extended his bounces. He fluttered about, daring me to catch him with the training blade.

I didn't know why he wore a pink feather boa draped around his neck. He usually played dress up with me, not himself.

He could only assume the blade's conformation when in the presence of something totally evil, like a being from another dimension—a demon. Hence the less lethal training blade that matched the true one in size, weight, and balance.

"Donovan's bio on the Web page mentioned an MBA from University of Florida. He's not married. No mention of a divorce or paying child support. Almost made the Fortune 500 list of most eligible bachelors."

I sensed a pattern in Scrap's movements. As he swooped up and to the right, I swung the left-hand blade to catch him on the downward spiral.

Only the boa tangled with the tines on the outside edge of my blade.

Fooled ya!

Scrap chortled, yanking his garment free, scattering tiny feathers through the air and into my nose.

I sneezed as he arced farther right, almost behind me.

I spun in place and caught his tail in the spikes, dragging him away from the support beam that would hinder my swing.

"You did what?" I laughed as I released him with a twist of the blade.

Timing is better. But you can't play in the battlefield. You can't hurt me in this dimension. Attack for real.

He bounced and tangled his tail around the staff at the opposite end. All of a sudden, he put on weight and form, dragging my weapon down.

I compensated and flung him back toward the stairs. He landed with a gush of expelled air, odiferous from both ends.

The boa lay at his feet. He snatched it up and wound it around his neck.

"You are such a flaming queen," I snorted.

Am NOT!

Scrap sounded genuinely affronted.

"Are, too! Why else would you wear a *pink* feather boa?"

B'Cartlin demons have pink feathered ruffs around their necks.

He fussed with the drape of the boa, getting it just right. It matched his pink skin perfectly.

You need to know their vulnerabilities.

"And how would you know?" I stood over him, still balancing the blade.

Last time through the chat room they were on guard.

He stuck out his receding chin.

"And just where is this chat room you mention but never explain?" A new tactic came to mind. I played it through three times, wondering if I was fast enough to make it work.

I'll take you there when you're ready. It won't make sense until then.

With a quick thrust I stuck the flat of the blade under his butt, scooped high, and twisted at the same time.

Scrap flew over my head and landed, face and belly flat against the far wall.

He slid down with a grunt, boa still in place.

"I thought you said I can't hurt you?" I dashed over to him, concerned when he lay there like a puddle of ectoplasm.

"Who are you talking to, Tess?" Mom called from the top of the stairs.

I cursed long and fluently under my breath as I stashed the Celestial Blade in the armory, a hidden cubbyhole beneath the stairs, and slammed the door. It latched automatically.

In the last second, I grabbed the very visible boa and hid it behind my back. Nothing I could do about the flecks of pink feathers scattered around the floor. I just hoped Mom wouldn't notice them in the dim light from a single bare bulb overhead.

"I thought you went shopping in town, Mom," I called up to her. I leaned against the door to my secret room and panted a moment.

Scrap disappeared.

"I finished, dear. I hope you are doing laundry down there. You know you are leaving again tomorrow and I don't think you have a clean set of underwear anywhere in the house." She floated down the steep stairs like an elegant lady descending to a ballroom. Of course she wore heels and pearls; a lady did not shop wearing more casual clothing. I'd never be that graceful. Mostly because I didn't work at it like she did.

"Laundry's all done." I pointed to the piles of folded clothing, sheets, and towels atop the drop table across the back wall—well away from the armory. Thankfully, I remembered to use the hand that didn't hold the pink feathers. I dropped it into the shadows behind the stairs.

Damn! A glimmer of light shone beneath the door.

Scrap, please turn off that light, I pleaded silently. *If you don't, she'll be in there cleaning. Not a single saucer of mold will be left. Ever!*

"Here, Mom, will you carry these upstairs for me?" I dashed over to the laundry counter on the opposite wall and handed her a pile of towels. I'd even fluffed them in the dryer an extra time so she couldn't complain about how old and threadbare they had become.

A nanosecond before she turned back to face the stairs *and* the armory, the light beneath the door extinguished.

I breathed a sigh of relief, and Scrap returned to my shoulder. He looked his usual gray with just a hint of pink. No boa.

"Oh, Teresa." Mom turned around quickly, as she had when I was a teen and she was trying to catch me hiding a package of condoms or cigarettes.

I returned her peering survey of me with innocence.

Her gaze lingered on my left shoulder.

I knew Scrap made faces at her. The longer her gaze lingered, the more I began to sweat and the stiller Scrap became.

"Yes, Mom?"

"Uncle George just called. We've changed family game night from Sunday to tonight so you can come."

"I have to pack . . ."

"You have an hour before dinner to do that. I'm fixing my special *ragout au vin.*"

"Mom, *ragout* is stew with wine, so if it's *ragout au vin,* do you double the wine?" I asked.

She snarled at me and retreated upstairs.

"I need your support tonight, Scrap," I whispered. "The only way they will let me get out of game night is if I answer every question correctly, even the sports and science questions."

You mean cheat? That's against the rules of the Sisterhood.

Scrap sounded enormously happy at that prospect.

You'd cheat your own family?

"With my family it's not cheating, it's survival. The rules of battle say survival comes first, honor and dignity second."

Donovan had said that last night.

I am not gay! What an insult. And from my babe, too. What would make her say that?

Imps can't be gay. Can they?

Ooooh, Mum would be murderously livid if she ever suspected one of her offspring leaned that way.

Maybe I should admit to it in Mum's presence just to put her knickers in a hot pink twist.

My babe doesn't care which way I lean. That's one reason why I love her so.

But I am not gay. I just like pretty clothes. That doesn't make me gay. I'm the weapon of a Celestial Warrior.

Tess is learning to think like a warrior. But will it be enough, soon enough? The fact that I grew a little bit after the abortive attempt to transform must mean that I will continue to grow each time we encounter evil. Each time the evil will grow worse, requiring more strength and agility from both of us.

Something looms just over the horizon. MoonFeather and her horoscopes can break through the veil of the future only a little. Only enough to see warning signs. Her talents help. Not enough.

Do I dare? Am I skilled enough to manipulate time to catch a glimpse of the future or the nature of our enemies? The least slip can trap me in that awesome dimension. The tiniest moment of inattention will make me vulnerable to the portal guardians. In the dimension of the future I have only my wits—no magic, nothing to help me.

The past is easier to view as long as I don't try to manipulate it.

That leads to total disaster.

Tess needs me tonight. Any test of my skills with time must wait.

Uncle George really needs a comeuppance at game night. When he feels superior, gloating over a triumph in the game, he searches Tess' house for her secret stash of cash just so he can afford to get drunk. If we beat him at game night, maybe he'll go crawl back into his hole and leave the money and my mold alone.

Now what can I do to keep Mom out of here?

I know, I'll persuade Standish the standoffish ghost to prowl down here rather than in the butler's pantry. Mom fears that ghost more than any of the others, mostly because he wants to be alone and howls like a werewolf when we disturb him.

Chapter 10

"Tess!" My old friend Bob Brown greeted me at the miniscule Pascoe Airport. He enfolded me in a hug worthy of the black bear he resembled, (or was it a Sasquatch, so frequently in the news of late?). Six feet tall, two hundred twenty pounds of muscle, thinning, curly black hair against tanned skin. For once he'd trimmed his beard. He had a BS in nuclear physics and an MS in health physics. He worked at the local nuclear reservation developing shields against radiation.

"You've lost weight, kid. There's hardly enough of you to gather to my benighted bosom."

"Forty-seven-and-a-half pounds," I chortled, still proud of the fact I'd kept off the weight the fever had wasted from my frame. "I think you're mixing metaphors again, Bobby," I laughed as I extricated myself from his arms. Tears came to my eyes unbidden. I hadn't seen my friend since Dill's funeral. A lot had happened since then. Quite a lot.

"You okay? Dill went so suddenly, and I didn't hear from you for so long, I was afraid you'd cracked up."

"I nearly did. But it's been nearly three years, Bob. I've finished grieving and moved on."

Yeah, right, Scrap mumbled from atop my laptop case.

"Ready to move on to me?" Bob asked hopefully. His nose worked like it itched. "Do you smell cigar smoke?"

"Wishful thinking, Bob. You gave up smoking ten years ago." I grabbed the handle of the wheeled case and dragged it, and Scrap, toward the baggage claim area. Bob had no choice but to follow.

"How many cons have we been to together since we met freshman year at Providence U, Tess? A hundred? Two? And you still don't love me enough to marry me."

"More wishful thinking. You're my best friend. Let's not spoil it." I waved a skycap over.

"You don't even trust me enough to carry your bags?" He pouted, but a smile tugged at his mouth. We'd known each other too long for us to take such banter seriously.

"I don't travel light anymore. Especially when you are tipping the skycaps," I teased.

"You really don't travel light anymore," he whistled as I claimed two oversized suitcases and three boxes full of books fresh from the publisher.

"One of those books has your name on it, the rest are for the dealer's room. There was a warehouse glitch in getting the order here in time."

"I tried to be easy on you with the schedule, Tess, so we can go filking." Bob loved sitting up in a ballroom all night swapping parody tunes and Celtic lays with all and sundry. I did, too, once upon a time.

"I haven't sung since . . . no, Bob, I'd rather not."

"Dill was a good man, Tess. Maybe you should sing something in memory of him. Get yourself some real closure."

"What? 'There's a Bimbo on the Cover of my Book'? That was his favorite."

"Is there a bimbo on the cover of your book?"

"Not this time. My publisher went tasteful for a change. They even spelled my name right."

For my first five books I'd written as Teresa Newcombe so readers could remember it and spell it correctly, though the copyright had always been as Teresa Noncoiré. When I had reemerged from my self-imposed exile, Teresa Newcombe was a fading memory among the powers that be in the book world. My publisher wanted a new name on the book he promised to push onto the bestseller lists. I decided to stick to my legal name. I'd never planned to take on Dill's name of Cooper. Fans had no trouble pronouncing or spelling Noncoiré after the book hit five best-seller lists including the *NYT*.

"A filk would be more appropriate for Dill than a hymn or dirge. Just promise to sing at my funeral." Bob hugged me again.

"Since I plan for you to outlive me by at least a decade, that might be a little hard."

"Oh, you'll come back as a ghost to haunt me at every con we've ever been to together."

Laughing, we made our way out to the parking lot, trailed by the overloaded skycap.

Bob drove into the porte cochere of the hotel five minutes from the airport. I got out without waiting for him or the valet to open my door. Eagerly, I arched and stretched my back, checking my surroundings for unexplained shadows as I had been taught by my Sisterhood. In the still warm night air of the high desert plateau of the Columbia River, I spotted a familiar cream-colored BMW across the parking lot.

Pointedly, I did not look closer. If Donovan Estevez had followed me here, he would find me. But he would not surprise me.

"Bob, are there any anthropology professors at the community college who specialize in local Indian lore?" I asked as I registered and the bellhop struggled with my luggage.

"Excuse me, I happen to have several anthropology degrees," a clipped voice remarked at my other elbow.

I closed my eyes a moment to master my irritation. Scrap bounced around the high counter, blinking shades of neon green.

"Guilford Van der Hoyden-Smythe." I turned to confront the tall nerd who had stalked me in Portland. "If you specialized in Pacific Northwest native lore, you might have had answers to my questions three weeks ago."

My dear friend held out his hand to introduce himself. "Bob Brown, I'm guest liaison and programming chair for the con."

"Call me Gollum." Van der Hoyden-Smythe reached across me and shook Bob's proffered hand vigorously.

Just then three people, two female, one male, wearing jeans and T-shirts and demon masks sauntered past. Very good demon masks at that. One had numerous tentacles dangling from wrinkled purple skin. I could not detect where the mask ended and their hair began. The other two had the furred faces of bats.

Bob draped an arm about my suddenly cold shoulders. He knew about my phobia. As long as they didn't show their wings, I'd be okay, though.

Hopefully.

Gape-mouthed, Gollum stared at them.

"Don't worry. That's rather mild for costuming at this con. Wait until the masquerade on Saturday night." I patted his arm in reassurance. He kept staring at the con goers.

"Part of the game is for them to stay in character, so don't be surprised if you hear them speaking nonsense words pretending it's a demon language." Bob said straight-faced. But not for long.

We both burst out laughing in memory of the time a Klingon had ordered a beer in Klingon at this very con five years ago. Bob and I had called the puzzled waitress over and suggested she serve the man prune juice. She did. No other Klingon dared order anything in any language but English after that.

I guess imitators aren't as tough as the real thing. Prune juice is, after all, a warrior's drink. They served it every morning at the Citadel of the Sisterhood.

I sobered instantly with that memory.

"I don't know any anthro profs at the college, but the guy who owns the Stalking Moon brew pub is full-blooded Sanpoil Indian—that's part of the Colville Confederation. He's full of tribal stories. We could have dinner and a tankard there," Bob suggested to both of us.

My senses flared. "Stalking Moon?"

"Yeah. Leonard Stalking Moon owns the place."

"Let the bellhop stow my luggage in my room. I'm starving. Take me to the pub now." I marched back out to the covered drive knowing both men would follow me.

Scrap landed on my shoulder, chortling and puffing away. I calmly reached up and took the cigar out of his mouth. It dripped pink slime as I tossed it into the bucket of sand placed outside for that purpose.

"Stay quiet, watch, and listen closely," I whispered to him.

I'll watch you fend off two admirers any day, he laughed. *This is going to be fun.*

"This is work," I whispered back as cold dread swept through me. I was getting closer to a battle with demons. "Special work that we have trained for."

We are never fully trained until we survive the first full battle.

"We've had one battle."

Fighting off that dog with a fireplace poker was not a true battle. Not a true test of our skills, our lives, and our vocation. But it is coming. Trust me.

Interlude

A warrior in training sends out pheromones that will attract every imp who can squeeze through the portal and all those on the loose. A kind of mating ritual was about to begin. But this joining of two beings had nothing to do with marriage and propagation. It had everything to do with survival.

Normally all the available imps will gather around the training field. The candidate bouts with her Sisters. She works up a sweat, straining muscles and ingenuity to score, something opens in her mind, and she will see an imp. Not all of them yet. But one. The special one she is most suited to meld with.

I had to be that imp. I had to fight off my bigger brethren so that I was the only imp on the field that day.

The imps who came to the choosing field that day were all fully grown, aware of their powers and their need to meld with a warrior. For imps are incomplete and without honor if they cannot bond.

But I am older than all of them. Stunted I may be in body, the runt of Mum's litters. My mind and ingenuity are far more developed than theirs. How else could I survive my one hundred two siblings? And Mum.

Life among imps is harsh. It has to be. Only the best survive. My sibs learned that from me the hard way. I knew I was something special because I had survived though I should have died a century ago when I failed to grow to full size.

Imps expect their brethren to fight fair. But life isn't fair. Demons don't fight fair. I pulled every dirty trick I could think of: gouging eyes, tying tails in knots to destroy balance, shredding wings with my hind claws while I dug out warts on faces. Whatever eliminated my competition.

When Tess walked onto the training field that day, strong, fit, and fully recovered, but inexorably scarred by the imp flu, only I awaited her. A torn ear, nearly severed tail, and beautiful bruises all over (two new glorious warts) but I was there.

"SO, THIS CITADEL SITS directly upon a portal between reality and the demon world," I said with a straight face. The night I had witnessed the Goddess in the sky had convinced me that something strange had happened that night. The warrior Sisterhood had some serious enemies. But I had yet to see any evidence those enemies were demons and not mortal predators.

Sisters Paige, Mary, and Electra nodded.

"And we are from the world of mortals, but this Citadel exists in neither that realm nor the one of demons; somewhere in between," I continued. Just to make certain I had the facts straight, as weird and unbelievable as they might seem. Seem to them. I had yet to be fully convinced. I wouldn't need much to push me either direction.

I had to concentrate. My mind had already begun constructing a new book, an entire series based upon what was going on here.

I'd started writing it on a lined spiral notebook with a stubby pencil. In the evenings, I told stories to the Sisters, making them a part of the story. Some thoroughly enjoyed the novelty. Others . . . ? Most of the older Sisters, especially Sister Gert, the leader, and those so entrenched in the life here and so long cut off from the world they had lost most of their memories of reality, scoffed and scorned and tried to get me to stop my tales. Those Sisters had no use for books, fiction or non. They had no television, no computers. No electricity to run them. And only a primitive plumbing system to provide sanitation.

I was bored out of my gourd except for my new book. And I'd only been on my feet and training a month. A total of three months here. How was I supposed to remain here the rest of my life and stay sane?

We occupied our days with training. This morning I stood easily in the middle of a sandy square, about five meters to the side, in the middle of the Citadel courtyard. The three arms mistresses all looked alike to me: medium height and stocky build with lots of muscles in arms, legs, and torsos. Not a bit of fat on any of them. But then, I didn't have any fat left on my body either. The fever had eaten it away and no matter how much I ate, I'd only regained about two of the fifty pounds I had lost.

After only a month of working out, my entire body had become whipcord lean and strong.

For the first time in my life, I was not pudgy. In fact, I was downright skinny. Ten pounds underweight instead of forty over. To my eyes I looked positively anorexic.

But I was strong. And gaining fitness and stamina by the day.

Paige, on my left, had a shock of black hair pulled back into a tight bun. Mary's wispy blond curls framed her face like an angelic halo. Electra had a bigger bust and lots of fiery red hair that clashed with her bloodred workout clothes. All three had long scars from temple to jaw to match mine. Theirs had faded to a thin white line. Mine still looked red, raw, and angry.

"If there is a portal, why can't it be sealed?" I asked. "And what's to keep demons from finding and opening another?" I needed those answers to satisfy my own curiosity as well as to plot the next scene in the new book.

The arms mistresses looked at each other. Some silent communication passed between them. "No questions," they spoke in unison.

Electra stepped forward one pace, the obvious spokeswoman of the group. "You'll stop talking and learn to fight properly when you face a Kajiri demon head-on with only a Celestial Blade for a weapon." She tossed me a quarterstaff with strange hooked ends.

I caught the thing easily. It balanced well in one hand.

"What kind of wood is this?" I asked, fascinated with it. The curved blades on either end seemed just as sharp as a steel sword.

"We call it imp wood. It is an exact replica of the weapon that will come to you when you face a demon. We are here to teach you how to use it." Paige picked up her own weapon, a duplicate of mine, from a nest of them at the edge of the sandy workout plot. She took a stance, feet spread, knees bent, back straight, staff balanced easily in both hands.

I mimicked her pose.

"Copy me move for move," Paige said. She raised the right end of her staff and thrust it forward.

My move blocked hers.

"Good. Again."

We played with the staffs for a good twenty minutes, increasing the speed and force of each move until we were both covered with sweat and my arms shook with the unaccustomed activity. The most intensive exercise I'd had yet at the Citadel. Any one day here gave me more work since I nearly failed physical education my freshman year at Providence U.

Then Mary jumped into the square with her own staff. The two of them went at me in unison. I barely had time to wipe the sweat out of my eyes when Electra took over for the two of them. She put me through my paces at twice the speed and ferocity of the other two combined.

My knees trembled, my heart beat overtime, and my lungs labored before she let me call a halt.

She'll do, a strangely accented voice called from behind my left foot.

I looked. No one stood behind me.

"Lower," Sister Gert, the head of the Sisterhood, commanded me. She sounded . . . disappointed or disapproving. I couldn't tell which. But then she didn't much like me because I wanted to know everything and anything about this place and the people here, all at once.

I looked at my feet.

A translucent imp, tinged with the same green as the fresh flower sprouts two plots over, stared back at me with huge eyes. His ragged ears flapped, showing off a rippled rainbow of colors along the serrated and torn edges. He grinned, showing pointed teeth beneath his snub nose. He rested his taloned paws on his pot belly. His tiny wings fluttered in the slight breeze.

I was so tired and dehydrated I didn't have enough energy left to panic.

"What is that?" I raised my staff ready to smite the thing.

"No, don't." Electra grabbed the staff away from me. "That's your imp. You need to ask his name."

"My what?" I rounded on the three. Each had a similar being perched on their shoulders. The imps took on shades of lavender. They looked larger, more fully formed than the little thing at my feet. And they all had full-sized wings that rose above their heads in sharp and hooked points. The tips of the appendages dipped well down the backs of the women whose shoulders they sat upon.

Even Sister Gert had one. Bigger than all the rest.

"We all have them," Paige explained. "Our imps."

"That sorry excuse for an imp is the only one that showed up to claim you," Sister Gert snorted, as if the imp reflected the sort of Sister I would make.

My knees gave out, and I plunked onto the churned sand at my feet. Between fatigue and shock I was done in, incapable of absorbing anything more.

The little imp hopped into my lap and stared at me in frank appraisal. I couldn't even feel his weight he was so insubstantial.

Can't fight demons sitting down, babe.

"Oh, shut up!" I buried my face in my hands, unsure if I should cry or laugh out loud.

"Ask his name!" Mary said quietly. "He's not fully yours until you exchange names, and we can't get on with your training until you have an imp."

"Okay, I'll bite. What's your name, imp?"

Scrap will do for now.

Did he speak or sneer?. I couldn't be sure which.

"Scrap? Because you're just a scrap of an imp?" The ridiculousness of the situation and my total exhaustion took me. I rolled on the ground unable to contain my laughter.

Sister Gert stalked off in high dudgeon.

I'd always wanted to use the word. Now I had the perfect example. And a place to put it in the book.

The imp—Scrap, I should say—pulled my hair and pinched me hard.

I sobered instantly.

Stop laughing, you miserable, no-good excuse for a warrior. Do you know what I had to go through to get here?

Only then did I notice just how battered and bruised he looked. I thought I was too tired to care about anything, even Sister Gert's disapproval. But my heart went out to the little beast.

"Sorry, Scrap."

"Your name," Sister Mary said gently. "You have to tell it your name."

"I'm Tess," I said, looking into Scrap's eyes. "That's Tess, not Teresa and not babe."

Right, dahling.

The thing wiggled and settled himself. Then he hopped onto my shoulder with a flutter of his stubby wings. They barely aided his ascent.

"I guess we are well suited for each other," I sighed. "What is it you do exactly?"

"He becomes your Celestial Blade when you face the demons in battle." Paige prodded me with her wooden replica weapon.

"Until a demon is present, you must train with imp wood." Sister Mary took a fighting stance.

Grab your blade, dahling, they're gonna attack.

I rolled and rose to my feet, blade in hand, in one smooth move, blocking three attacks within as many heartbeats.

The melding has begun.

Chapter 11

Vampire bats do not suck blood. They make tiny cuts in the skin of large birds, cattle, horses, pigs, and upon occasion, humans. Then they lap the blood from the wounds.

"Leonard Stalking Moon, this is my good friend Tess," Bob introduced me to the owner and brewmaster of a local pub.

I shook hands with the stocky Native American, not much taller than I, older by at least a decade. Hard to tell with his near hairless mahogany skin. He wore his sleek black hair in two long braids. A harelip scar marred his upper lip.

He looked me up and down with the same intensity I gave him.

"Are you any relation to Cynthia Stalking Moon?" I asked quietly, hoping Van der Hoyden-Smythe was too occupied ordering drinks and pizza for all of us to hear my question.

"My second cousin's daughter." He finished his appraisal of me and pointed to a photo of a smiling adolescent girl behind the bar. Cynthia's picture stood out among the dozens of photos of happy patrons.

"She looks happy," I said. She also looked less gaunt and strained than she had at the park. But that was an unusual situation. "Is she with you yet?"

"Yes, thanks to you, Tess Noncoiré. I hope you know how special is our Cynthia," Leonard replied almost in a whisper. "My daughter Keisha wanted her. She has fancy degrees and works in a museum, but she lives in Seattle. Cherry and I thought Cynthia would be happier here."

"She told you about me?"

"Everything." He looked closely at my left shoulder, then nodded.

I gulped. Had he seen Scrap? If so, did he know what the imp represented?

"My family, my entire tribe, owes you much," Leonard said, handing me a foaming glass of ale with a strange purple cast. "On the house. A very special brew with huckleberries, only for family and special friends. Very special friends who are almost family. For you, Bob, and your friend, everything is on the house tonight."

I smiled my thanks to him.

"Your thanks are appreciated but not necessary. I was just doing my job," I demurred.

"I know. Tomorrow, you speak to the high school and middle school English class. Cynthia will be there. She will thank you personally." He smiled hugely, showing an endearing gap between his upper front teeth and a twinkle in his eye that reminded me of MoonFeather.

Then I noticed a necklace of some sort tucked beneath his shirt. Only a little bit of knotted hemp showed around his open collar. MoonFeather had shown me a similar one in a book. That was a shaman's knot. Leonard Stalking Moon probably did see beyond this reality.

"You and I will talk more later. About just how special Cynthia is." I looked pointedly at his necklace.

He blushed and tucked it deeper beneath his short-sleeved sports shirt so that it didn't show.

"Will you sit with us a few moments? We have questions about the dog."

"In a bit. I have other customers right now." He moved to the end of the bar and served several more drinks.

"What was that about?" Bob asked, jostling my elbow so that I almost spilled my mug of beer.

No way to avoid telling him at least some of the tale. He'd never believe most of it.

"Well . . . let's sit down first." I wended my way between scarred and scuffed tables to the booth Gollum had claimed. The new building worked hard at looking old and rustic with rough planked walls and floors. The many windows were high and curtained, the lights electrified oil lamps.

"What did he say?" Gollum asked the moment I sat down across the table from him, next to Bob.

"He'll join us in a bit. I think he knows something about the dog."

"What dog?" Bob asked.

I let Gollum fill him in. Thankfully, the man left out the crucial point about Scrap becoming a poker and any reference to the Sisterhood of the Celestial Blade Warriors.

As Gollum finished, he took off his glasses and scrubbed his face with his hands. He looked weary.

For the first time I could look into his pale blue eyes. Really look. Our gazes met, and trust flowed between us as if we had known each other for ages.

Or perhaps in another time and dimension.

Those thoughts shocked me. I filled my books with ideas like that. I never considered that it could happen to me. Could happen in reality, anywhere outside the pages of a fantasy book.

I leaned against the high straight back of the booth and closed my eyes. Closed Gollum out of my thoughts.

"So, you followed Tess here just to find out about a stray dog?"

I didn't add that Gollum had stalked the dog across three or four states.

Bob shook his head incredulously. He also moved his hand to cover mine, laying claim.

His hand was warm and comforting. The contact lacked the electricity of Donovan Estevez's touch.

Naughty, naughty! Scrap chortled. *Letting poor Gollum believe you are taken.*

He slurped some of the foam off the top of my glass.

I made a casual gesture, as if shooing away a fly, that sent Scrap sprawling onto the floor, under the feet of two couples getting up to dance.

He had to scramble to keep from getting crushed.

Of course, he could have popped into another dimension. But then he might miss something.

"What's so important about a stray dog?" Bob asked. He downed a considerable portion of his porter. "Send a sharpshooter after it. No more problem."

"Trust me, Bob, this is no ordinary stray dog." I considered my next words carefully. Bob might be an avid reader of science fiction and fantasy, but his belief in the supernatural was limited to his Christian religion.

"Bob, this dog is like something out of my books. Beyond the reach of an ordinary sharpshooter. Beyond the size and strength of any mortal dog."

Both he and Gollum stilled for a long moment.

A tingle grew out of the base of my spine. I looked about the pub, peering into the shadows. I expected to see the dog, green slime dripping from its jowls.

Scrap turned bright pink and took up a defensive position near my hand.

Leonard Stalking Moon narrowed his eyes and lifted his harelip in a snarl as the front door opened.

I half stood, ready to face the demon dog we had been discussing.

Donovan Estevez sauntered into the pub as if he owned it. He brought with him two young ladies and a young man. From their T-shirts, I recognized them as the kids with the demon masks. Thankfully, they'd left the masks off for a public appearance outside the con. The bartender—not Leonard—carded Donovan's friends but let them enter.

Donovan surveyed the room, flashing that brilliant smile.

I relaxed instantly, and my belly warmed. Nothing to fear here. The tingle of warning evaporated and I waved in greeting to a man I considered a friend and wanted as a lover.

Scrap remained quite bright as he popped out of this dimension.

See ya later, babe, when stinky man is not around.

I knew I should pay attention to Scrap's implied warning. I knew it. Yet Donovan's welcoming smile and my blossoming affection for him clouded my senses. He and his friends sat at the table adjoining our booth and proceeded to monopolize the conversation. I didn't care. My weekend was complete.

Bob and Gollum faded in significance.

Leonard Stalking Moon avoided our table for the rest of the evening, and I learned nothing new about the dog.

The stinky man drove me away. He came too close to Tess and drove me away. What is he? There is nothing in imp lore to account for him or his friends.

Leonard Stalking Moon knows about me somehow. He must be a shaman. I wonder if I can communicate with him. He might know something about Donovan. He might be able to tell me how to stay close to Tess when he is around. I know that she needs me.

Even if she does not think so. All he has to do is smile and she succumbs to his every wish.

But I have noticed something. I will try something when she is alone.

DONOVAN ESCORTED ME back to my room when we'd all eaten and drunk our fill. I thought I'd have trouble ditching Bob and Gollum, but those two seemed to have bonded. They had role-playing games they wanted to check out.

The three young people in Donovan's wake evaporated.

The huckleberry ale was wonderful, leaving me mellow.

Now that I had him alone, Donovan filled my vision and my thoughts. Perhaps tonight I might, just might, get over my lingering inhibitions and doubts. Perhaps tonight I'd let him stay with me in the huge suite paid for by the con.

He held my hand in the elevator as it creaked noisily to the third and top floor of the sprawling hotel. At my door he lifted my hand to his lips. His eyes met mine in silent inquiry.

Heat flooded my face and a little thrill sent moisture to places in my body I thought I'd forgotten in the last two and a half years.

"Would you like to come in for a drink?" I couldn't believe my voice sounded so breathless and . . . anxious.

Inside the living room of the suite Donovan pulled me into his arms. Our mouths eagerly sought each other.

I melted under the firm pressure of his mobile lips. We came up for breath. My balance deserted me. He held me firm against his long, lean body.

We came together again in a searing kiss. His fingers tangled in my hair. I delighted in stroking the length of his black braid. No fair that his hair was prettier than mine.

In that moment I didn't care about the mystery that surrounded him. I just wanted him to hold me, make the delicious champagne bubbles coursing through my blood go on forever.

We stumbled toward the sofa, too intent on touching each other to care where we landed. He braced his weight on his elbows on top of me, eagerly exploring my neck with his wonderful mouth. The buttons of my cotton knit shirt fell open with just a touch. I yanked his shirt tails free of his jeans the better to run my hands up his hairless, muscled back to his broad shoulders.

A touch of shyness made me reach behind me to turn out the lamp on the end table. As I fumbled for the switch on the base of the lamp my fingers brushed the antique comb. It fell to the floor.

How had it gotten there? I hadn't even unpacked yet. My luggage was piled at the foot of the bed in the other room.

Before I could think of an answer, my skin cooled and my brain cleared just a little.

"Don't turn away from me now, L'akita," he whispered.

"Just for a moment. Not anymore," I answered on a spare breath. His gaze latched onto mine, and I lost whatever stray thought or doubt had flitted through my mind.

The world dissolved in a flurry of kisses and caresses. Our clothes landed in a tangle on the floor.

We came together in a glory of sensation. He coaxed and teased me into ever-heightening explosions of joy.

Replete, we lay cuddled together for a long time on the sofa. We didn't need words, we just needed to lay there with our arms about each other, my head tucked between his shoulder and his chin.

Eventually, we moved to the shower where we came together again.

Then we tumbled into the big bed, content to use only a third of it.

Sometime in the middle of the night he reached for me again. I opened to him eagerly. We slowly explored new ways to delight each other. Then as we fell asleep, he mumbled something into my hair.

I thought he said, "I love you, L'akita."

But I couldn't be sure.

I was too exhausted to react. Instead I savored a special warmth beneath my breastbone.

I might be falling in love with him, too.

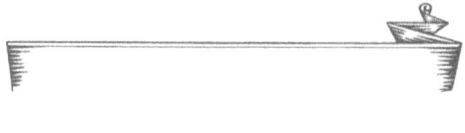

Chapter 12

Scientists give bats names containing the word chiroptera, Latin for handwing. Most of a bat's wing structure is supported by the elongated five-fingered hand, including a thumb.

Dawn crept around the edges of my perceptions. I cracked an eye half open. The digital clock showed big red numbers somewhere around six-thirty.

Donovan's arm lay across my waist, heavy, possessive, welcome.

I basked a few moments in the aftermath of being thoroughly loved by a very handsome man.

My mind spun and my fingers itched to write, as they did every morning about this time.

And my bladder was full.

Time to get up. I lifted Donovan's arm and wiggled out from under. He mumbled something, and he reached for me again.

"Later," I said as I scooted to the edge of the bed.

Something hard jabbed me. I squeaked and looked about for the offensive object.

The antique comb lay beneath me. I grabbed it with the intent of throwing it across the room in irritation.

Something in the luster of the gold knotwork grabbed my attention.

I sat up to put a little distance between Donovan and myself.

"Second thoughts, L'akita?" he whispered. He placed his hand on my thigh.

"It's been a long time. I haven't been with anyone, wanted to be intimate with anyone, since my husband died." I turned the comb over and over in my hands, examining it from every angle, falling in love again with the delicate filigree along the back. The abstract design suggested flowers, perhaps Celtic knotwork. I couldn't be sure. It seemed to change with each new slant of light.

"A long time to be alone. A woman as beautiful as you should not be alone." He lifted my hair and kissed my neck. "You aren't alone anymore."

Delicious shivers ran up and down my spine.

Not knowing what else to do, I twisted my hair up and secured it with the comb.

I shuddered as a stray draft worked its way through the French doors and wrapped around me. More than a draft. A ghostly presence. I'd lived with ghosts in the house on Cape Cod for too long not to recognize it, and I felt my mood change.

"I'm sorry, Donovan. In many ways, I still feel married to Dill. I feel like I've betrayed him." A cold lump gathered in my belly.

"A live man I could compete with. A ghost I cannot." He withdrew from me physically and emotionally. "The time will come, L'akita, when you banish this ghost. Only you can do it. When you do, I want to be the first man waiting in line for your affections. Your passions." He dropped a kiss on top of my head and departed. At the door he blew me a kiss.

Something in his posture, the swagger in his walk, something sent a frisson of fear into my throat, threatening to cut off my breathing. The indirect lighting gave him a visible aura, part a golden luster inviting trust, part black and impenetrable.

I swallowed deeply to master my fear and confusion.

"Donovan, were you one of the bat people in San Jose two weeks ago?" I knew he had been. I needed him to admit it.

"You recognized me?" He came back into the room, pulling on his clothes.

"Your posture, the way you walk." I gulped, not certain if I could ever look at him in the same light again. The delight his long-fingered hands had given my body turned to revulsion.

A bat. Anything but a bat.

How had I forgotten the bat family last night when I succumbed to the desire that still plagued me?

Two of the bat children tried to steal my tote. Had he fathered either one of them? Or both? And, if so, where was their mother?

"You had other issues. We had not been introduced. I had family with me. My family can be overwhelming." He smiled crookedly.

I laughed a little. "So can mine." I had to know. "Were any of those children yours?" I put on a bright smile, as if I had thought they were cute in their horrid bat costumes.

"No. Nieces and nephews, and one a half sister. My father took a new and very young wife. I have not yet had the luck to meet a woman I wanted to have children with. Until now."

That thought lingered between us for several meaningful, almost wonderful heartbeats. It changed our relationship completely. A quickie at a con wasn't going to be enough, or the end of it.

The blackness around him competed with the gold. What was going on? Who was he really?

"I'm glad Coach introduced us."

"A lucky happenstance."

"I won't have doubts forever, Donovan."

"I'll plan on it, L'akita. I'll catch up with you later. At the con. You have a panel at two?"

"I'll look for you."

The door snicked closed with barely a whisper.

I felt colder and lonelier than I had in a long time.

"How could you, Tess? How could you betray me with *him!*" Dill said, sitting beside me.

He didn't startle me. I knew he was a part of the cold drafts swirling around my body and my heart.

"Don't you like Donovan?" I asked. "Do you want me to be alone the rest of my life?" Anger began to boil up inside me. Anger that he still had such a strong hold on my emotions.

Anger that he had deserted me by dying.

"You promised to be faithful to me as long as we both shall live."

"You aren't alive anymore. You died in my arms, Dill!" I jumped up and threw a robe over my naked body.

I had to get some perspective, some distance from this specter.

"I'm not completely dead, Tess. I can come back. You won't have to be alone, you won't have to waste your affections on the likes of *him*. All you have to do is get rid of the imp. Then I can be with you always. I can be your weapon as well as your lover."

I paced. What did I truly want? Who did I trust? The man I had loved so well in life, and in death, or the man that sent my senses soaring and engaged my mind? Logic began to percolate in my foggy brain.

"How?"

"How what?" Dill returned.

I peered at the insubstantial form sitting on the oversized bed in the sumptuous suite. He looked just as I remembered him from the last night before the fire; clad in jeans and a western-cut checked shirt. Hiking boots on his narrow feet and a Stetson perched on the back of his dark, glossy head. No trace of soot or of strain marred his face. His skin had color, a ruddy tone darkened to bronze by hours spent hiking in the sun in search of geological specimens.

And I could see right through him. I could never embrace a ghost as I had a living man.

"How could you become a weapon? Would you be the Celestial Blade?"

"Nothing so mundane, lovey." He gave me his special smile, the one that reminded me of Donovan.

But the sight of his grin no longer melted my knees or drove logical thought from my head. The magic was gone. My vision was clear.

He was dead.

I wanted to cry that only a ghost would call me that now. Donovan had called me "L'akita." I didn't know what it meant, but it sounded special.

"I would be different. Better, more effective," Dill insisted. "You won't need the imp in battle or that traitor in your bed."

"Show me."

"I can't."

"Why not?"

"We are not in the presence of great evil."

"You're lying."

"Tess! How could you. I love you. I could never lie to you."

"Because I could always tell. From the first moment we met, I could tell when you stretched the truth. After that, you never dared lie to me, even when you came home late with the smell of tequila on your breath."

A memory startled me. We had both drunk a lot during those short three months of our marriage. Dill more than me, though. I could barely remember a time when one or both of us didn't have a drink in hand.

I shuddered at the thought that perhaps the great love of my life had been nothing more than a drunken haze.

"I can see that you need more time. You need to experience more evil and the limitations of your imp before you can fully embrace me. Before I leave you, remember all the books I made you read when I discovered how you felt about bats."

Knowing facts about the ugly critters hadn't helped my phobia, but I did remember odd things now and then, like the chiroptera—the handwing bone structure that supported the wings.

Donovan and the bat children all had very long fingers.

But his knees did not rotate backward like a bat's so that they can launch into flight from hanging upside down. I knew exactly how Donovan's knees were shaped. I'd kissed the back of them and tasted the salty sweat of his thighs.

Dill vanished as swiftly as he had come.

I wrapped my arms around myself trying to still the cold trembling of my limbs and my chin.

"Scrap, where are you? I miss you."

Right here, dahling. Never far. Just sometimes out of reach. That man drives me away.

"Which one?"

The one who doesn't smell right. A ghost has no smell.

"Did you ever stop to think that maybe you can't be close to us because he is meant to be my lover and we need a little privacy?"

I know how to be discreet. I know when I should pop out for a minute.

"How about for an hour?"

Lots of things I can do in an hour. Or overnight. If I thought you were safe without me. I don't think you're safe with that man. If he is a man.

"What is that supposed to mean?" Oh, how I ached for that man. I really wished now I hadn't driven Donovan away with my blasted sense of guilt and grief.

Scrap didn't answer me. I was left to shower and dress and prepare for the day alone.

Chapter 13

Seven o'clock in the morning and I paced the lobby of the con hotel. I hadn't slept after Donovan left and Dill visited. Now I waited for Bob to pick me up for a breakfast meeting and then take me to the high school. My mind spun in odd loops of wishful thinking and bewilderment. Pacing burned a little adrenaline but didn't help my mind.

A battered pickup wheezed into the porte cochere. I raised an eyebrow as Leonard Stalking Moon swung out of the driver's seat and entered the lobby with firm and confident steps. He held himself erect and proud and ready to confront anyone who might try to kick him out of the lily-white establishment.

No one challenged him as he walked right up to me. "We need to talk. You need breakfast and transportation."

"Bob?"

"Is sleeping in after a long night of gaming with your friend."

I chuckled at that. I'd pulled a couple of all-nighters with role-playing games in college. Then I channeled all of that creative energy into my writing and learned to keep normal hours. Bob only indulged in the need to game at cons. But he could cope, almost thrived, on about four hours of sleep during the entire weekend. I needed my beauty sleep.

Not that Donovan and I had slept much. My body tightened in memory. Then I banished the longing. Time to investigate Cynthia and the monster dog.

Leonard drove me to a small family café across the street from the high school. We settled into a booth near the window with large cups of trucker-strength coffee. There were as many Native Americans among the customers as there were ranchers and truckers. Maybe they were all ranchers and truckers.

"I know that Cynthia is special," I began once we'd ordered. "What kind of special that the dog singled her out?"

Leonard looked out the window a long moment. His eyes focused on something I couldn't see, possibly something in his mind or another universe.

"The blood of shamans runs strong in our Cynthia." He fingered his knotted necklace.

"Why would a dog need a shaman?"

"The story is long and old. We do not share it with outsiders, or those who have no shamanic learning."

I cocked an eyebrow at him and waited. Scrap mumbled around a mouthful of mold he found deep in a crevice in a broken tile in a far corner.

One good thing about my imp: he'd leave nothing behind for a health inspector to find and quibble about.

"We do not see Warriors of the Celestial Blade outside the Citadel often. What makes you so special that you do not need your Sisterhood to guide and support you?" he countered.

Touché!

"I'm a pain in the ass who asks too many questions."

Leonard chuckled. "Estevez will like that even less than does your Sisterhood." He sobered slightly. "Be careful around him, and his companions, Tess Noncoiré. They are both more and less than they seem."

"Why? He appears trustworthy." And beautiful, thoughtful, and kind.

And a magnificent lover.

"Estevez has a captivating smile that stifles questions."

I stifled my sharp retort. No sense offending this man. He had information I needed. And, from the looks of things, I'd have to pry it out of him bit by tiny bit.

I nodded acceptance of that explanation. I'd be wary of the perfect smile next time.

"Tell me about the dog." Better to change the subject than dwell on my mixed emotions about Donovan Estevez.

"I can say little. But trust me. My people have more at stake than you. We work to bring the dog under our control and our protection."

The waitress delivered our food. Simple pancakes, eggs, and sausage. The huckleberry syrup reminded me of the hint of an undertaste in the ale Leonard had served last night. Flavor fit for the gods.

I used the few moments of silence to think of a way to get more information from him.

"The dog is a killer. I watched it murder two adolescent boys and maim a third trying to get to Cynthia."

Leonard blanched a little beneath his dark copper skin. "Innocents fall victim in every war. Some die at the hands of the enemy, some from friendly fire."

"What is this war? The dog is evil, and I am trained and commissioned to fight evil wherever I find it."

"We fight the ultimate war of good against evil, Tess Noncoiré. Who is good and who is evil is sometimes not clearly understood by either side. The dog is on the same mission. Please do not pursue him with your Celestial Blade."

I trust him, Scrap said crawling out from under the table.

So, I guess I should too.

Leonard refused to say anything more on the subject. We left a few minutes later so that I could speak to the eight thirty creative writing class.

"UNCLE LEONARD SAYS I don't need to talk to you if I don't want, but I want to. I want to thank you. I need to know that you are okay," Cynthia blurted out as I left the classroom. The third one of the morning.

I'd spoken for three hours on the joys of writing and the need to learn to express yourself well on paper in everyday life. The classes were the usual mix of bored-to-snores and enthusiastic participants. A few woke up when we started plotting a book as an exercise. I expected to see entries from them next year in the junior writers workshop at High Desert Con.

I considered my work in the schools as payback to the people who helped me when I was first getting started.

Cynthia had sat quietly in the back, the new kid in school without familiar bonds yet. She'd also had the seat closest to the door so she could pop up beside me the moment I walked past her.

"I appreciate your concern, Cynthia. Are you safe and happy with your family now?"

"My father's cousin has taken me in. He has legal custody now." She dropped her head and a shy smile spread across her face. "I like it here. It feels like home. We will visit the reservation soon, so that I never forget that I am Sanpoil."

One thing I'd learned in my reading, the people we called Native Americans preferred to be called by their tribe if possible.

"Good." I gave her a quick squeeze around the shoulders. "I need to talk to you about that dog. Something really weird is going on with it," I whispered. "Are you sure he didn't try to hurt you?"

She nodded, gulping. "He only hurt my friends because they wouldn't let him get to me. Then he just tried to pull me along with him, not hurt me."

"He tried to pull you along where?"

Cynthia shrugged and ducked her head.

Then I turned to catch the questions from the teachers and students who had followed me out of the classroom.

"Excuse me, Ms. Noncoiré," Principal Barbara Mitchell, a comfortably chubby woman in a no-nonsense pinstripe suit, charged along the hall. She grabbed my elbow and separated me from the gaggle of lingering students and teachers.

She smiled warmly as she tried to assume a casual air.

My spine flared in warning. Scrap turned a darker pink.

The moment we were out of earshot she hissed in my ear. "We are about to go into lockdown. If you need to leave the campus, I suggest you do it now. I've called Mr. Brown for your ride."

"What's wrong?" I immediately shot an anxious look toward Cynthia.

"Some suspicious characters have been seen lurking on the fringes of the campus. They're wearing weird masks."

I started to relax. "Probably just people from the con trying out their costumes." But why here? Two miles from the hotel. Why now? Then my mind flashed to the too-real demon masks worn by Donovan's friends.

I kept my uneasiness and let it fine-tune my senses. Something strange was going on.

"A witness reported guns and knives. I've called the police."

Some costumes required weaponry to complete them. Con rules usually required a peace bond on them—a red twist tie or tag marking a promise not to brandish or unsheathe the weapon—while within convention boundaries. Who knew what kind of mischief they could cause near a school. Why, why, why?

"We have a strict 'no weapons' policy. Not even toys. This is serious," Principal Mitchell continued.

"Rightfully so. Children need to learn that weapons are not the norm, in spite of television cop shows. Good luck. I'll just slip out now and you can make my apologies." We shook hands.

Then I called over my shoulder, "Find me at the con, Cynthia. We'll talk."

But I didn't leave the area. While I waited for Bob, or Leonard, or whomever to arrive, to drive me back to the con, I circled the school campus on foot.

Too much weirdness was going on. And my spine continued with that flare of warning.

Keeping to the side streets, Scrap and I patrolled, wary, ready to fight off whatever might menace Cynthia. All of the houses dated to the World War II era, with tiny yards. A lot of them were duplexes. Clear evidence that the three cities had barely existed before the Hanford Nuclear Reservation started up during the war.

Maybe those demon kids are mutants from the radiation? Scrap mused as we peered between houses and kept our eyes open to any hint of movement.

Scrap shied at the presence of a tabby cat.

I nearly ran after a German shepherd dog on the loose.

Other than that, we saw nothing suspicious.

Whoever, whatever, had caused the alert had disappeared.

Bob was early for a change and had to wait for me.

"I just needed to stretch my legs," I excused my tardiness.

He shrugged and put his pickup in gear.

"How about lunch at the Stalking Moon Brew Pub?" I wanted to talk to Leonard some more about that dog.

But Leonard's assistant manager ran the pub that day. The owner didn't show the entire hour and a half we lingered over sandwiches and beer.

Chapter 14

"Bob, you do this to me every con you program," I whined, looking at my con schedule.

"What?" He opened his hazel eyes wide, innocent. Innocent as a kid with his hand in the cookie jar.

"You open the con with the sex panel and make me moderate." I only half complained. This opening panel was always well attended and set a comic mood for all the other panels. At least this year Bob had put a writerly spin on the topic. "How much is too much detail?"

"Who better than you? You write some of the most sensuous love scenes in fantasy. All your male readers drool over you." He waggled his bushy black eyebrows suggestively.

I could only laugh.

Two other respected writers shared the panel with me. One male, one female, guaranteeing a mix of genders among the attendees. Surprisingly, the mix of ages was equally diverse. Maybe we could actually get a little bit serious and talk about adding sex to writing without tipping over into erotica or porn.

"What is the difference between erotica and porn?" Gollum asked from the front row right after introductions.

"Men write porn," Jim Blass, the male on the panel, replied straight-faced. "Change the author's name to female and it suddenly becomes erotica."

Big laugh all the way around. That set the stage. We kept it light and suggestive without slipping into graphic detail. A few of the questions actually focused on the writing and not the interpretation. I didn't even blush when Donovan appeared among the standees who couldn't find a seat at the back of the room.

"Where do you get your inspiration?" asked a leather-clad Goth girl at the back of the pack. She carried a copy of *Imps Alive* under her arm. Her black sleeveless vest-style blouse couldn't close completely over her ample breasts.

Then I did blush.

"I'm sure you'll have plenty of offers for a research assistant," Jim Blass said into his white-streaked beard.

"Or if that doesn't suit you, you could buy a vibrator and rent some porn," I suggested. That set off a new round of laughter and suggestive nudges. On that note we concluded the panel.

Donovan sought me out for an early dinner before the opening ceremonies and succession of parties and dances afterward. We found a small circular booth near the back of the open coffee garden of the con hotel—the same restaurant from the con in San Jose, I swear. Tall potted plants grew in a box separating us from the view of con goers outside the restaurant. People coming into the restaurant would have to scan every booth and go around the service area to find us.

In this semi-seclusion, our hands reached for each other beneath the table. We scooted closer, forgetting to look at the menu.

He lifted my hand and kissed my fingertips. Small thrills coursed through my body. My eyes lost focus as heat and effervescence filled me. I basked in the excitement generated by our bodies pressed close together; anticipating what was to come.

I gazed into his dark brown eyes and lost myself in their depths. Every thought, every molecule of my being concentrated on him. I could almost read his mind.

A wait person hovered on the edge of my peripheral vision. "Chef's salad and iced tea," I said, not taking my gaze away from Donovan. Always a safe order at a con hotel.

"The same," Donovan echoed, caressing my hand, his attention solely on me.

Thankfully the waiter (ess?) retreated.

Donovan leaned closer. His mouth waited a hair's breadth from mine.

I closed the distance. His kiss was soft, exploratory, tentative.

I longed to deepen it. Discretion held me back. We had all weekend to get to know each other better. While the promise of sex simmered just below the surface, we both seemed more interested in the emotional intimacy developing between us.

"Hey, there you are! Donovan, Tess, can we join you?" Donovan's three young friends called from across the restaurant in voices loud enough to be heard in the next county.

"Ignore them," Donovan growled.

"A little hard to do when they are surrounding us." I jerked away from him and smoothed a napkin across my lap. A wave of cold emptiness threatened my equilibrium. I sipped at my iced tea and fussed with sweetening it and squeezing a lemon wedge over it to cover my momentary disorientation.

"Can't you send them away?" I murmured under my busyness.

"Sorry. Their parents are clients. I promised to look after them."

"They are old enough to go to a bar. They are old enough to take care of themselves."

"Not according to their parents. Tess, I'm sorry. I can't afford to offend their parents." He captured my hand again and tried to bring my gaze back to him.

I waved to Gollum just beyond the plants at my back. "Join us," I called.

"I'm meeting Bob, but we'll both be over in a minute."

"Did you have to?" Donovan asked, very much annoyed.

I heard Scrap chuckle in the back of my mind.

Keep him off balance, Tessie. He deserves it.

I hadn't seen much of the imp since returning from the school. I wondered what was keeping him busy.

What does that mean?

No answer.

Donovan's friends—I never did learn their real names, they insisted on gibberish sounds as their con names—pulled up chairs, filling the table. I frowned at them, but they didn't budge.

Gollum and Bob elbowed them aside and slid next to me on the banquette. I felt like the filling in a cookie squashed between Gollum and Donovan.

And that set the tone for the rest of the con.

The weekend passed in a blur of activity with my entourage in tow at every event. Panel discussions, writer workshops, I judged the costume competition, no bats this time. Donovan wore jeans and T-shirts like a normal person. We all partied. Leonard Stalking Moon presided over a keg at a reception held for the visiting authors and musicians and other special guests of the con. He was always too busy to discuss anything other than the amount of foam topping each cup of beer.

No sign of Cynthia. I looked for her at every panel and party. If she came to the con, she kept her distance. I even sent Scrap to look for her. He came up empty.

Donovan and friends—he was always in the company of those blasted friends—came to my panels, my reading, and my autographing. He produced old and battered copies of my first books for my signature. Since they were all out of print, my estimation of him rose and the tension and longing between us climbed, too. He came to the parties but was rarely more than an arm's length from his three masked friends. Bob and Gollum did their best to stay between Donovan and me.

The dance Donovan and I performed trying to carve out some time together became almost funny.

The tension between us continued to mount, along with the frustration.

I wanted him, but I knew I needed to spend more time getting to know him before we enjoyed a replay of Thursday night.

Scrap kept a low profile.

Dill did not return, even in my dreams. Maybe I was finally moving on. Maybe the grieving process had run its course.

But . . .

Bob dragged me into the filk circle. I couldn't sing. My throat closed every time I even thought about it. Dill had loved this part of cons and we had harmonized easily, my soprano against his lovely tenor.

Donovan and friends partied and danced rather than sit still long enough to enjoy the filk.

By this time both Gollum and Bob had a few beers in them. They joined the music with lusty—and slightly off key—bravado. Their near instant friendship warmed my heart. I'd learned to like Gollum even if he was a bit stuffy and pedantic. Then someone struck up a ballad and Gollum took the lead line with a beautiful light baritone. All the singers faded out just to listen. Afterward, he blushed and stammered and kept quiet for the rest of the evening.

Sunday morning I had a few minutes to breathe, so I joined the mock battles in the hotel courtyard. All of the weapons were "boffered" or padded and blunted to avoid injury and a dozen gym mats had been duct-taped together on the ground. (Did I mention that a con cannot be run without two dozen rolls of duct tape?) I selected a quarterstaff wrapped in acres of bubble wrap and duct tape. It lacked the Celestial Blades at the ends but weighed and balanced much like my weapon of choice.

To my surprise, Donovan appeared opposite me with a long broadsword made from cardboard stiffened with a dowel down the center and wrapped in duct tape. The demon children hovered in a semicircle behind him, but off the mats.

"Care for a rematch, L'akita?" he asked.

His voice slithered over me like hot massage oil.

I focused on his mouth, felt myself pulled toward him. I needed to kiss him again. I needed to feel his arms around me.

Two hundred people around us and two meters separating us kept our mutual sizzling heat down to a slow burn.

All of the disappointment and frustration of the weekend rose up like a living entity. We wanted each other. This bout was only the foreplay.

Donovan selected a gaudy football helmet in orange and green to protect his head.

His three companions stood behind him, still masked. Outside the pub, I hadn't seen them without the masks all weekend.

I chose a helmet in pink and purple to match my lavender slacks and sweater. Bob and Gollum moved behind me, almost as if they needed to back me up in this mock battle.

Appropriately, the bloodmobile had parked at the far edge of the combat area. A lot of cons have blood drives—they aren't all fun and games—but the symbolism of the truck struck my funny bone.

"A little different this time, L'akita," Donovan said. He smiled showing his very white teeth against his dark skin. But not as bright as the silver wings of hair at his temples. He looked more tanned than I remembered, his hair darker and longer.

My focus narrowed and my heartbeat quickened. My body told me I needed the practice. My heart told me I needed a long roll in the hay with the man.

"No fencing strip and no rules to confine me." I smiled as I swung low, to my left, aiming for his knee. A quick sidestep and I pivoted out of reach of his counterattack. He thrust his sword forward in parody of the sexual act.

We both grinned and circled each other, seeking an opening.

"She looks so skinny and fragile. She'll get hurt," Bob whispered.

"She's fast and strong," Gollum answered, also in a whisper.

Only then did I realize an even larger crowd had gathered to watch the Guest of Honor in a weapons demonstration. I'd talked a lot about writing realistic battles this weekend.

Donovan came at me low. I swung the staff high, clipping his helmet as I danced out of his way.

He shook his head to clear it. "You surprise me, L'akita. Where did you learn that move?"

"Not from Coach Peterson." I engaged his sword once more.

A flicker of movement to my left, and I knew Cynthia Stalking Moon watched from the fringes of the crowd. Finally. I hoped she had something to tell me about the dog, some tribal legend or shamanistic secret knowledge.

Donovan caught my right arm with a vicious sideswipe. I went numb from elbow to fingertips and almost dropped the staff.

Dammit, I needed to talk to Cynthia, find out what she and her family knew about that dog. Donovan wasn't about to let me free of this bout until one of us lay in the dust or both of us lay naked in bed.

I had to postpone any other encounters we might desire. All because of the damn dog and the near continual itch at the base of my spine.

Very well. "No more Miss Nicey-Nicey," I muttered. He tended to lean forward and overreach. I pressed him to the edge of the gym mats with half a dozen fast strokes. He met them, barely, retreating a step or two with each block and parry.

"Interesting strategy, L'akita," Donovan said. He sounded surprised at my ferocity.

Then, as he panted and considered my next attack, I caught him from behind, between the shoulder blades. He stumbled forward. I swept the staff in front of his knees and knocked his feet out from under him. He went down onto the gym mats with an "Ooh."

He lay there long enough for the officials to count him out. They began selecting and arming the next opponents.

I kept my hand on the quarterstaff. For some reason I felt I needed it close.

Gollum rushed to my side. "Congratulations!" he gushed, patting my shoulder.

"Quickly. Cynthia is over by the bloodmobile. We've got to talk to her." I glanced down at Donovan as he struggled to sit up and remove his helmet.

He cocked his head at me. "You were not so fast and sure on the fencing strip, L'akita." He flashed his teeth at me. My knees nearly melted.

"No rules and restrictions here. No sportsmanship and honor. When I need to defend myself, I fight dirty." I offered him a hand up anyway.

"Later," I whispered, then eased my way through the crowd, Gollum and Bob in my wake.

Chapter 15

My skin tingled from the exercise, and my right arm still ached from the hard blow I'd taken. I shook it out as we moved. Surprisingly, I kept hold of my quarterstaff, as if it belonged to me. My eyes searched every shadow and between parked cars for signs of the girl. As we rounded the bloodmobile, I spotted her edging away.

"Cynthia, please don't run away from me. We need to talk." I held her shoulder gently and tried to make eye contact, tried to reestablish the fragile friendship we had begun outside the high school writing class.

"Uncle says I don't have to talk to you, if I don't want to," she said in a meek voice.

"No, you don't have to talk to us. But it would help me find the dog that attacked you if you would tell us what you know. It would help me prevent that dog from harming another little girl. What's in the tribal legends about that dog?" I tried to keep my voice bland and un-threatening. I picked nervously at the duct tape holding the bubble wrap on the staff until I had one end exposed and a long loop of twisted padding hung free. It was sort of like the compulsion to pick at an itching scab.

Somehow, I breathed easier with every inch of tape I freed.

Cynthia pressed herself against the van, making herself as tiny as possible.

"I don't know. Those are stories told to the hunters by the shaman." She kept her head hung low and her eyes on the ground.

"But you have listened, haven't you, Cynthia?" Gollum took up the litany of persuasion. "Your encounter with the dog makes you a warrior. Warriors should not be excluded from the legends. They need to know them, they need to know how to fight the legends."

"Legends aren't real," Bob scoffed.

"Some legends are," I countered. "Some legends come to life when we least expect them."

"What are you saying, Tess?" Bob looked around warily. He shuffled and shifted as if he expected a boogeyman to crawl out from under the bloodmobile.

"I'm saying, Bob, that some of the things I write are real. It's not all fantasy. And right now, Cynthia is in the middle of something important." I caught his gaze, hoping he could read the truth in my eyes.

"I thought so. What can I do to help?" He half grinned at me and nodded his acceptance. "Gollum and I had some interesting talks this weekend."

"Watch my back."

"Always, love. You know this means you have to marry me now, to keep the secrets in the family."

I sighed in exasperation. I couldn't tell anymore if he was serious or not. I didn't have time to puzzle it out.

Finally, Cynthia lifted her gaze to mine.

"You gave me a flower for my husband's grave. That was kind and thoughtful," I whispered, strengthening our ties. "We were both lonely and grieving. That's a powerful connection, Cynthia. We have common ties to this dog."

"Legends do come to life," Cynthia whispered. "The dog and the old woman. There's a blanket that must be saved. It must be rewoven or mankind will shrivel into dust without honor."

"What did you say?" I wasn't sure I'd heard her correctly.

"The old woman weaves the blanket of destiny. The dog protects the old woman from the demons who need to steal the blanket."

"Look out!" Bob yelled as he pushed me to the ground.

Then I heard the growls and the scrabble of sharp claws on the parking lot.

"Scrap! Celestial Blade. Now!" I held out my hand, desperately hoping my imp heard my plea. All I had was the padded quarterstaff.

Even as I spoke, I rolled out from under Bob. "Protect the girl."

Then I faced the dog. I took a guarded stance.

So did he.

I centered my weight.

He bunched his muscles.

I lifted my lip in a snarl of defiance.

So did he.

I twirled the staff, and circled, never taking my eyes off the dog. The staff shifted. The looping tape and bubble wrap hardened, sharpened.

Dog followed my moves until his back was to where Bob and Gollum huddled over Cynthia.

The staff lengthened, turned silvery. Twin Celestial Blades curved and flowed from the ends. Scrap's puckish face blinked at me from the shiny metal.

He'd done it! For the first time in our partnership he fulfilled his potential.

We faced a demon, the personification of evil.

We swung into action, moving the dog away from his intended prey. He leaped and reared, avoiding the blade. Came at me sideways. Green drool oozed from his long-jowled, square muzzle. Red blood oozed out of a long gash on my forearm.

I gulped and blinked. And pressed on, ignoring the burn that ran all the way to my shoulder and into my brain.

I pressed him, back and back until I had his measure.

Then I swung the right-hand blade to connect with his neck. He dashed past me. I nipped his tail and flank.

A tiny victory. I breathed easier, but I didn't have time to bask in glory.

Dog took a piece out of my calf. Blood dripped. Pain engulfed my entire leg. I wasn't sure if it would support my weight.

My stomach knotted in determination.

Dog turned and snapped at the blade. I whipped it out of his reach. And stumbled to the left, leaving Bob, Gollum, and Cynthia exposed.

Donovan's demon children edged closer to them.

Hastily, I regained my footing,barely, and swiped at Dog, moving his attention away from the others.

We circled again, feinting and dodging.

Dog bunched his muscles for a leap.

I swung the blade to meet him.

Dog dove beneath me toward Cynthia.

The demon children made the same leap. They and Dog landed upon Bob's broad back, fangs ripping through flesh, knives flashing.

Screams.

Shouts.

Blood. Too much blood.

I ran, blade sweeping toward the dog.

Gollum rose up and kicked the dog in the belly.

The monster released his grip upon Bob and turned, growling at his new enemy.

I lashed out with the Celestial Blade. Tears blinded me. I cut a long gash along the dog's ribs.

He yelped, turned on me, saw the blade. He bared his teeth and growled. But his eyes remained upon Cynthia who cowered beneath the bloodmobile. He barked once and loped off.

I threw the blade aside and reached for Bob. Blood gushed from a dozen wounds. His face looked gray beneath his tan.

Gollum ripped off his knit shirt and pressed it against Bob's jugular. Some of the blood slowed. Not enough.

The demon children backed off, looking confused. "We were trying to protect Cynthia," they protested over and over.

"Don't you dare die on me, Bob!" I cried.

"Someone call an ambulance," Gollum yelled over the shouts and merriment on the other side of the van.

"Get a doctor. The bloodmobile. Nurses. Med techs. Anyone!" I barely dared breathe as I tried to staunch the horrible wounds.

The demon children faded into the mass of people drawn to us by the sounds of chaos and the scent of blood.

"Sing for me, Tess," Bob murmured. His lips barely moved. "Sing at my funeral."

"You aren't going to die. I won't let you." Too much blood seeped around my makeshift bandages and my hands. Too many wounds.

Too much blood.

The smell nearly gagged me. Still I did my best.

"You know which hymn to sing," Bob breathed.

"If you live, I'll marry you. But you have to live."

"Just sing at my wake." Blood foamed at his mouth. His lungs labored and rattled.

Then he smiled as he looked up into the brilliant autumn sky with wide blank eyes.

Chapter 16

"Where's the girl?" Gollum shouted into the chaos.

"Tess, L'akita, what happened?" Suddenly Donovan knelt beside me and enclosed me in his arms.

I leaned my head back onto his shoulder and let the tears flow.

Someone moved Bob's dead weight from my lap. All I could do was huddle in on myself; let Donovan's warmth take care of me. I couldn't do it for myself.

Gollum, thank Goddess, answered questions, organized a defensive barrier, and kept people away from me. All the while he kept asking after Cynthia.

A medic slapped bandages on my two bleeding wounds and slid a blood pressure cuff on my arm. The bite of the band jolted my senses back to reality. I had to ignore the gaping hole in my gut and do something. Bob was dead. A vicious dog from another dimension had killed him. Only I had the tools and the knowledge to keep it from happening again.

Bob was dead. Just like Dill. Was this to be a pattern? Were all the people I cared for doomed to die horrible and painful deaths before my eyes?

Did I dare care for anyone?

Cynthia was missing. And so was the dog.

Body heat returned. Clarity flooded my mind with the same tidal wave as a jolt of coffee.

Donovan must have sensed the change in my body tension. He slid away from me. I barely noticed.

"Those wounds don't look too bad. Just grazes. But you really need a rabies shot to make sure," the medic said, inspecting the areas beneath the bandages. They'd already begun to close.

"Which way did the dog go?" I asked anyone who could hear me.

Shrugs all around.

"Gollum?"

"North, I think. Forget the dog. I can't find Cynthia."

"She's with Leonard, or she's with the dog. I'm going after the dog." I jumped to my feet, knocking the crouching medic on his heels. My leg buckled, and I stumbled. I might heal fast and clean, but the dog was a demon. His bite would fell the healthiest of big men.

"Not now, miss." A deputy in a sheriff's uniform stood squarely in front of me, one hand on my shoulder steadying my balance. "That's my job. Get in that ambulance and go to the hospital. Change your clothes, but save them. They may be evidence. Someone will come to you and finish questioning you."

"Is anyone looking for that dog? It's a killer. Six bodies in three states by my count." I shrugged off the ambulance and the rabies shot. No germ would dare infect my body after the imp flu.

Modern medicine had nothing to combat demon toxin. I needed Scrap to do that.

"It's being taken care of, miss. Now, if you refuse medical treatment, return to your room and rest. Drink some coffee and calm down." He turned his back on me.

"The deputy is right, L'akita." Donovan cupped my elbow with one hand. His fingers dug into the flesh of my upper arm painfully.

"But..."

"I'll look into it." Gollum speared me with an intent gaze above his glasses, which had, of course, slid down his nose. Then he grabbed me in a quick hug. "Scrap needs to recover. He needs you and privacy," he whispered.

I didn't have time to question him before Donovan literally dragged me back into the hotel.

A decidedly subdued crowd gathered as close to the doors as possible. They peered intently at the flurry of police activity, the coroner's van, the ambulance.

Halfway to the elevator another deputy appeared at my side. "Did the deceased have family?" He held a notebook in front of him, poised to write down everything I said.

"I have an address on my laptop. It's in my room." Along with Bob's work number and a myriad of other details.

Details. I could handle details. Then I wouldn't have to think, wouldn't have to anticipate adding yet another ghost to the ones that already visited me.

Cold. I am too cold. As cold as if I had returned to the realm of imps. But I'm hiding beneath the bloodmobile. I can only shiver and watch. I wounded a beast that I should have protected. A man has died. I should have protected him even more.

Donovan's demon children had as much to do with his death as the dog. They were all going for Cynthia, but Bob got in the way. I do not think the demons wanted to protect Cynthia. I do not think they are merely humans wearing masks.

Tess mourns. She's as fragile as a frozen rose and may break if I don't return to her soon.

But I am too cold. I can't move. I can't jump from here to there. I've got to eat. The thought of food turns my tummy.

We're hunting the wrong beast. I knew it the moment my blades cut into the flesh of the dog and drew blood. This is no demon. This guy's on a mission to stop evil.

So who's the bad guy who allowed me to transform? Whose evil became stronger than the barrier around Donovan that keeps me away?

Why didn't we know about the dog before?

Why did Bob have to die before we discovered this? He didn't need to die if we had known.

He did not need to die.

If I do not move, I will die.

I'm too cold to move. Too tired to comfort my warrior. Too hungry to live.

I need a cigar. And a beer.

"THIS IS MORE THAN JUST a job, or a duty now. This is personal!" I screamed into the crisp desert night. The balcony railing outside my hotel suite bit into my hands where I gripped it. My leg and arm hurt like hell, but I needed the pain to take some of the hurt out of my heart. If I rested just a bit, propped the leg up on pillows, I'd relive the nightmare, watch Bob die in my arms again.

Just as Dill had died in my arms.

I stomped with the hurt leg just to make it hurt more.

I'd changed into a loose caftan that didn't rub on the bulky bandages on my right arm and left leg. My sweater and slacks were ruined by Bob's blood. So was Gollum's shirt. The police had them, testing them for DNA.

The police had asked endless questions. Donovan had deserted me to tend to his demanding demon children. I'd made numerous phone calls to Bob's family and workplace. Scrap sulked silently beneath my bed in the other room of the suite. He must have been as exhausted and depressed as I was.

Cynthia had disappeared along with all trace of the dog.

Only Gollum remained at my side.

I scanned the skies for a trace of the Goddess to tell me to go ahead and seek out that bloody dog. But it was the wrong quarter of the moon and storm clouds blotted out the stars.

Anger continued to boil through me. I'd cried my tears, nursed my wounds, washed away the stink of death with a shower. And now I had to *do* something.

But what?

"So, you finally admit that you have a duty to hunt this dog, other than your personal connection to his latest victim," Gollum said quietly. He lounged in the armchair just inside the French doors. His legs stretched out onto the coffee table. An empty beer bottle dangled from his hand. His third. Or was it his fifth?

I'd had two myself, then switched to scotch. I needed the burn down my gullet to remind me that I lived.

"You seem to know more about me than mundane people are supposed to know," I replied cautiously. Secrecy had been pounded into me by the Sisterhood. If people knew how many demons crossed the portals between dimensions, we'd have mass panic on our hands, witch hunts, and major interference from the xenophobic military.

How could we do our work properly without secrecy?

"I have made my life's work tracing folklore and legends about the supernatural back to the source," Gollum said. He pronounced each word carefully as if afraid he'd slur them.

"A little hard when most of the stories began before recorded history," I snorted. I wanted to scratch beneath my bandages but knew I shouldn't. If only Scrap would recover enough to lick the wounds, they'd heal faster and cleaner. Had he drunk the beer and OJ I'd ordered for him?

"Hard to trace, but not impossible." Gollum raised the beer bottle to his mouth, discovered it was empty, and replaced it with one from the mini fridge, then took up his same pose and the conversation as if the interruption had never happened. "It's surprising how many current stories of magic, hauntings, and miracles have their sources in the dim mists of time. More surprising how often the source has remanifested in modern times, and throughout history."

He ran the last two words together, then corrected himself, on guard against any appearance of being drunk.

How much could the man drink?

"You're a demon hunter." I'd been warned about people like him. Fanatics who misinterpreted facts, sometimes deliberately, to prove their point. They also seemed intent upon murder and mayhem in the name of ridding the world of demons.

Pity, I'd come to like Guilford Van der Hoyden-Smythe.

"You could say I hunt demons. I prefer to consider myself a seeker of the truth. An archivist. Someone needs to record this hidden history."

"Like your grandfather?" I still lusted after that musty old book. Maybe Gollum wasn't as bad as most demon hunters.

"You could call it a family tradition." He pushed his glasses up and peered at me mildly. "Much as your calling tends to run in families."

Back to the issue of the Sisterhood of the Celestial Blade Warriors, just when I thought I'd neatly side-stepped it. I thought briefly of MoonFeather. She'd understand about the Sisterhood. I didn't take her for the warrior type, though.

She fought battles against society with calm, balance, and restorative herbs. Though I'd heard stories about how she could tongue-lash officious clerics and leave them bleeding in their own aisles.

But her cats? Try crossing her threshold without an invitation and you'd swear at least two of her nine cats had demon origins.

Then again, I wasn't the warrior type before the infection had opened new pathways in my brain, and the training had awakened suppressed instincts.

I returned Gollum's stare, refusing to make a comment.

"I've seen the Celestial Blade," he commented. "I watched it dissolve when it rolled beneath the bloodmobile. I can also detect the telltale half-moon scar on your cheek."

Standoff.

"You said you'd seen a reference to the . . . Celestial Blade Warriors." There were also Brotherhoods, or so I was told.

"One oblique reference in a text that escaped burning by the Inquisition in the seventeenth century."

"And this book came into your possession how?"

"Family secret," he said on a big grin. "And I'm the last of the family." He took another gulp of beer.

"Cynthia said there was a blanket that must be recovered or humanity will shrivel and die without honor." I couldn't remember her exact words, but this sounded close. "Does that ring any bells with you?" I wandered back into the suite and headed for the mini bar. I needed more scotch. That might calm the ache in my wounds and numb the pain in my heart.

Damnation, I shouldn't drink hard stuff when I hurt so badly, inside and out. If I started drinking now, I might not stop.

I settled for a beer.

"Let me think a moment. The blanket does sound familiar." Gollum took off his glasses and leaned his head back. His closed eyes twitched as if he read the insides of his eyelids or dreamed deeply.

I plopped into the matching armchair and studied my beer bottle, a local microbrew that tasted faintly of huckleberries. I looked more closely at the label. "Stalking Moon Brew Pub." Leonard must have sent over a six-pack when I was out of the room.

Why was he avoiding me? Had Cynthia returned home safely?

Suddenly Gollum sat bolt upright, eyes still closed. He began speaking in tongues.

I grabbed my dictation recorder, separate device from my phone with a removable chip so I could store more than what my phone could hold, and switched it on. Whatever he said in this dreamlike state might be important. Or maybe he was just drunk.

After chanting a lengthy recital, he remained absolutely still and silent.

"What does it mean, Guilford?" I asked quietly, careful not to disturb his trance. I'd never seen anything like this, and I'd seen a lot of strange things over the years, feigned and real.

He opened his mouth and repeated the chant. This time in English.

"In the bad lands between here and there and nowhere, in a deep ravine that no one can find, lives a woman older than anyone can remember, older than any other person. All day long she weaves the blanket of life. She uses the old style of weaving with gathered goat wool, cedar bark, porcupine quills, and hummingbird feathers. All day long as she weaves, she imparts to mankind honor and dignity, courage and moral strength.

"Beside her sits the Shunka Sapa, her dog that is bigger than a wolfhound, uglier than a mastiff, and meaner than a pit bull.

"Each evening when the old woman puts aside her weaving to stir the stew of life that feeds her and all mankind, the dog rips out what she has woven that day. For if she ever finishes the weaving, the world will come to an end. There will be no more life to weave."

Gollum slumped down into the chair and began to snore.

I switched off the recorder.

"Something to think about." I went into the bedroom and switched on my laptop.

For the rest of the night I poured my grief and my thoughts into my work. I wrote and wrote until I, too, slept, slumped across the table, the cursor still blinking, awaiting my command.

Chapter 17

I'm hungry, Scrap wailed in my ear.

My stomach growled as I straightened up from sleeping hunched over the desk. I automatically wakened the computer and saved whatever I had written last night to both the hard drive and the flash drive. I even emailed the new work to myself as a backup. Then I pocketed the little flash drive.

"Food?" I had to think about that for a moment. "I guess I'm hungry, too." I looked at my rumpled caftan. "I need a shower before I do anything."

Room service? my imp asked hopefully.

Yesterday's events came flooding back through me. Suddenly I wasn't hungry anymore. I wasn't interested in doing anything.

I slumped back into my chair and stared at the empty computer screen; my suddenly empty life.

Scrap jumped to my left shoulder and rubbed his face against my cheek, the first show of affection from him since he came into my life.

I liked him.

"I loved him. Best friend doesn't begin to describe what I feel."

Uh, Tess, we need to talk.

No sarcasm, no "babe" or drawled "darling." Something was up.

"Spill it, imp."

The dog is not a demon.

"What do you mean, 'he's not a demon'? He killed my best friend! He's left a string of dead bodies and maimed children across three states and a province of Canada!"

He's not a demon. I tasted his blood. He's one of the good guys on a mission. The innocents got in the way.

"If he's not a demon, how could you transform?"

I don't know. I just know the dog is one of the good guys. We should be fighting with him, not against him.

"And why should I believe you?" I stared at the translucent blue being incredulously. Heat flooded my face. Anger roiled in my stomach.

I'm your imp. I can't lie to you.

"You won't even admit that you're gay. You won't tell me anything about your home world. Why should I believe anything you say?"

Trust me, please.

I marched into the shower without answering him. The sharp spray drove a little of my indignation out of me. But only a little.

"Dog's one of the good guys, my ass!"

Dog had killed Bob. Nothing could make me believe the beast was anything other than a demon, or fill the vacancy behind my heart.

I ripped off the bandages on my leg and arm, almost welcoming the ripping hurt from adhesive resisting me. The wounds were still raw, still burning, but not weeping. I was so angry with Scrap I couldn't ask him to lick the wounds to make them heal faster. I didn't bother covering them again.

If the dog were a demon, the toxin in his saliva would make those wounds a lot worse.

"I've still got the scar from the first time he bit me."

I shut out Scrap's further protestations. He was wrong about this. I knew it in my gut and my heart.

He was just plain wrong.

With my hair still damply springing into tight curls, dressed in jeans, a long-sleeved blouse, and walking shoes, I strode into the living room of the suite and froze in surprise.

Gollum peered over a map spread on the coffee table. His hair tumbled into his eyes and looked endearingly rumpled. He pushed idly at the glasses that slid down his nose.

I'd forgotten about him.

"Been awake long?" I asked, as if he usually slept in my armchair. I wasn't really in the mood for banter, but I didn't need to take my anger at Scrap out on Gollum.

"A few minutes. Long enough to find this map among your freebies from the hotel. Must be nice getting the best suite in the hotel. I didn't get a map," he grumbled, never looking up from his study. He acted as if he did usually sleep in my armchair.

I couldn't allow this to become a habit. He might have become a partner in my quest to find and kill the dog, but I wasn't about to let him into my life.

Him or anyone else, I thought as I remembered another man I had let sleep a lot closer to me than the armchair.

Once.

Donovan.

He might become my next great love, but he had deserted me in favor of the adult children of clients.

I couldn't bear to love another man and lose him, or have him killed.

"Tell me what's so interesting about that map over breakfast. I haven't had anything but coffee and booze since . . . since breakfast yesterday."

"Good idea." As he unfolded his gangling length, he knocked the map askew.

"Where's my dictation drive?" I scanned the area around the coffee table. The map lay flat, without a telltale bulge beneath it.

"Is it important? I might have knocked it off when I cleared the table. I don't remember."

He's as oblivious to the world as you get when you write, Scrap snorted.

"We can listen to it when we get back. It's very interesting." I didn't want to talk to Scrap right now.

"What's on it?"

Briefly I explained his trance, his speaking in tongues, and finally chanting an explanation about the dog.

"Tell me the legend while we eat. I don't remember a thing. I think I had a bit too much to drink."

He opened the door to the corridor to find Donovan about to knock. Behind him stood his three friends still wearing their masks.

A burning sensation flared up my spine. Scrap hissed and blinked out.

"The con's over, kids. Time to come back to reality," I said. All my disappointment that Donovan had left me before I was ready to cope on my own welled up.

He looked very handsome in the morning. His eyes held concern. A new spate of tears threatened.

I let the anger overwhelm them.

Donovan snapped his fingers behind his back. The kids retreated down the hall and around the corner.

"I have to explain. The kids saw the dog going for Cynthia. They were trying to protect the girl. But Bob got in the way of both of them. The police have ruled it an accident. No blame on the kids," he said all on one breath. His gaze was riveted on mine.

I gulped. The thought that Scrap might be right warred with my grief and anger.

"So? You've delivered your message." We stared at each other. Longing and disappointment poured out of both of us.

"I thought I might offer to buy you breakfast, but it seems you already have company." Donovan sneered with disapproval. He turned his back on me, his shoulders drooped a little. Not enough.

"Sorry; you lost your chance yesterday. Where were you, by the way, when a rabid dog mauled my best friend, and the police interviewed me for over two hours?" He'd comforted me for an extremely short period of time, then deserted me for business reasons.

Demons take his business.

Scrap hissed at me from the other room. He sounded peckish. He needed food. And so did I.

I pushed past Donovan, not giving him a chance to answer. I made certain I didn't look at him too closely and fall victim to his enchanting smile. A mesmerizing smile.

Gollum pointedly checked the door to make certain it was locked, then politely took my arm and led me to the elevator.

Over a double order of strawberry waffles with whipped cream, eggs, and bacon I related as much of the story Gollum had recited as I could remember. It filled in a few of the blanks in Cynthia's rambling version.

Scrap slurped at the orange juice and beer I had ordered for him. I might be mad at him, but I couldn't neglect him. The waitress didn't even raise an eyebrow at the order. This was a con weekend, after all.

Gollum eyed the level of the beverages as they slowly lowered without me taking a drink.

"The name of the dog?" he queried, making notes on his phone with the rubber tip of a pen. He typed almost as fast as I did on a full keyboard.

"Shanka something."

"That doesn't sound right. No language I can pinpoint."

I watched Donovan and his friends, sans masks, come into the coffee garden and take seats at the opposite end from us. They seemed remarkably subdued.

"Just how many languages do you know?"

"English, French, German, and Latin; a smattering of Greek and Aramaic. I read Sanskrit and Sumerian."

"Is that all?" I asked dubiously.

"For now. I've never had occasion to learn any Native American tongues. I wonder if Leonard Stalking Moon could point me to a Sinkiuse tutor."

"How long will that take? In case you haven't noticed, the dog attacks are getting more frequent and more vicious."

"Two to three weeks to get a basic vocabulary and grammar. Another month, maybe two, to truly master it." Gollum seemed preoccupied with pouring huckleberry syrup on his pancakes.

"Is that all? Two or three months? Most people need years to master a foreign language."

Gollum shrugged. "When I hear the recording, I'll have a better idea of what we are dealing with."

"What were you doing with the map?"

"Tracking the dog. Are you finished? I'm anxious to hear the recording."

I sighed and signed the check. But I made sure I finished the last of the carafe of coffee. Stars only knew when Gollum would come up for air long enough to think about eating again.

"You listen while I pack. The con only pays for my room until noon today. I have to decide where I'm going next," I said as I opened my suite door. "After the funeral on Wednesday."

I froze in the doorway. Inside, all the cushions lay tossed about the room, furniture rested upside down and askew.

Interlude

"Get off him, Sage!" Before the last word left Tess' mouth, she used her imitation Celestial Blade to sweep the much larger and more aggressive imp off my back. The fricking bully landed in the dust beside the training ground with a whomp and a gush of air.

I immediately jumped to my feet and snarled at the dominant imp.

Sage flew up to eye level with Tess, teeth and talons bared.

"Enough, Tess," Sister Gert commanded.

"She's a bully," Tess defended her actions. "Where I come from, we do not tolerate bullies." She did not add that Sister Jemmie, the companion of Sage, was also a bully who cheated by sharpening her training blade. She liked hurting others but could not tolerate a single blow to herself.

I crawled across the sand of the training ground to sit at Tess' heel and nurse the bite wound on my forearm and the tear in my stubby wing tip. I'd had worse injuries from my fellow imps. They didn't like it that I, a runt, had invaded their turf. This was the first time Tess had witnessed them in action, though.

"This is not where you come from, Tess," Sister Gert reminded her. "We train for war."

"Since when are imps the targets of each other in our war against demons?" Tess rubbed at the welt rising on her left thigh where Sister Jemmie had slashed at her with the sharpened blade.

I liked that Tess defended me, rather than herself. I needed a few moments to recover. Imps can push toxins into their saliva—the better to slay demons with. Or we can make them antibiotic specific to healing our companions. If I wasn't careful, the open wound on my arm might fester and I'd lose the use of it.

Precisely what Sage and her ilk intended.

They'd do anything, including crippling a Sister to send me back where we came from.

"The imps have a social order we do not understand. They have to work it out for themselves," Sister Gert dismissed the problem. "Now get back to work. We can't afford to tolerate sissies in our order."

"Then why don't I see any other imps attacking each other?" Tess muttered under her breath.

Because I'm a runt and should have died from the cold back home a century ago. But the Sisters will never know that if I can help it. The other imps won't talk about it because they are embarrassed that a mere scrap of an imp survived the portal and managed to meld. I make them look weak in comparison.

I took the opportunity to hop over to one of the irrigation springs and wash the wound.

"Sage is not only a bully, she's ugly, too," Tess continued. "Covered in green warts."

Tess had yet to learn that we imps consider warts the most beautiful and seductive part of us. I wanted more than my mere three. Tess could use one on the end of her nose, but humans might object to that.

She took one step to the side and swung her blade at Sister Gert, shouting "En garde." In one smooth move she hooked the leader's blade out of her hand and pinned the woman across the throat with the staff.

"We train for war, Sister Gert. Always be on your guard."

"You will regret your insolence, Tess. You are not a Sister yet."

"I'm beginning to wonder if I want to be."

"HIDEBOUND, PRETENTIOUS, cliquish, bullheaded . . . bullies! I exhausted my vocabulary of maledictions against the Sisterhood. Midnight, huddled in the gatehouse while the wind howled and dry lightning raged outside the Citadel was not my favorite time. But it was the only time I had any privacy from the Sisters. That night I needed privacy to rant and rave and pound my fists against the wall.

I no longer counted Scrap as an intrusion. In just a few short weeks he had become so much a part of me, almost like my conscience, that I felt incomplete the few times he slipped off on his own business.

I presumed that on this stormy night he returned to whatever dimension speeded his healing.

When I stopped for breath, I heard a different pounding, weak and rhythmical. Not like a tree branch scraping. There weren't any trees outside the citadel. This was the high desert of the Columbia Coulee in Eastern Washington. Tumbleweed, sage, and stunted juniper were about all that grew naturally here. Maybe a few grasses if you looked hard enough.

I braced myself for the blast of wind and opened the gatehouse door. The feeble light of a shielded lantern revealed no untoward shadows on the inside of the gate. I stepped the two yards to the spy hole in the middle of the double doors, ten feet high and six wide apiece.

A lone figure slumped against the door, pounding weakly with a loose fist. "Let me in. Please let me in," she wailed.

Red suppurating sores on her face told me more than her own words ever could.

I heaved at the crossbar that sealed the door against the elements as well as enemies.

"What are you doing?" Sister Gert hissed in my ear. She leaned on the crossbar, keeping me from lifting it.

"There's a woman out there. She's sick."

Sister Gert peered through the spy hole. "She's not one of ours." She kept a heavy hand on the barrier.

"She's infected. Just like I was. We have to let her in." I tried to open the door anyway. I didn't have the strength to overcome her pressure added to the bar's weight.

"The infirmary is full. Three of our daughters returned from the outside, and three more who haven't had the chance to go to school. We can't take in another."

"Did it ever occur to you that maybe this recent epidemic is the Goddess telling us that we need more warriors? That maybe the demons are gearing up for a major push and we need every woman who can be infected?" At least that was how I'd write the current scenario. I had yet to see a demon or the supposed portal and was more than a bit iffy on the belief business.

What kind of God or Goddess would allow my beloved husband to die after he'd gotten me to safety from that horrible fire?

Sister Gert and I stared at each other, neither willing to move.

"You know nothing about it."

"I know that I can't leave her out there. She'll die."

"She'll die if we let her in. We don't have enough medicine and caretakers to treat our own."

"I'll take care of her. I'll venture into the nearest town for antibiotics. But we can't let her die out there alone."

"Are you willing to give up your place here to make room for her?" There was more to that question than I wanted to think about right then.

"I'll move into the gatehouse. I'll tend her fever there if there are no beds in the infirmary."

"Think on this, Tess Noncoiré."

"I don't need to think. I need to help a Sister in trouble."

Sister Gert stepped away from the gate.

I shoved the crossbar out of the way with a bang and flung the gate open.

A woman about my own age with silvery-blond hair and fifty or sixty too many pounds on her fell into my arms. She was sopping wet and smelled of the heavy mineral salts in the string of lakes that used to be the riverbed of the ancient Columbia. I staggered beneath her weight as I dragged her into the gatehouse. Getting her onto the cot took more effort. Sister Gert watched but did nothing to help.

I knew nothing about medicine, only that I needed to get her fever down. Her polyester shorts and tunic would not tear. I resorted to a knife to cut away her soaked clothing. Then I wrapped her in the rough blanket and rubbed her skin dry.

Sister Serena appeared at my elbow. She still wore a sling on her right arm from the demon battle five months ago. "She's in bad shape, Tess. I can't lance those festers. You'll have to do it," she said, with more compassion than Sister Gert had exhibited.

I gulped back bile. No matter how much gore I wrote into my books, when it came to the real thing, I was very squeamish.

"It's not nearly as bad as demon gore, Tess. You have to do it." Serena opened a sterile pack and began swabbing the woman's face and a spot under her breast with the orange stuff they use in hospitals. It smelled like a hospital at least. Then she opened a second pack containing a scalpel.

"Shouldn't I scrub or something first?"

"No time. If we don't lance it now, the infection will go inside and she'll die horribly within a few hours. Put on some gloves."

That might help. At least I wouldn't have to touch the foul-smelling goo with my hands.

"Where are your nurses? Your *trained* helpers?"

"In the infirmary, doing this same chore for another Sister. They have their hands full and then some. It's just you and me, Tess, for this outsider."

I gulped, tried not to look too closely at what I was doing as I followed Sister Serena's instructions. A neat slice along the outside of the fester that ran from her temple to the jaw.

"Have you noticed that your scar is longer and more jagged than any other Sister's?" Sister S commented. "Women who come to us from the outside wait too long. They don't know what they are dealing with. By the time they get to us, the infection is deeply embedded, the fever so high, they are on the brink of going mad." She kept up a detailed conversation as I worked, trying to keep my mind off the grisly nature of the chore.

"Outsiders are harder to treat; they have a longer recovery because they do wait too long. But it makes them better warriors in the end. The changes in their bodies and their minds are more profound."

"I was nearly mad with grief before the fever hit."

"The grief made you vulnerable to the infection." Sister S directed me to sit before my knees gave out. Then she deftly produced sterile pads to soak up the smelly residue that oozed out of the wound. She might have trouble using her right arm again, but she was getting good with the left.

"Are we all mad here?" A question I'd long wanted to ask. A psychiatrist would have a field day with every woman in the citadel as well as their stated purpose in life.

"A good question."

"Sister Gert doesn't like questions. She doesn't like me."

"Sister Gert is under a lot of stress. Not much has changed here in almost three hundred years. We don't get a lot of outsiders. Since I finished my residency in trauma surgery and returned, we haven't had many cases of infection. Rarely more than one at a time. Rarely more than one a year."

"Three hundred years? There were only Indians here then."

"You'll have to do the stitches, Tess." She handed me a curved needle already threaded from another sterile pack.

I got to my knees shakily. Stitches I could do. Just like fancy embroidery, or mending a difficult rip in upholstery or curtains. I'd done those chores often enough under Mom's direction.

"In the beginning our warriors were of native stock, women who needed to be warriors but were excluded from that occupation by their society. Later came the native widows of fur traders, their half-breed daughters, then some missionary women who did go mad on the frontier. Now we're a thorough racial mix."

I had noticed some African and Asian features among the women.

While Sister S filled me in, I set fifteen neat stitches down our patient's face and another five beneath her right breast.

"No matter what Sister Gert says, you were sent to us for a reason, Tess. The Goddess chooses wisely."

"Sometimes I think I was sent here just to shake things up."

"Change does not come easily to us."

"I've noticed." Did I accept change any more easily than the Sisters? I just wanted to go home.

Without Dill, did I even have a home?

"Change is what drives the world, Tess. Change is part of the human condition. People change. Lives change. Lives come and go. The only constant in life is change. Without change, we do not grow, we do not evolve. The demons are evolving, and so must we. Do not allow Sister Gert to drive you away."

Chapter 18

"My map!" Gollum cried as he dashed into the room. "My book!" I headed for the bedroom and my laptop.

"Intact," we both said when we met in the middle.

"What's missing?" he asked, pushing up his glasses and peering about.

"I'll check. You call security."

I didn't dare touch anything in case I disturbed evidence. The laptop seemed intact, the flash drive was in my purse, and I'd emailed my latest work to myself this morning. An old habit. Plus a new habit of saving the work online. I backed up everything, not taking a chance on losing my livelihood. Anything else could be replaced.

But nothing seemed missing.

"Did you ever find your dictation recorder or the chip?" Gollum asked. He braced himself on both sides of the doorjamb to the bedroom and leaned forward.

"No, we were going to listen to it when we came back."

"Where did you leave it?"

"On the coffee table. Did you look under all the chairs and the sofa?"

"Yes. They've been overturned, the carpet is dusty under where they sat. Except for a rectangle about two inches by three that's been disturbed."

I gulped. "Who would want my note dictation?"

"An aspiring writer out to steal your ideas and publish before you?"

"If that were the case, they'd take the laptop with the full manuscript on it."

A knock on the open door to the suite interrupted my next thought. A man in a dark suit, crisp white shirt, and blue-and-green paisley tie entered.

He took one look at the chaos and pulled his cell phone from a belt clip. "I have to call this in to the police, ma'am," he said and autodialed a number.

The next two hours evaporated under a barrage of questions and paperwork with the same city policeman I'd talked to the day before.

"Seems like trouble follows you, Ms. Noncoiré," Police Sergeant Wilkins said. He wrote copious notes on a tiny tablet.

"A string of bad luck." I smiled sweetly at him.

The hotel manager stood by, wringing his hands as another officer made a bigger mess searching through the debris for evidence. He dusted everything with a fine black or silver powder hoping to reveal fingerprints on light and dark surfaces. A useless task. I'd hosted a writers workshop in here Saturday morning and I doubted the place had been properly cleaned since.

Scrap thoroughly enjoyed following the officer about, diving into piles of clothes and blowing on the fingerprint powder. This room might never get clean again. I wanted to laugh at my imp's antics but didn't dare.

"Ms. Noncoiré," the manager said, "we will gladly move you to another suite, at no charge for tonight. We are terribly sorry for the inconvenience."

"Thank you, a regular room will be fine. I'd like to stay until the funeral." I figured the price of a regular room for three nights ought to be about the same, or less than a suite for one night.

"Of course. Of course. We hope this inconvenience in no way impinges upon your opinion of our hotel or the chain . . ." He babbled on.

Scrap, I whispered with my mind. *Find that dictation machine and the chip.*

About time you asked, babe. He puffed on a cigar that sent the police officer sniffing all over the suite for the source. This was a nonsmoking room.

"What was so special about the recorder?" Wilkins asked after a long pause of considering his notes.

"Nothing really. Just notes about some scenes I plan to write. Some native folklore I recorded." And that bizarre channeling episode of Gollum's.

Could someone have stolen the device for that?

Fine. If someone else wanted to chase the dog and put him out of my misery, let him.

"Yesterday was the second time you fought off that marauding dog," Wilkins said, almost an accusation.

"And the second time the dog had selected Cynthia Stalking Moon as his victim. But Bob Brown got in the way. He died protecting that little girl." Maybe the police would give the girl some protection.

"You saying there is something special about this girl?"

I shrugged. "Ask her uncle, Leonard Stalking Moon."

"Now I happen to know Leonard Stalking Moon. And I knew and respected Bob Brown. A lot. So why don't you tell me what's going on."

"I don't know," I replied earnestly. "I wish I did. Then I could track down this monster and kill it before it harms someone else. Why don't you ask Leonard and his ward Cynthia?"

"Maybe I'll do just that, except Leonard reported the girl missing last night. We'd put out an Amber Alert, but haven't got any proof she was kidnapped. No proof of anything. She just vanished right after Bob was killed. Care to comment on that?"

My heart beat rapidly and my spine burned its entire length. My throat closed.

My fault, my heart screamed.

I swallowed back my panic. Panic would not save Cynthia.

I'd panicked the night Dill died. I might have saved him if I hadn't panicked.

My fault!

"I only can say that I believe Cynthia is in grave danger." And I had to help her. I couldn't let another person I cared about die because I failed to act.

WHERE ARE WE HEADED?" I asked Gollum as he turned his battered green minivan onto a state highway headed north.

"You need to get away from that hotel." He signaled a tricky merge and managed to squeeze between two SUVs that didn't want to give an inch to any other vehicle.

I grabbed the handrest and held on for dear life as he accelerated and passed the macho cars. Maybe I shouldn't watch.

"So, we are out of the hotel. Where are we going?"

"A little resort town on a mineral lake about two hours from here."

My skin grew cold and my lunch turned to lead. "Half Moon Lake," I growled. "About ten miles from Dry Falls."

"We are on the same wavelength."

"No, I've been there before."

"I drew a line connecting all of the reported dog attacks, including two in British Columbia that didn't make the local news. Dry Falls and Half Moon Lake are almost exactly dead center."

"That's in the very ancient streambed of the Columbia River. The dry coulee. Aeons ago, an ice dam backed up millions of cubic acres of water . . ."

"Lake Missoula," he interrupted me.

"Yes. Periodically, the dam would break and flood the river all the way to the ocean, gouging the terrain. The last time it changed the course of the Columbia. The coulee was left with just a string of spring-fed lakes with heavy mineral content." I recited what I could remember of the lessons Dill had taught me on our last fatal trip together.

"Why do you know so much about the local geology?" Gollum looked over at me and almost rear-ended a pickup with tires taller than me.

"My husband and I went fossil hunting in the canyon that used to be the largest waterfall in the world—four times the size of Niagara—but is now just another cliff in the desert."

"Husband? I'm sorry, I didn't realize you're married." His face lost animation, and he shut down his emotions.

"Dillwyn died the last time we came this way."

"Sorry."

So was I.

We rode in silence for another fifteen miles. Gollum slowed to the speed limit and obeyed all the traffic laws, thoroughly pissing off numerous drivers who all honked and passed us with angry gestures.

"I figure the dog is ranging around the area. The cave of the old woman must be around Dry Falls or Half Moon Lake," Gollum broke the silence.

"Why is the dog ranging if his job is to rip out the weaving every day?"

"The old woman must be dead and he needs to find a new weaver . . . that's why he goes after adolescent girls of Native American blood."

"If the old woman has ceased to weave the blanket of life, what will happen to humanity?" My insides grew colder than they did when I remembered that I might have saved Dillwyn Bailey Cooper if I had acted in time.

"We have to make sure the weaver and the blanket are restored."

What was this "we" business?

Chapter 19

"You should wear your hair up in the comb more often," Gollum said an hour or so later.

The road ran straight and boring for mile after mile, and we'd run out of conversation fairly quickly.

"I like the comb, but it's not always comfortable." Self-consciously I patted the golden filigree that still held most of my curls in place. I wasn't used to compliments. Especially from geeks.

Donovan complimented me often. From him, it seemed natural, a part of the relationship. From Gollum? I wasn't sure what kind of relationship I had with him, if I had one at all.

"You look more glamourous in it." Gollum grinned as he sped up to pass a farm truck. "Maybe it's the desert sun, but it gives you a golden aura."

Listen to him, dahling, Scrap commented from some distance. I hadn't actually seen him since I sent him to retrieve the tape. *The comb has magic in it.*

I wondered what kind of magic. Other than outdated ideals that women were more glamourous in days gone by when they wore their hair up and their skirts long.

We drove through steepening hills covered in sage and rock and not much else. Then, as we drove around a bend, the town of Half Moon Lake appeared out of nowhere. All eight blocks of it.

The town rested at the tip of the crescent mineral lake. Along the inside curve of the lake, next to the highway, I spotted RV parks, campgrounds, and aging resort hotels, including the barren ground where the seedy Life Springs Motel had burned three years ago. New homes and a golf course spread around the outside curve up onto a ridge. Atop that ridge, new construction of a wood and stone monstrosity marred the picturesque and craggy skyline.

I studied that new construction rather than take a chance of espying the place where my husband had died. The log construction Mowath Lodge had grown up beside and around the original motel. Only a cement slab remained where it had burned to the ground. I didn't care. I wanted out of this town and away from my memories.

I'd lost two men I loved.

"There's a crowd gathering around that log building," Gollum said. He slowed the van and pulled into a parking space beside a restaurant. The last place Dill and I had eaten a meal together.

He'd had the fish. I had the steak. The buttery taste of the baked potato that accompanied the meal lingered in my mouth.

"Looks more like an angry mob than a crowd," I replied, doing my best to hold the memories and the tears at bay.

"Let's ask while we have lunch," Gollum said. He killed the engine and sat staring at the milling throng of men and women.

The pattern of their movements became clear. Two factions. One side: men dressed in slacks and knit shirts and expensive athletic shoes. The other side: all had dark hair, coppery skin, worn denim, western cut shirts and boots.

The whites versus the aboriginal natives.

I felt like I'd been dumped into a bad B Western movie. John Wayne or Roy Rogers should ride over the hill at any moment.

"Do you see any sign of the dog?" I asked. While I made a production of stepping out of the van and stretching my back, retying my shoes, straightening my shirt, I took the time to study the faces on the tribal side of the brewing confrontation. No sign of Cynthia or the huge dog. Scrap said he was less a monster and closer to a kindred spirit, on a mission and not knowing quite how to accomplish it.

But he'd killed Bob and some innocent children. He was a monster by any definition despite his supposed mission.

I wanted to kill him, or at least take a big piece of his hide for the death and misery he had caused.

"Cynthia's not here," Gollum replied. He looked as if he'd made an inventory of every face and noted it down for future reference. "Can you make out what they're saying?"

"Not really. Something about overstepping bounds and violating permits." Food interested me less than the scent of fear and creeping violence in the air. I wished that Scrap would return from . . . wherever.

My feet wandered toward the simmering crowd. Gollum followed me. He kept pushing up his glasses and looking around as if threatening monsters could jump out at us from any of the sun-drenched buildings or from behind a scraggly tree. Ancient cottonwoods mostly, drawing moisture from the spring-fed lake.

I'd forgotten the salty, fishy smell of the place. One of the oils in the lake came from decaying and fossilizing fish left over from the flood twelve thousand years ago. That layer of oil remained fixed in the water. None of the layers in the lake mixed. No currents, no movement.

A thick crust of mineral salts frosted the coarse black sand beach; a beach that extended a good fifty yards farther back from the water than I remembered.

My fingers itched for a weapon.

"You're draining all of the wells with that fucking resort," a man wearing a shirt with the golf course logo on the left breast shouted and raised his clenched fist.

"You were only going to build a spa, not a full-blown casino and hotel," a woman accused, adding her voice to the crescendo.

The noise rose and fell like ocean waves that wanted to swamp me and drown my senses. At the same time a tingling awareness coursed through my veins.

Where in hell had Scrap gotten to? I might need him if things turned ugly.

Uglier.

Gollum edged closer to me. I didn't know if he wanted to protect me or hide behind me.

"If we want to build a casino, who are you to stop us?" yelled a slender, well-groomed man on the native side of the fray. "You owe us water, land, and respect for what you have done to our people."

"Respect, my ass," snorted a woman on the white side. "Lazy buggers who don't know how to work for a living. Can't even clean up your own yards."

"How are we going to feed and water our cattle if you damn Indians drain all our wells?" asked a wiry little man with leathery skin. Only his blue eyes and sun-bleached hair beneath his Stetson separated him from the "damn Indians" in appearance.

"The casino isn't even up and running, and my water's down by half," the man from the golf course said. "I'm gonna lose a million bucks in greens fees if I can't water my grass."

A younger Indian woman tugged on the arm of the man beside her. "Why *did* we agree to the casino? All we really needed was the spa. We could survive very nicely on the money we'd make from a spa."

That statement told me more than all of the shouting. Something strange had happened in this town. Something manipulative.

"Tess," Gollum said quietly, touching my arm.

I made a conscious effort to relax my fists and take the tension out of my face and shoulders.

"Look there." He jerked his chin to the doorway of the log building beside us.

A dark-haired man with the smooth coppery skin, flat face, and almond eyes so prevalent on the tribal side of the conflict stood watching every move. He remained stolidly aloof from the conflict.

"I sense a connection between him and why these people gathered here." I gestured to the octet of modern log lodges scattered around this collecting point. I didn't remember these buildings from my last visit three years ago. Each lodge appeared to be a four-plex, two rooms up and two down, built from massive tree trunks at least two feet in diameter.

I searched for a sign. The grand two-story edifice the watcher had come from announced to the world in big carved letters "Mowath Lodge. Office." It overlapped onto the foundation of the burned out Life Springs Motel.

"They rebuilt. Bigger and grander," I said quietly. My knees and hands began to shake.

If Scrap were here, would he be able to help me sort out my own emotions from those of the crowd? Would wading into the fray with fists and feet flying make me feel better?

"What?" Gollum asked.

"I've got to get out of here. Now."

He stared at my cold face. "You are looking a little pale. Let's get some lunch."

He took my arm and led me across the street to a café. It looked run down and weather-beaten, like so much of the original town. Only in the last ten years had tourism and the mineral qualities of the lake drawn outsiders to exploit the sleepy town's only resource. New Age herbal stores now nestled cheek by jowl with antiques and oddities, shamanistic counselors, and massage practitioners. The café stood out like a withered old lady among aggressive professional women. The age of the building seemed embedded in the cracked linoleum.

We took a table by the window. Gollum sat facing the Mowath Lodge. I kept my back to it.

"Do you want to talk about it?" he asked. His eyes centered on mine but flicked to the view out the window periodically.

"The foundation of the two-story office," I said flatly.

He nodded.

"That was the original motel. An old and run-down place. A firetrap." I gulped back my tears. "It burned three years ago. Dill and I were staying there. He didn't make it out."

"Oh." His eyes flicked back to the scene playing out across the street. They strayed there more often as we worked our way through huge hamburgers with homemade rolls, thick-cut fries, and milkshakes made with real ice cream.

With food like this in my system I could fight dragons. But not my own personal demons.

I felt a weight against my belt purse. Quicker than thought I slapped the thing and prepared to knock a thief flat.

My hand encountered air.

Watch it, Blondie. You almost knocked me back three dimensions, Scrap snarled.

He looked exceedingly gray and I had to peer hard to actually see his outline. He was barely into this dimension.

"Are you okay?"

"What?" Gollum asked, instantly alert.

"Scrap," I mouthed.

Hungry, my imp said in a whisper of a breath.

I searched frantically for something he could and would eat. All the food here was fresh, the inside of the building scrubbed clean, the outside so dry and dusty no molecule of mold would dare try to take hold. Desperate, I signaled the waitress and ordered a beer and OJ.

"Did he get the chip?" Gollum asked sotto voce.

Donovan in his cream-colored BMW (his own or a rental?) had just stopped in front of the Mowath Lodge. He angled his long legs out of the car and flashed his brilliant smile at the angry mob.

An immediate hush came over the noisy crowd. The smell of incipient violence melted out of the air.

What kind of magic did Donovan have?

That smile?

Very like Dill's smile.

Some kind of connection flickered across my mind. Then I lost it. So I plowed forward.

"Screw the recorder. Something more interesting just showed up." I threw a twenty on the table and dashed out the door. "You stay there until the beer and OJ are gone," I threw over my shoulder to Gollum.

A look of intense relief settled on the face of the Indian in the doorway. I sensed then that he had been guarding the door. For some reason I did not know he feared outsiders entering the room behind him.

This was just too much of a coincidence.

There are no coincidences in imp lore, Scrap reminded me around a mouthful of liquid. His voice sounded weak, but better than when he'd first showed up.

Donovan climbed the three steps to the wide deck of the office and spoke to the guard in quiet tones before I could catch up to him. Then he passed inside without a backward glance at the suddenly dispersed crowd.

"What just happened here?" Gollum asked, out of breath as he caught up to me. Scrap hovered behind him. He looked the same washed-out orange as his juice.

"I don't know. But I think I need to find out. Something about the man doesn't ring true," I replied.

Goddess! Why had I been so dumb as to let him into my bed?

"I could have told you that Thursday night back in Pascoe," Gollum said, straight-faced.

I glared at him. Friend he might have become. But he had no right to pass judgment on the man I found very attractive. As well as mysterious and irritating.

"Donovan!" I dashed through the door before he or his guard had a chance to close it in my face.

Gollum slid in behind me.

Scrap returned to the restaurant to slurp up more beer and OJ.

Before I could say a word, I stopped short in the lobby of a small office. Inside the room containing a desk, an oversized swivel chair, and one small, straight, uncomfortable-looking visitor chair, I spotted, hanging on the wall, the most magnificent example of Native American weaving I could imagine.

Something clicked in my memory.

"And the old woman weaves the blanket in the old way. The way it was done before the white man came. She uses wool gathered from the sheddings of wild goats, cedar bark, grasses, and bird feathers. She has nearly completed the blanket except the binding for which she uses porcupine quills. Only the binding remains unfinished . . ."

"What language are you speaking?" Gollum hissed in my ear.

"English. It's the only language I know besides French."

"She speaks a dialect of the Lakota," Donovan said. His voice was as tense as his neck. His eyes narrowed to mere slits.

What was going on here? I thought I spoke my natal language.

"Are you stalking me, Tess Noncoiré?"

My senses sizzled under Donovan's scrutiny.

Goddess! He looked sexy, even strained and harassed as he was now.

"I was about to ask you the same question, Donovan Estevez." I yanked my eyes away from the blanket. But the pattern remained burned into my memory. Grayish-brown background from the goat wool with an abstract design in greens and cedar. Brilliant red, black, and blue from the bird feathers highlighted the arcane symbols within the weaving. I knew they had to be symbols. They just had to be.

"I live and work in this town. You don't." Donovan challenged me. He leaned slightly forward as if ready to engage in another duel.

That answered the car question. It was his.

The light from the window behind him made a golden corona around his head. An aura braided with black darker than his hair.

The aura I could explain as a trick of the light. But not the darkness that entwined with it. Was I seeing a true aura that reflected his personality?

I hoped not.

Our gazes locked once more. But I retained control. I clung to the burning anger in the pit of my stomach and the questions teasing my brain rather than succumbing to the weakness in my knees and the warmth in my breast.

"I brought her here as a tourist, to get away from the hotel and the scene of her friend's death. We had no idea you had any connection to Half Moon Lake." Gollum edged between me and Donovan, leaving me free to examine the blanket.

"Or the controversial casino," I added.

Laid out flat and held that way by fossilized rocks and pen holders, on the desk that nearly filled the tiny room was a roll of architectural plans labeled "Half Moon Casino."

"That mob came near to exchanging blows several times in the last hour. Then you show up and they just drift apart as if drugged into a mindless trance. Care to comment on that?" I lifted my eyebrows and stared at him but kept part of my gaze on those plans. I didn't dare study the blanket.

Or ask why Donovan had it.

If it was what I thought it was, and the unfinished porcupine quill binding led me to believe it was, then the dog and probably Cynthia Stalking Moon couldn't be far away.

My spine began to tingle. Scrap hovered in the middle of the outer office, mostly recovered and glowing a pale pink.

That stinky man keeps me away from you, he glared at Donovan. *You act different around him. Let's split this scene, babe.*

When I met Donovan at the *salle* back on Cape Cod, Scrap had said that Donovan smelled funny to his imp senses.

The silent guard moved to stand in front of the blanket. He jerked his head toward the door, then looked pointedly at the plans on the desk.

"This is a private office, Tess. I have to ask you to leave now. But I'll meet you for dinner at Don Giovanni's Restaurant at eight. We'll talk then."

"I'm going back to Pascoe. If you want dinner, look for me in the hotel coffee garden about six." I turned on my heel and marched out.

Scrap thudded onto my shoulder the moment I cleared the office.

I got the recorder, babe. It's damaged. But you don't need it now.

"Gollum needs to hear the recordings. He needs to know that he recited the legend in a language he doesn't know he knows."

Tough. Scrap winked out again, leaving me with more questions than before.

Chapter 20

My babe would be horribly shocked if she ever learns where I found the recorder. She would want to go charging into the lion's den, or rather the nest of the Sasquatch guarding the chat room and the hiding place of the thieves. She is not ready for what I suspect the demons are planning. The entire Sisterhood combined is not ready. The stinky man's demon children stole the recorder for reasons I can only guess. They hid it near the portal to their home dimension. I don't know why they didn't destroy it.

Seems like those super-special masks weren't masks at all. They're half-bloods—Kajiri. Their proximity at the time the dog attacked was why I became the Celestial Blade so easily. The dog is no demon. The dog is the enemy of demons.

I didn't recognize one of those demons from imp lore—a dozen tentacles, four inches long at least, dangling from each purple cheek. Maybe Gollum knows. Maybe they're a whole new kind of demon mixed from several tribes with a bit of human thrown in.

They hid the recorder well. I had to wrestle it away from a black Sasquatch who had sworn to protect it with his life. He didn't die. By tomorrow he will kinda wish he had. I hooked his face with the talon on my wing elbow. He nearly ripped my tail in two. The battle cost me two of my three warts, but it earned me one more.

I am worn to the bone and must recover.

Beer and OJ are nice, but they are not mold. I can't find a scrap of mold in this entire desert. Oh, for a neglected air conditioner! Or better yet, a neglected cup of coffee laced with heavy cream.

I would know heaven if only I could have a fat layer of mold growing atop a thick layer of real cream.

"Well, we found the blanket. But where is the dog?" Gollum asked as we headed south down State Highway 17.

"More important, where is Cynthia?" I replied, hugging myself against an autumnal chill that only I felt. Scrap had not returned to me. Or if he did, I could not see or sense him. Without him, I'm not whole, and I don't think properly.

There was something important just on the edge of my perceptions that I couldn't grasp. I needed Scrap, dammit!

"Cynthia is with the dog," Gollum stated with some authority.

I looked at him sharply. "How do you know that?"

"Logic. If Dog needs to find someone to continue weaving the blanket, and he's gone after Cynthia twice, then she is his choice. Dog needs to get Cynthia and the blanket together." He shrugged and fiddled with the radio.

"Cynthia has shaman blood in her. Leonard admitted as much. It must be very strong for the dog to want her so badly."

I fished the damaged digital recorder out of my sweater pocket where Scrap had dumped it. Without bothering to look too closely, I retrieved the chip and slipped it into my phone.

Sputters and pops came out of the speaker for many long minutes. Then Gollum's trance-induced voice came through speaking the alien language.

He cocked his head and listened closely. "Are you sure that's me?"

"Very sure. I was there." Some of the phrases sounded familiar.

Then my voice came through asking him what he'd said.

His voice returned in English for about two sentences. Then nothing but the whirring of the phone skipping around to find a cluster of useable pixels.

"Know anyone who can fix that?" I asked.

"Not here. Back in Seattle."

"Bob will . . . would know." Damn. I blinked back a new spate of tears.

"What's your connection to Seattle?"

"Are you sure the blanket is the one we want?"

We asked at the same time.

"You first," he said as he swung around a slow-moving pickup loaded with hay.

"My mom raised me to be a proper French housewife. I can cook when I want. Sew when I have to. But I also know a lot about knitting and crocheting. I can even do *la frivolité.*"

He quirked an eyebrow in question.

"Make tatted lace." I had to search for the English word. Mom never used it if she could pound the French one into me. "In short, I know something about textiles. I recognized the porcupine quill band that is unfinished. And that thing wasn't woven on a modern loom."

"Okay. In answer to your question, I taught for a year at UW in Seattle. Adjunct work, no tenure track. Stayed on for a while because I like the city."

"Where's home?"

"Upstate New York when I can't go anywhere else."

I laughed. I had similar sentiments about Cape Cod. More because of my relatives than the place. "Dysfunctional family?"

"Dysfunctional mother. She wanted me to become a financial advisor for her family's investment group. I chose to follow my father's family business."

"Which is?"

He clamped his mouth shut.

He passed another car, this one going over the speed limit, rather than answer.

"You know a lot about me, even without me telling you. How about some equally shared information," I demanded.

"Your Sisterhood didn't tell you about the archivists?"

"No."

"Ask them." He punched the stop button on my phone. Then he tuned the radio to a country and western station—the only thing we could receive out in the middle of nowhere. He turned up the volume so loud we couldn't converse if we wanted to. And he clearly didn't want to.

One thing I'd learned during my travels: when in doubt take it to the con com.

The convention committee was still in the middle of packing up from the long weekend. The computer gamers clung to their last few minutes of screen time. I poked my nose into the secluded conference room they had made their home.

"Anyone know someone who can salvage a damaged dictation chip?"

A bevy of techno-geeks swarmed around me, all begging for the chance to prove themselves the geekiest. Three of the eight were female. The gender ratios had changed in the last decade. Most were under the age of twenty.

"Hey, weren't you the babe hanging out with Bob the other day?" asked a middle-aged man with a very round belly and thinning hair, the only "adult" in the crowd.

"Yes," I replied hesitantly. Of all the children consulting over the damaged chip, he seemed the most stable.

"I worked with Bob. He was a good guy." The man shook his head and frowned. "Dave Corlucci." He offered me his hand.

"Tess Noncoiré." I shook Dave's hand with conviction. "Yes, Bob was a good man. A good friend."

"This got anything to do with the beast that mauled Bob?" one of the kids asked. He poked his head up out of the huddle for a moment.

"Perhaps."

"Then we gotta do this. We gotta crack the tracks for Bob's sake." He dove back into the consultation.

"We'll have this for you tonight." Dave gave me a thumbs up and joined the consultation that made its way over to one of the computers en masse.

"Tonight? So soon?" I edged closer to the blob of helpers.

"No prob," one of the female voices piped up. She couldn't be over fifteen, with black lipstick, exaggerated black eyeliner, and ragged black T-shirt and jeans. She meandered off into a spate of techno babble that left me more confused than when I came in.

With the recorder safe in their hands, I made my way back to my new room—considerably smaller than the suite—and put in a call to MoonFeather. I took the coward's way out and had my aunt tell Mom why I wouldn't be home tonight. I had no doubt that any leftovers in my fridge would find their way into the hands of one relative or the other. Dad paid my bills online for me, out of my checking account. He also kept track of my few investments. I didn't have a compelling reason to go home yet.

Donovan did not show for dinner. Why was I disappointed? In my head I should have dismissed the man as a lost cause romantically. Another part of me yearned for his touch.

Gollum disappeared in search of a library, and possibly Leonard Stalking Moon.

I retreated into my work.

Once again, I fell asleep over my laptop. This time I awoke in the wee small hours of the night. I wasn't alone.

Dill, my ghostly husband, sat on the edge of the bed, not three feet from my armchair at the round table by the window.

"Have you deserted me already?" he asked.

"Wh . . . what?" I pushed tangled hair out of my eyes (I'd dispensed with the comb hours ago) and peered at him, trying to find some point of reference; something, anything that would tell me if the love of my life was truly there, or just a dream. Nightmare.

"Dill . . ." I reached out to him.

He scooted away from me.

"Don't touch me. You are tainted by that . . . that halfling." He sounded nearly hysterical. Dill, always calm, logical, organized; hysterical?

"Halfling? What are you talking about?" The only reference I could dredge up from my tired brain was hobbits. J.R.R. Tolkien had referred to hobbits as halflings.

"Don't go near him, Tess. Beloved, Tess, I can't stand to watch you ruin yourself with him," Dill pleaded.

These extreme emotions could not come from the man I loved.

Then another half-memory clicked in. Donovan owned Halfling Gaming Company.

"Are you talking about Donovan Estevez?"

"Don't even say his name. He's tainted. He's selfish. He's a traitor to everyone. He lies. Don't believe a word he says."

I'd already come to a similar conclusion but didn't want to believe it.

Either my face showed my reaction, or Dill's ghost read my mind. He calmed down instantly. "You know the truth in your heart, Tess." He caressed my hair with a translucent hand.

Frissons of otherworldly energy tingled through my body. I forced myself not to shudder. This was Dill. He'd never hurt me. He loved me.

And I loved him. Still. Even after three years of separation by death.

"Let me stay with you, Tess," he begged. "I can watch your back better than the imp. I can take care of you. If you just accept me, the veil of death will no longer separate us."

I did not want to explore that. Somehow bringing him back to life seemed a violation of . . . of life, fate, the natural order of things. That was the stuff of romantic fantasies. Even I didn't write that nonsense.

"Can you lead me to the dog and Cynthia?" I asked the only practical question I could think of when all my heart wanted was to accept his proposal.

He disappeared without a backward glance.

Someone knocked loudly on the door.

"Hey, is this some kind of demon language?" the black-clad girl geek asked before I'd opened the door all the way. She and her clones surged into my room without further invitation.

"No, it's not a demon language. It's a subdialect of Lakota," Gollum said, right behind them. He had on his "teacher" face, and I knew he'd spout a lot more information given the chance. Subjects, he'd talk about. Himself, he would not.

Dave Corlucci planted a laptop computer next to mine; a much fancier and slimmer one than mine. I was sure it had all the bells and whistles available at the moment. It booted up in a matter of seconds rather than moments. Then with a flourish and many grand gestures, he took an external hard drive from the girl who had been first through the door and inserted the cable into one of five ports. Five USB ports! I could barely imagine how much multitasking I could perform with such a luxury.

Before I had time to banish lingering questions about ghostly Dill, Gollum's disembodied voice came through the computer. I heard once again the gibberish, trying to make sense of the syllables.

Gollum made rapid notes into his phone, shaking his head. "I don't remember any of this. How?" He looked up at me in disbelief.

"You were drunk," I replied.

Then the voice on the machine switched to English. Gollum listened more intently, still making notes.

"Interesting. I remember seeing a Masonic jewel once. It had a carved head of Isis, in black onyx, set in an ivory crescent moon. Below that, dangling within the curve of the moon, was a five-pointed star representing Sirius—the Dog Star. Isis, a form of the Mother Goddess full of wisdom, like the old woman weaving the blanket. And Sirius, connected to the dog-headed god Anubis; the god who first taught mankind language, astronomy, music, medicine and the ways of worship. This legend smacks of Universal Truth."

"Cool," from the Geek Chorus. Happy smiles spread among them along with many high-five hand slaps and other arcane gestures.

"Can you transfer that file to a flash drive?" I asked. "I have several blank ones."

"Of course. We've got three backups," Dave chortled. "It's not a big file. I single gig should be plenty of memory."

"What do I owe you for this? It's wonderful."

"This was for Bob," Dave said hesitantly.

"How about autographed copies of your book?" one of the boys asked.

"One for each of us?" one of the girls looked at me hopefully.

A small enough price with my discount on the surplus books. That much less weight to haul home. "They're yours." I dug eight copies out from the box stored by the door. The dealers at the con had made a considerable dent in the copies I'd brought with me, but I still had half a box left after giving out the eight.

I signed the books and ushered the wonderful computer whiz kids out the door. The moment the latch clicked, Gollum replayed the file.

"What am I listening for?" I asked quietly.

"This." He turned up the volume.

At the moment his voice switched to English in the background I heard the door open quietly.

I had to look to make sure the noise was on the drive and not the actual door to my room.

"Someone else heard the story," he said.

"Someone who has something to gain, or lose big time, by us investigating the dog and the blanket."

"Your friend Donovan has the blanket."

"So where is he hiding Cynthia and the dog?"

"I don't think he has them."

"What makes you say that?"

"He's still trying to keep the blanket a secret. He wants the dog to bring Cynthia to him."

"What if he wants to keep the blanket away from Cynthia and the dog?" Where did that thought come from? Dill had called Donovan a traitor and tainted. If Donovan wanted the blanket to remain stagnant, then he wanted humanity to stagnate as well.

I shivered.

"Scrap!"

No answer. Where had the imp gotten to?

"Scrap?" I called again. "Scrap, please come back to me."

He popped into this dimension, hovering on extended wings between Gollum and me.

What do you need, babe? He removed his cigar from his mouth and blew visible smoke rings into my face.

I coughed.

"Why can't I see him?" Gollum asked, coming around Scrap to stand beside me. He peered into the air with and without his glasses.

"You haven't been infected with the same fever I had." I touched my scar tentatively. I barely remembered the lancing pain from having the infection cut out. I had full gagging memories of doing the same for Gayla, the woman I'd let into the citadel under protest from Sister Gert. Only the monsters I fought in my delirium remained real to me.

Or maybe they were real monsters. The fortress of the Sisterhood guarded a dimensional portal. I might have fought real demons trying to slip past their vigilance.

"Scrap, where did you find the recorder?" I asked as pleasantly as I could. I didn't want him running away again.

Don't ask, babe. You won't like the answer. He paled and shrank in size until his wings would no longer support him in flight. He dropped to the table beside the laptop. But he did not flee.

"I need to know, Scrap."

One of the demon kids from the con had it. Scrap almost became invisible. He wouldn't look into my eyes.

I smelled his cigar as the only evidence that he remained with me.

I repeated Scrap's words for Gollum.

"If one of those brats knew Donovan had the blanket and overheard me reciting the legend, then he, or she, took the recorder to protect Donovan," Gollum mused.

"Possible. But that doesn't tell us why the demon child sneaked into my room at the crack of dawn in the first place."

"Jealousy?" Gollum asked. One of his endearing smiles flashed across his face.

I snorted. But I blushed at the same time. Donovan was one sexy man. The girls in his con entourage could very well have a crush on him and want to pull some prank on me to discourage tentative and now dead romance.

Be careful, Tess. Not everything is as simple or as obvious as it seems. Scrap turned bright pink then winked out.

I took that as my cue to send Gollum on his way, and I went to bed.

Since Dill had visited me earlier that night, I did not expect him to pop up in my dreams again.

He did.

Interlude

My babe's dreams are private. She would not allow me to enter them even if I could. Once in a while, when she is distracted, I can nudge her to certain actions.

Or I can listen to her rave during her nightmares.

I wish I had known this Dill person who haunts her. Waking and sleeping, he comes to her. I cannot see him, cannot hear him in her dreams when he is most powerful.

The other ghosts talk to me. They play with me and plan tricks on Mom.

Dill acts as if I am absent when he shows up—uninvited.

That is how I know that Dill does not mean well by my babe.

Human men talk a good line. Especially to women they want to possess. Knowing when to trust them is difficult. Trusting any human other than my babe is difficult for me. I know them too well. She does not.

How can I help when I cannot enter her dreams and he can? He has magic when she dreams of him. He can influence her. That does not bode well for either my babe or me.

I just hope she has enough sense not to follow him into that half world between life and death. That realm is much like the chat room that leads to other dimensions. A very dangerous place for the living and for the dead. Choose the wrong door at the wrong time and you become demon fodder.

The nightmare began again.

ONCE MORE I DROVE THROUGH a dream landscape that became more real by the heartbeat. I proceeded north, through the massive rock formations that twelve thousand years ago had been the streambed of a much larger and deeper Columbia River. Now only a string of mineral lakes marked the ancient coulee.

I drove and drove, barely able to see the twisting road through my tears. Paroxysms of grief racked my body and my mind.

Two days before, I had buried Dill. Two days before, I had laughed at all of his jokes recited by his friends, but not his family. Three days before, Dill's family had refused to acknowledge me as a member of the family and threatened to sue me for Dill's life insurance and his portion of the family business.

I let them have the business.

Fever sent chills through my body and distorted my vision even more. I knew I should pull off the road and sleep. I knew it. And yet I kept driving. The road was narrow and twisting with no shoulder and few gravel turnouts. Darkness fell.

I remembered seeing lights out on one of the lakes. I remembered glancing over. Oncoming headlights blinded me.

I missed the curve. My car kept flying forward, off the road, over the cliff. Into the lake.

I did not care. Without Dill, I did not think I had anything worth living for.

My car plunged deeper and deeper into the lake at the base of the dry falls. Before the last Ice Age changed the course of the Columbia River, water poured over these cliffs in the largest waterfall in the world.

Now only a small lake winds around the base of the eroded rock formations.

I plunged deeper than the water, into another world. Another dimension.

Monsters met me with clubs and poisonous talons. Tall hideous shapes that barely resembled human beings. Short, oozing, squiggly things. Worse than the nightmares created by Hollywood.

They reached for me through a darkness lit only by the green and yellow gleams from their eyes.

I fought them off with my purse, my fists, my feet, and my teeth. I fought myself, knowing how easy it would be to die here. But if I did, then I could never return to my own dimension. I'd wander endlessly in this timeless space, always fighting off the monsters.

I'd never be reunited with Dill in any afterlife.

Gradually, my fever abated. I had periods of lucidity when the Sisterhood of the Celestial Blade bathed my brow and fed me broths. How I got there, I did not know, then.

During these periods of half-waking I became aware of a searing pain along my face, across the top of my belly, and beneath my breasts. I slipped back into my fever dreams almost gratefully to escape that pain.

Doors to other worlds opened off to my right and left. Huge bronze doors with iron bars across them. Tiny glass doors that revealed impossibly green meadows filled with flowers in bright hues never seen by a human eye. Normal wooden doors that opened an enticing crack.

I had but to choose the proper door and the nightmare, the pain, and the loneliness would end.

How could I choose? I didn't have Dill beside me to guide me.

Then he appeared, not as I'd seen him last, hideously burned with his skin peeling away, flesh cooked, blood oozing through his cracked visage, bones poking through his flesh.

He was whole, clean, handsome, and loving. He pointed to the tiny glass door that led to a fairyland of too brilliant colors and lovely dancing figures. I could never fit through the opening, even in this realm of distortions.

I stood there, long dangerous moments in indecision. All the while the monsters crept closer. I realized they had become wary of me. I knew I could defeat them, but I would not emerge from their realm unscathed. I needed to escape.

Dill beckoned to me anxiously. He mouthed words I could not hear. His gestures became more frantic.

I took one step toward him and the escape he offered me.

Then a tiny figure bounced across the landscape. It had one horn, elongated earlobes, and a hump upon its back. Other than that, it appeared vaguely human, maybe a lizard dancing on its hind legs. It kept its eyes closed as it played a haunting and wistful tune on a flute held in front of it rather than to the side. Seeds dribbled from its hump. Wherever a seed landed, light blossomed out of the darkness. The music was decidedly not European. Still, it enchanted me.

"Don't listen to Kokopelli," Dill shouted to me.

But Dill didn't have his normal voice. I heard deep guttural growls beneath his words, and I knew that this was not my Dilly who enticed me into a land where I could not survive. My Dill spoke in smooth, melodic tones. Almost like he was singing to me.

And when he sang, the world stopped to listen.

"Come with me, and we will be together forever. Come, lovey. Come to me. Our love is eternal. Death cannot separate us." He held open the door to the impossibly beautiful fairyland.

Little winged beings flitted from flower to flower. I could get drunk on the perfume that wafted toward me on an ethereal breeze.

But that wasn't Dill talking to me. That was another demon who had taken on his face and form. I couldn't trust this dimension.

So, if the demons did not want me to follow the little guy with the flute, then perhaps, just perhaps . . .

I followed Kokopelli through a narrow slit of a door made of a rough deer hide. The tight confines squeezed my oversized butt and breasts.

A demon grabbed my arm, pulling me back into the darkness. I resisted. The demon pulled harder, nearly dislocating my shoulder.

Kokopelli played a faster tune that made me want to dance.

I broke through into reality, my normal reality, with a squishy sound like popping wet bubble wrap.

A woman wearing surgical scrubs and mask, (a doctor?) leaned over me. "Welcome back," she said. "I see our treatment was successful."

"What treatment? Where am I?" My voice sounded raspy. The movements of my jaw made me aware of a tightness and dull ache along the whole right side of my face.

I reached up to touch the soreness.

The doctor grabbed my hand. "Best keep your hands off the wounds for a few days. You had a serious infection with a very high fever. We had to cut out the sources of the infection. I've stitched and bandaged them, but we can't risk a secondary infection. That might kill you." Her voice was smooth and matter-of-fact. I couldn't place an accent, regional or foreign.

Fever explained the nightmare dreams. I hadn't truly battled demons. They hadn't truly slashed me with their poisonous talons.

"Where am I?" My nose detected the pervasive smell of disinfectant.

"In the infirmary," the doctor replied.

"Which hospital?" I choked the words out. My throat was too dry.

The doctor held a glass of water with a bent glass straw to my lips. I sucked greedily. She took it away from me all too soon.

"Not too much at once. We don't want to upset a very empty tummy."

She hadn't answered my first question. But I had more.

"How long was I out of it?"

"Five days."

That must have been some fever. "Recovery?"

"Oh, you will mend quickly now that the infection is gone. In fact, you'll be stronger than before once we feed you up and rebuild some muscle tone. I think you'll like the new you."

"I lost some weight?" I asked hopefully. I'd always had a rather round figure. The loss of a few inches on my hips could only improve things.

Why bother? Dill was gone. Gone forever. Keeping a svelte and sexy body no longer mattered if he wasn't there to appreciate it.

Thus began my yearlong recovery and training to become a Warrior of the Celestial Blade.

Wait a minute.

This memory/dream was different.

Chapter 21

Of the nearly one thousand recognized bat species only three may be classed as "Vampires."

I sat bolt upright in my hotel bed some three years after I had battled demons in my fever dream. I had battled those fever demons alone. Dill had not been there, either as a ghost or a corpse.

Why was I rewriting things in my memory?

Sleep fled, lost mist in the sunshine. So did any memory of why I might have added Dill to the recurring nightmare of my time between dimensions, keeping demons from slipping past the guard of my Sisterhood.

Talk to me, dahling, Scrap ordered. He shifted a very stinky cigar from one corner of his mouth to the other.

I grabbed it away from him. "This is a no smoking room, you idiot. You're going to get me thrown out of this hotel."

Then talk to me. Maybe I know something you don't.

"Fat chance." I drowned the cigar in the sink, then wrapped it in tissue. In the morning I'd dump it in the ash can outside the hotel.

You never know what I know.

"It was just a nightmare."

The same nightmare that haunts you month after month. I was there, babe, even before you could see me. Tell me about it.

Did I really want to relive that nightmare long enough to talk about it?

If you talk about it, you will purge your mind of the worst of it.

"I've heard that."

So I sat cross-legged on the bed with a glass of water and a box of tissues and talked.

Scrap stayed a normal grayish green, nodding his head as he listened attentively.

The tightness in my chest eased and my eyes grew heavy. I trusted Scrap with my secrets. Hell, he was my biggest secret.

So why couldn't I trust him when he said Dog wasn't a demon?

Because Dog had killed Bob.

Think on this while you snooze, Tessie babe: Why does Dill want you to reject me and go to him? What can he do for you that I can't?

"He can love me."

Scrap winked out in a huff.

I slept dreamlessly through the rest of the night.

TUESDAY MORNING DAWNED bright and cold. The air smelled clean with just a hint of mint and sage on the wind. More than just a breeze. On the Columbia River plateau the wind always blew. Air masses shifted from here to there endlessly, without regard for human concerns.

Bob had loved the land. A real desert rat, he backpacked through the treeless local mountains and the trackless Cascades.

I think one of the reasons I had never married him was that the desert scared me. The emptiness, the loneliness. The silence deep enough to break my heart. People and monsters I could fight. Only with Dill had I found beauty beneath the relentless sun and seen color in the barren rocks.

An empty day loomed before me, as empty as I perceived the desert. Bob's funeral was tomorrow. A funeral I had no part in planning. Bob had been my closest friend, but was not my lover or my family. I could pay condolence calls on his parents and sister. Nothing else.

You could sing at his funeral, Scrap reminded me.

I couldn't see him, but that didn't mean he wasn't close.

"I can't sing anymore." Not since Dill died.

Can't or won't?

"Is there a difference?"

You tell me.

A loud knocking at my door ended that pointless conversation.

Donovan stood in the hallway bearing a single red rose and a sheepish look. "Can we talk?" he asked.

"Over breakfast. Have you eaten?"

He was right. We needed to talk.

I didn't want him in my hotel room. My bedroom. Not again. Yet.

"No. I left home before dawn and drove straight here. Breakfast would be good."

I grabbed my purse and my key card and met him in the hallway. He gave me the rose. I buried my nose in it, suddenly shy, but warm and comfortable in his presence, just like I had been back at the *salle* on Cape Cod.

In a public place I could trust him. Alone? I didn't think I could trust myself.

We walked the long length of the hotel in silence, a scant three inches separating our shoulders and our hands. Together and yet . . . not yet.

We sipped coffee while we waited for our orders. Scrap hadn't showed up, so I didn't order his favorite beer and OJ.

"Tess."

"Donovan." We spoke at the same time.

"You first." I gestured.

"I reacted badly yesterday, Tess. I'm sorry." He looked up at the plants growing around the ceiling beams rather than meet my gaze.

My suspicions hovered on the edge of my perceptions. Then he smiled and I relaxed.

"The truth is, I need to know which tribe approached you to try to get the blanket away from me. I saw how closely you studied it. More than just a tourist's interest."

"What?" Of all the explanations that was the last one I expected. "No one approached me."

"Are you certain? Maybe that Van der Hoyden guy said something. He's an anthropologist. Maybe one of the tribes approached him to authenticate it."

"I am certain, Donovan. My interest in the blanket is . . ." Goddess, how did I explain it to someone who didn't know about the Sisterhood and my imp? "My interest in the blanket is deeper than possession by any single person or group. It's the stuff of legends. I need to study it. Research it. Make sure it is protected."

"For a book?" He looked hopeful.

"Very likely." I already had a fantasy novel outlining itself in my head. The first volume in the series—the one that had made the best-seller lists—was based on fact, though I'd never admit it publicly. Why not one of the sequels?

"I'm glad. The truth is, several tribes have applied a lot of pressure to get the blanket into one of their museums. But it's a family heirloom. It's protected in a temperature-and-humidity-controlled environment, behind museum-quality Plexiglas, out of direct sunlight. I've got provenance going back to the first written records in this part of the country."

Not so long ago. Europeans didn't bring reading and writing to this part of the world until the early 1800s.

Could the old woman, the weaver, have been dead that long?

I doubted it. The dog would have been looking for a new weaver before this. And probably found one. But if he hadn't found a weaver, his activities would have passed into local legend more readily. Sort of like Sasquatch.

Something hummed along my spine with that thought.

The number of lies Donovan told me mounted up.

So why did my blood sing every time he came near?

Our food came, interrupting my train of thought. The tingling at the base of my spine calmed.

"Who is this Van der Hoyden person anyway?" Donovan asked around a mouthful of Belgian waffle. "I have to admit I'm jealous. He spends more time with you than I do."

"He's . . ." How did I describe him? "A colleague. Sort of a research assistant." I ducked my head and tucked into my omelet with Hollandaise sauce, sausage, and pancakes.

"I wish you wouldn't spend so much time with him. I don't trust him. Who is he and where did he come from?"

Good questions. I'd asked them many times of Gollum and received only vague answers.

Yet I trusted him more than I did Donovan.

"He's been a friend," I replied lamely. He had stuck by me after Bob was killed while Donovan attended to the adult children of his client.

"How about I ask around and see if I can find you a real research assistant, a grad student or something?"

"I don't know..."

"We'll talk about it later."

We ate in silence a moment.

"Tell me about your husband?" Donovan looked at me hopefully.

"I'm not sure..."

"I'd like to scope out my competition. Were you married long?"

"Not really. He died quite suddenly. A fire."

"You must have known him a long time, then. High school sweethearts?"

"No. We met here at High Desert Con three years ago. He taught geology at the community college. He transferred to Cape Cod Community College after we married, was due to start spring semester. He didn't live that long. Bob Brown introduced us."

Donovan stilled like his entire being listened for clues to something.

"Does this ghost of a man have a name?" he asked after several long moments.

"Dillwyn Bailey Cooper. Dill."

"D. B. Cooper?" he asked on a grin.

"You know the legend?"

"The first guy ever to have the audacity to hijack a plane, hold it for ransom, and get away with it. He's a local folk hero."

I laughed. "My Dill was too young to be *that* D. B. Cooper. But maybe his father, who was also D. B. Cooper, as are his mother, brother, and sister—before she married. They did come into a lot of money without explanation and bought a furniture and appliance store."

"How mundane. You'd think with a name like that they'd open a pub or a hotel, or something more exotic."

"Mundane. That's a good way of describing them." For the first time in a long time, I laughed while talking and thinking about Dill and his family.

"I have some business in town this morning, Tess. But I swear I'll be done by lunchtime. We'll spend the rest of the day together. Get to know each other better." His eyes pleaded with me as he signaled the waitress for the check. "How about we take a picnic down to the river. I'll show you where Kennewick man was found." He mentioned a thousands-of-years-old skeleton found on the Columbia River banks, almost intact. Legal wars raged for more than ten years as to tribal rights to bury the bones with respect and scientists' rights to study them.

"Sounds like fun." I smiled up at him.

"What will you do this morning?" He toyed with the red rose that lay between us on the table. Almost a pledge, certainly a token that something strong kept bringing us back together. If I could ever learn to truly trust him Still I lusted for him.

"Work." I shrugged. "I can write anywhere, almost anytime."

Suddenly Donovan broke off a long portion of the rose's stem and tucked the flower behind my ear. My left ear, isn't that supposed to be the side that symbolizes a woman was married or betrothed—taken, anyway?

"I like that better than the comb. More natural. It suits you." Then he kissed me lightly, scooped up the check, and left. At the cash register he blew me another kiss.

About time he took off, Scrap complained. He popped into view in the middle of the table, inspecting coffee cups and juice glasses for residue. *Nothing left for me.* He pouted.

"If you'd stick around more, maybe I'd get you something to eat. Guess you'll have to make do with mold in the air conditioners." I grabbed my purse and headed back to my room and my laptop.

I've cleaned them all out! Scrap hopped to my shoulder. *Witching into your Celestial Blade is hard work.*

I ignored him.

Maybe Gollum has some beer in his room.

"Where is Gollum by the way?" Now that Donovan had left, I wanted to discuss the blanket with my friend.

College library. Been there most of the night.

"Good place for him."

The itch to write crept through me, fast becoming a compulsion With both men out of my hair, I could get some serious writing done. And think about the questions I had for Donovan and Gollum when next they darkened my door.

Something perverse made me keep the rose behind my ear when Gollum showed up a couple of hours later with a stack of printouts from tribal databases all over the country. The jerk didn't even notice.

But Donovan frowned when I jammed the comb into my hair as we left on our picnic.

The time is coming when my babe will understand that Dog isn't our enemy. Soon she'll listen to me calmly and rationally and form a plan. Two days ago, when the dog killed Bob, wasn't the time for her to get what Dog's all about. Two days ago she was in danger of drowning in her grief like she did when Dill died.

She still wears her emotions on her sleeve. Only with Mom does she hide her feelings. But then she's always done that, even before she had secrets to keep. I wouldn't tell Mom anything either. She reacts more volatilely than my babe does.

But that time comes, too, when Mom will have to be told. Dad would never understand, and we'll keep him in the dark. MoonFeather, on the other hand, is a ripe candidate to help us.

That is if my dahling babe doesn't do something stupid like fall in love with the stinky man who I can't figure out.

Chapter 22

Ten o'clock the next morning found me tearless, sitting in a middle pew of the Catholic Church in Kennewick, Washington, a few blocks west of the con hotel in Pascoe. The two cities blended into one, along with Richland, the third city in the area.

I wore the little midnight blue dress that suited all occasions and I never traveled without. Bob did not approve of black or tears at a funeral any more than Dill did. Funerals were meant to be celebrations of a life.

So, I sat alone for almost half an hour before anyone else showed up. Alone with the memories of the man who had shaped more of my life than Dill had.

Memories washed over me like a sneaker wave at the coast. Good memories. Bob in our Freshman Western Civ class at Providence U, totally at sea in the mass of historical information. I helped him study. He tutored me in math. We went to our first con together in Boston. He introduced me to science fiction. I introduced him to fantasy. We went to another con together. And another. We learned to filk together.

We graduated together, then went our separate ways, only to meet up again at other cons throughout the country. He built a career at the nuclear reservation. I built mine in publishing.

Always there was that deep and abiding friendship uncluttered with sexual tension. We might have been good lovers, but knew each other well enough that sex wasn't important between us.

I breathed deeply, aware of the emptiness in my life. But I was refreshed. I remembered Bob with joy and thankfulness for that wonderful friendship. I regretted his passing, but not our time together.

Why couldn't I remember Dillwyn Bailey Cooper with the same sense of gladness and thankfulness? Whenever I thought of Dill, I wanted to cry and scream and rant, and dive into the depths of the lake at the base of Dry Falls to escape the emptiness of my life without him.

Friends from cons all over the Pacific Northwest nodded to me as they took their seats in the church. A few stopped to say "Hello," and condole with me. Bob's coworkers gave me curious looks. I heard their whispered questions. "Is she the famous one?"

None of them asked if I was the one who had caused Bob's death.

Guilt and anger gnawed at me. I should have saved Bob. If I were faster with the Celestial Blade . . . If I'd thought beyond . . . If I'd thought at all rather than just reacted.

Scrap plopped into my lap. His skin looked brighter blue against my dress. *You look bluer than I do, dahling,* he said, puffing on a thin black cherry cheroot.

"Bad pun, Scrap," I whispered to him. My anger vanished. My life wasn't so empty after all. No matter which path I took, I'd always have Scrap with me.

Where do we go from here? Scrap climbed onto the back of the pew in front of me and surveyed the growing crowd of mourners.

"I'll let you know when I know."

Further conversation was cut off by the entrance of Bob's family, escorted by a priest. The service began and I lost myself in the beauty of the familiar ritual. The responses came naturally to me. Mom and Dad had raised me Catholic even if I'd stopped attending church after Dad moved in with Bill. I even managed to choke out some of the songs and chants.

A filk group got up and played some of Bob's favorite pieces and two of the hymns. They looked meaningfully at me. I shook my head. No way could I sing the piece Bob loved above all others. "Ave Maria."

I turned and left the church before the Eucharist. I felt everyone's eyes on me. That did not matter. I'm not certain I'd have stayed even if they hadn't expected me to sing.

I didn't believe in that God anymore. I didn't really believe in anything. Music had been a large part of any kind of faith I might have had.

I doubted I'd ever sing or believe again.

Scrap remained oddly subdued.

"I think we need to go back to Half Moon Lake," Gollum said as he followed me out. "The dog is going to show up there sooner or later."

"This is my job, not yours," I snapped. I wasn't in the mood to be pleasant to anyone.

"Consider me an objective observer who will report back to the proper authorities." He remained beside me, matching me step for step.

"No." I planted myself in the middle of the sidewalk. "You aren't coming with me unless you come clean. I am sick and tired of your half statements and cryptic answers. Who are you and why are you following me?"

He clamped his jaw shut.

"Fine. You're fired." I turned on my well-shod heel and marched back toward the hotel and my luggage.

"Tess, you can't fire me. You need me."

"No, I don't."

He continued to offer me arguments in favor of us teaming up. I refused to hear a thing he said. The more he argued the more My heart hardened against him, against Donovan, against... every other man in my life who kept secrets.

"Tell me what I need to know and I might...*might* listen to you."

He said nothing.

Righteous indignation propelled me all the way to the car rental booth. All they had left was a huge SUV. White. I took it though I hate big vehicles. Then as I signed my name to one form after another my hand began to shake.

I kept right on signing. I'd finish this on my own, with only Scrap for help. That's the way I was supposed to work. One Sister, one imp. We'd find our demons and fight them back to their own dimension, then return to our normal everyday lives. Alone.

People I cared about couldn't desert me if I never let them into my life.

LOCALS IN HALF MOON Lake tended to hang out at the bar down the street from the Mowath Lodge where I booked a room—hey, it was the only lodging in town, dirt cheap, and I could watch Donovan's office from my front deck. I began to wonder if gaming software had anything to do with gambling machines—now run by computers rather than gears and levers.

I couldn't see Donovan's suite from the bar. But it was dark anyway. This town rolled up its sidewalks at suppertime.

That would change when the casino opened. People could lose money there three shifts a day. The local unemployment problem would evaporate with the locals taking care of those determined to dump money into slot machines and roulette wheels and card games.

If the casino employed locals. In some places Indian casinos only hired other Indians; bringing them in from other tribes and locations rather than hire any "white" folk.

With the tension I'd witnessed earlier in this town, I guessed the casino would hire outside.

But if the casino used up all the local water, the locals would lose doubly, no irrigation for livestock and the few crops. And no golfers at the lushly green resort at the southwest end of town.

I took a seat in a booth in a back corner where I could watch the local gathering and not have to worry about anyone approaching me unobserved. Before leaving Tri-Cities, I'd stopped at the mall and outfitted myself with distressed jeans, boots, and cotton shirts, the better to blend in with the town folk. A little fussing and oily hair products straightened my curls and made my hair long enough to pull into pigtails. Darker makeup and pale lipstick completed my disguise. A careful observer might recognize me, but not strangers. Scrap gave me a gentle aura of familiar friendliness.

A few people half waved and smiled as I entered, then ignored me. Hopefully, they would keep their conversations normal rather than clam up in the presence of a stranger.

I needed to hear the local gossip about the casino, Donovan, and any dog sightings.

The waitress let her eyes glaze into boredom as she took my order for hamburger, fries, and beer. No one else ordered the overpriced limp salads, so I didn't either. The chilled beer came with a frosty mug. I drank from the bottle, like the locals. It was good and slid down my dry throat like balm on a wound.

The beer was the tastiest part of the meal. I'd downed three and a half of them—Scrap drank a fifth and the half I left in my fourth bottle—before I heard anything new in the conversation that rose and fell around me.

"Those fuckin' Indians can't drain the water table if we blow up the casino," a man whispered in the booth next to mine.

"I got some dynamite left over from building my irrigation dam," another man said quietly. "Fat lot of good it did me. Ain't no water left in the creek to dam."

"Don't even have to bomb the casino. That hillside is riddled with caves. All we have to do is plant a little bit of explosive in one cave. It'll undermine the foundations. Make it too unstable to build anything up there."

I shivered with that. The cave where an old woman had woven the blanket of life had already collapsed (according some of Gollum's research) and started this entire chain of unfortunate events. I had to do something.

What could I do to stop them?

Whisper campaign, Scrap said. Then he belched, having drunk his entire beer and eaten all of my greasy fries.

"Nice to see you are back to normal," I replied sotto voce.

Nice bugs in the lake water.

"I didn't think anything could live in that heavy mineral mixture."

Microorganisms in the top layer that doesn't mix with the heaviest minerals at the bottom—sort of like the cowboys and Indians in this town.

"Meromictic," I said. "That's what Dill called it when the layers of lake water do not mix."

Anyway, the microscopic shrimp are better than mold. And there is mold in the air conditioners. I could live here.

"Don't get used to it. We're leaving as soon as I can find Cynthia and get her away from Dog."

Won't happen unless you rescue the blanket and find a new weaver. Dog is on a mission. He's one of the good guys.

I snorted in derision. "Dog killed Bob and a bunch of other innocents. He's not one of the good guys."

Sometimes innocents get in the way of an important mission. If they don't step aside, they become casualties of war.

I decided to ignore that rather than think too hard. But the idea sounded good for the book.

Don't forget that the demon children were as responsible as Dog for Bob's death.

"Let's start that whisper campaign against the idea of blowing up the hillside under the casino." Something to do rather than think too hard. I wanted to blame Dog.

Hell, I wanted Donovan's demon children to be innocent so that he would be innocent.

"If you set dynamite in one of those caves, any one of those caves, the whole hill will slide into the lake. The town will close down without the lake," I said as I slipped onto the seat next to the conspirators, beer in hand. Flirtatiously, I took a cowboy hat off one middle-aged and paunchy rancher and set it on my own head. The brim hid my eyes and shadowed my face.

The men leaned closer to me. Lust and hope crossed their faces.

"I know enough about geology to tell you, you're better off sabotaging the building materials. Then you get an inspector out from Olympia to declare the construction shoddy and unsafe."

"Estevez has got all the inspectors in his pocket. Pays them better than the state does," Paunchy grumbled.

"The local inspectors, sure. But what if we demand the state bring in someone new? This is a big construction project. Local guys don't have enough experience to know what's being done right or where Estevez is sliding beneath building codes," I countered.

Three men raised their eyebrows. "Who do we know with enough clout to get that done?" Paunchy asked.

"Let me send an email." I returned the hat and slid out of the booth. Scrap clung to my back, making me look a lot broader and taller than I truly was.

No gossip about a big ugly dog in town. But he'd be here. And I'd be waiting for him when he arrived. Then I'd let these guys blow up the whole town if they wanted.

If they blow up all the caves, Dog will have nowhere to put the blanket and the new weaver. He'll go after Cynthia again.

"Oh, shut up, I didn't want to hear that."

Chapter 23

Bats use echolocation to find food and avoid obstacles.

My feet took me north to the end of town and a little east to the dregs of the housing. About half the dwellings were tiny abandoned structures—sanitariums left over from the heyday of the lake as a healing place, before modern medicine. I found the Wild Horse Bar in a ramshackle building with a stone foundation made from rocks rounded and smoothed by water action, and wooden additions that took off at weird angles.

The tribal contingent hung out here.

Scrap, can you darken my hair and skin a bit? Few of the locals appeared to be full-blooded aboriginal. I could get away with Caucasian features but not my New England fairness.

A slithering like gel flowing over my head made me shiver in revulsion.

Done, dahling.

I stepped into the bar and ordered another beer, fully intending to let Scrap drink it. I'd had enough fuzziness for one night.

The jukebox played the same country western music as at the other bar, the linoleum floor looked just as ancient. It smelled of spilled beer and crushed peanuts and the ever-present fishy smell of the lake. Other than the fairly universal dark hair and dark eyes, this could be the same bar I had just left.

Except the patrons were not quite as drunk. I knew alcoholism was a big problem on the reservations. I watched the bartender—who might have been a Leonard Stalking Moon clone including the harelip—cut off a sullen young man. He had three beer bottles in front of him. The well-groomed middle-aged man I'd noticed in the crowd the other day pushed a cup of coffee at the man. The waitress pulled the drunk's keys out of the pocket of his tight jeans and handed them to the coffee pusher.

These people took care of their own.

I took a table in a corner and ordered a beer.

"Estevez had no right to fire me from the construction crew!" the drunk slammed his fist on the bar.

"He had every right if you showed up drunk, Billy," Good Dresser said, plying another sip of coffee on the man.

"But I wasn't drunk. I swear it, Joe. I didn't start drinking until after he fired me." Drunk Billy looked sullen.

"Then why were you late? Two and a half hours late by my reckoning," Joe prodded.

"Mellie has morning sickness. I didn't want to leave her until her stomach settled."

"Let me talk to Donovan in the morning," Joe said. "You need to go home to Mellie. Sam will take you." Joe snapped his fingers at a youngish man hovering behind Billy. "You can come back in the morning to get your pickup."

Sam led a still grumbling Billy out the door.

A collective sigh of relief went around the room.

"Anyone else got a beef against Estevez?" Joe asked. He didn't look happy.

"The bastard promised me long-term carpenter work," the man next to Joe said. "Replaced me with one of his own cronies who doesn't know a finishing nail from a sander. Demoted me to unskilled labor at half the wages."

"Who's he?" I whispered to the waitress when she brought my foaming glass. I jerked my head in Joe's direction as he handled more complaints.

"Joseph Long Talker. He's the only lawyer in town," she replied on a chuckle. "Even the whites have to go to him or drive into Ephrata for a more expensive guy."

Within a few minutes I understood that Donovan hadn't made himself popular with either side in this town. Arrogant and self-serving with the whites; not living up to his promises of good employment and overbearing with the aboriginals. My distrust of the man rose, and I vowed never to be caught in the net of his smile again.

Remember that the next time he tries to charm you.

Donovan did seem to have the ability to make me forget my resolve. All he had to do was smile . . .

Just like Dill had.

I jerked into new awareness. Dill had charmed and manipulated me much as Donovan did.

Anger at both of them seethed within me.

"What kind of magic does he have?" I whispered to Scrap, who still had not appeared.

I wish I knew.

If Scrap didn't know, then we were both in trouble.

AFTER BREAKFAST THE next day, I sent emails to friends in Seattle who might get an impartial and unbribable inspector out here. I called Leonard. He sounded anxious, and weary. Still no sign of Cynthia.

"Donovan Estevez has the blanket in his office," I said.

He replied with a string of invective I didn't want to translate even if I could.

"Watch him, Warrior. Watch him close. Cynthia will come there soon. The blanket is a lodestone. The forces of good and evil will circle around it in a never-ending dance. You must keep it that way. No one side can dominate. I charge you, Warrior, with Cynthia's safety until a balance is achieved."

He hung up abruptly, leaving me with more questions than when I started.

I needed to stretch my body and think, push it to more vigorous activity than sitting in cars on endless drives through boring country or sitting and eavesdropping. I left my room and walked along the lake edge on the far side, beneath the casino. It was early yet, and Donovan's posted office hours were ten to two. Bankers' hours. I wondered what he did there. Maybe he spent the rest of his day at the construction site. I'd have to take a look up there eventually. Not today.

The Mowath Lodge sat at the southern tip of the lake. The golf course spread out south and east of the lodge. A dozen sprinklers watered the manicured greens. The town hugged the inside or eastern curve with its sandy beaches and easy approaches. I followed the shoreline as far as I could to the west and the outside curve of the water until the beaches became cliffs.

Houses with irrigated lawns fell away to shacks hidden behind tumbles of reddish-brown rock. A few scrawny goats and cats seemed to be the only inhabitants of these dwellings. Occasionally, I spotted a bit of laundry on a line behind the house, a diaper, dish towels, socks, not much else.

Long strides took me quickly beyond the developed lakeside into rough and rocky terrain. The salty sands became shallower. The cliffs came closer and closer to the water's edge. I looked up and up and up along water-scoured rock with deep crevices and ravines. This land was planned on the vertical.

I tried to imagine what the area would look like if the Columbia River had not changed course twelve thousand years ago. Deep water everywhere, I guessed. The river had dug channels four-and five-hundred-feet deep in places when the glacial floods happened. The amount of water needed to fill the coulee boggled my mind. I concentrated on finding some of the caves the river had carved out of the rock.

"Not much here, Scrap," I said, poking my nose into a shallow ravine. "Might as well turn around."

Not so fast, Blondie. Look up and to your right fifteen degrees.

I did and saw a shadow that was probably more interesting than the narrow crevice at beach level.

"I'll have to climb onto rocks to avoid the water," I complained.

The old woman wouldn't live in a place accessible to just any tourist out for a stroll.

"What if there are bats living in there?"

You'll survive. They'll be sleeping now. It's broad daylight.

"Still . . ."

Climb, babe.

Scrap pulled my hair harder than any bat could. At least, he didn't tangle his talons in it.

As I pulled myself onto the first boulder, a good twenty-five feet high with convenient hand and footholds in the rough surface, I spotted the dark shadow that had no business being on that cliff face. The sun shone directly onto that area with nothing between the light and the rock to cast a shadow. I climbed with more enthusiasm.

I'd look inside and hoped this was the one. Then I wouldn't have to chance any more exposure to bats.

Sure enough, the tall, narrow shadow proved to be an opening into the rocks. Scrap scampered in ahead of me. I shifted my daypack from my back to my hand and turned sideways to slither in.

With a high-pitched screech, Scrap came tearing back out, claws extended. *Bats!* he yelled.

I screamed louder than he did and backpedaled to the edge of the rocks and almost took a dive into the water.

Just kidding! Scrap laughed. He lay on the boulder rolling around in uncontrollable laughter.

"Very funny," I snarled. My heart was in my throat and beating double time. I could barely breathe.

But I had to admit the sight of Scrap making an ass of himself was funny. I began to chuckle. And soon I had to sit while I let the laughter take control.

Eventually we calmed down.

Still friends?

"Maybe."

The first cave was shallow and empty.

We trudged on, climbing three more boulders in search of the next cave. *Found one.*

I pulled myself up to the next level, arms shaking to support my weight as I heaved upward and scanned the cliff. Sure enough, Scrap had found another shadow that didn't belong on the flat surface in full sun.

I entered cautiously, wary of Scrap's tricks. He behaved himself.

A low cave spread out just beyond the opening. I had to crouch to avoid hitting my head while my eyes to adjusted to the new darkness.

My bare arms chilled, and a frisson of . . . something crawled across my nape. The interior darkness seemed artificially deep and oppressive. A perfect home for bats.

A sense of someone—or something—else filling the cave pressed me against the wall. This place was old beyond ancient. I wasn't wanted here. I had intruded upon someone's privacy, someone's sacred place. A sanctuary.

Take off your sunglasses and hat, babe. You'll see better.

Scrap snapped insubstantial fingers and produced a morsel of flame on a chubby pawtip. This he applied to the end of a cigar. He began puffing away, producing clouds of aromatic smoke.

That otherworldly sense of another presence vanished.

I choked and coughed. When my lungs and eyes cleared, I saw evidence of rockfall along one side and the remains of an old campfire up against the back of the cave. I touched the bits of charcoal. They crumbled to dust without the least scent of burned wood.

A very old fire.

Rock chips littered the ground around the site. They might have been detritus from arrowhead knapping. They might have been just bits of rock. I didn't have the training to know the difference.

I don't like this place, Tess. It's old. There are ghosts here.

Scrap radiated waves of defensive red, ready to transform if needed. He levitated himself into the cave opening, as if he intended to flee.

"Ghosts, I can deal with. It's bats that scare me."

These ghosts should scare you. They scare me.

"Any ghosts that haunt this place can't be any worse than the ghosts that terrorize my dreams," I replied. But I, too, crawled out into the sunshine. Immediately, I felt a weight lift from my chest, and I breathed deeply of the crisp autumnal air.

"I'm missing something, Scrap." I gulped greedily at one of my water bottles from the daypack.

My imp perched upon my shoulder without saying anything. But he took on shades of pink as he watched and thought.

I sat on the long bench of rock with my back against the cliff and stared into nothing. Quiet times like this were part of the everyday life within the Citadel.

Part of me longed to go back to those simple days of training and meditation, of companionship and learning. Sure, I'd had my problems with the powers that be. But there were good times, too. I'd made a few friends.

Serena, the doctor. Gayla, the woman I'd rescued and nursed through the imp flu. Paige, my trainer in the use of the Celestial Blade. If I sat here long enough, absorbing sunshine and quiet, maybe my mind would open up and give me some answers.

Answers to questions like: Where were Dog and Cynthia? How could I get the girl away from the monster dog when I found them?

I look three long breaths, making certain I exhaled as deeply as I inhaled. With my eyes closed and my mind open, I sent my thoughts searching for an equally open mind.

Images of the lake and shore reversed on the inside of my eyelids, light and dark swapped places, as did red and green. I let the scenes develop and dissolve, not concentrating or dwelling on any one of them.

My muscles twitched, demanding action. I let them twitch but ignored the need to stand up and move.

This was the hard part. Sister Serena had tried very hard, but in vain, to instill good meditation habits in me during my training.

You have questions, daughter.

A voice came into my mind: gentle, calm, serene.

I nearly jumped out of my quiet in surprise. I didn't often manage to contact anyone at the Citadel.

Many questions. No clear path to find answers.

Not so much words as symbolic images of a path broken by boulders, booby traps, and diverging trails, all marked with question marks.

Trust in dreams, my child.

My dreams are troubling, filled with demons.

As are mine. We live in troubled times. We are challenged often. Besieged. Many of us are wounded or dead. Dreams are our only truth.

The sense of another mind in my head vanished abruptly.

I opened my eyes, startled by the brightness of the sun on the water. I felt as if I'd just awakened from a long sleep.

"Trust my dreams? What does that mean?" I'd had a lot of disturbing dreams of late. Did the message mean that Dill truly was a ghost who haunted me? Should I trust him?

Or should I be wary of the demons that stalked me in my dreams and in real life?

Scrap shifted uneasily on my shoulder. His movement made me lift my gaze from the depths of the lake and the whirlpool of my thoughts to the buildings across the water from me. About half a mile away, on the inside curve of the lakeshore, children played on the swing set of the public park while adults in bathing suits caked their bodies in the salt-encrusted sand or waded in the oily water.

The salts caked the dry sands for about twenty feet above the waterline. Another thirty feet of dry sand stretched above that. Evidence that the water level receded? Was this a seasonal retreat after a long, dry summer, or did the construction of the casino divert enough water from springs and creeks to deplete the lake?

That was a lot of water. The lake was two miles long and one across.

And the casino and hotel were still under construction. What would happen to the water level when six hundred toilets and showers started operating?

To my right, my own room at the Mowath Lodge sat back from the beach. My balcony looked out over the water, as did the room next to mine. Each of the eight log lodges contained four suites, two up and two down. All of the rooms had lakeside views.

The old motel, where Dill and I had stayed, the building that had burned, had been designed just like a normal motel, a single long building, two stories, doors on the street, windows and balconies facing the lake. Just because it was built with a log facing didn't make it anything other than what it was, a motel.

I liked the new design better. It must have cost the earth to rebuild with the massive logs and unique wooden interiors. Did the insurance money cover all the costs?

Maybe someone had made a lot of money off the insurance when the old building burned. Who?

If I knew that, I might have a clue as to why my husband died.

Donovan seemed to be in charge of an office. Not the hotel reception office, though. That was in a small single room cabin at the edge of the grounds. Did he own the building and delegate hotel management? Or did he just rent office space?

Before I could follow that thought any further, a flicker of movement inside my suite caught my attention. Maybe it was just a reflection off the glass doors and massive windows. Maybe not.

I stood up and cupped my hands around my eyes to reduce the glare off the water.

Movement definitely. Reflection or inside, I could not tell.

"Time to go home, Scrap."

Home to Mom's burned cookies? he asked hopefully, glowing green.

"No, the lodge. I need to check out that sense of movement inside my room. Then I need to do some research into the history of this region and the geology and water table. Good thing every room has a data port and wireless Internet."

Along with microwave, mini refrigerator, and coffee maker. You need more coffee.

"You mean, you want to drink my leftovers when they get moldy."

Who, me?

Scrap turned a cute and innocent lavender.

I began searching for the safest way off this rock. If I turned around and backed down . . .

A shot rang out from above me. A bullet pinged against the place I had sat seconds before.

Rock shards sprayed and ricocheted.

I ducked. Not fast enough.

Burning pain seared my upper right arm. A sharp sliver of rock penetrated my sleeve.

Blood dripped and stained my blouse.

Darkness encroached from the sides of my vision. I grew hot and chilled at the same time. Up and down reversed.

A second shot landed beside my left boot.

I barely clung to consciousness as I crawled into the cave full of hostile ghosts.

Chapter 24

I sank to the ground inside the cave, clutching the ricochet puncture on my upper arm, careful not to wiggle the long sliver of rock that protruded. It burned all the way to my fingertips and up across my shoulder into my neck.

Damn! I still had tender wounds from the dog attack. If I wasn't careful, I might lose strength and stamina when I most needed it.

Slowly I pinched the shard of rock and slid it out. A good half inch of the pointed edge came out red. Blood flowed freely down my arm.

Pressure, babe. Apply pressure, Scrap whispered.

I couldn't see him. But I followed his advice. Basic first aid. Pressure and elevation. No way could I lift the wound above my head. The arm was just too heavy and hurt more with every movement.

Let me help, Tess. Scrap sounded worried as he popped back into view, a pinkish haze that glowed slightly. He ran his tongue around the edges of the wound and across it.

I had to look away. Too close to vampirism for my taste.

The intense burn dissipated and retreated. Now I only ached from neck to elbow. The arm was still too painful to lift.

I fumbled for a bandanna I'd stuffed into the pack. It was sweaty and dirty from where I'd mopped my face and neck. Better than nothing. With only a few missed tries, I managed to wrap it around the wound. With my teeth and my good hand, I tied it reasonably tight, then clamped my palm across it and pressed.

The bleeding slowed to an ooze while I leaned my face against the cool rock wall and tried to stay conscious.

"Who, Scrap?" I finally whispered. Even if I had the strength to speak louder, I didn't want the sound of my voice to carry and alert the shooter to my location. Caves did strange things to acoustics and might amplify sound in a weird direction.

Don't know.

Scrap stubbed out his cigar in the remnants of the fire.

"Can you go look?"

Not with you bleeding. Can't get more than six feet from you. Even if the stinky man showed up right now, he couldn't force me away from you.

"Oh?"

Code and honor and magic tie me more closely to you when you're wounded or under attack.

"So, what do we do?"

Wait.

"For what? For an assassin to come looking and find me?"

Three misty forms oozed out of the walls. No features, no definition. Just blobs of white. They hovered in front of me. My vision must have been playing tricks on me. Shock and blood loss.

I gulped. Once again I had that overwhelming sense of unwelcome.

Just then I heard small rocks falling and a body flopping around on the cliff face. "She can't have gotten far," a man said in a deep, guttural voice. He sounded like the Indian who had guarded Donovan Estevez's office.

I froze in place. Specters in the cave or an enemy with a gun outside?

The ghosts grew in size and took on the vague outlines of short, muscular humans. Male or female, I could not tell. Modern or ancient remained just as elusive.

I was betting on ancient.

"I told you, I don't want her hurt," Donovan said.

What was he doing out here?

Good question, babe. What is the stinky man up to?

More scrambling among the rocks. The voices still sounded far above me. The ghosts shifted their eerie attention from me to the men outside.

"But she was spying on our operation," the other man replied.

"Spying on the casino from down here?" Donovan sounded a lot closer now. Closer than his guard. "Come now, Quentin. Even you aren't dumb enough to think she could see anything from below."

"The office, boss."

I didn't need to see the men to know that Quentin pointed across the water toward the Mowath Lodge. I *had* seen movement in my suite.

Donovan said something in a language I did not understand, full of hisses, clicks, and grunts.

Scrap's ears pricked and he turned brilliant red, as if he needed to transform into the Celestial Blade.

The ghosts melted back into the cave walls.

"What?" I mouthed to Scrap.

You don't want to know.

"Yes, I do!" I insisted without sound.

"Next time, ask me before you shoot. Tess Noncoiré dead is a whole lot more trouble than alive."

"If you say so, boss. I still think she should meet with an accident."

"No."

"I could make a fire look like an accident. Like when that Dillwyn person died."

Shock robbed me of breath.

I needed to run out and confront the man, demand what he knew about my husband's death.

Scrap kept me in place by suddenly becoming heavy on my shoulder.

Tears crept toward my eyes.

Quentin knew how Dill had died. He implied that he had set the fire.

Anger banished my chills.

I needed to know more, hear more.

Fear for my life kept me rooted to the spot. I began to shake all over.

"What part of 'no' don't you understand, Quentin?" Donovan's voice became strained.

I imagined the lines of anger creasing his face.

A long moment of silence.

My blood ran cold. Donovan's henchman was talking about killing me. Just two days ago Donovan had plied me with champagne, caviar, and strawberries dipped in chocolate on a picnic.

"Well, she's long gone now. We might as well return to work. We're behind schedule as it is," Donovan said.

"You going ahead with construction without that inspection?"

So, my email and phone call had done some good.

"Inspectors aren't worth the paper their credentials are printed on," Donovan sneered.

"This one sounded serious and important. He can close us down if he doesn't like what he sees."

"I'll see to it that he likes what we are doing." Donovan moved away.

I counted to one hundred in the unnatural silence that followed.

"Check to see where they are," I finally whispered to Scrap.

He winked out and back in less than a heartbeat. *Halfway around the lake, still in full view of here,* he reported. He hovered close to me, wings working overtime as he peered through the gloom at my aching arm.

I leaned my head back against the cave wall while I gathered my strength.

The bleeding has stopped. You'll start to heal soon. Imp spit does the trick every time!

"But it still hurts. And it's weak. I'm going to have a hell of a time climbing down those rocks." I drank deeply from the water bottle.

Power Bar, babe. You need some protein.

"I need answers. What was that language Donovan spat out? I didn't think a human voice box could wrap around some of those sounds."

Absolute silence from Scrap. He tried to fade into nothingness, but I was still hurt and he was still bound to stay with me.

"Spit it out, Scrap."

You don't want to know, he repeated.

"I'm getting tired of hearing that."

His glamour of irresistible male potency is not natural.

"Tell me something I don't know." Cold fear and adrenaline washed over me, replaced by an ugly sense of—I didn't like myself very much in that moment. Donovan had *used* me. He'd used some kind of unnatural magic on me.

And I fell for it.

"I'm gonna kill that guy when I see him next," I ground out between clenched teeth.

Not a good idea, Tessie.

"I know. He's got money and connections. I'd bring a whole hell of a lot of trouble down if he turned up dead with me holding the gun. At least now I know I can't trust him."

You'd be better off with Gollum. I like him.

"Guilford Van der Hoyden-Smythe is a pest and a nuisance."

That's why I like him.

"He also knows languages. Maybe he's know what Donovan said, if I can repeat the words."

Might be native. Might be demon, Scrap mumbed.

"You are no help at all! At least, go check again and see if they are out of sight. I need to get out of here and then find a drugstore so I can properly clean and bandage this wound. Don't want infection setting in." My emergency med kit was in my own car, at home. Too bulky and extensive to carry with me. The small first aid kit I kept in my suitcase wouldn't cover this large a wound.

Scrap snorted even as he poked his head out the cave mouth. *You can't get infections anymore. And it's all clear.*

"Don't suppose I could go back to the Citadel and have Serena fix me up?"

We both have to earn our way back in. You haven't even killed one demon yet. We've got a ways to go, babe.

The story of my life. What I truly wanted was always just beyond my reach. Like answers and saving Cynthia.

"Au revoir," I called to the ghosts as I crawled out of the cave. "Mind the store until I get back."

In that moment I knew I'd be back. With questions. Or maybe just to wait for Cynthia to show up with the dog.

I DIDN'T HAVE THE ENERGY for disguise and subterfuge that evening, so I dined in the steak house next door to the lodge. This place catered to tourists and wealthy retirees in the big houses around the golf course. The chilly evening gave me the excuse to wear a bulky sweater with my jeans to cover the bandages on my upper left arm.

Donovan apparently ate there, too. He straddled the chair opposite me, leaning over the back, without invitation.

"Why are you here, Tess?" he asked without preamble.

"Research. I'm setting a new book in a place like this. Add one monster out of local folklore to that lake and it makes a perfect setting. I like the idea of the water layers never mixing, not in twelve thousand years."

"You've been here long enough to gather all the books on local geology and take pictures of every rock formation." He tapped the book on local Indian legends I'd been reading before he so rudely interrupted me. I hadn't found anything on the dog or the blanket.

Not that I minded staring at his handsome face rather than rereading the same paragraph over and over because I couldn't concentrate.

Stop that! I admonished myself. *He's using that weird mojo again.*

"You could go home in the morning," he said with a sexy smile.

Was that an invitation to spend tonight with him before I went home tomorrow? My bones wanted to melt despite my resolution to never trust him again.

Mentally, I slapped my face to rid my brain and my libido of all those stray thoughts.

"I'm fascinated with that blanket hanging in your office. It's obviously very old. What's the story behind it?" I had to think about something other than the way his mobile mouth curved over his teeth, how that mouth tasted, and molded to mine.

"The blanket is a family heirloom."

"I'd like to buy it from you."

"It's not for sale."

"Then tell me more about it. Where did it come from? How was it woven? Why is the binding unfinished?"

Donovan looked up sharply and frowned at some newcomers at the door.

"Doesn't this town have animal control laws?" a stranger shouted. "I swear that dog was ready to chew through my *closed* car windows."

I turned around and stared. Just an ordinary middle-aged couple going to fat and wearing too much turquoise and silver jewelry with their polyester slacks and matching golf shirts.

Their frowns and scowls showed their disapproval as much as their words.

The hostess murmured something soothing to the couple.

"I've got to go. I hope to see you in Cape Cod next time I'm there. But not around here, Tess. This town can be dangerous. We have our own monsters to deal with, and they don't have anything to do with your fantasy books" Donovan slammed his chair back and dropped a kiss on top of my head. "And I prefer your hair down, like it is now," he murmured and stalked toward the door.

I waved the waitress over. "Serve that couple the drink of their choice on me," I said quietly, nodding toward the strangers who had had a dog encounter of the close kind.

When the drinks arrived, I picked up my own glass of wine and moved my chair to their table. "I'm so sorry you had such a terrible fright from that dog. He's so big and dangerous. I don't see why the authorities don't just shoot him," I said in my most sympathetic manner.

"You seen him, too?" the man asked.

"Just before I came to dinner. Bigger than a wolfhound, uglier than a mastiff, and meaner than a rabid pit bull."

"That's him alrighty. Vern and Myrna Abrams." He stuck his hand in my face for me to shake.

I took it limply. "Teresa Newcomb," I replied, giving him my first nom de plume. "Where did you see the dog?"

"On the road into town, not ten minutes ago."

Already dark out.

"Was there anyone with the dog? You'd think if someone owned him, they'd be chasing after him, trying to catch him."

"Just a little girl. Looked like an Indian, dirty and scruffy. She yelled at the dog, and he seemed to pay attention to her, but he just kept coming right at the car, like he didn't see it. Woulda run right over us if I hadn't hit the brakes."

The waitress arrived with my steak. I told her to put it on my table. I'd learned enough. No sense in disturbing this couple further.

"We're staying at the Mowath Lodge, number seven. Where're you staying, Teresa?" Myrna Abrams asked.

I gulped. They had the suite right next to me. So much for privacy. "Number six," I admitted reluctantly.

"Maybe we'll see you around, take the cure together. I hear the water works wonders on arthritis. Bet you've got a nice case of bursitis going in that shoulder the way you favor it," Myrna gushed.

I smiled and picked up the book I'd brought to read with my dinner.

At least Cynthia was still safe and communicating with the dog.

Interlude

Patience, dahling. You need patience to survive in this world, *I counseled my babe. She sat with her legs folded beneath her, hands resting on her knees, palms up, eyes closed, and a frown upon her face. Half a dozen other trainees sat with her in a circle. Sister Martha marched around them. Her voice droned out the litany of meditation.*

Concentrate. You have to concentrate.

Tess wasn't listening. She was bored. I could tell. She'd been here in the Citadel eleven months now. She'd mastered every physical exercise and blade technique they threw at her. She even threw some new ones into the mix—and got into trouble for it.

But this simple relaxation and thought mastery eluded her.

I couldn't blame her. I tended to snooze through these sessions, too.

Today Sister Gert observed. That did not bode well for us.

"SISTER TERESA, WHAT do you think you are doing?" Sister Gert demanded.

I cracked open one eye to make sure she meant me and not one of the other newcomers. The way she scowled I was pretty sure she meant me. She'd used my real name, the one I only allowed my mother to call me.

Sister Gert was *not* my mother.

"I'm trying to concentrate." That was what Scrap had advised me to do, wasn't it?

"You cannot meditate with your shoulders hunched and your face screwed up like a dried prune. Now what were you thinking about? Not the exercise, certainly." Sister Gert stalked over to my position in the circle.

"Actually, I was thinking up a new plot for a book. But the character of the villain has me puzzled. Would you like to model for her?"

Not the most diplomatic thing to say. Obviously.

Sister Gert grabbed me by the collar of my cotton shirt and hauled me to my feet and out into the slightly warmer corridor. At least part of the Citadel had south-facing windows that absorbed some of the winter sunlight and heat.

Thank the Goddess. My butt was numb from the cold stone floor in this cold stone room without windows. My back ached from sitting straight for so long without support. My mind was threatening to desert me from sheer boredom.

"Insolence cannot be tolerated here!" Sister Gert clenched her fist as if she wanted to slug me.

I almost welcomed it. She wanted to hit me. I wanted to hit back. And then I wanted to leave.

"We are a tightly honed fighting unit. You must learn to obey without question in order to survive the next attack."

"An attack from what? I've been here almost a year and there has only been one fight. I wasn't allowed to watch or participate. I've never seen a demon and I've yet to see the supposed portal." My fists clenched, too.

"You do not believe?" Sister Gert looked at me incredulously.

"No. I do not believe in your demons, or your Goddess, or anything you've taught me." Except for Scrap. He was the only part of this entire experience that seemed real.

A translucent imp from another dimension was the only thing real here.

Maybe I had gone mad in my grief over Dill.

"Come with me." Sister Gert marched down the corridor toward the central tower building. I'd been in the ground floor of that building once or twice. Just an armory. Nothing more. I had my own personal replica blade and Scrap. I didn't need anything more from there.

Sister Gert yanked open the heavy wooden door with iron hinges, locks, and crossbar. The thing weighed more than the two of us combined, yet she moved it with ease.

My estimation of her strength and abilities went up, even though I'd rarely seen her on the practice field.

The armory smelled of dust and cold. Afternoon sunlight streamed in through high windows on all four walls. Bright blades in numerous shapes and sizes from ornate daggers to broadswords to scimitars to pikes gleamed. Well-oiled, sharp and deadly.

"A case of AK47s would kill a lot more demons a lot faster than blades," I said, admiring the weapons anyway.

"Wouldn't do a thing against a demon," Sister Gert snorted. "Specially forged blades are the only thing that will penetrate their hides."

"Specially forged?"

"With magic."

Can't you feel it, babe?

Scrap stared at the weapons array with longing.

"Feel what, Scrap?"

"The magic. The aura. The specialness," Sister Gert answered for him. She stared at a broadsword with awe.

They looked like any other sword I'd seen at cons and SCA events. Only sharper.

Sister Gert ended her rapt study by whisking a tacky piece of dirty carpet off the floor near the center of the room. Then she beckoned me to help her lift a stone trapdoor. It came up with surprising ease to reveal a flight of narrow stone steps heading into darkness.

"From here we must have absolute quiet. Your life depends upon this." She fixed me with a stern glare.

Scrap turned bright red and gibbered something unintelligible. I guessed it was some kind of prayer, or curse, in his own imp language.

I nodded my agreement. Then I followed her down the stairs, stepping lightly, breathing shallowly of the hot moist air that rose up from the depths of the basement.

At the base of the stairs, when the diffuse light from the upper room dwindled to almost nothing, Sister Gert produced a very modern and powerful flashlight. The beam shot forth from the lens to reveal a large room, big enough for forty or fifty Sisters to swing their blades all at the same time.

I couldn't figure out what heated and humidified the room. We were in the high desert, barely fifteen inches of rain fell a year. This was the middle of

December when outside temperatures rarely ventured above forty. This room should be cold and dry. Very cold and very dry.

Sister Gert shook her head and frowned a warning as I opened my mouth to ask my questions.

Scrap prodded my mind to remind me to obey.

Then the flashlight picked out iron-and-brass fittings on a round door in the wall. At least twelve feet in diameter. It looked to be one solid piece of metal. Nothing decorative about it, just a solid barrier between here and there.

As we stood there, the door began to vibrate and glow red with a new blast of wet heat.

Scrap turned scarlet.

Sister Gert grabbed my arm and we both hastened upstairs.

The cold air in the armory was a welcome relief. Briefly. Then the goose bumps on my arms rose and I shuddered with more than cold.

When the trapdoor was back in place and the carpet hiding it once more, she heaved a sigh. "That is the portal. Just going into that room was dangerous. The demons smelled us. They wanted to break through and taste our blood."

I sensed her genuine fear.

Believe her, babe, that is one mean place to be.

"What keeps them from breaking through?" I finally asked. I didn't like the way my voice shook. Something was down there. But I still didn't know precisely what.

"We do not know. For many, many generations the Sisterhood has been charged with the duty to guard that portal. All we know is that upon occasion, demons breach it. When they do, we must fight them back to their own dimension and close the portal once more." Sister Gert led me out of the armory, back into the sun-lit corridor.

"Well, shouldn't we find out what seals it and what breaks it so that we can do a better job of keeping it closed?"

"Ours is not the place to question, only to fight."

"Well, that's stupid."

"There are others who keep this information. They will tell us if we need to know more."

"How long has it been since you've heard from these 'others'?" I couldn't stand still any longer. This woman had blinders on and refused to look beyond them.

"Questing into other realms is more dangerous than allowing demons to breach the portal and come into this world."

"How do you know that if you've never done it?"

She looked at me in bewilderment, not understanding what I asked or why. "We leave that to those who know better than we."

"But how do you know that these 'others' still exist? How do you know they have the best information and pass it along? How do you know . . ."

"It is very clear to me, Teresa, that you do not belong here. I hate to waste one who is chosen by the Goddess, but you must leave here. You will never be worthy of the title 'Sister.'" She marched off. I don't think she had any other gait than marching.

"Who said I wanted to be a 'Sister' in the first place?"

Time to keep your mouth shut, Tess. We're in big trouble here.

"What can they do, throw me out?"

Yes.

"That is bad how?"

We will be utterly alone.

"Sounds good to me. I could use a little privacy now and then."

Chapter 25

Shouts and gunfire awakened me just as the first rays of sunlight poked above the hills to the east of Half Moon Lake. Friday morning, my second full day in this dusty little town.

I dashed out of bed and peered out the front windows, heedless of my lack of sleeping attire. A quick glance through a slit between the drapes showed Donovan and Quentin barring their door to Dog and a decidedly grubby and disheveled Cynthia.

Quentin had a big handgun. A very big handgun.

Dog had a slight graze on his left flank, like a bullet had bounced off his hide. Bullets wouldn't touch a real monster from another realm. Sister Gert had been most adamant on that point.

I couldn't dress fast enough. Clad in jeans and a sweater, without underwear or shoes, I ran across the courtyard to Donovan's office suite.

"Don't hurt him, Sapa!" Cynthia yelled as she grabbed the dog by the scruff of the neck.

"Outta the way, girl. I'm gonna shoot the fucking dog!" Quentin yelled back.

"Forget the dog, protect the blanket, you fool!" Donovan joined the fray. He looked as if he'd slept in his clothes. His rumpled hair and heavy eyes only made him look more attractive and vulnerable.

I couldn't let my heart stutter in utter awe of the man's beauty. I had to get the girl away from the dog.

Dog, Sapa she'd called him, looked into Cynthia's eyes with utter devotion and backed off two steps. The killer I loathed with every atom in my being looked just like any other oversized puppy in need of an ear scratch.

I came to a stumbling halt, suddenly aware of the gravel cutting my feet. "Everybody shut up and hold still," I commanded as sternly as I knew how. I put on my schoolteacher face—I had teaching credentials in history and lit, and had substituted in numerous inner city high schools in New England before I met Dill. It paid the bills while I tried to build a writing career.

Strangely, the crowd obeyed me. Even Sapa turned his attention toward me for two heartbeats. Then he looked to Cynthia once more for confirmation that he should obey me.

Good move, Tess. Stop and think before you get everyone into more trouble.

Scrap chomped on one of his favorite black cherry cheroots. He looked mildly pink. There was evil afoot but nothing imminently dangerous. Still, he stayed back by the doorway of my suite. The barrier that existed between Donovan and him was back in place.

"Can you talk some sense into these men, Tess?" Cynthia asked. A little-girl plaintiveness returned to her voice and posture. She didn't want to be in charge, even though Sapa thought she should be. Someone needed to be in charge of that dog.

"Donovan, I suggest you allow the dog into your office. He won't hurt the blanket."

"Are you crazy, Tess? He'll steal the blanket again. It's unique, worth three fortunes. And it belongs to my family." He stood firm, arms crossed, chest heaving in agitation.

"I know how unique it is." I took my eyes off the dog and shifted my gaze toward Donovan. A glare of pure hatred crossed his face. Before I could blink, the malevolent expression vanished, replaced by his completely charming smile.

But I had seen something in his eyes that broke his spell over me. At least temporarily.

"As long as Cynthia is nearby, Sapa will merely guard the blanket for her."

"What's she mean, boss?" Quentin asked. He kept his handgun leveled on the dog. I didn't know the caliber, only that it was an automatic and the muzzle looked very large and powerful.

"Never mind. Let the dog and the girl inside, but keep your aim on the dog at all times. If he so much as drools on that blanket, shoot him." Donovan turned back into his suite.

I counted his stomping steps. Fifteen of them. Then I heard an interior door slam.

"Go with Sapa, Cynthia," I said quietly. "I'll be right behind you. As soon as we get the dog settled, I'll take you to my room. You can bathe and have breakfast."

"I . . . I don't know if he'll . . ."

"Sapa knows you need food and rest. He'll let you come with me. Won't you, Sapa?" I forced myself to scratch the dog between the ears. His shoulder was as high as my hip. But he reacted just like any other dog, sighing and leaning his weight against me as he luxuriated in the caress.

Remember, he isn't totally responsible for Bob's death, Scrap reminded me. *If the demon children didn't have knives aimed at Cynthia, Dog would not have attacked. Bob got in the way of both.*

"It's not over between you and me, Dog, but for now I'll let you live. For Cynthia's sake."

In moments the dog had curled up below the blanket and rested his massive head upon his paws. He looked up when I led Cynthia out the door. Then he settled down again.

"Quite a show, Ms. Newcomb," Vern Abrams said from his half of the deck that spread in front of our suites. "Thought you believed the dog to be dangerous." He looked at me with suspicion and not a trace of the previous evening's camaraderie.

"Most dogs are only dangerous when they or their pet humans are attacked," I replied. I dragged Cynthia inside and slammed my door, putting an end to the next question I could see forming on Vern's lips.

I'd figure out who he was and what he wanted from me later.

Scrap's words set me to shaking. What if Dog *was* one of the good guys?

Right now, Cynthia needed a bath, new clothes, and food. I was the only one who could give them to her.

"Interesting development, the dog and the blanket together with a new weaver," Guilford van der Hoyden-Smythe said. He'd parked his long, skinny body on the sofa in my suite and propped his big feet up on the log-and-tree-burl coffee table. The television blared the twenty-four-hour news station. He fingered my antique comb, shifting his attention between it and the TV.

Damn. I knew I should have locked the door behind me.

Chapter 26

When I'd settled Cynthia in the tub and ordered breakfast for three from the steak house, I planted myself between Gollum and the TV that fascinated him.

"Why are you here?" I asked when he finally realized that I blocked the screen from his view.

I smell cat. Do you smell a cat? Achoooooo!

That was the least of my worries.

"I think you'd better watch this next news segment," he replied.

Frowning, I turned to watch an all-too-familiar scene. SWAT teams camped outside a chain-link fence and a scattering of low featureless buildings. Police tape, crowds of media trucks, and cameras littered the rest of the high desert landscape. The anchorman's voice over the live pictures droned on about the militants inside the abandoned military facility—unnamed, of course.

I'm sure I smell a cat. Scrap turned a nauseating shade of puce and sneezed again.

"Software mogul Donovan Estevez, as spokesman for the C'Aquilianish Tribal Council, released this statement yesterday evening."

Donovan replaced the unnamed military facility in an unnamed location on the screen. A time and date stamp of yesterday, late afternoon, *after* his minion shot at me, showed in the lower left hand corner of the screen. He stood before a bouquet of microphones, wearing a pristine white shirt and tie. His long black braid, decorated with those eye-catching silver wings at his temples looked just as respectable as the rest of him—an image I'm certain the tribe chose deliberately.

I'd never heard of that particular tribe, though.

"More than one hundred forty years of abuse of treaty rights by the U.S. government must end," Donovan said most pleasantly, as if discussing business over tea. "We of the Confederated Tribes of the C'Aquilianish Nations," he went on to name several other tribes I did not recognize. None of them resembled the Colville tribe he claimed as part of his ancestry. Each name had more of the unpronounceable clicks, pops, and hisses I'd heard Donovan use in his curses the day before.

"We do hereby declare war on the United States Government," Donovan continued. "We currently occupy this military base and have taken possession of all the weapons stored here. We have set up further defenses with armament purchased out of tribal funds."

His speech went on and on.

I stared at the TV in disbelief, mouth agape.

"They can't possibly win. What can they hope to gain? They're insane," I said over and over again.

"Or they are desperate," Gollum replied quietly.

"Or they are being manipulated."

"'Those aren't any tribes I've ever heard of," Cynthia said from the doorway to the bedroom of the suite. She wore one of my jogging suits with the cuffs and sleeves rolled up.

"Me either," Gollum said, his accent more clipped than usual. He leaned forward, peering at the TV screen intently. "And I've done a lot of research into tribal legends and mythology this last month."

Breakfast arrived. Gollum paid for it out of a thick wad of bills.

I raised my eyebrows at the sight of the cash.

"Family trust fund, just kicked in," he said as he started to make coffee.

I'm going to find that cat. I hate cats. Another sneeze. *How can I scent out evil with a cat clogging my nose?*

We all tucked into the meal provided by the steak house. Steak and eggs and pancakes for Cynthia, bacon and eggs and waffles, traditional, not Belgians (air-filled) for me, more sausage and eggs and French toast for Gollum. Cynthia wolfed down most of her food, including two glasses of milk and sixteen ounces of orange juice. But she barely touched her steak.

"Um, Tess, would you um, mind . . ."

"Go ahead and give it to Sapa. That's why I ordered such a big one. I figured you'd want to share."

"Thanks." She wrapped the meat in a napkin and bounded out the door, barefoot and happy.

"That's an incredible bond between her and the dog, considering he kidnapped her and killed two of her friends back in Alder Hill," Gollum mused.

"They adore each other. Sapa is the family that was stolen from her when her parents died." How did I know that? "I don't think she really fit in, even after Leonard Stalking Moon adopted her. She needs that dog as much as he needs her." And I needed to call Leonard.

"But she can't stay here. She needs adults to look after her, school, clothes, friends, all the normal things adolescents have," Gollum insisted.

"In her culture she is a woman. I don't know how this is going to turn out, and as much as I hate leaving that dog alive, right now we have to keep Cynthia and Sapa together. We also have to call Leonard and let him know she is safe."

"Are you forgetting that Sapa is a killer?" Gollum and I stared at each other. The vivid memory of two dead boys at the skate park and another maimed rose up in ghastly detail in my mind's eye. The perfect recall given me by the fever was as much a curse as a blessing.

Then I remembered Bob. My dear friend. I choked and nearly gagged on my tears. I could almost smell Bob's blood on my hands, on my clothes, in my hair, everywhere but in his body where it belonged.

The weight of his head in my lap was all too real.

Remember Donovan's demon children and their knives. Were they trying to protect Cynthia or kill her?

"Why would they want to kill her?"

She is The Weaver.

I had to relate the snippet of conversation to Gollum.

"Sapa has killed, but only to achieve the mandate given him centuries ago. He had to find a young woman of tribal blood to weave and maintain the blanket—for the good of all humanity." As much as it felt like betrayal of Bob's memory, I had to acknowledge that Sapa would never hurt Cynthia, his chosen weaver.

Gollum sighed and nodded. "I can stay a few weeks and look after her." He pulled out his phone and started tapping in notes.

"Scrap, what's my schedule?" I called into the thin air. I hadn't seen the imp since he'd gone cat hunting. He probably got distracted by hunger and was in the lake feasting on micro bugs.

Clear for most of a week. Then you have to go to World Fantasy Con in Madison, Wisconsin.

"Crap. I forgot about that." Both my agent and editor planned to attend the mostly professional con. I was up for an award. I really needed to go.

Gollum's got a cat. He can't stay if he has a cat. I won't let him.

I relayed my schedule to Gollum, remembering that he couldn't hear or see Scrap. I didn't care about the cat. "Let's just hope we can wrap this up in a week."

"Where'd you get this?" Gollum held up the comb.

I snatched it from his hand. "It's an antique I picked up somewhere." I twisted up my hair and jammed the comb in. It seemed to fit better every day. But I also noticed more and more transparent and brittle hairs came out with it each time I removed it. My scalp hurt, too, as if a cat had run its claws over the surface.

I couldn't wear it as often as I liked, or I'd lose all my hair.

"It has a glamour of magic about it. Only a few antique stores in this country would be able to handle something like that. Do you remember where in your travels you found it?" Gollum moved around behind me to study the thing.

"Magic," I snorted.

Listen to him, babe. And find out why he has a cat in his room. Scrap sounded decidedly stuffy.

"Magic," Gollum said firmly. "I wonder what sort of magic."

So do I.

Cynthia came bounding back in, still happy. "Sapa thanks you for the steak. He was really hungry." She plunked back down at the table and tucked into her remaining pancakes. "Oh, and Sapa reminded me that the mean man thinks he has a claim on the blanket, but he doesn't really."

"What?" Gollum and I said together as we stared at her.

"Long ago, in the time of our oldest grandfathers, when Coyote still walked the earth, the gods gave the blanket to all of the tribes so that they would learn honor and dignity and compromise." Cynthia fell into a kind of chant.

I thought she might be channeling this legend much as Gollum had channeled the original, but her eyes remained bright and her face animated.

"The blanket didn't always work, humans being what they are, so when the Columbia River changed course, and chaos ruled, the demons from beneath the lakes and rivers stole the blanket. Humans took a long time recovering from the awesome floods, but when they did, they missed the blanket and the honor and dignity and compromise it helped us hold onto. So, three warriors from each of three different tribes went down below the lakes. The nine warriors had many adventures and six of them died. But the remaining three, one from each tribe, captured the blanket from the demons and returned it to humanity. This time it was entrusted to the best weaver in all of the tribes and she and the blanket were hidden where no man could find them with the dog Shunka Sapa to guard her and the blanket." She finished and drew a deep breath.

"I think that's everything Sapa said to tell you."

"How does Sapa communicate with you, Cynthia?" Gollum asked the question that burned in both of us.

"In my dreams. We travel in my dreams, too. I don't remember walking a step, but each night when I'd fall asleep curled around Sapa, I'd dream deep and long, then in the morning I woke up miles and miles and miles from where we were. And I didn't get hungry either."

"Cross-dimensional travel. I've read about it in a number of legends. Rip Van Winkle comes to mind." Gollum looked as if he'd embark on a lecture longer than Cynthia's story.

Time is just another dimension. Cynthia may have matured ten years or more in five days, Scrap whispered in my ear. He didn't appear.

Obviously, he was still hunting the cat. Why, I didn't know.

Trust your dreams, Sister Serena had said to me yesterday. *My* dreams, not Cynthia's.

I think that's what she said anyway.

"Why didn't we know about this part of the blanket legend, Cynthia? We only had the part after humanity got the blanket back." I diverted the conversation.

"Coyote made people forget the early part, so we wouldn't get into trouble with the demons." She finished her meal and went looking in the mini fridge for more juice. "I've got to get back to Sapa and study that blanket." Cynthia dashed out again before I could object.

"I don't like the implication that Donovan comes from a family of demons," I muttered into my coffee. But that would explain a lot. Especially his potent male mojo that melted my knees and sent my logic flying in the wind.

"What makes you say that?" Gollum asked. He got up to make a new pot of coffee. The in-house machine only brewed about two cups at a time.

"He claims the blanket is an old family heirloom and he's deathly afraid the dog will steal it. Again."

Chapter 27

"Okay, if Donovan is a demon, why don't I just kill him? That's what I'm trained to do." And that would take away the annoying temptation to jump his bones and screw his brains out.

I might also get rid of some of my own self-disgust for succumbing to him.

"No!" Gollum leaped up in protest. The table rattled. His plate rocked. The remnants of his coffee sloshed over the rim of his cup.

"Why not? He's a demon." I shouldn't have any remorse about killing a demon. I had to forget that Donovan looked and acted like a man; that he kissed me like a man in love.

Find out about the cat. I hate cats. Cats are evil.

Scrap tugged at my hair, but I ignored him. Cats weren't important.

Waddya mean they aren't important. They are as evil as demons!

"We don't know for sure that Donovan is a demon, more likely a half blood, possibly only a liaison. True demons can't shape-change into human form in this dimension," Gollum said, studying the muted television. I noticed, he'd turned on the closed captions.

"Then how do demons breed with humans?" I asked.

"They kidnap them and take them back to their own dimension where they appear very human and very charming," Gollum replied.

"And you know that how?"

"Old family tradition. We study demons." A long pause while he bit his lip and thought long and hard. "We also study those who can kill them."

Meaning me and my Sisterhood. Brotherhood, too, I supposed. The Citadel ruled by Sister Gert wasn't the only one in the world.

231

"If Scrap can transform into the Celestial Blade in Donovan's presence, then he's a demon. That would explain why he couldn't become anything more lethal than a fireplace poker when I first encountered Sapa. Sapa isn't a demon. But Scrap did transform fully when the dog kidnapped Cynthia." I had to avoid mentioning that Sapa had killed Bob during that encounter. I wouldn't be able to continue thinking, let alone talking if I dwelled on my best friend's death. "Donovan and his three demon children were right there."

"Whatever Donovan Estevez is by blood, he is a legal citizen of the U.S. He owns a business. A *BIG* business. People will ask questions if he dies. His death will be investigated. You, my dear, will be arrested and tried for murder."

"I am not *your* dear. But you have a point. So what do we do?" I paced restlessly, needing to feel the Celestial Blade or a fencing foil in my hands, needing to lash out at something. "I'm going for a run. You do what you do, like finding out how and why Donovan is involved in the casino, and the Indian movement to declare war on the U.S. Then call Leonard." I might as well make use of Gollum while he insisted on annoying me with his presence. "Oh, and while you are at it, figure out how you are going to explain to me why I've let you back into my life. I still don't want or need a partner."

I ripped out the comb, not wanting to lose any more hair than I had to. Let him study the magic in it.

When I came back an hour later, winded and glowing with sweat, Gollum had set up his own laptop—much more expensive and powerful than mine—on the coffee table and was studying an Internet page filled with arcane symbols. He was so intent upon his study that he didn't acknowledge me when I came in. Nor did he turn his head as I stripped off my sweats and wandered into the bathroom wearing only my bra and panties.

A true geek if I ever saw one.

"Guilford, this is *my* room. How about some privacy?" I poked my head out of the bedroom door and glared at him.

"I can go back to my room, directly below you, if you insist." He stretched and yawned, never taking his eyes off his computer screen. The TV continued to broadcast the world news on the tall stand above him. At least he'd muted the blasted thing.

"Oh, my Goddess!" I stared at the TV. Without regard to my dishabille, I moved to stand directly in front of it.

"What?" Gollum stood up beside me. The TV was about eye level to his tall frame. I had to crane my neck a little.

"That shot of the abandoned military facility Donovan's 'Indians' took over." I pointed at the latest account of the story.

"What about it?"

"In the background, caught in the sidelight of the setting sun."

"A lot of desert."

"And a casino under construction. The military base is right next door to Donovan's casino. Just outside the city of Half Moon Lake. I've got to check this out." I hastened toward the door.

Gollum grabbed me by the shoulders. "After you shower and you get dressed, we'll both go up to the casino and check it out." He pushed me back toward the bedroom.

I followed orders, my mind spinning with thoughts and possibilities.

"By the way, I like that you color coordinate your underwear," Gollum called after me.

I half laughed. I'd clung to the tradition of the Sisterhood. Bloodred bra and panties to remind me of the demon blood I was commissioned to spill.

"But I don't like that wound on your upper arm." Gollum stopped me just before I stepped into the bathroom. He peered at the raw flesh that oozed a little blood, left over from the bullet ricochet. "How did this happen?"

"It doesn't hurt anymore, and it will heal by tomorrow," I replied defensively. "Nothing to concern you."

"But it does concern me."

"It's none of your business until you tell me why you are still here getting in my way. You find a way to tell me when I get out of the shower, or you are out of here, along with the cat that Scrap hates." Anger heated my face and pulsed through my entire being. The wound throbbed anew.

I slammed the door in his face.

"I'M WAITING FOR AN explanation," I said, freshly showered and dressed in jeans, sweater, and boots. Cloud cover had moved in and turned the high desert into a cold place hunkering down toward winter.

Ask him about the cat.

"This isn't easy for me, Tess."

"Fine. Then grab your computer and the other detritus of your sojourn in my room and get out of here." I grabbed my purse and fished out the keys to my rental car. The big honking white SUV. I hated driving the gas hog, but it was all the rental agency had left.

Don't be so harsh on him, Scrap admonished me as he blew a particularly odiferous smoke ring into my face. Then he farted.

I had to lean away and fan the air in front of my face.

I like him, Scrap explained. *Except that he has a cat. If he stays, the cat has to go.* He fluttered near Gollum's shoulder but didn't alight. Maybe he couldn't sit on anyone's shoulder but mine.

"Okay, best I blurt it out before I lose my courage." Gollum fidgeted, shifting from foot to foot. "Secrecy is a hard habit to break."

Meanwhile, the news coverage showed a flurry of shots exchanged between Donovan's "Indians" and the SWAT team. Three military helicopters and a squad of Marines had been added to the chaos.

"Then blurt and stop hedging. I need to get out to the casino and see what is really going on." I juggled the car keys between my two hands.

"My family has monitored the Orders of the Celestial Blade for over four hundred years. We do the research for them."

"But you never fight the demons yourselves?" Why hadn't anyone told me about this?

"Upon occasion. My dad lost an arm to a demon. He claimed he lost it in Viet Nam when I was two. Mom never quite forgave him for that. He didn't even admit it to me until last week."

I raised both eyebrows at that.

"My grandfather told me about the family trust—the trust to seek out and aid your Sisterhood any way we can. Mom insisted they were all just tall tales born of Gramps' over-fertile imagination. But I knew he told the truth."

I stared at him for several long moments, not certain I wanted to believe so simple explanation.

"Have you ever fought a demon?"

I bet he lets his cat do it for him. Cats are mean.

"No."

"Have you ever seen one?"

"Just the kids at the con. By the way, they are half-blood Kajiri demons, according to my research."

I shuddered at that. Paige, Mary, and Electra, the arms mistresses at the Citadel, particularly feared Kajiri demons.

"Why didn't you just come out and tell me this when we first met?"

"I had to be sure you are what you are."

"You seemed more certain of it than I did."

I looked at my keys, wondering what to do next. What to ask next. "Are you officially attached to any of the Orders of the Celestial Blade?"

"No."

"So why are you here?"

"We . . . my grandfather and I had been led to believe that all of the initiates had died out. There haven't been any authenticated demon sightings in over thirty-five years, not since the battle that took Dad's arm."

"Of course not. They all hang out at SF cons and win prizes for their costumes that aren't really costumes at all."

Donovan had won a hall prize for his bat costume. Meaning he wore the costume but did not compete in the masquerade. Was it truly a costume?

We both sighed at our ignorance at High Desert Con. We could have taken out three demon children if we'd only known.

"So why did you seek me out? Why didn't you just take a teaching position at some obscure college and forget about the Sisterhood of the Celestial Blade."

"I read your book."

"Crap."

"The family trust fund supports us when we are assisting members of your order. Gramps reopened it as soon as I told him about you. It hasn't been touched in decades. I can access the money for all our expenses until this matter is settled."

"Thanks, but I can pay my own expenses."

"I've already paid the hotel for our two rooms for two weeks in advance. This place is cheap."

I brushed past him.

"You need me, Tess. Not many members of your Sisterhood venture outside the Citadel once they are initiated. You are alone in this fight. You can't contact them for help. You can't go back there until you have done their dirty work for them."

No phones, no computers, no running water, or electricity in the Citadel. I had only an occasional and spotty mind contact with Sister Serena. And no true control over that.

"The Sisterhood is fully occupied in guarding the portal. They don't have time to help me."

We are challenged often. Beseiged. Many wounded and dead, Sister S had said.

Or had I imagined it.

No, the contact had been real. And clear. Demons on the move meant trouble everywhere.

"In the year you spent in the Citadel, did you even once engage in battle at the portal? Did you even hear about a battle while you were there?"

"One. But I wasn't allowed to participate. And they showed me the portal."

"But you never saw a demon or fought one. They've abandoned you, Tess. You sink or swim on your own."

A fitting metaphor since we bordered on a lake.

Was it the same lake I plunged into during my hallucination/dream/ memory.

I glanced out the window to the room's balcony and the view of the lake beyond. I saw only a reflection of the cliffs towering above the water on the western curve of water.

"This lake that might be its own portal to a land of demons. I think I crossed into one when I first contracted the fever.

"You can scout with me *today* if you want. But I'm driving."

Chapter 28

We found an unpaved road that wound up the hill on the west side of Half Moon Lake to the ridge where the partially built casino sat like a squashed spider. All of the regular roads were blocked off by state police and the military. Heavy trucks carrying construction materials had churned this rutted dirt trail into a mess. I had to engage the four-wheel drive to get up the steep road. For the first time ever I was glad to have the SUV.

"I brought your comb. I think you should wear it," Gollum said, peering through the dusty windshield.

"Why don't you wear it?" I had trouble concentrating on getting through the next pothole that looked big enough to swallow a tank. Thankfully, the SUV was bigger.

"Because it is *your* comb. However you came by it, it was meant for you. The rightful owner is probably the only one who can access the magic."

He's right.

"Okay, okay. But not right now. I need both hands to get us up this hill."

The main casino building in the center rose two full stories with framing for another two atop it. Satellite buildings sprawled around it with only the skeleton of connections among them. Construction trailers, heavy machinery, stacks of wood, and other building supplies lay scattered about as if a tornado had hit the area. I couldn't see any sign of activity or people anywhere near the place.

I stepped out of the car. Even the ever present wind had stilled, as if waiting in ambush for the unwary. I could have written this scene. And I didn't like what I did to my characters when I did.

I don't like this, Tess.

No sarcasm, no cigar, no "babe." Scrap was worried.

"Let's do this when there are people around to ask questions of," Gollum said quietly. He stood with the door open, ready to duck back into the car at the first portent of trouble.

I'm made of sterner stuff. Or maybe I'm just stupid.

I stepped away from the car and walked around the first pile of construction debris. It smoked. The crew had burned the scraps as they went. I hadn't been around construction projects much, but that seemed wasteful. At least in textile projects you never knew when a small leftover piece would correct a mistake or fill an unexpected gap or highlight a finishing touch.

I kicked at the smoldering mess. It wasn't all wood pieces. Something metallic caught my eye, and something else . . .

"Tess?" Gollum called.

I whirled to face him.

"Can we go now?"

"No. Something is wrong. It's the middle of the day, not yet lunchtime. It's not raining. Where is everyone?"

"Maybe they are with the 'Indians' taking over the abandoned army fort."

I could see the ten-foot-high chain-link fence topped with rolls of razor wire a mile or more behind the casino. The horizon was a long way away up on this plateau, distorting my sense of distance.

I looked across to the back side of the abandoned—and now reoccupied—buildings. Even they seemed stagnant, waiting for someone to move, or fire the next shot.

"Do you have any binoculars in the car?" Gollum asked very quietly.

"Emergency travel bag behind the driver's seat," I replied in a whisper. I didn't need the binoculars. Scrap fluttered before my eyes, beet red, ready to transform.

We'd all spotted movement along the back of the buildings. Hunched-over forms that moved with a stiff gait and heavy fisted hands that brushed their knees. Thick fur, both dark and light, covered their bodies.

Sasquatch.

Demons.

Teenagers, Scrap snorted. *Unstable and unpredictable. Violent.*

I remembered a few high school misfits whom I'd reported to social services, during my teaching days for the same reason.

My skin prickled, and tension built along my spine. The otherworldly figures opened a door by scratching at a keypad near a seemingly blank space of wall. They slipped through the opening, then closed the door. It blended into the gunmetal gray walls so well, I doubted I could find it if I stood directly in front of it.

Scrap faded a little. But he still retained a battle-ready attitude and redness.

The air thickened. Then I heard the distinctive *whopp, whopp* of a helicopter flying low and close. The stealth-black vehicle was above me before I saw it.

The wind from its blades tried to push me flat against the ground.

Scrap winked out.

I held my ground.

"You have entered a restricted area. Get into your car and leave immediately," a voice boomed from speakers mounted on the skids of the helicopter.

I stared at the black whirling machine above me, slightly stunned by the wash of noise and that we had seen no signs restricting the area outside the fence.

"Come on, Tess, we've got to get out of here." Gollum beckoned me.

Of course, the military and the SWAT teams would have cleared the area if they expected a firefight to remove Donovan's "Indians."

I took one step toward the car.

The demons emerged from the hidden door once more.

I pointed furiously at the activity, willing the officials in the helicopter to look in that direction.

A hideous buzzing noise erupted from a bulb on the front of the helicopter along with a sizzling blue light.

Incredible lancing fire assailed every muscle in my body. I collapsed in a writhing blob of pain.

Disaster! I can't find my babe's mind.

Medic!

Oh, my, what do I do?

She's gone. I can see her body. But her mind is gone. Worse than before she had the imp flu. She can't reach me. I can't reach her.

It's as if she no longer exists. Has she died?

Without her I will die.

Without me she will die.

I feel myself fading.

Is this the end?

Chapter 29

"Lieutenant, this reaction isn't normal," a disembodied voice said into the chaos that had become my mind.

"Keep her restrained, corporal. Medics are on their way," a deeper voice growled.

I tried to ask what had happened. My mind and voice seemed to belong to separate entities. Every muscle in my body seemed disconnected from the rest of me.

If this was a dream, I didn't want to trust it.

"She's still twitching and unresponsive, lieutenant," the first voice said. "That's not normal. Instructions on that weapon say that victims should return to normal within thirty seconds of the blast."

"This is a prototype, not the standard police issue taser," the second voice, the lieutenant's, said.

Okay. That sizzling blue light and hideous buzzing was a taser. Some kind of super-duper taser designed for military use. I made that much sense of the conversation.

Coherence began to return to my thoughts. But my muscles still twitched and ached and refused to listen to the rest of me.

Muffled grunts and thumping came from my left. I tried to turn my head but failed to make the connection.

"Lieutenant, the other vic is trying to say something. He might have information as to why the lady had such an abnormal reaction to the taser."

"Keep him restrained and gagged. These two are obviously terrorists connected to the hostiles inside Fort Snoqualmie." The lieutenant brooked no interference with his orders.

The other "vic" must be Gollum. I wasn't alone. But where was Scrap? I could really use his ears and eyes right now.

A door opened and then closed. I managed to focus my eyes long enough to see a rectangle of brighter white around the door for just a few seconds. Then there was a shifting of bodies, a rustle of clothing, and boots scraping on a vinyl floor.

That told me I'd been moved from the casino site. Indoors somewhere. That would account for the lack of background noise, especially the roar of helicopters.

Hands upon my wrist. The cold metal mouth of a stethoscope on my chest beneath my sweater.

"Vitals are normal," a new voice said. Probably the medic the lieutenant and corporal expected. "Must have been some strange and individual neurological reaction to the taser frequency. She'll come around eventually. I'll shoot her full of tranquilizers before she hurts herself with those convulsions."

No drugs! Scrap screeched in my ear.

"No," I managed to squeak. "No drugs." I had strange reactions to drugs since the fever that marked me as a Warrior of the Celestial Blade. Maybe the fever had changed other things in my brain as well.

Tranquilizers will kill us, babe.

I couldn't see Scrap. I should. Why couldn't I see Scrap?

Because you're only half alive and so am I.

"Sorry, miss. This will make you feel better, and keep you from hurting yourself."

I concentrated very hard on getting out the next few crucial words. "Drugs make worse. I'm weird," I choked.

"Huh?"

"The lady said no drugs. Now put that syringe away," Gollum said in his most clipped accent, as if speaking to a child.

How did he get loose from the gag?

"Really, sir," the medic protested.

Then I heard the sounds of someone choking, a scuffle, shouts. A thump. A body fell hard across my middle.

I forced my eyes open. Gollum lay across me, glasses askew, silver-gilt hair tangled, muscles limp.

Suddenly my body stopped twitching and my mind connected everything up.

I rolled out from under Gollum and came up to my knees, elbows out, ready to jab someone in the throat. Handcuffs hindered my movements but didn't stop me.

The medic and the lieutenant lay collapsed upon the carpeted floor. The corporal—I presumed the youngest of the trio with two stripes on his camouflage jacket was the corporal—cowered against the metal wall of the small room. He held his pistol—a long and wicked-looking instrument—by the barrel. He must have used the butt to hit Gollum over the head.

An ugly lump bled a little on the back of my friend's head. Gollum's face looked a little raw, like someone had rubbed it with sandpaper—or ripped off a wad of duct tape.

Corporal Bolo, at least I thought that was the name embroidered on the pocket of his fatigues, gulped and tried to disappear into the wall.

He was mortal and mundane and couldn't get any farther away from me.

"Don't let him hurt me, lady," he pleaded.

What had Gollum done to put the fear of God into this boy? This military corporal who still had a gun!

"Get these handcuffs off me, and we'll leave you mostly intact," I replied, trying to sound a lot fiercer than I was. He had the gun after all, even though he still held it by the barrel.

Nice try, babe, but I wouldn't be afraid of you, Scrap sneered from the region of my left shoulder. He was back.

I'd never been so grateful for his smelly, rude, nosy presence in my life.

Glad to have you back, babe. Wondered if we'd survive this.

"Who . . . who's smoking?" the corporal asked. "This is a nonsmoking area. We've got a lot of sensitive equipment and . . . and firepower stored here." He stared at his own gun and fumbled it around until he finally pointed the business end roughly in my direction.

I rolled my eyes at Scrap.

Toss the cigar, imp. You're more trouble than you're worth. Where have you been?

No answer, but the cigar smoke disappeared.

"Just get these handcuffs off me. Please."

I looked down upon Gollum's sprawled figure. He'd be uncomfortable with his restrained hands tucked under him in that awkward position. If he were conscious. That lump on the back of his head looked painful.

"And off my friend, too."

"Look, lady. We were just doing our job. You're terrorists. We can't let you loose." Corporal Bolo's chin quivered a bit and his voice threatened to crack.

"What makes you think we're terrorists, Bolo?" I asked as I did my best to stand up. My knees were still a little weak and my balance sucked, but I made it upright without falling over. I held out my hands as if I expected the man to produce a key and release me.

"You . . . you sneaked up behind us in a white SUV rental. That's a profile car."

"Sheesh!" I rolled my eyes and stared at the ceiling.

"I'm a novelist doing research. The white SUV was the only rental available in Tri-Cities."

"Is that why you had a case of books in the back of the SUV?"

"Duh."

Gollum groaned. His eyelids fluttered open. He looked at me, unfocused and puzzled. Then his face cleared of befuddlement and he reached a hand to touch his wound. But his hands were still cuffed together and underneath his body. He moaned and lay still again. But his eyes remained open, searching, taking in every detail within his range.

He was no normal professor-type geek. I knew he hadn't told me his entire life story and I began to wonder just what he wanted to keep secret. And why.

The medic and the lieutenant also began to wake up. They grabbed their throats and coughed shallowly several times before completely rousing.

Before I could think of a way to talk myself out of this mess, the door to the outside banged open.

"Get in there, you terrorist bastard!" a Marine sergeant shouted as he shoved Donovan inside the tiny hut. A quick glance told me this was a portable trailer moved on site—probably painted camouflage—as a command center.

Donovan stumbled up the one step to the inside, cursing and spitting blood. His shoulders hung at an awkward angle with his hands cuffed behind him. Blood dripped from his split lip, his left eye had nearly swollen shut. The bruising would become a rainbow of colors before long. His white shirt was ripped at the shoulder seam and filthy. A jagged cut showed through the torn knee of his dress slacks. He looked like he'd been beaten, rolled in the mud, and hung out to dry.

Couldn't happen to a nicer guy.

So why was he still the sexiest man in the trailer?

Ta, babe! Too much demon smell in here. He's been around demons. I gotta go find them.

Scrap winked out.

"Tess, thank God you're okay," Donovan gushed. He winced as he dropped to his knees beside me.

"Traitor!" I hissed. Hard to do without any esses in the word, but I managed.

Gollum grinned, then quickly blanked his expression again. He still surveyed the room warily from his position at my feet.

Scrap pressed his nose against the tiny window above the door from the outside.

"What?" I mouthed to him.

I'll say something when I've got something to say, babe. He chomped on a cigar but didn't light it. *You're not bleeding, I can go scout around for you.*

Stay right where you are, I ordered him.

He left anyway. But that's Scrap, as independent as I. He couldn't get along with the other imps any better than I got along with the Sisters who partnered them.

"I couldn't help it, Tess. They kidnapped me. They forced me to be their spokesman," Donovan continued his litany of innocence.

He was so sincere I almost believed him. Almost. We had a lot of trust issues to work out.

"Define 'they,'" Bolo barked, finally gaining courage in the presence of backup.

"That mob of crazed youngsters who think they can take on the world and win. What do you expect from unsupervised, and undisciplined teens with unlimited access to pot, beer, and pizza," Donovan spat, literally. A wad of blood and spittle and a tooth came out of his mouth. It looked like a normal human tooth.

"So why didn't they keep you?" I asked.

"I don't know." He had the grace to look abashed and drop his gaze.

"Did the demons do this to you or the Marines?" Gollum whispered.

"The Marines." He was silent a moment, then looked at us both in surprise. "Demons?" he mouthed.

"They aren't exactly Indians." I smiled too sweetly.

Donovan shook his head. "They are Indians. I've known a lot of them all my life."

"I don't doubt you've known them most of your life." Standoff. "How'd they force you if they didn't beat you?" And how long had they been teens? He looked forty.

"They threatened to burn the casino. I've got every dime I own tied up in that project. One more delay, one more bad inspection and I'm ruined." He looked up with those big dark eyes framed by beautifully long lashes and pleaded with me to believe him.

My heart, and my innards threatened to melt under those eyes.

"Don't believe him," Gollum muttered as he struggled to sit.

"Well, I don't believe any of you," the lieutenant sneered. He struggled to his feet and sat (collapsed?) onto a typing chair in front of a console full of monitors and keyboards.

I ignored the tactical displays because I didn't understand them and didn't have the concentration to figure them out.

"We've got to bust out of here," Donovan whispered.

I was sure everyone in the trailer heard him. The sergeant just leaned against the door and grinned, inviting us to try. He wanted to hit someone almost as much as I did.

"Not on your life, Donovan. We stay put until these people realize that they made a terrible mistake and release us. I'm not spending the rest of my life on the run from the U.S. government. I have a life and a career." I sank down to sit cross-legged next to Gollum.

He still didn't look real healthy. His complexion remained pasty, and his eyes still rolled out of focus occasionally.

"If you two are so innocent, how come tall and lanky attacked us?" The lieutenant leaned forward, almost falling off his chair.

"The medic wouldn't listen. He was going to give Tess a drug that would kill her," Gollum replied. He looked the lieutenant directly in the eye. Few people could do that and lie effectively. "Sweetheart, we've got to get you a medical bracelet so emergency personnel know which drugs you're allergic to." Gollum patted my cuffed hands with his own cuffed hands.

I wanted to snarl at him that I wasn't his sweetheart.

He frowned at me until I almost heard him beg me to play along.

Reluctantly I decided to let him lead the way. Maybe he had a plan. I sure didn't.

Chapter 30

The door rattled. We all looked to see how many more bodies wanted to squeeze into the trailer.

"Background checks coming in on monitor four, lieutenant," a private said as he poked his head inside. He looked askance at all of us, counted bodies, sitting and standing, on the floor and at the workstations, then backed out.

Lieutenant Vlieger (thank the Goddess these guys all wore name tags) swung around on his chair and clicked a mouse. The center monitor flashed a picture of me—my most flattering publicity photo with soft lighting and fuzzy edges that disguised my untidy hair and imperfect makeup—along with a bunch of text.

Vlieger switched his gaze from me to the monitor, peering ever closer to both. "I guess that could be you," he finally admitted.

"Well, thanks," I said. Sarcasm dripped from my words thicker than it did from Scrap at his most polite.

"Your hair is quite a bit lighter now," he said half apologetically.

"Women dye their hair," I returned. Only I hadn't. It had only gotten lighter since I'd been wearing the comb. I wondered if the translucent hairs it pulled out were the transformed darker strands, leaving only the fairer blond ones.

That comb was certainly weird. Wish I knew what its magic purpose was.

Vlieger scrolled down the screen until he came across the cover for my book. "You wrote this?" He pointed.

"Every last word."

"Guess that explains the case of them we found in the back of the SUV."

I rolled my eyes. "Don't think I'm going to give you an autographed copy," I muttered. "That is, if you can read."

"Easy, Tess, we want him on our side," Gollum whispered and patted my hand. He was getting too used to that proprietary gesture.

"May I check your blood pressure again?" the medic asked, almost meekly. He held up a cuff.

I nodded and held out my arms.

He maneuvered around our sprawled legs until he could crouch beside me. While he pumped up the cuff and monitored a digital readout, Vlieger continued to read every word of my bio.

"Sheesh, not even a traffic ticket," Vlieger said out loud. "What are these organizations you belong to? They might be subversive."

"A bunch of writers banding together so they can have legal advocacy funds and medical insurance are very subversive," I replied.

He scrolled further down. I guess he found explanations for the acronyms for romance authors, science fiction writers, and novelists in general.

"If you are so squeaky clean, Ms. Noncoiré, then why did you disappear for a year?" He tapped a blank portion of the screen.

"I was in retreat while I researched and wrote that damn book."

"Right after a dubious marriage."

"My marriage to Dillwyn Cooper was legal, binding, and . . ." I choked. "And real."

"Easy, Ms. Noncoiré," Medic Lawrence soothed. He pulled me back down into the sitting position. "Your blood pressure just rose sixty points. That's not good."

"Did her blood pressure go up because she was lying?" Vlieger looked hopeful.

"This isn't a lie detector," Lawrence said. He was too calm, too collected, too bland.

I didn't trust him. That blood pressure cuff just might be the latest thing in lie detection.

"She was really mad at you for questioning her marriage. My educated guess is that she was telling the truth." Lawrence kept his eyes on his equipment, not meeting Vlieger's malevolent gaze.

Vlieger turned back to his screens. "Homeland Security says you're clean, Ms Noncoiré. I trust that you aren't a terrorist or security risk. Take the cuffs off her and let her go."

"What about Gol . . . Guilford?" I figured they wouldn't appreciate his nickname. Or understand it.

"We'll get to him." Vlieger clicked the mouse and read silently.

We waited.

He muttered and snarled to himself.

We waited some more. And fidgeted.

"What haven't you told me about yourself?" I asked sweetly. Too sweetly.

Gollum shrugged. "I practice tai chi every morning." He smiled weakly, apologetically.

Scrap peered through the window again. *Gollum smoked marijuana in college. Says so right on the screen,* Scrap chortled. *They're gonna put him away for ten years for that!*

Scrap, we all smoked marijuana in college. Probably even the lieutenant there.

Oh. Scrap sounded disappointed. *Even you, babe?*

Even me.

"There is a little matter of two years in Africa working for the Peace Corps," Vlieger turned back to pierce Gollum with his gaze.

"I gave back to the world." Gollum shrugged.

"Says here you come from old money in upstate New York. Why'd a guy born with a silver spoon in his mouth condescend to grub in the dirt with a bunch of primitives?"

"Like I said. I felt I needed to give something back to the less fortunate. Money isn't always enough. Besides, it gave me a chance to study some of their myths and folklore firsthand. I wrote my master's thesis on what I learned." Gollum's grip on my hands turned fierce. He was hiding something. Possibly something even Homeland Security couldn't find.

Something I needed to know.

Vlieger gave his attention to the screen once more. "Two more Masters degrees and three Ph.Ds. and you haven't applied for a tenure track position at a college or university?" He raised his eyebrows.

"Old money from upstate New York. I don't have to work, so I take on short-term teaching positions in interesting places. When I find the right place to settle down, I'll consider something more permanent." His grip on my hand softened. Whatever he had to hide was in those two years in Africa, not in his recent career.

"So why are you here?" Vlieger kept up his interrogation.

"Helping Ms Noncoiré research a new novel." Gollum grinned and scrunched up his nose in an effort to push up his glasses.

Vlieger was out of his chair and grabbing Gollum's shirt at his throat in less than a heartbeat. "Why were you both poking around the casino construction site? Today? When we'd closed off the entire area because of terrorist activity nearby?"

No one else moved.

No one breathed.

Except Scrap. He lit his cigar with a flamelet on the tip of his thumb. Then he blew a huge smoke ring toward the sergeant at the door. Good thing the door was still closed and Scrap on the outside.

"We need to speed this up or turn on the air-conditioning." The sergeant fanned the air in front of his face. Some of Scrap's smoke did get through. "The air's getting stale in here. Smells of old cigars and . . . oh, my God, who farted?"

This time he did open the door and let in some of the cool desert air.

Scrap remained outside, eyeing Donovan with a fierce hatred.

Donovan eyed the door longingly.

"We did not know the area was closed," Gollum explained patiently. "There were no signs on the construction road, no roadblocks. We wanted to talk to some of the people in favor of the casino. Heaven only knows we've talked to enough people in town who are against it."

"All fodder for the writing mill," I chimed in. "Conflict is the essence of plotting. I need more conflict in my new book."

Donovan shifted as if ready to get his feet under him and dart out the door.

I kicked him. He glowered at me.

I wondered what *he* had to hide. Maybe something in the background check coming up on the computer screen. It took a lot longer for it to scroll down to the bottom than Gollum's had. Even if Vlieger kicked me out right now, I doubted I'd go. I needed to know more about Donovan Estevez.

WE WAITED. CORPORAL Bolo took the handcuffs off both Gollum and me, but left them on Donovan. Vlieger had said we were free to go, but he didn't kick us out and neither of us made a move toward the door. Lawrence kept fussing over me with his blood pressure cuff and stethoscope.

Scrap popped up and down by the window, laughing at us mere humans.

It's a circus out there. Neither side seems to know how to fight this war, he chortled. *Some of the media trucks are packing up and going home. Not enough action.*

Finally, Vlieger's computer beeped. "Took long enough," he muttered.

We all leaned forward.

Vlieger read the screens without comment. Screen after screen rolled past. I saw blurred photos; some looked like they'd been downloaded from news services.

"Homeland Security wants us to hold on to you a while longer, Mr. Estevez. You two can go."

Did I dare ask what was on those computer screens?

"I'm ruined." Donovan slumped. He looked smaller, more human, and more vulnerable than I'd ever seen him before.

And sexy as hell.

"Come on, Guilford." I didn't want to raise questions by calling him Gollum in this crowd, and I certainly wouldn't call him sweetheart. "We need to check on Cynthia."

"Don't even think about stealing the blanket," Donovan snarled. "My people are armed and guarding it with their lives."

"I wouldn't dream of committing a crime." I opened my eyes wide, trying to look innocent. Though that was precisely what I was thinking. "But who will defend your claim to the artifact in court while Homeland Security has you locked up on suspicion of terrorism?"

I grabbed Gollum by the elbow and decamped as quickly as I could.

Fresh air never smelled so sweet as that windy hilltop in the high desert on a cloudy autumn day. Sage and dust and something sharp, like cedar cuttings... no juniper and a desert pine.

The air scintillated like fine lead crystal in the unfettered sunlight. A heady mixture that deserved a painting, or a song, except for the ugliness of all construction sites, and chain link fences robbing the plateau of its natural beauty.

A series of pops and bangs sounded off to our left.

The sergeant pushed us down one step into the dust. "Down! Those damn Indians are trying to break through our lines."

I choked down an admonishment that the term Indians was not politically correct. Or accurate.

Bullets whizzed over our heads. They pinged against the trailer and smacked into the dirt.

I cringed and cowered with my arms over my head, trying to make myself as small a target as possible.

Gollum landed on top of me. His weight became a reassuring barrier between me and a weapon I could not counter.

Scrap, what do we do now?

Hide!

He turned bright red and elongated, thinning, ready to transform.

Another spate of gunfire. I couldn't fight guns with the Celestial Blade. Scrap and I were useless.

The bullets intensified on both sides.

I watched in stunned horror as a bullet crashed into Corporal Bolo's forehead.

He looked stunned for half a heartbeat. A dark hole appeared between his eyes. His blood and brains splattered against the trailer wall behind him. Then he slumped to the ground, dead before his knees crumpled.

Chapter 31

Up to twenty million bats have been known to live in a single colony inside a cave—Bracken Cave in the central Texas hill country.

Donovan burst out of the trailer, automatic weapon blazing like some movie action hero. I half expected him to spout words in Austrian. He aimed at the figures gathered on the other side of the fence. "Stupid Kajiri fools. Too impatient. Too violent. Too young to know your ass for a hole in your heads. Everything I've worked for—ruined!" he screamed as he marched forward.

Young men and women on the other side of the fence fell bleeding. Crumpled rag dolls thrown into the dirt by Donovan's bullets. Their blood smelled like water tasted when tainted by heavy mineral salts—like the lake.

That's what these demons smell like, the lake. Donovan smells different, Scrap said, puzzled. *Demons are close, their evil counters Donovan's mojo. We need to go into action, dahling.*

Not until they stop shooting! I protested.

"Stand down, Estevez!" Vlieger shouted. Wisely, he stayed in the doorway of the trailer, ready to duck back inside the dubious shelter should Donovan turn that horrible weapon on him.

Donovan paused. His gunfire sputtered to a stop. No one was firing back. No one was left inside the compound to fire back.

"Stand down and hand me the weapon, Estevez," Vlieger ordered, like he was speaking to one of his own Marines gone berserk.

An ugly sneer marred Donovan's handsome face. But the tip of his gun lowered. His finger on the trigger went slack.

"Hand me the weapon." Vlieger stepped down from the doorway. He placed a gentle hand on Donovan's shoulder as he eased the heavy gun out of his hands with the other. Keeping his eyes on Donovan, Vlieger handed the gun to the sergeant.

"Let's go back inside and talk."

"Just lock me up and throw away the key," Donovan said sadly. He looked toward the half-built casino with longing near despair.

"Good place for you, Donovan," I said as I crawled out from under Gollum. "The siege of the fort is over." So why was Scrap still hovering so close to me? Donovan's presence should chase him away.

Already I could see Marines breaking through the front gates, weapons at the ready. No one stirred among the fallen defenders.

"Your crews can get back to work. You've only lost one day of work." I kept up my soothing tone. "That is, if you can afford the legal fees for the brace of lawyers you're going to need to defend you on murder charges.

He turned his bleak gaze back to me.

"The people he just killed are terrorists who declared war on the U.S. I doubt any charges will be brought against you," Vlieger muttered. "Damnit all, I was hoping to see you fry."

"Promise you won't steal the blanket until I get clear of Homeland Security?" Donovan flashed me one of his charming half smiles.

That might be a very long time. I couldn't promise him that. I clung to my doubts and distrust with a will as strong as imp wood.

"We'll talk when Lieutenant Vlieger is done with you. I'm sure he'll understand that you couldn't have been part of the takeover." He wouldn't kill his own people just to prove his own innocence, would he?

A demon would.

Shaking and numb at the same time, Gollum and I stumbled to my rental car, or what was left of it. The Marines had been very thorough in their search for anything incriminating. The seats lay strewn about the ground. My books had been ripped to shreds. The vehicle sat on its axles, the wheels and tires stacked nearby.

"Who's going to pay the damage on this?" I screamed. My usually healthy checking account suddenly seemed vastly inadequate to deal with this. I sank onto the ground and stared dumbly at the mess.

Tess! Scrap screamed at me.

Before my butt hit the ground a long arm wrapped around my neck and pulled me back.

I leaned into the arm, thinking it must be Gollum come to console me.

Scrap dropped into my hand and began to stretch and thin and . . . and solidify.

Alarmed, I slammed my left elbow backward. I connected with hard cartilage and bone. And fur. Not a normal chest.

Curved blades extruded from Scrap's head and feet. Close enough.

I flipped the Celestial Blade over my head and stabbed the blade into what should be a demon head.

I missed.

A thick gun barrel pressed into my temple.

"Put the blade to rest, or I kill you before you can breathe again," a deep bass voice growled at me.

I CAN'T RISK IT, BABE, Scrap apologized and winked out of view.

"He was hiding behind the tires, Tess," Gollum explained. He fidgeted and tried to ease around behind me.

"Stay put, teacher man," the demon said, pressing the gun tighter against my skull.

I gulped. Sweat broke out on my brow and my back.

How could I fight a gun?

"Everybody stay put, or I waste the chick," the demon shouted.

I felt him shift his grip on the trigger.

Instantly, every Marine within view froze. Even those behind the fence.

"What does he look like?" I mouthed to Gollum. He may have crept closer. I couldn't tell. My whole being shook so badly the world seemed to tremble in fear.

"He's human," Gollum replied in a whisper.

I glanced sideways at the pile of bodies on the other side of the fence. They looked human, too. And there seemed to be a lot fewer of them than when Donovan had first blasted them with his automatic weapon.

"Wh . . . what do you want?" I asked the man who held me hostage. My brain finally kicked in, though my feet and hands itched to take him out any way I could, despite the risk to my own life.

"I want all those fucking Marines out of our home base," he yelled.

My ears rang from the volume of his demand.

"And I want everyone to clear a perimeter half a mile from the fence."

The closest Marines edged away from us. Gollum stayed put. He might have come an inch or two closer.

I couldn't see how he'd do any good with that honking big gun muzzle pressed against my head and probably a hair trigger for a jumpy guy.

Prayers. I should have said a prayer. My mind remained blank. I didn't believe in God anyway. Why should I call for help now when He or She couldn't give any?

"And we want a million dollars and Fort Snoqualmie declared an independent and sovereign nation, separate from the rest of the country," my captor added.

"I'm not worth that much," I said, wishing I could joke my way out of this.

"Someone will come up with the money. You're a celebrity, after all."

"The U.S. government doesn't negotiate with terrorists. They'll kill me when they storm the fort just to get rid of you."

"Let 'em try," my captor chortled. "Now everyone out of our way. I'm taking her inside. All those Marines in there need to get out now."

"Take me instead of her," Gollum said. He stepped a little closer.

I gulped. I tried to shake my head no, but the gun barrel kept me immobile.

"You ain't worth a damn, teacher man."

"My family has money, influence in government. I'm more valuable than she is."

"But she has fans who will make a big stink in the press."

He prodded my back and pushed me toward the gate.

Again, I noticed the pile of bodies was smaller, down to two or three. Where had they all gone?

"Gregor, no!" Donovan called from the trailer. "This is about our people, not about any of them. Do you really want to involve outsiders?" He stepped down the one stair to the ground and approached us.

Gregor swung me around, putting my body between himself and Donovan. He began backing up until we pressed into the fence. "This has gotten bigger than you, Estevez. Bigger than me. We have a homeland now, right here at Fort Snoqualmie. No one will dare take it away from us. This woman is our guarantee of that."

He pushed and pulled me along the fence until we reached the gate.

A dozen Marines filed out, all holding their weapons away from their bodies, hands away from the triggers.

My heart pounded so hard and fast I couldn't think beyond keeping my knees locked and my body upright. I could almost taste the metal of the gun and bullets.

Gollum and Donovan kept pace with us as we sidled along.

"Gollum, go take care of Cynthia. And call Leonard. Oh, and call my agent. And I guess you should call my mother. But whatever you do, don't speak French to her. The numbers are on my cell phone."

"Got it. Why shouldn't I speak French to your mother?"

"Just don't."

Scrap, what the hell do we do? I implored my imp.

We play along until the moment is right. I'll be right here with you, every step of the way.

"Don't try anything, lady," Gregor whispered. He yanked me into the compound. One of his friends—risen from the pile of bodies?—slammed the sliding double gate closed.

"We've got guns trained on you from every corner of the compound. And we've got this." He held up a long rope of mistletoe and holly twined together by vines of ivy.

"So?"

Scrap gagged and held his throat as if strangling. He turned a sickly neon yellowish green, then winked out.

"Scrap!"

"Didn't know about imp's bane, lady?" Gregor laughed. He released his death grip on me.

I sank to my knees. Tears streamed down my face and my body shook uncontrollably. What else could go wrong?

Chapter 32

Bat mothers nurse their young. Specially adapted milk teeth in the young—teeth that are shed after weaning—allow the babies to cling to Mama's nipple even during flight.

"Everybody back inside," Gregor commanded. "They've got snipers all around, just waiting for the right moment to pick us off." He grabbed my hair in one of his oversized fists and dragged me toward an opening in the fence.

I stumbled along in his wake, too shocked and numb to do anything else.

My total awareness centered on the gun barrel now pressed against my spine.

And my thirst. I hadn't eaten or drunk since breakfast. How many hours ago?

"You guys got any beer in here?"

"What do you care, writer lady? You aren't going to live long enough to appreciate our beer," one of the resurrected demons off to my left said.

Gregor jammed the gun tighter against my spine. I raised my hands in surrender but couldn't keep my mouth shut.

"The whole point of taking me hostage is to keep me alive so that those on the outside have hopes of getting me back." I stopped short of the doorway into the main building. A gray, squat, ugly place with few windows and no grace. "Kill me, and they have no reason to answer your demands. Kill me, and you give them an excuse to nuke the entire place."

"She's right, Kaylor," Gregor mumbled. "Gotta keep her alive and happy until the outsiders do something smart or incredibly stupid. Then we kill her."

"Then bring out the beer, boys. How about some sandwiches, too?"

"Better than that. We got pizza."

My mouth watered.

Okay, I'm a slave to my stomach. I think better when I've been fed.

As they shoved me against a pile of packing crates that held a microwave and mini fridge, I remembered to pull the comb out of my pocket and jam it into my hair.

The world seemed to tilt, and colors jumped out at me as if I was tripping on LSD. Why hadn't this happened before? Maybe because there wasn't anything unusual to see before. I saw a halo or aura of fur surrounding each of the demon faces.

Sasquatch.

The boys, they all looked to be in their late teens, young enough to have no sense of judgement at all, had made a cozy nest for themselves out of brightly striped blankets in a ghastly color scheme, oversized pillows, and packing crates. The place had probably been a warehouse or a hangar originally.

I arranged a couple of pillows to support my back and butt. My captors faced me in a semicircle, boxes of pizza and six-packs between us. The smell of warm bread and tomato sauce made my stomach growl.

"I bet you boys don't have food this good where you come from," I said, offhandedly, as I drowned my third piece of pizza with my second beer.

Kaylor stilled and stared at me with a what-do-you-know-about-that expression. He wasn't the brightest bulb in the pack.

"Hey, I'm a Warrior of the Celestial Blade. It's my job to know where you boys come from."

"We aren't 'boys,'" Gregor said. He sounded very offended.

"No, you're not." I'd seen their like at hundreds of cons over the years, too old to have a parent in tow, too young to truly be ready to face the world on their own. But they had enough experience to think they knew everything there was to know.

Teenagers.

They all looked smug and satisfied, and ever so macho.

"You're demons, halflings, really."

"Don't call me that!" Kaylor screamed. He crouched, ready to spring at me, paws and talons at the ready.

Gregor had to hold Kaylor with both hands to keep him from climbing over the pile of pizza boxes to rip my throat out. He hadn't managed to morph his hands/paws completely. His fingers looked preternaturally long, tipped with talons as long as my hand.

"Writer lady, we don't like being called 'halflings,'" Gregor warned. His canine teeth elongated, hanging down below his lip. "We eat humans for lesser offenses."

None of these guys had a lot of control over their morphing.

"Well, I don't like being called 'writer lady.'" I stood up, hands on hips, glowering at the contingent of young demons. "And I thought you kidnapped humans for breeding purposes, not food."

They all exchanged uneasy glances.

Gregor's eyes slitted vertically and turned yellow before he regained control over himself. "We are Kajiri. What are you?" he finally spat. His saliva was still green, but his eyes and hands returned to a more human appearance.

My heart flipped and beat a few extra beats. Kajiri? Could that be just the name demons gave to half-breeds?

"I'm Tess. A writer by profession."

And a Warrior of the Celestial Blade by a fate I didn't choose.

I sat down again on a fuchsia-and-pea-green blanket on the cement floor, feigning casualness.

Gregor reached for another piece of pizza. His eyes dropped out of confrontational mode. "Pizza and beer are better than human blood," he muttered. "Most of the time."

Kaylor still looked ready to pounce and eat me.

"So, Donovan is also Kajiri?" I might as well make use of my time here.

"Yeah, Kajiri, like us. But he ain't Sasquatch. He's Damiri. They're pansies. Disdain eating humans, pride themselves on their ability to maintain a human form and get educated in your universities. They like blending in with the enemy. Some even try to forget where they really come from," a shorter and lanky fellow from the back of the pack said with derision. "And they're all richer than Bill Gates."

"No one is richer than Bill Gates. How would an ignorant human tell the difference?"

"The Damiri are tallish by your standards, about six foot, and darker. They tend to go to fat if they don't watch it. But they are more deadly in a fight." Gregor seemed truly interested in educating me. "Their natural form is similar to your bats."

I blanched and lost my appetite.

"Donovan is tall and dark, but he certainly hasn't gone to fat," I choked out. But he liked bat costumes at cons. Was it all a costume?

"He works out," the short and lanky one said.

"They get those silver wings of hair at about age thirty, but the rest of their hair never goes gray."

"Their names always start with a D and end with an N."

In less time than it took me to inhale, an image of Dillwyn flashed before my mind's eye. He'd just turned twenty-eight, a year older than me, when I met him, and lost him three months later. He had about two white hairs on each side of his full head of dark hair. Right at his temples. The same place Donovan had silver wings of hair.

He'd been about an inch taller than Donovan, too.

I'd fallen for him within minutes of meeting him.

No.

Impossible.

My imagination running overtime. I am a science fiction/fantasy writer after all.

But... I needed more information. Facts not innuendo.

"Where'd the pizza and beer come from?" I asked rather than think those horrible thoughts. They had a microwave and mini fridge plugged into the wall. "Come to think of it, where is the electricity coming from?"

The first thing the Marines and SWAT teams outside would do is cut off electricity and water.

"We've got our own sources," Kaylor said smugly. His eyes dropped to the floor.

"From underground. You're bringing up resources from the underworld."

Silence.

I'd hit the nail on the head.

"I don't remember seeing any pizza parlors or bars the one time I ventured into the underworld."

"You only made it as far as the chat room. That's a scary place if you aren't used to it," Gregor said.

"Chat room?" I raised both eyebrows in astonishment. I'd heard Scrap use that term before.

"That's what we call it," the short and lanky one said. Short being relative. These guys were big. Sasquatch. All of them well over six feet. I wondered if full-blooded or fully grown Sasquatch were in the eight-foot range as legend suggested.

"It's the room just beyond the portal where you get to choose which dimension you go to. Anybody can get into the chat room. Getting into a dimension not your own takes real talent. Never known a human to manage it," Gregor said. He seemed to be warming up to me.

I wanted to ask if this chat room was where demons seduced their breeding partners. That might explain the Beauty and the Beast legend. But I didn't want these angry young men to think I was coming on to them by asking too many questions about breeding.

"Time to set the watch," Gregor changed the subject. Then he switched to that strange clicking and hissing language as he pointed to six of his fellow demons.

Those six rose reluctantly, each grabbing another piece of pizza and an extra beer. They disappeared into the shadows. Within a few moments, six different demons reappeared, all carrying new stores. They settled in to eat with only a quick glance and dismissal of my presence.

They all wore jeans, western-cut shirts, belts with big buckles and boots, much like the tribal members I had seen in town. They all had dark hair, but not the jet black I expected of aboriginal genetics. And they all smelled of the oily, mineral-laden water, including the ancient fish oil, from the lake.

"Mind if I go off into a corner and sit by myself for a while?" I asked.

Gregor waved me off to the left, away from the microwave and fridge.

I took the bright pink blanket and a pillow with me. That cement floor was cold. Once I'd made myself comfortable—much easier than I expected, but then I'd had a few beers, well more than a few on a nearly empty stomach—I closed my eyes and breathed deeply. Maybe, with luck, and a lot of concentration I could reach out with my fuzzy mind and find . . . "Sister Serena?"

The fuzzy image of my friend and doctor at the Citadel appeared before my closed eyes. The image came and went sporadically, like a hologram shorting out in an SF movie.

"What ails you, child?" she asked into my mind.

"I am a hostage of two dozen Kajiri demons. They have strung imp's bane around so Scrap cannot find me. I need help getting out of here."

"Kajiri demons!" She sounded alarmed, looking about frantically. "How did two dozen Kajiri slip past the portal?"

"I think they came through a long time ago. They are very familiar with this world; very comfortable here. They admit to being half-breeds."

"Impossible. Demons cannot breed with humans. Your information is faulty. Perhaps they are Kmera demons. Our brothers to the east have been lax in guarding their portal. They age and do not recruit new members."

"No. They definitely said Kajiri."

"I have to go. There's more activity around the portal." She snapped out of my awareness so fast I thought she might have panicked.

That was a concept I had trouble getting my imagination around. Sister Serena never panicked. She was always calm, always clear-headed, always willing to answer my questions.

Now what did I do?

Wheee! Tessie, look at me.

I swung merrily from rafter to rafter. Lighter than air. Hardly any wing needed at all. Whee!

Hey, babe, you aren't looking at me.

Oops, forgot. She can't see me through the miasma of imp's bane.

I jumped onto a rafter beside a bat. A big fella. We stared at each other for a while. Kinda hard since he was upside down.

So I went upside down, too, clinging with my toes. What a rush. Blood in my head and in my eyes. Everything looking weird and wonderful.

Bat got bored. I think he said his name was Morris or was that Morrissette and a she? Anyway, he went back to sleep. Too bad. He was kinda cute. So I tried watching my babe for a while. She wasn't doing much, meditating. How boring.

Time to slide down the walls and give those Kajiri a scare. A tweak to their ears here, a pinch to a bottom there.

But they don't scare easily.

So I hang in front of one of the guards and make ugly faces at him. He can't see me either. He's got a braid of mistletoe, holly, and ivy around his neck.

Weird. None of those plants ever put a foggy wall between my babe and me before. She's a nut at Christmas and drapes the whole house in greenery. Must be the way they braid and knot the stuff.

Who cares. I'm going back to the rafters. I can see the world from here. The world could come to an end—and I wouldn't care!

Interlude

SOON AFTER I'D BEGUN training seriously, a night of a waxing quarter moon came around. The Sisters all gathered in the courtyard for their ritual. I stood aside with a new initiate, Alunda, still recovering from her fever. We wouldn't be allowed to participate until we finished our training and went through some kind of ritual blessing from the Goddess.

This night, the Goddess did not appear. The portal had not been breached.

I helped Alunda back to her infirmary bed. Her black skin glistened with sweat from the effort of standing. Sister S hastened in and fussed around her, taking her temperature and blood pressure, clucking her tongue, and showing her best bedside manner.

The warm, cozy, charming atmosphere Sister S created tugged at me. I wanted to linger, be one of her patients again. Not because I was sick. Because I was lonely. And bored. I needed mental stimulation, a book to write, animated discussion on hot topics. Even the evening news on TV would help.

None of that happened at the Citadel. Here, life revolved around training, recounting past battles, working in the garden, and sleeping.

Reluctantly, I retired to my solitary cell in the dormitory. No books. No radio. No CDs. No TV. Nothing but myself and my purloined notebook and pencil.

Trouble was, I had no idea where the story was going. I needed an ending to drive the story forward. So I played with words and graphs and character development until loud voices and laughter drew my attention.

A party seemed to be growing in the common room. I slunk out of my cell and down the hall to the big room where twenty women lounged about on sofas, overstuffed chairs, and big cushy pillows. A keg of beer stood in the corner. Sister Paige played bartender, drawing glass after glass.

I joined the line for this rare treat. Sister Gert probably allowed the keg in this one dorm because the Goddess had not appeared. The rest of the dorms were on watch. I wondered if the single keg just wandered from dorm to dorm each month.

The beer tasted funny, too heavy and yeasty for me with bits of floating vegetation. Homemade with a crude filter. Maybe they'd used the recipe found in the Hammurabi Code. Maybe the Sisterhood had written the code for the ancient king of Babylon who codified every aspect of life he could think of, including how to make beer.

Don't you like beer, babe? Scrap looked at me wistfully. He snuggled next to me in the armless chair I found off to the side.

"Sure I like beer. Just not this beer." I didn't have to whisper to keep this conversation private. The stories and songs in the center of the party had become rather raucous. No one could overhear us unless they sat in the narrow chair with us.

Can I drink it?

He looked hopefully lavender.

I held the glass for him. The liquid disappeared at an alarming rate.

I wondered if there was a limit on refills. Then I noticed a lot of the Sisters fed beer to their imps.

More, Scrap demanded.

"Say please."

He stared at me malevolently.

None of the other imps have to be polite.

"But you're my imp, and I like to live life in a somewhat civilized manner. That requires a degree of polite-ness just to get along."

Scrap fumed in silence a moment.

Oh, okay. May I please have some more beer?

"Sure, pal. I'll get it for you."

I had to duck beneath swooping imps to get back to the keg. Sister Electra had taken over at the tap. Her flushed face matched her flame-colored hair, and her eyes glazed over a bit. Her imp hung from a drawing of dry falls on the wall by one elbow talon. Electra and the imp swayed in rhythm to a discordant tune the imp sang.

I looked back at Scrap. He perched on my chair, hands crossed over his pot belly and tiny wings folded neatly against his back. He swiveled his floppy ears, catching every nuance of the conversations. Oh, well, if he got drunk and had a hangover in the morning, maybe he'd learn not to indulge. I let Electra refill my glass.

The party went on and on. I told story after story, each more fantastic than the last, fishing for the right ending for the book I wrote. Nothing worked for me. My audience seemed to appreciate them, though, singing battle songs in the right places and dirges in others.

Scrap drank glass after glass of beer, keeping pace with the other imps.

"Why aren't you as drunk as those idiots?" I asked, leaning back to avoid two imps fighting a mock battle using plastic straws for swords. (Some modern conveniences made their way into the Citadel. Sister Gert made a trip into the nearest town once a month in an unobtrusive four-by-four pickup. I had no idea where the money came from.)

Because you aren't drunk.

Interesting. "So if I'm hungry, so are you. If I'm tired, so are you. If I get drunk, so will you."

Yeah, something like that. He belched and let out a huge yawn.

I couldn't help but echo that.

We retired long before the party even began to wind down. I was still bored to tears. And I hadn't learned anything new. The Sisters drunk told the same stories they told sober. And frankly, I could write more exciting stuff with one hand tied behind my back. If I could just find the right ending.

Chapter 33

Some bats can live up to thirty years. Even small bats live considerably longer than other small mammals.

Sitting in that drafty warehouse in the middle of abandoned Fort Snoqualmie, I'd give my eyeteeth for a cell phone. Or my laptop. Or even an outdated PDA. But the Marines were probably jamming cell phone signals, my laptop was back at the lodge, and my cell phone was in my purse, which Gollum had.

How many minutes was he running up explaining the unexplainable to my mother and my agent.

"Close the door, dammit," I snarled at the young Sasquatch who escorted me to the restroom.

He snarled back, showing his teeth.

"At least turn your back. Don't you guys have any sense of privacy?"

"Can't have you climbing out the window, writer lady."

"Fine," I growled back at him. I stomped into the middle stall which had no window above it and slammed the door. The catch was broken. Somehow I managed to hold the thing shut with one hand as I crouched over the throne, thighs straining until they trembled. No way was I going to let my butt touch the stained and broken seat.

My headache throbbed, worse than any hangover I could imagine. What do you expect? All they had to drink around here was beer. And the fumes from the joints they smoked were thick enough to swim through.

No wonder I was cranky.

And I hadn't seen Scrap for hours. I missed him. Part of me wanted to wither up and cry from missing him.

My mind began to spin with new ideas for my book. My fingers wanted to beat on the keys of the computer. I needed to get this down before I lost it.

The adrenaline rush from new ideas cleared my head some.

That made me want to write even more.

I finished my business and took a few extra moments to solidify my thoughts on the book. Then I stomped back to beer-fume central.

"Gregor, I don't suppose on your next trip out for supplies you could slip into the Mowath Lodge and liberate my laptop? Or a pad of paper and a pen." I asked as nicely as I knew how. All those years of Mom beating good manners into me must account for something.

"I'll try." He shrugged and curled up on his pillow and promptly went to sleep.

They all went to sleep. Except for the guards outside who brandished their guns in my face when I poked my head out the door to check out the landscape—or a means of escape.

So I returned to the central space where I paced, trying to keep the words and images in my head. As I paced, I managed to kick a couple of the braids of imp's bane into the fire the boys kept burning in the middle of the warehouse. The smoke vented naturally through the original heating ducts.

Autumn had settled in, and the desert air grew cold at night. The cement floor and vast open spaces held the cold. I hated to think how hot and stifling this place would be in summer.

My head cleared a little. I tossed another bunch of mistletoe, holly, and ivy into the fire, curious at how they'd bound the three plants together.

My head cleared a little more. I caught a glimpse of movement in the rafters. Scrap.

Plans flashed in and out of my head.

After about an hour I decided I should sleep, too. I might never know when I'd need to be rested and ready to roll.

"TESS, YOU HAVE TO HELP me," Dill whispered in the dead of the night.

I stilled every muscle, every thought. Had I truly heard the soft voice next to my ear?

Then I felt him, a warm, comforting, solid body curled up against my back.

Another dream?

I pinched my thigh hard enough to bruise. The old superstition proved true. My leg *hurt* and Dill remained.

"Dilly, my love." I rolled over, throwing my arms around my husband. Desperately, I wanted to submerge myself in his dominant personality, give over all the troubles and decisions to him. As I had when he lived.

"Make it all go away," I cried.

"We can do that now, lovey. The imp no longer stands between us. All you have to do is renounce your vows to the Sisterhood of the Celestial Blade, and we can be together again. Just like this. Together we will be invincible." He kissed me hard upon the mouth.

I melted into him, opening my mouth to his demanding tongue. He held me tight. I drank in the touch of his hands against my back. Too long we'd been apart. Too long I'd been alone.

"Where have you been, my Dilly?" I kissed him hungrily on cheek and neck and mouth.

"Drifting, lost. Wanting you. Join me now. All you have to do is renounce . . ."

Something in the desperate pressure of his fingers against my back sent warning tingles up and down my spine. The fine hairs in the small of my back stood straight out.

His hands were cold as ice. Literally. Cold enough to burn through my sweater and cotton shirt. The place on my neck where his tongue made enticing circles just beneath my ear was cold and dry. Not the cold of chill air touching a wet spot. It was the ice of another world.

"Don't pull away from me, Tess. Please," he pleaded.

I pulled my head back enough to look into his deeply shadowed eyes.

"I can't bear it if you reject me just because I'm dead, Tess."

That sentence chilled me more than his touch.

"What is this about, Dill? Why now? Why didn't you come to me three years ago when I cried myself into a fever in my grief?"

"I wasn't offered the deal until now." His gaze dropped away from my face.

I lifted his chin with one finger. His skin felt dusty and fragile, as though if I pressed too hard it would slough off like the layers of a fine pastry.

"What deal?"

"If you get rid of the imp and renounce your vows, you and I can be together. Forever. I get out of limbo. You won't be alone anymore."

In other words I had become a threat to some . . . *thing* since surviving the imp flu and acquiring Scrap.

"I can't trust that kind of deal, Dill. I'm sorry. But you are dead. Giving you life again is . . . wrong. There aren't any 'get out of jail free' cards once you're dead."

"But I'm not dead, Tess. Not completely anyway. Can't you feel how alive I am? It's the imp. He's tricked you into thinking I'm dead."

"You died in my arms, Dill. You said you loved me with your dying breath. I held your body until it grew cold. I buried your ashes in the pioneer cemetery in Alder Hill." I choked on a sob. This was it. I had to finally admit to myself and to the ghost of my husband that Dill had died.

I traced the lines of his face lovingly one last time. "Good-bye, my love."

Resolutely, I turned my back on him and closed my eyes. The solid presence evaporated.

I took one last tear-filled glance over my shoulder. A man-shaped column of black mist drifted away and passed through the solid cement block walls.

This isn't the end, Tess. I won't let you get away from me. Ever. You're mine in this life and the next.

I AWOKE WITH A START near midnight as the watch changed. I shuddered in memory of the all-too-real nightmare. As I shifted position, the new bruise on my thigh reminded me of every last touch and word of Dill's visit.

New loneliness and despair opened holes in my soul.

A band of teenaged, half breed Sasquatch had taken me hostage. Imp's bane kept Scrap from my side and made him drunk. I was on my own with little hope of seeing tomorrow, let alone living out the rest of my life.

Maybe I should have taken Dill's offer.

But that grated on every nerve and scruple I had.

New supplies of pizza and beer arrived with the change of guard. A repeat of lunch. Couldn't these guys find some steak or tacos or even peanut butter and jelly? Would a glass of water or cup of coffee kill them?

My bad mood and headache returned. I tore the comb out of my hair, bringing a handful of crystalline strands with it.

Immediately, the room dimmed, colors faded. The boys looked like normal boys. The aura of fur, talons, and teeth became echoes of my former vision. After a few minutes they faded altogether.

But my headache didn't.

I stuffed the comb back into my hair. Everything brightened and the auras came back.

So that was the magic of the comb. That was why I'd felt the chill of the grave in Dill's touch and seen it in his eyes.

I couldn't wear the blasted comb all the time because of what it did to my hair and scalp.

I stuffed it back into my pocket. I knew these guys for what they were now. I didn't need it.

Now that I knew what to look for, how would Donovan appear with my vision cleared of demon glamour?

"ANY NEWS?" GREGOR ASKED the newcomers. I hadn't seen Gregor take a watch yet. Obviously he was the leader.

"All quiet out there. Marines, SWAT, and press still camped just outside the fence. A lot less press. The news is absolutely quiet after one mention of our demands. Heard one of the Marines say they'd put a clamp on coverage," the underling replied.

Gregor cursed long and fluently in his own demonic language. Then he cast me a malevolent glare.

After the meal we dispersed to our separate nests again. The boys slept as if they were just normal teenagers, sleep, eat, eat, sleep, occasionally take responsibility for a watch, nothing more, nothing less. If they'd had video games, a few would probably zone out on those, taking breaks only to eat, sleep, and take a turn at watch.

I have a very low boredom tolerance. I'd reached mine several hours ago. I tried calisthenics until Kaylor yelled at me to quiet down.

Another day passed without change. Was this the second or third? I'd lost track. More pizza and beer. I wanted coffee. I needed coffee.

I feared for how Scrap managed without me.

I feared for how my mother reacted to Gollum's phone call.

I feared I might go insane.

I kept the fire going with the piles of brush the boys brought in and an occasional braid of imp's bane. Couldn't burn it all at once in case they noticed. It was something to do and dispelled some of the autumnal chill settling into the room.

Hey, babe, I'm drunk and you're hungover! Scrap's voice came through the thickness in my brain. *And our best friend is a bat named Morris. A mighty cute bat at that. We might get somthin' goin'.*

I rolled my eyes at his rambling. "How can I have a hangover and you don't? You can't get drunk unless I get drunk, and I'm not drunk."

Great, just what I needed. A drunken Celestial Blade when I was going to need it most.

Who cares. Whoee!

I sensed a rush of movement like riding a roller coaster. The vertigo made me stumble. I caught myself just before I stepped into the fire.

The imp's bane burned brightly. That must be it. Either the plant combination or the separation gave me all the symptoms of a hangover.

Yuck. I went back to my corner and tried to sleep.

Then, around noon, the watch changed again, and new supplies of pizza and beer arrived along with my laptop.

"Thank you, thank you, thank you," I gushed all over the young demon who carried the black sanity saver under his arm. "And the flash drive, too! You are wonderful." I kissed the boy's cheek, and he blushed a bright purple.

I fell upon the computer with a vengeance, totally ignoring the greasy aroma of fresh tomato sauce and cheese with too much garlic in the sausage and pepperoni. Not a vegetable in sight.

Idly, I munched on a piece of lunch while I plugged the thing into the only outlet I could find. The boys didn't really need the microwave. Then I booted up the computer. Within minutes I was so absorbed in writing that I didn't notice the beer shoved into my hand or the second piece of pizza someone handed me.

My conscious brain remained paranoid enough that I set the computer on automatic backup every five minutes. That way, if the power blew, I'd still have most of my work. No telling how reliable the electrical source was coming from the other side.

Twenty pages and several hours later I came up for air. My watch said midnight. Not a demon was stirring.

I got up from my blanket and packing crate and began to prowl and stretch. The pizza was cold, but the microwave took care of that once I switched plugs. The beer was warm but there was more in the fridge. I wandered around the warehouse of a room inspecting my captors for more individual characteristics. True to type they were all leanly muscled, well beyond medium height for human males in the fifteen to twenty age range.

I stuck the comb into my hair for a moment.

Their skin and hair colors . . .At first glance their skin ranged from palest Nordic Caucasian to the dark olive of the Mediterranean, with a suggestion of Negroid in a couple of them. Upon closer inspection I saw that they had no beards. By this time all of them should have needed a shave. We had basic plumbing and most of them showered and used the toilets—utilities purloined from the underworld. But I'd never seen them shave. What I saw as skin was actually a light fur, mottling from cream to black.

Not human. I had to remind myself that none of these "boys" was fully human. They were demons, unpredictable, probably violent.

I backed off from my inspection of Gregor and stumbled over a clump of plants. The imp's bane. It had begun to wilt and lose its brightness. What did these guys expect? They hadn't watered the stuff.

I threw the wilting branch into the fire. It burned rapidly. Several more of the bunches joined it. I left enough scattered around so my current depletion of it wasn't too obvious.

Time for a snooze.

Chapter 34

A drug company has recently patented a new blood thinner called Draculin, developed from research on natural anticoagulants in vampire bat saliva.

"Hey, look what we found!"

I woke up, still groggy, headachy from the lack of caffeine and fresh air.

And from Scrap's absence.

The boys gathered around the watch change near the back entrance to the warehouse.

I checked the laptop and pocketed the memory stick out of habit before rolling to my feet.

The ebb and flow of bodies changed enough to reveal a smaller figure huddled in on itself in the center.

"Leave her alone!" I screamed, dashing forward. I ripped young men out of the pack until I could wrap my arms around Cynthia Stalking Moon.

"Out of the way, bitch. She's fair game," Kaylor snarled.

"She's too young for you, Halfling," I sneered back at him. The fine hairs along my spine stood on end. Scrap was close and ready for a fight.

I saw a pink blob above me. A few knots of wilted imp's bane lingered in odd places around the edges. I sincerely hoped he'd be able to break through the invisible barrier to come to my hand as a fully charged weapon.

Kaylor's eyes morphed to yellow with a vertical slit. His fingers elongated and grew horny nails. His mouth and nose grew into a long muzzle with way more teeth—very sharp teeth—than most primates had. His posture crouched and his paws brushed his knees. Black fur shone through the brown glaze on his head and on his body.

Cynthia screamed.

I slapped the demon's muzzle. What else do you do with a beast that refuses to obey?

Startled, Kaylor sloughed off some of his demon aspect. For half a moment a bewildered teenager stared at me.

"We don't take women below the age of consent," Gregor snapped at Kaylor. "That's the rules. Good rules. They keep us safe." He elbowed his way to Cynthia's other side. "Take the kid over to your nest and keep her there," he hissed at me.

His clenched fists and authoritative attitude kept the beasts at bay. For a moment. Long enough to drag a sobbing Cynthia over to my corner.

Halfway there I kicked another bundle of imp's bane into the fire.

The demons were too busy snarling and snapping at each other to pay attention.

"How did this happen?" I whispered to Cynthia the moment we had an illusion of privacy.

"I don't know," she wailed, clinging to me. Fat tears slid down her cheeks and made her dark eyes look overly large and bruised.

"Where is Sapa?"

"I don't know." She buried her face against my chest, fists wrapped in my sweater as if she clung to a lifesaver.

Maybe I was a lifesaver for her. I had to be. No one else was left.

"Let's just sit here for a while and think this over while we calm down."

The demons began to circle us. Feral. Hungry. Growing bolder by the minute.

"Back off, boys," I ordered.

They paused in their cautious circling. But only for a moment.

"Hey, she unplugged the microwave for her stupid laptop!" Kaylor snarled. He ripped the wires from the outlet. He held them up and ripped the plug free of the connection with a twist of his large hands.

I swallowed the gibbering fear that wanted to climb out of my throat into a screech that would put a banshee to shame.

"Into the corner, Cynthia. Stay right by me." Cautiously, I moved us to a place where walls protected our backs.

"Scrap, you available yet?" I kept my eyes on the Kajiri. They took on more and more aspects of their demon nature, the Sasquatch of legend, and yet not. More deadly than imaginable.

Legends claimed that the bigfoot—bigfeet?—were more benign than these monsters.

Which came first, the demons of another dimension or peaceful forest creature? Were they related, or parallel evolution.

Not ready yet, babe. Getting there.

Shit. No weapon but myself, and a little girl to protect. From rape. Or worse. From being eaten.

How could these boys still be hungry after all the pizza and beer they'd consumed?

They were teenagers.

Blood appealed to something more primal in their make up.

The central fire sent a new waft of pot smoke into the air. It helped relax the teens but also sharpened their appetites.

Tall cement block walls comforted me where I could feel them behind me. A smaller flank to defend and protect.

Cynthia still sobbed.

Kaylor edged closer. He kicked my laptop aside. The machine crashed into the wall. The case split down the lid.

Another demon jumped on it until it shattered.

"Now that makes it personal," I snarled. Boiling hot anger replaced the sinking emptiness in my gut. At least I had the flash drive to continue the project.

Provided I lived through the next ten minutes.

Kaylor laughed and dropped all pretense of humanity.

I kicked his snout with the heel of my boot. Then stomped upon his foot. They had earned the nickname "Bigfoot" for a reason.

He backed off, snapping and snarling.

A second demon lunged for my throat. I twisted and hit his chest with my shoulder. The jolt raced through my body. My head ached and my left arm went numb.

He landed heavily and yipped.

Before I could catch my breath, another dove for my leg. He grabbed my calf in massive jaws and sank in his long teeth.

Green saliva burned through my jeans to my flesh, like acid in chem class, only worse. My leg threatened to crumple. Already weakened and off balance from the shoulder, I knew I'd not last long with six demon bigfoots ready to attack.

"Forget the bitches. I found something better," the youngest of the pack announced from the main doorway.

The demons turned their attention toward him—all except the one worrying my leg.

I slammed the side of my hand across his spine, just behind his head. He let go.

We both stepped apart, nursing our hurts.

Cynthia gulped and clung to my belt loop. The small warmth of her body cowering in the corner eased my heavy breathing.

Then we looked to see what had distracted the demons.

The young one held up the raggedly severed head of a man by his long black braids.

A look of horror and pain was frozen into the tired face. A harelip scar split open.

Fresh, bright blood dripped onto the floor where it pooled and spread.

"Uncle Leonard," Cynthia whispered through a new spate of tears and choking sobs.

The smell of blood filled the warehouse.

Two dozen demons gathered around the boy with the head, drooling green ichor as they licked at the dripping blood.

I gagged and nearly lost two days' worth of greasy pizza and beer.

Chapter 35

Spectral vampire bats make a purring sound when held.

"The body is outside. We got fresh meat for dinner!" the boy chortled. All of the demons surged out the door.

"Come on, Cynthia, we have work to do to get out of here." I grabbed her by the hand and limped toward the nearest clump of imp's bane.

Damn, that leg hurt. I needed Scrap to lick it before the boys returned and I had to fight. "Gather up all of these and throw them in the fire. Quick."

She stood beside me paralyzed with fear and shock.

"Move, kid, or we die with your uncle." I slapped her face just hard enough to get her attention.

Her big brown eyes teared. She gulped but nodded.

We ran, well, she ran, I had to drag that leg, about the huge room, collecting the bundles of twined mistletoe, holly, and ivy. Dozens of them. And I had already destroyed dozens. What had the stuff done to Scrap?

My plodding footsteps drowned out the sound of two dozen demons slurping and slathering over the dead body of a man who deserved more respect and honor in his death than this.

I cast the last bits of trailing ivy leaves into the fire just as Gregor wandered back into the room, back in human form. He wiped blood and flesh off his mouth with the back of his hand.

Even he, the leader and most reasonable of the pack, was not immune to his nature when presented with a fresh kill.

"You will be the first of your kind to die." I snapped my fingers. Scrap appeared on my palm, already half extended into the Celestial Blade.

"Can you help the leg first?"

No time, dahling. Do the best you can.

I twirled the shaft in both hands, like a baton while my imp completed his transformation. His grinning face leered back at me from the shining metal of the curved blade on the right side.

Let's kill the bastards.

Scrap couldn't hide his morbid glee.

"My thoughts exactly." An invigorating tingle started at the base of my spine and shot up and out, filling me with resolve and purpose. Adrenaline overcame the need to favor my leg.

A bat swooped across my field of vision.

I screamed and tried to hide beneath the Blade.

It's just Morris come to help. Isn't he cute?

I whimpered.

Morris won't hurt you, but that blond Sasquatch will!

Gregor dropped to all fours and leaped across the room in three bounds. The last one launched him up and forward, directly at me.

I had no choice. I had to swallow my fear. Murmuring prayers to any God or Goddess that might hear, I met his attack with a curving swish of the staff. The right-hand blade sliced neatly through his neck. His body collapsed and twitched. I yanked the blade free of muscle, bone, and gristle.

Green blood dripped onto the floor.

"Oops! I'm wearing the wrong color underwear."

Kaylor appeared at the door at the head of the pack. Two or three could enter at a time, no more.

I had my work cut out for me.

The lead demons saw Gregor's still twitching body and snarled a warning.

Too late. The left-hand blade severed Kaylor's spine in midback. He yowled in pain and confusion as his body convulsed. He scrabbled around in a circle lying on the ground. A stench arose as he lost control of his bowels and bladder.

He didn't stink any worse dead than alive.

"Next time, take a shower before you attack someone."

Another circle of the blade to adjust my grip while the surge of demons halted just outside my range.

The bat flew back and forth between us.

I clenched my jaw and locked my knees so I wouldn't run screaming into the corner. Not that I could run. But I could stand, as long as I watched my balance and locked that left knee.

"What's the matter, boys, afraid of one angry human bitch?" Sarcasm always hid my fears and hurts best.

A third demon tried to slip under the twirling blade. He lost a leg and rolled out of the action.

Behind you, babe.

Without thinking, I extended my twisting of the shaft to my back and clobbered a lurking demon.

Four down, only twenty to go.

We can hold out longer than they can, Scrap reassured me.

I wasn't so sure.

Three of the demons melted away.

Three more jumped forward. I shoved the staff to meet their chests. They dropped back, winded but still breathing.

The bat dove and tangled its claws in their head fur, yanking hard as it flew up.

The Sasquatch squealed loud enough to wake a Marine out of a dead drunk.

Better them than me. I had no hope that the Marines would come in time to rescue me. Their weapons wouldn't do more than bruise these guys.

"Left!" Cynthia screamed.

My blade flew back and forth, up and down. Two more stinking bodies littered the ground. Exhaustion crept up my arms to my shoulders and back. My leg burned all the way to the hip. I paid heed to only the next demon. My vision narrowed and turned red.

I even forgot the bat.

And then my swirling blade bit nothing more substantial than air. I stumbled at the lack of resistance.

The Celestial Blade lost substance.

Eight demon bodies lay piled around me. I caught a glimpse of a cinnamon-brown fuzzy butt tucked between hind legs disappearing out the back door as the last of the Kajiri slunk away.

Energy and strength drained out of me. Scrap disappeared. I bent double, hands on knees, gasping for breath.

Cynthia touched my back. "Tess, there's a commotion at the gate."

"Of course there is. Rescuers always come a day late and more than a dollar short." I rose to my knees. Cynthia helped me stand. I stiffened my spine and turned to face the Marines pouring into the compound.

To mask the shock and horror tremors that filled my body and mind, I whistled a jaunty tune that I couldn't name, placed Cynthia's arm around my waist while I leaned on her shoulder. Together we marched (limped) out to meet the Marines.

I stumbled at the doorway and fell into Gollum's arms.

Totally off balance, I dragged us both to the ground. He rubbed my back and held my shoulders while I vomited and retched way beyond empty.

Chapter 36

"How did the demons get Cynthia?" Showered and dosed with three cups of coffee, I sat on the sofa in the living room of my suite with Gollum. Cynthia stretched out, sound asleep, with her head in my lap. Neither one of us wanted to let go of the other.

Scrap had shown up long enough to lick the hideous wound on my leg. My blood revived him a little. Enough for him to take on color and pop out to feed elsewhere.

"I don't know what happened. I'm sorry. I should never have left her alone," Gollum apologized for about the fiftieth time. "She was with Sapa over at the office. She must have been returning here, after dark. They grabbed her between the two buildings."

He took a big gulp of coffee. "Leonard showed up. I called him like you said I should. We went over to the office to get Cynthia. She wasn't there. Sapa was agitated. Pacing, growling at everyone, unwilling to leave the blanket to Donovan's goons. Leonard took off."

"He must have hiked up the hill to Fort Snoqualmie and sneaked in under the radar of the Marines," I said on a regretful sigh. "The boys caught him inside the fence and . . . and their demonic nature took over. They couldn't stop themselves." My coffee threatened to come up again as I remembered all the gory details.

We endured an eternity of silence, wrapped in our own thoughts and horrors.

"Is this what my life is going to be like from now on? Horrible deaths and torture for people I like and respect, and then I have to go out and kill monsters who appear to be just misguided teenagers on the outside."

"Innocents you don't know will die, too. More of them will die if you do nothing. The demons are on the move. Somehow, they've found a way around the guarded portals. This rogue portal must bypass the chat room." Gollum stared into his coffee cup as if startled that it was empty. "Either that or the Warriors of the Celestial Blade have become incredibly lax and complacent."

"I don't think so. From what little communication I've had with the Citadel, they seem besieged. Under heavy stress and pressure at the portal they guard."

"Feints to keep the Sisters from noticing their use of the rogue portal?"

I shrugged. We sat in silence a while longer. Chills took over my body, upsetting my stomach again.

"I quit. I've had enough blood and gore to last a lifetime. Cynthia is safe. The blanket is safe. This job is done. I quit." I rose, settling Cynthia's head on a pillow, then headed toward the bedroom, still limping. I needed another shower.

"I don't think it works that way, Tess," Gollum said quietly. "What are you going to do about Scrap?"

"Send him back to his own dimension. He can pick a new warrior." A hole opened in my emotional gut. Scrap had filled a big part of my life in the last three years. He'd helped me stop thinking about Dill every minute of the day and get on with my life and my career.

"I've got a book to finish. The demons destroyed my laptop. Can I borrow your machine?" I'd lusted after the top-of-the-line computer since I first saw it.

"No backups?"

"Backups!" I dashed for the pile of dirty clothes in the corner. A search of my jeans pockets turned up the flash drive. "Thank Goddess for long habits." I sank to the floor in relief. For a minute I'd feared it lost or destroyed in the battle.

A bit of my depression left. I could work. I'd forget while I worked.

For how long?

"You are wrong about Cynthia and the blanket. Neither of them is safe as long as Donovan Estevez has possession of the blanket," Gollum reminded me. "Humanity may not be safe while Estevez has possession of the blanket.

I think the blanket is the seal to the demon portals. No one is working on it, so the seal is weak."

"Where is the bastard, by the way? Do the Marines still have him, or has Homeland Security taken over?"

"He's free. They let him go. Apparently, his story of being blackmailed by the 'terrorists in search of a homeland' held up. I believe he went back to his house."

"Which is where?"

"On a lake island between here and Dry Falls. I hear it's guarded like a fortress."

"How . . . how did the Marines explain the demon bodies I left behind?"

"I don't think they did. They probably swore themselves to secrecy and burned the remains before the press showed up. What little press they allowed in. Most of the reporters—the legitimate ones anyway—packed up and went home with a story Vlieger spun and altered dramatically."

We sat in silence again, I on the floor by the dirty laundry, Gollum in the armchair with his big feet on the coffee table.

"You should get some sleep," he said quietly.

"I don't think I dare." Every time I closed my eyes for the briefest of moments, I lived again the sickening sight of demon Sasquatch lunging for me, their fangs dripping green saliva; their dead bodies dripping green blood; Leonard's severed head dripping red gore.

I lunged for the toilet, vomiting again. The stink nearly set me to retching again.

Vaguely, I heard a telephone ring. I didn't care. I just wanted everything to end.

"Your mother," Gollum handed me a cell phone while I lay on the floor, resting my cheek against the cool tiles.

Limply, I held the tiny receiver to my ear.

A spate of angry, garbled French stabbed at my brain.

"You spoke French to her!" I accused Gollum.

"What was I supposed to do? She reverted to it when I gave her the news that you'd been kidnapped. Really weird dialect of it, though." He shrugged and left me in private with my mother and the crude invention of a language she thought she spoke.

I let Mom babble on for several minutes, picking out an actual phrase now and then. When she finally wound down, I replied in English, reassuring her that I was indeed safe, I had not been harmed. But no, I was not coming home on the next plane.

After a bit of negotiation, she agreed to ship me some clothes so I could attend the World Fantasy Convention in a few days. And yes, she would file a claim with my insurance company for the loss of my laptop.

Or rather she'd tell my sister Cecilia to tell my dad to do it. Maybe I should call him in the morning and make sure the message got through. Cecilia was good at "forgetting" things that might help me.

We talked for a long time. Slowly, I absorbed my mother's love for me. Warmth returned to my limbs. My stomach settled; the horror began to fade.

Despite her eccentricities, her irritating habits, her need to manipulate and control, my mom loved me. And I loved her.

When my world and balance tilted back toward normal, I allowed her to hang up.

"Scrap?" I called when we finally disconnected. "Scrap, what's my schedule?"

No answer.

The imp, my best friend, had to recover in his own way, much as I did.

"Gollum, get on the Internet and order me a new computer. My credit card is in my purse. I'm going to bed."

Only then did I notice the fat, fluffy white cat sitting in his lap. The beast blinked green eyes at me. It opened its mouth in a satisfied grin as if he'd just swallowed the canary.

I hate cats, Scrap whimpered into my mind. He sounded stuffy and insecure.

Chapter 37

"If the blanket is a metaphysical seal on the demon portal, why don't the demons just burn the blanket?" I asked at dawn as I stretched out in preparation for a run.

Gollum roused himself from where he'd fallen asleep in the armchair, his laptop across his knees, the screen gone black in sleep mode. He looked all tousled and vulnerable, approachable, likable.

Then he adjusted his glasses back onto his blade of a nose and put an impenetrable emotional barrier between himself and the world.

His cat peeked out from beneath the chair. I hissed at it.

It hissed back at me.

If the beast was keeping Scrap from me, then I wanted it gone. I'd spent too much time without him in that creepy warehouse at Fort Snoqualmie up on the plateau.

"You say something?" Gollum looked just a little baffled and confused, but his eyes focused clearly.

I wondered briefly if he truly needed the glasses.

I repeated my question.

"For the same reason they didn't destroy it the first time they took possession of it." He straightened up and placed the laptop on the coffee table. Idly, he reached down to scratch the cat's ears. It leaned into his caress and purred.

"Which is?" I asked, ignoring the interplay between the man and his pet.

For a moment I wished Scrap were more tangible so we could pet and cuddle like Gollum and his cat.

"I haven't figured that out yet. But there has to be a reason why the demons protect the blanket even if they work just as hard to keep it out of the hands of a weaver."

"I'm going for a run. You might wake Cynthia. We'll go to breakfast when I get back."

Our charge still slept on the sofa. At some point he'd placed a blanket over her and she had cuddled into it, looking once more like the child she was rather than the tortured adult she had been forced to become yesterday.

"Thank you for taking care of her."

"Breakfast, yes. Good idea," he mumbled. The cat meowed, demanding its own meal.

"She'll be safe here for a while. You can go back to your own room and clean up. You know you could have slept there last night. And feed the cat there."

"You might have needed me. I expected you to have nightmares." He lifted the cat and held it close to his face, all the while scratching its ears.

"I didn't." I'd had nightmares. But I'd dealt with them in my own way, by outlining the next scene of my book in my head. If all those horrible things happened to my characters, then perhaps I could persuade myself they hadn't happened to me.

I couldn't dismiss the burning demon wound. It would leave a scar. I was growing a collection of them. I'd run on it anyway. If I let it interfere with my life, then the demons had won.

"Scrap seems allergic to that cat. I can't afford to compromise his well being."

My slow run through town and along the lake, with frequent breaks to rest my leg, cleared my mind. While my feet made slight indentations in the salt-encrusted sand I looked for traces of the cave I had found across the water. Too many cracks and crevices defined the landscape for me to find the specific spot where ghosts had loomed and Donovan's minion had shot at me.

All the while, the briny scent of the lake water filled and refreshed me. People had been coming here for many generations to find healing in the waters. A lot of them had stayed to continue the beneficial effects of both the lake water and the slow, low stress, pace of life here.

Until Donovan decided to build a casino.

I could see men swarming over the half-finished structure today. He hadn't wasted any time getting back to work.

Maybe his primary concern was merely the financial commitment to the casino. Maybe he was merely another victim of the overzealous demon children.

Maybe he was more.

I had no way to tell at this point. My focus had to be to keep Cynthia and the blanket safe. Permanently.

I turned away from the lake, crossed the deserted highway, and sent my feet pounding along a dirt trail. Memories of my first visit to this area flooded through me.

Dill grubbing in the dirt for a choice geological specimen and coming up with a near perfect arrowhead. We'd exclaimed over the treasure, hugged, and kissed.

Sister Mary showing me how to properly hold a bow and nock the arrow with a similar broad arrowhead. "It won't kill a demon, but it will slow him down while your imp rests," she explained patiently as she guided my hands to find a proper aim for the straw target fifty yards distant.

Dill patiently climbing a rock face, expertly seeking hand and toeholds. I waited anxiously at the base of the cliff, my heart in my mouth as he braced himself with one hand and his feet, tiny pickax in his dominant left hand. Dirt fell into my face as he chipped away the effluvia that held a fossil in place. Then his wild and exultant slide back to me with an ugly lump of rock in his hand that looked like every other rock but delighted him.

Sister Electra sparring with me, forcing me to push myself beyond my physical and mental limits. Me shouting in triumph as I finally found an opening in her defenses and sent her sprawling on the ground, both of us panting from the effort and wiping sweat from our eyes.

My ankle twisted on the uneven trail and my weakened leg nearly gave out on me. I turned around and headed back toward the lake. My body told me I'd had enough exercise. My mind rebelled, wanting more physical effort to help banish the memories.

Little puffs of red dust sprang up with each pounding footstep. The dust was real. Here. Tangible. Just like the black clouds scudding across the sky to the west, obscuring the top of a nameless peak. A flash of lightning revealed jagged and tortured rock formations. The sharp smell of ozone replaced the dusty dryness, purging the air and my mind of the past that tried to rule my thoughts and actions today.

MY RENTAL SUV WAS PARKED in front of my room at the lodge when I returned. Lieutenant Vlieger in crisp fatigues, along with a man wearing a dark suit and sunglasses, sat on the steps leading to my room. The suit positively screamed Homeland Security or FBI. They rose, as one, at my approach.

"Ms. Noncoiré, on behalf of the Marine Corps, I extend to you an apology for the ill treatment we gave you. We have restored your car and offer you a check for the destruction of your personal property." Vlieger almost saluted as he proffered a slim white envelope.

"Thank you," I replied. What else could I say? "Tell me," I said after staring at the envelope for a moment. "Why did you have to trash the car?"

"Profile vehicle. White SUVs are a favorite among certain terrorist groups," the suit replied.

"My Marines were careful to disassemble the vehicle and keep the parts in order. We put it back together without damage," Vlieger added. "You should not have to pay for any damages to the rental agency."

"Whatever." I tried to push past them.

"Ms. Noncoiré, we do have a few more questions for you." The suit snaked out an arm to block my passage.

"Your questions will wait until after breakfast." I stared at his arm as if it offended me and smelled bad.

"The security of our nation may be at stake."

"It will wait until I've eaten. Or do you want me fainting in your lap from low blood sugar?"

"The lieutenant and I will join you."

"Does he have a name?" I asked Vlieger.

"Ben Miller," snapped the suit. He had fewer manners than Scrap.

Ten minutes later, Gollum, Cynthia, and I took places in a booth across the street at the steak house. I wore my hair twisted up in the comb. I wanted to see everything and everybody for what they were.

An aura surrounded Cynthia's head. In just the right light I almost detected an ancient woman of great wisdom overlaying her personality. Scary and yet satisfying. She was easing into her role as the weaver. Or her shamanistic heritage was showing through.

The suit and the Marine were forced to take places at a table adjacent to us. They had no compunction against moving the table so that it butted up against our booth and effectively blocked our exit.

Miller finally removed his sunglasses and placed them in his breast pocket. He turned pale brown eyes on me, assessing me, trying to peer past my reserves into my soul.

That was something I allowed no one. Not since I'd left the Citadel anyway. I forced my face into neutral, but felt my spine stiffen and tingle with wariness.

Where the hell was Scrap?

At least I couldn't see anything unusual or otherworldly around either of them.

"Ms. Noncoiré, explain to me the significance of the—er—rather interesting bodies we found inside Fort Snoqualmie," Miller stated rather than asked the moment the waitress had taken our orders. He didn't seem concerned that she hovered nearby with a full coffeepot ready to pour while she eavesdropped.

I looked at Gollum for inspiration.

He shrugged. "You might as well tell them the truth. They'll put their own spin on it anyway."

Cynthia and I both raised eyebrows at him.

"Illegal genetics experiments that failed. The monsters ended up killing each other."

"That's what we thought," Miller said, taking a long drink of the super-strength coffee, black, no sugar.

The waitress must have used the pot they reserved for local law enforcement rather than the milder one she used for tourists. I had to dump extra cream and sugar in mine to make it palatable. Scrap would have loved the leftovers.

Where was the imp anyway? I'd never known him to stay away this long. Even when the imp's bane separated us, he hovered close by. Or, rather, played in the rafters. I had a brief vision of him swinging from them like Tarzan swooping through the trees.

But then he'd never had to recover from such an extensive battle with demons before.

I missed him.

"What about the bodies of the men we, er, Estevez shot?" Vlieger burst into the conversation. He, too, took his coffee black with no sugar.

I wondered if coffee had become the new contest to prove manhood.

"More genetics experiments and Kevlar, or maybe the new carbon fiber armor. You didn't kill them. In the confusion they melted away to nurse their wounds. They'll be back to fight another day."

Thank Goddess our food arrived. The waitress took her time refilling coffee cups.

"What about the kid? What's their interest in her?" Miller spat. Or was it an accusation? Every statement or question seemed to be an accusation.

"My name is Cynthia Stalking Moon," the girl jumped in. She faced the man defiantly, demanding he acknowledge her as a person and not just a victim, or thing.

"Where do you fit into this puzzle, Ms. Stalking Moon?"

"I . . . I don't know for sure. I think they want my DNA. I come from a long line of shamans. We have . . . powers." She lied. I knew it. Gollum knew it. Did Miller?

On the other hand, maybe she didn't lie. Maybe Sapa singled her out because of her genes; more than just being of Indian blood, she might be a direct descendant of the old woman who had originally woven the blanket. The old woman had to have been a shaman to maintain the power of the blanket.

Curiouser and curiouser.

"I'm the last of my line," Cynthia added. That was true enough. "The last of the great shamans with special powers of insight and prophecy." She fell into the now familiar chant of her people reciting old legends.

Miller looked askance at that statement.

"There are more things on this earth than you can perceive with your limited imagination, Miller," I added, trying to sound spooky and cryptic like an old horror film. Then I took a big bite of toast so I wouldn't have to say more.

"The study of anthropology has revealed a number of instances when humans have been able to reach beyond the realm of what we call reality to tap powers and secrets." Gollum put on his professor face and proceeded to expound in big words and the most boring tone I'd ever heard. Usually, he had more animation with his favorite subject.

But then, this was information that Miller didn't want.

Vlieger, however, looked very interested. He'd been there and seen some pretty weird things yesterday.

"As you explore Fort Snoqualmie, you might be looking for a back door, probably underground," I said casually. "The boys kept bringing in fresh pizza and beer. And pot. Lots of pot. And Cynthia." And they always smelled like lake water.

I examined Cynthia speculatively.

She shrugged and mouthed, "Later."

"Where is this genetics lab?" Miller demanded. He'd barely touched his sausage, pancakes, and eggs.

"I have no idea. Why don't you ask Donovan Estevez?"

"Maybe we will. In the meantime, don't leave town." Miller pushed back from the table, giving me an exit.

"Sorry. I have professional commitments in Madison, Wisconsin. I'm flying out of Moses Lake with connections to Seattle on Wednesday." I sat placidly eating my own meal. "I'll be back Sunday night, maybe Monday early depending on the weather, unless my agent has other plans and projects that demand more time."

Miller threw two twenties on the table and stalked off.

Vlieger scooted closer, all traces of yesterday's antagonism vanished. "So, what really happened up there?"

"My kidnappers are demons who came through an underground portal. I allowed them to keep me hostage so I could learn their true motives for claiming the fort. When they kidnapped Cynthia and tried to molest her, and killed and ate her uncle, I called up my imp from another dimension and slew them one and all," I said with a straight face. "Well, maybe not all of them. I think a few retreated back down the portal."

Vlieger burst out laughing. "Good one. I can see why you write fantasy fiction. With your imagination, you'll go far. I kept one of your books by the way. One of the damaged ones that we paid for. Not bad. Not bad at all."

He, too, threw a twenty on the table and left.

Gollum and I breathed a big sigh of relief in unison.

Chapter 38

I'm going to kill that cat.

Cats are evil.

I'd just finished a good feed in the lake and returned to my babe to find the cat crouched in the middle of Tess's bed, waiting for me. If I dare move from this shelf above the bed, it will attack. If I leave the shelf, I have to abandon access to the box of tissues. The longer I stay the more my nose runs. My eyes are swelling shut.

I can't smell anything!

I don't have the strength yet to fly.

It just stares at me, unblinking, with those vicious green eyes, like I'm a mouse or something. It won't even tell me its name.

"That's a secret," it says. "That's precious," it says.

Big honking deal. How important can a name be? I mean, even the demons tell people their names.

Gollum has been duped by this cat. It is not a pet. It keeps Gollum as a pet. Gollum is not evil. But that damned cat is.

If I could transform, I'd kill the beast.

Not enough strength or rest. I need to eat more. Where is my babe? She'll give me beer and OJ. That always helps.

But I can't get past the damn cat. Achoooooo!

And then, as if by magic, he leaps from the bed. In two bounds it lands in Gollum's lap where he collapsed in a near boneless heap. The cat has stolen all his starch.

I knew it. It is an evil thief of human energy.

"You know, Tess, if I don't start weaving on that blanket, humanity is going to lose its integrity, dignity, and honesty," Cynthia asserted, hands on hips, feet grounded soundly, and head cocked in that all-knowing teenage way she had.

I'm afraid I snorted at her statement. "When have you noticed a lot of integrity, dignity, and honesty in humanity? Have you watched the news lately?" I mimicked her stance.

"My point exactly. Sapa should have gone looking for a new weaver a century ago. But the old woman was still alive, just not very effective."

We entered a staring contest. All the while, my feet itched to show her the cave where I believed the old woman had lived and worked.

"Those qualities are already woven into the blanket," Gollum said, peering up from a book. He had a pile of them around "his" chair in my living room. And the bloody cat in his lap. He seemed to have moved in, except for his clothes and toiletries. "Humanity can still tap into those qualities, if they choose. The blanket has another, deeper purpose that we need to address."

"Such as?" both Cynthia and I asked.

"Such as sealing a portal to the demon dimensions. It is precisely the integrity, dignity, and honesty of humanity that allows the portal to be sealed." He returned to his book as if he'd had the last word.

"A rogue portal that the Citadel doesn't know about because it was sealed centuries before the Citadel was founded, and bypasses the chat room," I mused. That would explain a lot.

"That still doesn't explain why Donovan doesn't destroy the blanket," I said.

"Because he's half human," Cynthia replied.

Out of the mouths of babes.

Gollum put down his book and stared at the girl. His hands stroked the cat in rhythm with his breathing as if the action helped him think. Or maybe the cat's purr soothed and ordered his thoughts. "Of course. If Donovan destroys the blanket, he destroys half of himself. He's not trying to go back to the demon world, nor is he trying to integrate completely with the human world. He wants a homeland for half-breeds, like himself."

"There's a story in history ..." The brief glimpse I had of an answer passed. "Come on, I need to show both of you something."

"I need to start weaving."

"You need to come with us." I threw Cynthia my running jacket and grabbed a sweater. Gollum could fend for himself.

An hour later Gollum boosted Cynthia and then me up the last boulder to the ledge outside the cave. Cynthia had delayed our trek by constantly stopping to gather bits of grass and plants, bird feathers, a tuft of animal hair, anything that might enhance the blanket when twisted together into a rough yarn.

Instinctively I looked up the cliff face, ready to duck at the first sign of observers with guns.

As Gollum hauled himself over the edge of the rock, he paused, still supporting himself with his arms and shoulders at an awkward angle. He was stronger than I thought. He studied the rocks beside his hands for a long moment before continuing up to our level.

"Looks like a bullet hit the dirt right there," he commented casually.

Automatically, I touched my arm where a rock chip had sliced me on the ricochet. It had healed cleaner and faster than the two dog bites. I didn't want to think about the demon bite. Scrap's ministrations helped, but it would still take a long time to heal. I had needed Gollum's broad shoulders and well-muscled arms to help me over the last barrier.

Why hadn't I noticed his strength before? He had to do more of a workout than just tai chi.

Gollum raised his eyebrows, keeping his eyes on my arm.

I nodded briefly, then turned to face the crease in the cliff. "In here."

"Doesn't look like much of a cave to me," Cynthia said skeptically.

"Trust me. It's bigger than it looks."

I paused before ducking inside. "Please do not reject us," I pleaded with the unseen guardians of this place. "We mean you no harm. We honor this place and will not desecrate it."

Then I swallowed deeply and entered the narrow defile. I didn't really expect the ghosts to heed me, but it couldn't hurt.

Goose bumps rose on my arms and back the moment I moved from sunshine to shadow; far more than the change in temperature from outside to inside would account for. Gollum shivered the moment he stood upright within the dim confines of the cave. Cynthia, however, poked into the ashy remnants of the fire without visible concern.

"An old campfire. So what. It could be two weeks or two centuries old." She shrugged and scuffed the dirt.

"Can you tell if it's old or new?" I asked Gollum.

He was already on his knees, sifting through the rockfall. In moments he had collected a hand full of . . . of pottery shards. They looked like rock chips to my uneducated eye.

"This looks precontact, but I'd need to do some tests in a lab to be sure. People are turning out some great fakes these days." He held up one of the larger shards with traces of pigment on it that might have represented a lizard, or a snake, or rippling water. Or it might just be a squiggle.

"If it's precontact, and the construction above caused the rockfall, can we get the casino shut down?" I asked.

"Probably. There's enough here to call the state archaeologist and get an investigation started." He came to one knee, ready to rise to his full height.

Suddenly, the temperature in the cave dropped at least another ten degrees. We both froze in place.

"What?" Cynthia asked, still oblivious to the eerie chill.

Mist developed around the fire, drifted a moment, then coalesced into three vaguely human forms.

I caught glimpses of long dark hair and feathers, bone beads and leather.

Pressure fell on my chest. My breathing came in short sharp pants. I had to leave. I had to go outside. There wasn't enough air in this place.

Gollum, too, breathed with difficulty.

"Leave the shards. We've got to get out of here," I panted.

"What?" Cynthia protested. Then her eyes grew large.

I saw understanding dawn in her gaze.

She smiled hugely and walked right up to the trio of ghosts. "Hi, guys, are you here to protect me?"

Tess is in danger. I can feel it. I have to brave the cat to go to my babe.

I have battled and bested all forms of demons in the chat room. I survived my Mum. I can handle one lowly cat.

"I am not a lowly creature," it deigns to advise me. Its tail swishes and churns. It narrows its eyes and bunches its muscles, ready to pounce.

"Tell me your name and I won't kill you, this time," I snarl at it.

"Sit still so I can kill you, imp."

That's it. I take a deep breath, unfurl my wings—grown quite a bit after the last battle, and I got six more warts—and leap.

I skim past the highest reach of the cat's paws, lean down, and grab a pawful of tail hair.

Gleefully, I pop over to my babe, trophy in hand.

Chapter 39

The Incas and Aztecs used slave labor to collect bat fur as clothing decoration. They probably used only pelts from large fruit eating bats as most do not have enough fur to make collecting economically viable.

The cave might have warmed a degree or two. Nothing more. Cynthia might feel at home here with the spectral guardians. Gollum and I still were not welcome.

"What?" Cynthia turned her big dark eyes on me once more. "They won't hurt you."

"Tell that to them." I jerked my head in the direction of the three solemn figures who had moved into a semicircle around the rockfall.

I heard mad laughter in the back of my mind. It sounded a lot, more than a lot, like Dill when he'd told one of his outrageous puns that insulted the entire world without being totally offensive because he touched a universal truth. He was good at that.

Suddenly I wondered why I had found his humor so endearing. In retrospect, he seemed immature and unsympathetic, almost racist. And definitely insulting.

The three native ghosts remained the only ones I could see. If Dillwyn was present, he wasn't visible. I chose to ignore him.

"Listen, guys, these are my friends. They take care of me in the outside world. I welcome them, so you should, too," Cynthia addressed her new friends.

They remained implacable.

"You might be a little more respectful of them," Gollum whispered. "Ghosts are not usually in tune with teenage flip attitudes and vocabulary."

Cynthia rolled her eyes. But she turned back to the ghosts and bowed ever so slightly. Just a token, barely a show of respect at all. "Listen, my friends, I'm the new weaver. Times have changed. I've got to live out there as well as weave the blanket."

"If we ever get our hands on it again," I muttered.

"*When* we get our hands on it again," Cynthia insisted. "The dog, Shunka Sapa, chose me. I am the new weaver. I need Tess' and Gollum's help. I invite them here. You have to accept them."

Where is the Shunka Sapa? Only the dog of the ages may reveal this cave to the weaver.

The feeling of menace increased. I really wanted out of the cave. More than that, I wanted Scrap to recover and return to my side. I didn't feel safe without him anymore.

"The dog is protecting the blanket. It was stolen from you when the old weaver died," Gollum answered for Cynthia.

Many times over the centuries the dog and his descendants have brought new weavers to us. Always the dog. Never has a weaver been disrespectful to us. Never has the weaver needed assistance beyond what we can give.

"Well, times have changed, guys," Cynthia retorted. "It's a whole new world out there. I'm about the only one Sapa could find who will respect you and the blanket and everything it stands for. Now either get with the picture or get lost."

Out of the mouths of babes. Or did I say that already? The misty ghosts faded for a moment. I sensed, could almost hear, an indignant conversation among them.

Abruptly, the cave warmed. Air returned to my lungs. The lifting of the pressure of unwelcomeness made me feel so light I almost lost my balance. Gollum staggered, too. I grabbed his arm and kept him upright.

I may have leaned in to him, holding myself vertical as much as helping him.

If you are to be the new guardians of the weaver, then you must dream and learn.

My knees turned to jelly, and I found myself on the cave floor, fighting a huge yawn.

I OPENED MY EYES TO find myself, Gollum, and Cynthia in a green landscape filled with sharp contrasts of rock and prairie, river, cliff, and plateau.

A steady rain pounded us yet didn't seem to get us wet. The sky looked black and ominous, but it was full daylight—or as bright as those clouds would allow.

"Where are we?" Nothing looked familiar. My sense of direction, up and down, right and left, forward and back, tilted about five degrees to the left. The colors altered by the same measure as well. And I didn't even have the comb with me. The slight tug by the North Pole on my senses had disappeared as well.

I shivered a little from the bite in the air. Early spring. I guessed the season by the depth of the green and the chill.

"I think the better question is, when are we?" Gollum replied.

Found you! Scrap chortled. He bounced into view, more solid and bigger than I had ever seen him. He stood about four feet tall instead of the twelve inches I was used to. His wings had grown, too; they reached high above his head and draped below his four-taloned feet. Something else was wrong, but I couldn't pinpoint it.

He waved a fist full of white hairs, then let them scatter to the rising wind.

"So that's what he looks like!" Gollum gasped.

"Hey, he's cute. Can I pet him?" Cynthia asked.

"He's a pain in the ass and not normally this big or solid," I snarled.

"As solid as you, babe," Scrap chortled out loud. "But only in this dimension. Time warps things."

"What is happening, Scrap?" My senses remained distorted, but Scrap was here. With Scrap, I could defend myself and my companions.

"You jumped a couple of dimensions," he replied.

"Where's your cigar, Scrap?"

"Wrong time, wrong dimension. No tobacco here."

"Then what do we have here?"

"Floods!" Gollum shouted. He grabbed Cynthia by the elbow and began running uphill.

I didn't wait to see what had alarmed him. Hot on his heels I registered a roar in the background. A roar that had been there ever since I arrived, but I hadn't noticed it as separate from my other disorientation.

We crested the closest hill. Instinctively, I looked toward the river that wound around the hills below us. If anything, the water level seemed lower than my first glance moments ago.

"Gollum, what's happening?" I pointed toward the water.

Sure enough, more and more damp rock on the cliff sides was exposed.

And the roar came from behind us.

I whirled around. Off in the distance, many miles away, I caught a hint of rapid movement.

A brown wall of water raced across the landscape, gouging out a new riverbed. It leveled hills. Boulders as big as houses tumbled like feathers. People, animals, villages—everything was swept up in the relentless surge of water.

"I think we are watching the flood that nearly destroyed my people twelve thousand years ago," Cynthia whispered in awe and terror.

"The ice dam over in Montana must have broken, releasing more water than fills all of Lake Superior in one gush. It's forging a new riverbed," I quoted one of the pamphlets I'd picked up in Half Moon Lake.

The old river behind us continued to drain away. Soon, only a necklace of mineral lakes would be left. We were probably standing on the site where Donovan Estevez and his demon cohort would build a casino twelve thousand years in the future.

"The real question is, why are we here?" Gollum asked. He peered through the onslaught of rain.

"Over there," Scrap said. He pointed north.

Movement. A long line of people trudging along the ridgeline, perhaps two miles away, approached us. Too far to see details.

But Scrap elongated and thinned. His head and wings took on a metallic cast. His wings became curved blades with spikes sticking out of the outside edge.

"Those are demons," Gollum informed us.

"I guessed. Scrap doesn't do his Celestial Blade thing unless a demon or great evil is present."

"Sasquatch demons," Cynthia breathed. "I bet they've got the blanket. Maybe we can keep them from stealing it."

"No," Scrap spoke from within the blade that balanced so easily in my hand. His voice sounded deeper, more solemn and filled with portent. "We can only observe the past. We cannot change it. In this dimension we are all as transparent to the inhabitants as I usually am in your true time and place."

I gulped and began swinging the blade, ready to defend myself and my companions.

"Won't work, babe." Scrap sounded his usual sarcastic self. "You can't touch these guys in their own time. They belong here. You don't."

"If it won't work, then why did you transform?"

"Because it is his nature," Gollum said.

The demons came closer. True demons rather than half-breeds, close to twelve feet tall.

I drew Cynthia and Gollum behind me while I continued to keep the blade in motion.

Sure enough, the lead Sasquatch, obviously male with huge testicles hanging between legs half hidden by auburn fur, clutched the blanket to his chest.

I peered closely at the textile as the demons passed us, seemingly oblivious to our presence. But some of the smaller Sasquatch, possibly half-breeds, looked about nervously.

The blanket looked more vibrant than I remembered, full of color from dried grasses, tree bark, bird feathers, and multicolored wild goat wool. Especially the bird feathers.

Maybe the blanket rippled because the demon who clutched it bounced as he jog-trotted along the plateau. Maybe.

But it looked to me as if it vibrated with life.

Three of the demons pushed ahead of their leader. They joined hands (paws?) in a circle and began chanting something in a weird language full of pops, clicks, and grunts. A very similar language to the one the demons who'd kidnapped me had spoken.

The ground beneath my feet rocked. I fought for balance. The land heaved. I had to jab the Celestial Blade into the rain-slick turf to stay upright.

Gollum and Cynthia flopped facedown, clinging to the grass with desperate fingers.

The demons seemed unaffected by the quake. But the three chanting ones broke their circle and stepped back. A jagged hole opened where they had been standing. A metal ladder led down that hole deep into the earth.

"The demon portal," I breathed. "Did you get that invocation, language guy?" I asked Gollum.

Abruptly, the world went black, and I tumbled into nothing.

Thank the Goddess I still had my hands on the blade.

Chapter 40

I came up blind and swinging.

"Easy, Tess. Back off." Gollum's voice.

Light glimmered around the edges of my perceptions.

"Did they get you, too?" I asked. Why did my hands feel numb and empty?

"We're back home, Tess. Back in the cave."

"Scrap?"

"I can't see him," Gollum said.

"I can't either," Cynthia chimed in.

"I can't see anything." I rubbed my eyes. A little more light. Concentrated in a vertical line off to my left.

Dimension blindness. It will pass. That was one of the Indian ghosts who had started this nightmare.

I closed my eyes and thought for several moments. *Yes!* The tug of the North Pole on my nerve endings was back. My feet found a rock-solid balance. I breathed normally.

Then I opened my eyes. I picked out a few more details in the cave. Rockfall, the pile of sherds Gollum had collected, the remains of an ancient fire that had burned for millennia until the cave-in killed the old woman and sent her dog in search of a new weaver.

That rockfall was the beginning of this entire adventure. A collapse caused by construction of the casino above. Construction directly on top of a demon portal that the Sisterhood of the Celestial Blade didn't know about.

They didn't need to know about it until a few months ago because the weaver and the blanket sealed the portal.

The blanket still existed. We had a new weaver. So why wasn't the portal closed?

Because Cynthia wasn't actively weaving the blanket and Sapa wasn't ripping out her new work each day so that the blanket was never finished. Finish the blanket?

The world comes to an end.

Stop weaving the blanket?

The demon portal opens and demons return en masse. That might well be the end of the world, too.

"I need a drink," I muttered.

"It's almost dark. I think we can safely go outside now without being blinded by the sun," Gollum said.

"Did you remember the incantation the demons spoke to open the portal?" I asked.

Gollum looked at me, puzzled. "I can't learn any language that quickly."

"But you spoke Lakota dialect when you channeled the legend." The myth might belong to all the Indian tribes, but apparently only the Lakota had recorded it and allowed the outside world to think it their own.

"I don't remember a word of it other than what I've learned from listening to the recording."

"Shit. I think we're going to need that incantation."

"But we don't want to open the portal, we want to close it, and keep it closed," Cynthia said.

"Demons aren't very smart," Gollum said, adopting his professor tone. "They probably can't remember two different chants. They'd use the same one to open and close the portal. Like the word 'Aloha' means both hello and good-bye."

"What day is it, Scrap?" I asked, stepping out into the twilight, grateful that the cave mouth faced east, and not west where the sun set. I couldn't find Scrap with my eyes or my other senses. He must have done his disappearing act again after transforming.

"My watch says Tuesday, October twenty-seven," Gollum replied.

"Shit. I've got to leave in the morning for the con. Let's go get a little bit drunk while I pack."

Three hours later, as I filled my suitcase with the clothes Mom had sent to me and drank from a bottle of single malt scotch I'd found in the local liquor store, Gollum entertained Cynthia with stories of ancient man in Europe. The cat perched on his lap as if it was seated on a throne.

I half listened, marveling at the man's talent for dealing with an adolescent who would really rather be with her monster dog.

Sapa still guarded the blanket over at Donovan's office. The guards with guns kept Sapa and me from stealing the blanket. The dog kept Donovan's goons from damaging or removing it to another location.

So why didn't the goons just shoot the dog? Because he'd been touched by the otherworld. Bullets would bounce off his hide, like they did with demons.

Balance, Scrap reminded me from his hidey-hole. *Even demons respect the need for balance.*

A loud argument next door interrupted my errant thoughts. I thought I heard echoes of Donovan's voice in the verbal melee. Specific words eluded me.

Anything that concerned that man now concerned me.

I placed a glass from the bathroom against the wall and pressed my ear against it, hoping to use the old movie detective trick to pick out the nature of the argument. The volume rose, but the words did not become any clearer.

When I stepped away from the wall, I noticed the volume had risen even without the aid of the glass.

Gollum and Cynthia were engrossed in an argument over the intelligence of Neanderthal Man versus Cro-Magnon. Gollum sipped at his glass of scotch quite regularly, and he slurred his words. Between the two of us, we'd drunk over half the bottle. I hadn't had more than one glass. No wonder Cynthia seemed to be winning the argument that Neanderthal was smarter than normally given credit for.

I stepped out onto the back deck overlooking the lake. A tiny slice of a moon drifted in the autumn sky surrounded by a blanket of stars. A fresh breeze ruffled the lake and brought the sharp scent of mineral salts to me—an odor I would now always associate with Sasquatch demons rather than the healing attributed to those mineral salts. The window in the suite adjacent to mine was open. About two feet of space separated my deck from theirs.

If I climbed onto the railing, I could step over the space and get directly beneath that window.

"We're cutting you off, Estevez. No more delays, no more money. We're through. If you don't come through in two weeks, we take over," Vern Abrams shouted.

"If you'd only listen," Donovan pleaded.

"We've listened enough to your platitudes and innuendos. No more," Myrna Abrams added. Her strident voice nearly pierced my eardrum.

Someone shoved the sliding glass door open, then rammed it closed again. Donovan stood at the railing gulping air. Even in the dim light, I could tell from his posture that he wasn't happy. Then he slammed his fist into the top rail. The varnished cedar pole, nearly three inches in diameter bent, almost buckled.

I stepped back into the shadows, unwilling to be a part of or witness to his violence. His physical strength alarmed me.

"Who?"

My movement must have alerted him.

"Just me. Tess. I couldn't help but overhear. I'm sorry. I wasn't deliberately eavesdropping." Like hell I wasn't. But I couldn't tell him that.

"Abrams is my banker. He's just refused to extend the financing on the casino. There's no way I can finish on deadline, thanks to those impatient and stupid fools. Homeland Security still has the construction site road-blocked until they finish their investigation. Heaven only knows when that will be." He took a deep breath to steady himself.

Did he mean that Homeland Security were the impatient and stupid fools, or the Kajiri—the half-blood demons?

"I'm ruined, Tess."

"Your software company?"

"Mortgaged to the hilt to finance the casino. My house, even the car. I . . . I'm . . . I need to be alone. I can't hope that you will learn to love me when I'm broke." He vaulted the railing, landing softly on the sand, then ran off into the night.

I gulped, more than a little confused. There was that "L" word. Call me a sucker, but there was more between Donovan and myself than I wanted to admit. He hadn't pulled the trigger or authorized Quentin to. But still . . .

Donovan had shot a lot of Kajiri demons. His own people. During those long moments of gun play he seemed as blood thirsty as. . . as a full blooded, Midori demon was reported to be.

I could never trust him enough to love him as he wanted me to.

Did he love me as he hinted?

I needed to break the spell that man had on me. Until I figured out how to do that, I needed to stay well away from him.

Maybe all I needed was to buy a vibrator and rent some porn.

Would I ever dare love anyone again? Dill had so dominated my emotions I hadn't thought I'd be able to look beyond the too-short time we had together.

Only now, after three years, was I able to look more closely at the whirlwind love affair, the blind devotion, the all-consuming love . . . or was it just lust?

I went back inside rather than face my own emotional demons.

Gollum sat straight up in his chair, eyes focused on something too far in the distance for me to pinpoint. A stream of nonsense syllables streamed from his mouth.

Cynthia tried to write down the sounds on the tiny sheets of memo paper provided by the lodge. I grabbed my brand new Dictaphone and turned it on.

Only then did I note that the bottle of scotch was nearly empty.

Gollum had been almost as drunk the last time he'd channeled a legend in a foreign language. No wonder he didn't remember it.

Chapter 41

Fruit eating bats drop seeds far from the source thus increasing the number of seedlings away from the mother tree.

Madison, Wisconsin, is a lovely city. What I saw of it. Flight options out of Moses Lake, Washington, connecting to Seattle were limited. I flew in during the wee small hours of Thursday morning. The hotel was . . . a hotel. I've seen too many of them to get excited about any of them.

"Tess, you look wonderful for having been kidnapped by terrorists," my agent Sylvia Watson gushed when we met for brunch that first morning. I'd had a few hours of sleep. She hugged me to her ample bosom. I found my face nearly smothered in her shoulder. She's *that* tall and she was wearing four-inch heels. I had managed to find a pair of flats that actually matched in my luggage when I stumbled awake ten minutes before. That left me at my normal five foot two.

"Wonderful?" I blinked at her blearily. "Where's the coffee?"

"Same old Tess. Brush it off, hide your pain, and pour it into your work. Makes for wonderful novels, Tess, but I worry about you. You need to talk about this, maybe see a counselor. Post traumatic stress syndrome."

"I have talked about it, Syl. Endlessly. To the Marines, to Homeland Security, and to my research assistant."

"That cute-sounding gentleman who called me? What is his name? Gordon?"

"Guilford."

"There something going on between you two? About time you found someone new. You've mourned Dill long enough."

"There is nothing going on between me and Gol . . . Guilford." Not while I lusted after Donovan, even though I couldn't trust the bastard any farther than I could throw him.

My cell phone bleeped out the opening phrase of the *Star Wars* theme. Sylvia raised her eyebrows.

I turned away from her as I answered.

"Tess, you didn't call me. Are you okay?"

"I'm fine, Gol . . . Guilford. I'm getting ready to eat brunch with my agent. I need to talk business with her." In other words, go away.

"I made some progress on the recording you made Tuesday night."

"Was it only yesterday?" My time sense and balance were off. This was . . . what, Thursday? So, day before yesterday. Yesterday had evaporated in long waits for airplanes, flurries to get onto airplanes, then long waits while flying. Over and over again.

"I think we've got the incantation to open the portal."

"Fine. Memorize it and translate it. I'll check back with you later."

"In an hour, Tess. I'm serious. You are in danger."

"I'll check with you *later*." I disconnected.

"What was that all about?" Sylvia asked, too curious to be polite. Maybe too pushy to care about being polite. That's why she's such a good agent.

"He was just giving me a progress report."

"Making sure you aren't with another man?"

I picked up my menu and pointedly ignored her comment.

I yawned my way through most of Friday and finally excused myself for a much needed nap and reemerged ready for dinner with Sylvia and some of her other clients. I wore the little dress Scrap had altered for the convention in San Jose. I got a few whistles from male writers and editors who knew me. A lot of makeup hid the still healing demon bite on my leg. Dark nylons couldn't cover it adequately.

We sat down together in a private corner of a Mexican restaurant three blocks from the hotel.

"I thought Howard Ebson was supposed to be here," I said as I looked around the small circle.

"The famous recluse?" one of Sylvia's other clients gushed.

"Infamous is more like it," replied a professor of psychology from out west somewhere. He wrote psychological thrillers with futuristic backdrops.

"He promised he'd show up on Sunday for the lifetime achievement award." Sylvia shrugged. "At least his lady friend promised she'd get him here. He doesn't talk on the phone to anyone anymore, not even me." Sylvia pouted, offended that her most famous client had shut her out along with the rest of the world.

Scrap finally showed up on the walk back to the hotel. I hung back a little to assess his color. Still a bit gray around the edges, but definitely closer to normal.

I don't like it here, babe, he said, chomping on his cigar. *Great dress by the way. New designer, dahling?* He winked at me.

"What's wrong?" I whispered, very aware that the psych prof also hung back from the crowd.

Don't know. Just feels colder than it should.

I'd noticed that the wind out of the north bit through my nylons to the still healing demon bite on my leg. I snuggled deeper into my wool coat.

Gotta feed some more. The moment we stepped into the brightly lighted hotel lobby, Scrap winked out.

"Time to party!" I called to the others. I suddenly needed a lot of people and noise around me. Body heat and the hot air from too much talk sounded wonderful.

My cell phone sang. Gollum checking in. His concern warmed me even better than the party. Make that parties. I hit three that night before my body's demand for sleep overcame my need to keep people close and unseen enemies away.

Chapter 42

S aturday became a close repeat of Friday.

For some reason I kept looking for the contingent of bat people. And not with my normal trepidation. Maybe the Morris critter back at Fort Snoqualmie had helped me get over my phobia. Maybe. I didn't count on it.

Resolutely, I went off to the next party, this one at the overflow hotel two blocks away. I needed to party, to reaffirm that life existed beyond the realm of demons and imps and secret warrior Sisterhoods.

I took a shortcut through the back parking lot since I was running late, no thanks to yet another call from Gollum. With a quick dash, I shouldn't need a coat.

This party was hosted by my publisher, so I wore a brand new black sheath covered in gold and iridescent sequins. Since this was the end of October in Wisconsin, I slung a lace shawl woven with metallic gold threads around my shoulders. Not much protection against the wind, but I should be okay outside for a few minutes. Tiny glass beads weighted the fringe of the shawl. The entire ensemble glittered gaily in the subdued light. I could hear the noise from the party in the small ground-floor ballroom half a parking lot away.

The soft grass verge between the two parking lots absorbed the sound of my high-heeled footsteps. It absorbed the raucous voices and music from the party as well.

Streetlights didn't penetrate here.

A hushed barrier grew between me and the rest of the world. The hairs along my spine tingled.

Mist covered the few lights I could see.

"Scrap?"

More silence. No cigar smoke. I couldn't even smell the booze, smoked salmon, and cigarettes from the party.

"Where the hell are you, Scrap, when I need you?"

A shadow appeared beneath a spindly tree to my right. It looked like it stepped right out of the tree. A shadow that had no being to cast it. I stopped and placed my feet *en garde,* or at least as close to that position as the straight skirt of my dress allowed. I hiked it up, almost to my hips to give my legs moving room. While I debated kicking off my shoes, another shadow appeared out of the matching tree on my left.

Retreat or advance?

Right shadow took the decision away from me. It moved away from the wall and placed itself between me and the party. It had three dimensions now, roughly humanoid in shape, though with no substance.

Left shadow crowded behind me.

What could they do to me if they had no substance?

The temperature dropped to freezing. Ice crystals formed on the grass and in the mist around the lights.

They could freeze-dry me and crumble me into stale coffee grounds.

I took off the shawl and whirled it over my head like a toreador cape. The weighted fringe made the thing bell out. Front shadow ducked.

Every creature is vulnerable in the eyes and in the groin, Sister Paige's voice came to me unbidden. *The trouble with demons is finding the eyes and the groin.*

Since these guys looked vaguely human, I kept the glass beads on the fringe as close to their eye level as I could—a full head above me. Were these guys more Sasquatch only halfway into this dimension?

Back shadow moved off to my side.

Still whirling the shawl, I lashed out with my left foot toward backside shadow. The spike heel landed near its groin.

It grunted painfully.

Before I could take satisfaction in landing a good one, front shadow advanced. It grabbed the shawl in one hand and reached for my throat with the other.

I ducked and plowed forward, ramming my head into its middle. It stumbled and went down.

It had substance after all.

Back shadow recovered. It lunged for my knees.

The smell of cigars sharpened in the frigid air.

"Goddess, Scrap, where did you get to?" I evaded the tackle, just.

Right here, babe.

I snapped my fingers. Scrap appeared in my right hand, elongated and sharpened in the blink of an eye.

I twirled the blade, cleaving mist. It hung in tattered streamers like shattered silk in a circle around me.

Shadows backed off.

I kept up my circular pattern, over my head, down low, in the middle, never giving them a chance to touch me.

They kept moving around and around me, looking for an opening, reaching to touch me so they could freeze me.

I kept edging closer to a tree, to protect my back.

Could they lose their third dimension and slip between me and the trunk?

I gulped, hesitated.

One of them dove low toward my ankles.

I stomped on its hand with my heel. It yelped and flowed backward, half mist, half solid.

Gut one of them, Scrap chortled gleefully.

"Bloodthirsty little imp, aren't you?" I followed suit with a long lunge and backhanded slash with the spikes on the outside curve of the blade. My skirt ripped.

Damn. The dress had cost a fortune.

I cleaved in two the shadow demon in front of me.

It screamed. The high-pitched shriek stabbed at my hearing and my sanity.

My shoulders hunched in an attempt to cover my ears. I couldn't drop the blade to use my hands.

The two parts of the demon toppled to the ground in opposite directions. Black liquid pooled out from both halves. The grass absorbed it like nourishing water.

I gagged on the scent of burning hospital waste mixed with sulfur and disinfectant.

The other shadow came at me from the left with a roar that could shake the eight-story building in front of me to dust.

I swung the blade. It backed off, turned to mist, and disappeared within itself.

The parking lot brightened. The temperature rose. Noise from the party oozed out of the French doors.

My teeth stopped chattering. But the base of my spine still tingled.

Using my Celestial Blade as a walking staff, I sauntered on toward the party, pretending nothing had happened, that the rip in my skirt seam, halfway up my thigh was intentional.

"Hey, Tess, cool weapon," one of my fellow writers called. He squeezed between people to come examine my blade. He wrote sword-and-sorcery fantasy and had a collection of blades, real and fanciful.

"Hi, Steve. I had this made up as a wall ornament, but it works really well as a prop at cons," I hedged.

Steve touched the spikes with tentative fingers. "Those are really stable. Surprising. You'd think metal that slender would wobble." He made as if to take the weapon from me.

I jerked it away from his reach. "I know you, Steve. You couldn't resist trying it out and it's way too crowded in here."

I propped the blade behind a potted palm and took Steve by the arm, steering him away from the Celestial Blade. Scrap could use the privacy to return to his usually invisible self while I partied.

But three hours later, the blade was still intact.

Scrap couldn't dissolve because a demon was present.

"Steve, walk me back to the hotel," I suggested around midnight. I knew almost everyone in the room. Who among my colleagues led a double life as a demon and a writer?

If that was the case, who was missing? Besides Howard Ebson and his lady friend. They were always missing.

"Sure, I'm about done in anyway." He eyed my Celestial Blade with longing. I kept it close by my side.

"So, who's going to win best fantasy novel tomorrow? You or me?" he asked.

"There are three other nominees," I hedged. I really wanted that award. I'd never won anything before.

"May the best *man* win," he countered as we shook hands.

"Where's Val, your wife?" I. suddenly went cold again. What if . . . ?

"Oh, she's tucked up in bed with a cold and the copy edits of my next book. She should be well enough to attend the awards brunch tomorrow."

I hid my sigh of relief. Who else did I need to be suspicious of?

Goddess, I hated suspecting my friends.

Chapter 43

"Gollum, I'm scared," I whispered into my cell phone at two in the morning. Only midnight back at Half Moon Lake, Washington. He was still awake, still working on the translation of the demon language he'd channeled.

"What happened?"

I could almost see him straightening from his slump in the armchair of my suite, pushing his glasses up his nose, and planting his big feet firmly on the plank floor.

"What do you call a shadow that takes on three dimensions and freeze-dries everything around it?" I tried for a flippant tone but failed miserably.

"I don't know. What do you call it?"

I rolled my eyes. He couldn't be that oblivious to my emotions. Could he?

My gut still churned with fear. Why now? Why were demons coming after me now? I'd been going to cons this last year, promoting the new book. Were the shadows local and opportunistic?

Or were they in communication with the Sasquatch and out to get me wherever they could?

"A pair of demons who tried to kill me," I informed Gollum. Sarcasm helped me quiet the roiling acid in my stomach.

Dead silence.

"Are you there, Gollum? Is the line still open?" Cell phones had a bad habit of dropping calls in Half Moon Lake.

Well, cell phones had that bad habit everywhere.

"Yeah, I'm still here. Describe them." He sounded clinically detached, once more the anthropologist deep into research.

I knew he opened files on his laptop—a twin to my new one. Trying to separate myself from the awful reality and fear, I matched his tone, giving him as much detail as I could. Surprisingly, I had observed more than I thought. I described shades of black, height, estimated mass, a clear description of how the surviving demon dissolved, and how it grunted when my spike heel connected with its groin.

"You have to get out of there, Tess. Come back now. Take whatever flight you can grab. Those freezing temperatures sound familiar. And dangerous. Something Scandinavian going back to the Viking era..."

"This is Madison, Wisconsin. It gets very cold here. And as for the next plane out... this is not Chicago or New York. Planes don't come and go at all hours here. I'd be stuck in the airport. Alone. For hours and hours."

"Better the airport with lots of people around. Demons won't attack where there are witnesses."

"I'm not alone here, Gollum. Any one of a hundred people could have stumbled across that attack."

"Get out of there, Tess. Rent a car and drive to Chicago."

"Alone in the middle of the night on the road? You call that safer? Besides, I have to stay for the awards banquet. My publisher paid for it. I'm up for an award. This is my career."

"I mean it, Tess. You aren't safe there. I think you might be dealing with Wendigo. Killing one of them is more dangerous than leaving both alive. They always hunt in pairs, with their life mate."

"I have to be here. And I won't be alone. Scrap just crawled into the temperature control unit under the window. He'll gorge on mold and be fine in a couple of hours," I said too brightly. Actually, Scrap resembled a wounded mole limping back to his dark tunnel.

"I don't like this, Tess."

"I don't like it either, but I have to do this. Tomorrow evening I'm on the seven o'clock flight to Chicago, then to Seattle and Pascoe. I should be back in Half Moon Lake by midafternoon."

"Call me. Every hour."

"In the morning, after I get some sleep."

"Every hour, Tess. In the meantime, I'll see if Gramps can call in some favors and get you reinforcements."

I snorted at the idea of two octogenarian anthropologists hobbling into a battle with canes against demon claws. "I'll call you when I wake up."

I did call him. But first I called Donovan to see what information I might pry out of him. If I admitted to being a Warrior of the Celestial Blade, would he admit to having demon ancestors? Not likely, but I felt like I had to talk to him. He was the closest contact I had to the demon world. He should know *something*.

He didn't answer his office or his cell phone. My heart sank toward my belly.

Being really stupid where he was concerned was getting old.

"EAT SOMETHING," SYLVIA admonished me at the awards brunch the next day.

I'd picked out crepes and eggs and sausage rolls from the better-than-average buffet. The fruit had tasted good and three cups of coffee had helped make up for the hours of lost sleep. For a few moments I felt almost human, almost normal. Then I remembered freeze-dried grass and tree bark. My appetite vanished. I kept harking back to the feel of the Celestial Blade biting into demon flesh and the sight of black or green blood spilling on the ground with the horrendous scent of sulfur and other noxious things.

I kept wondering who in the room might be a demon and who I had killed last night. I scanned the crowd constantly, wondering who was missing. The comb in my hair, despite a tender scalp and a few more brittle hairs, revealed only normal auras. No extra shadows or braids of black within the variety of colors.

The awards portion of the day wouldn't start until after we'd all eaten, about an hour from now. It couldn't come soon enough.

"I wonder where Val got to?" Sylvia asked, looking toward the untouched place setting across the round table from me.

"Val Littlefield? Steve's wife?" I gulped. No wonder Steve had had such an intense interest in the Celestial Blade. But he'd touched it. I didn't think a demon—even a halfling—could touch it with impunity. And I'd asked him to walk me home last night!

"No. Valerie White. The new author I introduced to you. You two share an editor as a matter of fact. Gryffyn Books bought her ticket to this brunch. The least she could do is show up." Sylvia searched the room, her mouth turning down in distress. "There really is no excuse for not showing up for a free meal with your agent and publisher."

Tom Southerby, the publisher of Gryffyn Books, wandered around the large room, networking rather than eating. We'd be lucky if he sat anywhere long enough to do more than say "Hi," before he took off again.

My stomach sank. I knew of a very good excuse why a new author might miss a free meal that could make her memorable to the publisher and launch her career to a new level. I'd killed her last night.

My cell phone sang again. Gollum, of course. I leaped to take it outside the banquet room.

"Jealous Romeo again?" Sylvia leered at me knowingly.

"Who else?"

The hush of the lobby outside the banquet room came as a relief from the constant noise of conversations and cutlery clanking against fine china.

Gollum continued his litany of complaint that I had not checked in with him every hour. I apologized and cut him off.

Then I stepped outside for a breath of fresh autumn air, lightly chilled and redolent with the scent of fallen leaves. I missed the trace of stale cigar smoke that used to pervade my life. Scrap's failure to recover from last night's ordeal added on top of everything else that had happened to us recently twisted my gut with apprehension.

Demons all over the country wanted me dead.

After about five minutes, the bite in the wind penetrated my good wool rust-colored suit—the one Scrap had wanted me to buy a new hat with a feather for.

Damn, I wish the imp would come back from his hidey-hole. There was still a shadow demon out there who wanted my blood.

I yanked open the door and stepped back inside, grateful for the relief from the wind.

Maybe my eyes took longer than usual to adjust from bright autumnal sunshine to a remote inside corridor of a hotel. They shouldn't have. Since the fever that had made me a member of the Sisterhood, my senses reacted more quickly than those of a normal person. The moment I stepped inside, I felt shrouded in shadows, chilled beyond the seasonal temperatures, dull and heavy.

Just like I'd felt before I cleaved shadow mists with the Celestial Blade.

Quickly, I inventoried my assets for another fight. No heels. No shawl weighted with glass beads. No energy.

And no Scrap.

The shadows began to coalesce around me.

"You killed my mate," someone whispered through the growing darkness. An androgynous voice. Menacing. "Your life is forfeit."

"Not today, buddy." I turned on my flat heel and dashed back outside into the minimal shadows of noon sunshine.

Half running, I made my way around the hotel to the main entrance. Knots of people laughed and joked and talked very loudly in the lobby.

If any shadow demon followed me, I denied it privacy for the kill.

Hunching my shoulders and dropping my head, I assumed a posture of meekness. One group of seven people had two other hangers-on who listened intently but offered no contributions to the conversation.

I joined them, sidling closer to the center, using these people as a human shield.

"Hey, looks like they've finished serving the overpriced brunch and will let us poor peons in now," one of the crowd said in a high squeaky voice.

Feeling like part of the wallpaper, I followed her back to the banquet room. Even Sylvia didn't notice me until I sat heavily in my chair and nibbled at a cold crepe stuffed with strawberries and cream cheese.

"Have you been running?" my agent asked. "You're breathing heavily."

"Sylvia, I think I just had a panic attack. Post-traumatic stress and all. Would you . . ." I gulped and swallowed heavily. "Would you stay with me while I pack and check out? Maybe ride to the airport with me?"

"Honey, I'll stay with you until we reach Chicago. I'm on the same flight as you that far. Then I'm scheduled to leave for New York an hour after you head off to Seattle, same airline. No problem." She patted my hand and waved my publisher back to the table as the organizers began the award ceremony.

Val, the missing new author, breezed in wearing swaths of floating rayon and more bracelets than I could count. She glittered and clanked and gushed apologies.

"Where's your husband?" Sylvia asked, after she'd hugged Val and kissed her cheek.

I'd had to publish three novels before I got that kind of affection from our agent.

"He'll be along in a minute. There's a glitch with our flight reservations." Val dismissed his absence with a wild gesture that almost took out the publisher's eye with one of her rings. It looked like a hinged casket, one of the "poison" rings so popular with the con populace.

If Val and her husband were the shadow demons, she might decide to eliminate me now that I was competition to her own career. Any con we had been to together before this, we weren't in the same league.

I kept looking around, too nervous to pay attention to the ceremonies that captured the attention of the entire room.

The presenters went through the long list of publications up for awards, short stories, novelettes, novellas, editors, artwork, anthologies and collections, even industry magazines. Finally, they came to the last and most coveted category, novels.

I gripped my chair with white knuckles and bit my lip. I'd never been nominated before. I'd never had a work sell well enough to gain this kind of recognition before. I really wanted to win, though I knew the voters in this contest favored obscure literary pieces over commercial successes.

"Ladies and gentlemen, I don't remember this happening before. For the category of Best Fantasy Novel of the Year, we have a tie," the presenter, an editor from a rival publisher announced. "The winners are . . ." dramatic pause while he opened the thick cream-colored envelope. "The winners are, Steve Littlefield for *The Dragons of Banesfield Manor* and Tess Noncoiré for *Imps Alive!*"

I sat there numbly, not daring to believe what I heard.

Sylvia pounded my back. Tom pumped my hand and pushed me up to the dais. I bowed to the thunderous applause as Steve grabbed the microphone. He said a few words I couldn't hear over the roaring in my ears, then he handed the mike to me.

"I . . . uh . . . I need to thank my agent Sylvia Watson, my editor and publisher Tom Southerby, and um . . . and my mom, as well as all the readers who voted for me," I stumbled.

I had to give credit where credit was due. Editors and publishers invested a lot of work and money in putting a book on the shelves. This was a big feather in Tom's hat.

Scrap loved hats with feathers. He should be here to share the moment, too.

I gave the mike back to Steve. He rambled on quite nicely, covering for me.

My attention riveted on the tall black man who took a seat next to Valerie White. He had to be at least seven feet tall and wore a conservative business suit.

Was he the shadow demon? If so, then who was his mate? Certainly not pudgy and flamboyant Caucasian Val.

I couldn't see their auras even wearing the comb.

If the Whites weren't the shadow demons, then who were?

Eventually the crowd let me sit down again. One more award, the previously announced lifetime achievement award to Howard Ebson, the recluse. More speeches and intros.

Finally Lilia David stood up to accept the award for Howard. She wore jeans, a flannel shirt, and hiking boots. Very inappropriate to the occasion. She mumbled some kind of apology for Howard. Everyone knew his reclusive nature. He hated crowds and ceremonies.

I barely comprehended a word she said. Her aura revealed layers upon layers of shadow shifting in the wind.

Last night, I'd killed her mate, Howard Ebson, the shadow demon.

While my babe is safe aboard the airplane, I have a little freedom to roam. I'd like to bust into the chat room and put the bad guys on notice they've caused a Sister enough grief. Next time we stop pussyfootin' around. Next time I won't be showin' no mercy.

Speaking of pussycats and no mercy, I've made plans for Gollum's little playmate. That cat is goin' down. I've earned a couple of new warts and my wings actually look like wings now instead of stubs. I've taken out shadow demons and I've neutralized a tribe of renegade Sasquatch. I'm ready for that cat.

But first I think I'll just zip back home for a moment and see if the garbage dump holds any more little treasures for Tessie-babe. She needs a little gift to make her feel better.

But I've got to be careful. She won't appreciate an old 286 CPU, like some people. Nor will she want a leather leash and slave collar with metal studs. Some of the Sisters might like them. But not my babe.

My babe has class. Like the comb. Now what other useful little talisman can I find?

Interlude

THE ENTIRE SISTERHOOD filed out of their various quarters. Each woman wore a red gown, all different designs, revealing or hiding cleavage, clinging or full, but all long and flowing. Each woman carried a red candle, not yet lit. Quite an impressive display when they gathered in the courtyard on the night of a waxing quarter moon. Seven initiates stood to one side, on a little dais. They all wore white.

Except for me.

Sister S had given me a new pair of jeans, a flannel shirt, low-heeled boots. Clothing for the outside world.

Sister Gert stepped forward. She wore her gown cut low on the bodice, empire waistline, and falling in straight folds to her feet. Thus clad, she looked younger, more vibrant, less stern than I knew her to be. She'd swept her short, blunt-cut hair behind her ears and secured it with a glittering barrette that might have diamonds and real gold in it. It looked very elegant and expensive. And old.

"Before we induct seven new members into our order, we must deal with one who is not suitable, but has certainly been chosen by the Goddess." Sister Gert's voice rang out, caught and echoed on the stone walls, compounding in volume and authority.

I firmed my shoulders and faced the assemblage with defiance. I'd not conform to their rules, so they wouldn't let me play their game. Fine. I didn't like them or their game. But I respected their dedication and their training. Even if I did feel like the entire thing was a bogus excuse to withdraw from reality.

A little more sanity, and they'd probably all fit in nicely with the con culture.

Easy, babe. There's a time to speak out and a time to hold your tongue.

Scrap stuck out his long, forked tongue, and grasped it between two talons.

I bit my cheeks rather than laugh at him, and thus at the Sisterhood.

"Teresa Noncoiré, you have been privileged to share many secrets with the Sisterhood of the Celestial Blade," Sister Gert said more quietly. But still her voice carried to the far corners of the Citadel. "We charge you to keep those secrets close to your heart, nurture them, and be aware that evil walks abroad, enemies to those secrets and all we fight for and hold dear."

Oh, my, she was serious.

I could only nod mutely. Otherwise I might laugh out loud. This was more solemn than the most serious of cults within fandom.

"Do you swear by all that you hold sacred to keep the existence of the Sisterhood secret?"

Swear it, Tess, or we'll never get out of here alive.

If the matter was so important, why was Scrap making faces at Sister Gert from his hiding place within the folds of her skirt on the ground?

"I so swear." In the face of the solemnity that graced every face and demeanor I could see, I had to agree.

"Do you swear to nurture your imp and prepare for the day you must combat evil and protect the innocent from its ravages?"

"I do so swear." And I did. Those were ideals I could agree with and follow.

"Then we send you forth into the world, a more complete and better woman than when you came here."

That was certainly the truth.

In the middle of the crowd, a Sister lit her candle and lifted it high. Then another and another of them saluted me.

Gulping back a sob, I held my head high and marched out the huge double gate of the Citadel. Alone except for Scrap. More than a little scared at having to face the world again. Saddened that I had to leave friends behind.

I had made friends within the Citadel. Friends I would cherish for a long time to come.

And we cherish you as well, Sister Serena whispered into my mind.

Thank you for championing me when no one else would, *came a farewell from Gayla, the woman I'd pulled in from the storm.*

Keep your guard up on your left. Demons will know it's your weak side, Sister Paige reminded me.

Remember to give your imp an occasional beer, Sister Mary added.

Thanks for telling us stories in the dead of night when our nightmares became too real. That was Sister Electra with her flaming red hair.

Questions have their place. Learn when to ask them, and when to accept what is, Sister Gert got in the last word. She even had a bit of a chuckle in her voice. *You gave us many things to think about, even if you are rash, impudent, and disrespectful.*

I laughed out loud and started up the refurbished car I had arrived in eleven months ago.

Chapter 44

"Where's Cynthia?" I asked Gollum the moment I entered my suite at the Mowath Lodge. Why was the place starting to feel like home?

Thanks to Sylvia's mother-hen presence, my return trip had been free of incidents, shadows, and other boogey-men. I wasn't ready yet to face them here where I knew they hovered.

"She's with Sapa. They are out collecting grass, bark, and feathers to weave into the blanket," Gollum replied, not even looking up from his computer screen. As usual, he was sprawled in the armchair with his laptop. I had no idea what the arcane symbols on the screen meant. The cat had squeezed itself around the computer and still managed to occupy most of his lap.

"If Cynthia and Sapa are out collecting, who's guarding the blanket?" I turned on my heel and began the march back to Donovan's office and the precious artifact. I couldn't stand still anyway. Something drove me to keep moving. Unpacking wasn't enough.

"The blanket is under lock and key and I have the key. I can't get into the office to take it. They can't break into where the blanket is without setting off an alarm." He held up a shiny brass key no bigger than his thumbnail.

"Who set that up?"

"I compromised with Estevez."

"How'd you twist Donovan's arm to get him to agree?" I couldn't imagine Gollum so much as threatening the man, let alone forcing a compromise.

Although I had a fuzzy dream image of Gollum near strangling a Marine medic to keep him from giving me lethal tranquilizers. That must have been a hallucination induced by fried synapses from the super-industrial-strength taser.

But then I had a flash of remembrance as he hoisted himself up rocks by the strength of his arms alone while Cynthia and I had to scramble with footholds and elbows and knees to get over the obstacles in front of the cave even after he boosted us up.

"I got the phone number of the state archaeologist and put him on speed dial." Gollum grinned and finally looked up at me. Even through his glasses, I could see the smile light his eyes with mischief.

"And Donovan will do almost anything to keep the state archaeologist from prowling around the caves beneath the casino." Part of me was delighted. Only part.

Goddess, I wished I could get over that man. Why couldn't I just admit to myself that he was half demon and not attractive at all?

Sad and vulnerable Donovan was more attractive than strong and confident Donovan. I still lusted after both of him.

One night with him didn't seem like enough.

And yet it was too much.

I'd never chosen bed partners indiscriminately before.

Dill, my husband, was the only man I'd slept with before a long series of dates and inner debates. With Dill, it was love at first sight.

With Donovan, it was lust at first sight, nothing more. It had to be.

"Tess, look what we found!" Cynthia bounded into the suite looking flushed, windblown, and happy. Happier than I'd ever seen her.

Once more my heart swelled with . . . with love for her. She had given me a flower for Dill's grave. Now she held out a pretty feather for my inspection.

A longing opened in my soul. A longing to keep this child/woman close and cherished; to protect her as a mother as well as a friend.

Possibilities . . .

"Let me see." I held out my hand for the long, dark tailfeather that looked black upon first inspection but glimmered iridescent blue when the light shifted.

"Magpie," Gollum said and went back to his computer.

A strain from "The Thieving Magpie" by Rossini drifted through my head. I couldn't think of a more appropriate feather to add to the blanket that had been stolen and recovered so many times in the past.

After a light supper at the café—I'd eaten so much restaurant and airline food in the past few weeks even Mom's cooking was beginning to sound good—Cynthia went back to the office and the blanket to sleep with Sapa. The two of them truly belonged to each other now and I had no idea how I could arrange for them to stay together with the blanket once we closed the demon portal.

She was still only twelve, and the state had very serious issues with a child who didn't have adult supervision and school.

"The blanket belongs in a museum," I muttered. An afternoon job demonstrating weaving in the old way might be the solution. If we could find foster parents and a school for her close to the museum.

"But there is no museum close enough to the portal to be of any use," Gollum reminded me.

An idea itched in the back of my mind but slid out of reach every time I tried to grab it. My body twitched more than the idea.

"Let me think about this for a while. Come on, let's take a walk." I grabbed Gollum's hand and hauled him out of his chair.

He slid the laptop onto the coffee table. The cat humphed and took up a roost under the highly varnished slab of burl wood.

We walked in silence a few moments, comfortable with each other and with the silence.

"If Donovan is keeping his office in town open, then he must be working on refinancing the casino," I mused as we climbed the steps to my suite an hour later.

I was beginning to wonder if Gollum actually had the suite below me. He didn't seem to use it at all.

The night was too fine, and I was too restless to stay inside. I wandered out onto the back deck, pacing. Inside, outside.

Maybe if I went for a run around the lake, I'd settle down. I hadn't had any serious exercise other than the treadmill at the hotel gym in nearly a week. The demon bite was healing, though it itched abominably.

My skin felt like it didn't belong to me. A run didn't sound right. I wanted Scrap beside me. I even missed his smelly cigar. My fashion sense wasn't complete without him.

I grabbed the deck railing with both hands and forced myself to breathe deeply. Three breaths in, exhaling completely each time. I tried a standing meditation to clear my mind so that I could pinpoint the source of my agitation. No way could I sit still long enough to do a proper meditation.

Three more deep breaths. I couldn't get rid of enough air. Everything clogged in my body and my mind.

Something outside myself nagged at my soul.

This was like PMS magnified by ten, except that I didn't get PMS anymore. Not since the fever.

Only once before had I felt this extreme and uncalled-for agitation . . .

The night I witnessed the Goddess manifest in the stars while I was still at the Citadel.

I looked up to where the waxing quarter moon floated in the sky. It cast a diffuse reflection across the surface of the murky lake.

The stars shone so brightly behind the moon I felt as if I could reach up and touch them.

A river of light streamed away from the top of the moon.

The Milky Way.

The constellation jumped out at me. The moon defined the curve of a lady's cheek. The Goddess Kynthia. The Milky Way became her flowing hair, drifting in a celestial wind. Two bright stars with a blue cast twinkled at me like eyes trying to communicate wordlessly.

Even as I blinked in wonder, the rest of Kynthia's face filled in with more stars. Her mouth quirked up in a knowing smile, reminiscent of the *Mona Lisa*.

"Guilford, get your butt out here!"

He slammed open the sliding doors and appeared at my side before I finished speaking. "What? What's wrong?"

"That!" I pointed to the wondrous event in the sky.

"The moon's up. So?"

"Can't you see her?" I couldn't take my eyes off the Goddess. "She's so clear, so dominant in the sky!"

"See what?"

"Oh, My Goddess!"

Kynthia only showed her face when the Warriors of the Celestial Blade needed to gather in defense. She warned us that the demons were on the move.

Quickly I scanned the horizon, wishing for supernatural vision or at least infrared goggles.

"There!" I pointed up and across the lake. In the few security lights around the casino on top of the ridgeline I saw movement. Many figures. Many figures carrying torches. Live fire in a desert that hadn't seen any rain in months.

"I need binoculars."

"Your binoculars won't help. But these will." Gollum produced a pair of the night vision binoculars.

I didn't waste time asking him where they came from.

"Two dozen beings up there. I can't tell if they're human or Sasquatch. How do I increase the power of these things?"

Gollum adjusted something on top of the heavy binoculars.

Images jumped into focus. "Sasquatch!"

"Tess?" Donovan called to me from the front of the lodge, followed by fierce pounding on the door. "Tess, where are you?"

"Back here!" I didn't move, didn't dare take my eyes off the demons until I figured out what they were up to.

"Tess, they've stolen the blanket. They've got Cynthia and the dog, too." Donovan rounded the building and stood below me on the verge of the beach.

I vaulted the railing and landed lightly, ready to run. Kynthia imbued me with power I didn't know I had.

"Scrap, get your ass back in this dimension. Now!"

"I didn't hear the alarm," Gollum said accusingly.

"They smashed it and cut the wires before they entered the office. They ripped the blanket off the wall, glass case and all. The dog attacked them. They just clubbed him over the head and picked him up. Cynthia, too. We've got to get that blanket back!"

Chapter 45

"We've got to save Cynthia." Images of Cynthia proffering me a flower for Dill's grave cleared my priorities.

"We'll help." The banker and his wife appeared on their deck.

"How?" I asked Donovan.

"They know everything. They can help."

"Number crunching won't help." I was already running to my rental car, another SUV, red this time.

Gollum grabbed the keys from my hands. "I'm better qualified at off-road driving," he informed me as he started the engine. I had no choice but to claim the seat beside him. Donovan and his friends piled in behind.

I burned with questions about the bankers. We rode in silence. Gollum took the rough back road up to the casino way too fast. My teeth jarred until my jaw ached. We bounced over ruts and dipped into potholes only to climb out the other side with speed and dexterity I'd never have managed.

Gollum certainly had more talents than I suspected.

I gripped the seat with white knuckles. The drive went on forever.

All I could think about was Cynthia alone and frightened. Kidnapped a second time by demons.

Demons who had clear access to a portal beneath the casino.

The road leveled out abruptly as we topped the ridge. Gollum jerked the emergency brake on before we came to a complete stop. I was out of the car and running a heartbeat later. Donovan came hot on my heels. The bankers and Gollum were only a step behind.

"Scrap, where the hell are you?"

I ran into a solid wall of Sasquatch. The stench nearly gagged me. My head felt too light and my knees too heavy.

I bent my head and rammed straight forward into the gut of one. He grunted as the wind whooshed out of him.

More bad breath.

But he backed up, giving me access to the backs of his comrades.

They must have been Kajiri—half-bloods. Not a one was over six-and-a-half-feet tall. Judicious kicks to knees and groins helped clear more space. I needed fighting room, with or without my Celestial Blade.

"Scrap!" I continued to call, whenever I had breath enough to spare.

Then, at last, a familiar whiff of cigar smoke cut through rancid BO and lack of mouthwash.

Scrap landed in my outstretched hand with a thud, already halfway into transformation. He clutched something bright and shiny, but I didn't have time to wonder about it. Whatever it was, it became part of the blade.

I cleared more space twirling him, giving him the centrifugal force to elongate. Together, we cut a swath through the Kajiri.

Over to my left I saw Donovan fighting tooth and nail with a pair of full-sized Sasquatch. He stayed human, no trace of bat wings. Why?

No time to wonder. The Sasquatch came at me thick and heavy.

The banker couple engaged their own pair. They'd grown teeth that might have looked adequate on a saber-toothed tiger, and long purple tentacles sprouted from their faces, like the kids at the con.

I didn't care as long as they helped me rescue Cynthia.

I caught a glimpse of Gollum wrestling another full-blooded demon for the blanket, still in its glass case. Cynthia clung to the monster's back while Sapa worried its feet. That was one big Sasquatch. It dwarfed all three of them combined.

Then the herd was on me. They brandished torches, trying to force me to back away from the casino building. I had no time to think. No time to worry.

But I did worry. There were hundreds of them and only a few of us.

I had to save Cynthia, and Gollum, and, yes dammit, Donovan, too, because I cared for them. Losing them would hurt as much as losing Dill.

My blade sang as I cleaved the space around me. The Sasquatch jabbed their torches at me. They had me on reach. I had them on reaction and timing.

I whirled right and caught a torch, spinning it up into the air like a fiery baton. The second half of my blade ripped out the throat of that demon.

The others backed off.

I breathed deeply, grateful for every lungful of precious oxygen.

Then I noticed the heat from the torches. Like a ring of fire, the demons closed upon me. My skin blushed red in the first stages of burning.

A jab from my left. I thrust and swung. One demon backed off, another replaced him.

And so we danced.

My shoulders grew tired.

The heat increased.

Scrap began to blur and lose his edge.

Desperate to end the fight, I lunged forward, thrusting out and back in one smooth move.

I gutted one demon and nearly fell onto the torch of the other.

Then I danced with my blade. Forward, back. High, low.

Two more demons met death. My blade darkened with their blood. The heat lessened. Scrap brightened.

The sage and tumbleweeds burst into flame, giving me brief flares of light to kill another demon. That one fell upon his own torch and screamed.

The stench of burning flesh and fur grew thick as fog.

I gagged. My shoulders grew heavy and felt as if they'd dislocate if I had to swing the blade one more time. My ears roared with blood pounding behind them.

The roar grew. Not just the laboring of my pulse.

A dozen pickups crested the ridge behind the casino. Their headlights blinded me.

"Who?" Donovan shouted above the noise of huge diesel engines.

"I don't know!" I shouted back. My heart stuttered a moment in fear. What if the Kajiri had called for reinforcements?

Then dozens of women swarmed out of the oversized pickup beds and out of the cabs. Imps filled the air, their wings beating furiously as they, too, elongated and transformed.

"Cavalry to the rescue!" Gayla shouted above the melee. "We figured out that the assaults on our portal were diversions against something bigger. We came to help."

My knees nearly melted in relief. My Sisters had seen the light and joined me in this battle.

New strength invigorated me. My heart swelled with gratitude and . . . and love.

Well, let's leave it at gratitude.

Gradually, we pushed the never-ending tide of Sasquatch back and farther back toward the empty casino buildings. A few dozen against two hundred. With the help of our imps, we prevailed as we were ordained to prevail over demons and evil forces.

Gulping air, foul as it was, I chanced a look around to see how my companions fared.

Donovan was down and bleeding but breathing. I couldn't find the bankers.

Sapa ripped at the throat of a full-sized Sasquatch. That demon clutched a hunk of hide and a hank of fur from Sapa's hip in its dying fist.

Cynthia and Gollum? I couldn't find them. Dared not take the time to look for them.

Then I heard Gollum's blessed voice. "They're going back down the portal. Quick! We have to close it!"

"How?" Cynthia asked weakly. I think she sobbed.

My heart cried out to her. I needed to hold her tight, and reassure her.

I needed to keep these last three demons from ever touching her again. My Sisters fought mop-up actions, finishing off the downed and wounded Sasquatch with bloodthirsty glee.

"The blanket, Cynthia! Weave the feathers into the blanket," I yelled.

One more demon down. Two left.

They threw their torches into the open piles of timber stacked beside the building and dove for the region of the portal.

Smoke and flame billowed up. The hungry flames licked greedily at this new fuel. The fire became a living wall between me and the last of my victims.

Then Cynthia and Gollum were beside me. Cynthia grabbed bits of Sapa's hair from the fist of a dead Sasquatch. Rapidly, she rolled it between her palms along with some tree bark and one of her treasured feathers. A crude thread extruded from her makeshift spindle. The quill tip of the feather became a primitive shuttle.

Gollum jumped upon the protective case of the blanket. Glass shattered upon impact. Not bothering to clear away the shards, he plunged his hand into the mess. He emerged with a bloody arm. The sharp edges of glass snagged the blanket, ripped holes in it, and finally released it.

Cynthia grabbed a hunk of fabric and began weaving her feather thread through one of the snags.

"The incantation," I panted. The smoke thickened making it harder to breathe.

"I need three people to say it," Gollum said. An edge of panic touched his eyes and his voice.

"I know it." Donovan half-crawled, half-stumbled beside Gollum.

"So do I," said Vern Abrams.

"Are you sure, Estevez? You know what will happen." Gollum looked him in the eye levelly.

Donovan swallowed deeply, closed his eyes, and grimaced.

"I know. We've got to do it. We can't let those stupid fools loose again in this area. Not any time soon anyway."

Gollum dropped the blanket across Cynthia's legs. She continued her weaving.

Sapa limped over to her and lay his great head in her lap. He was hurt badly, but I thought he'd live.

Myrna Abrams staggered over to me. Blood dripped from a nasty gash in her forehead. Her teeth, like her husband's, had retreated, along with her tentacles.

My Sisters gathered behind me, leaning on each other in exhaustion. Some had taken wounds. I barely registered that they all had survived.

Gollum took the hands of Donovan and the banker. They circled again and again clockwise as they chanted the weird language full of pops and clicks and unpronounceable syllables.

"What are they doing?" Gayla whispered.

"Sealing the rogue portal," I replied and draped an arm about her shoulders.

We stood there, propping ourselves upright with our blades, trying to breathe the heavy air through exhausted lungs.

The land heaved beneath my feet. A great rumbling roar near deafened me. I let go of Gayla and braced myself.

I blinked in the fiery light as the casino crumbled and imploded. A gaping hole in the earth opened and swallowed the entire building, extinguishing the fire.

Then the earth settled back into place.

In moments all that was left of Donovan's empire was a pile of ash and shattered dreams.

Chapter 46

Here, babe, I found a new treasure in Mum's garbage dump.

I dropped the shiny bit of metal into Tess' outstretched hand the moment I managed to shrink back to my normal self. A little hard with the bankers still hanging around, but they are good folk even if their great-granddads were demons. And their two kids didn't kill Bob. It was the bat child. I remember it clearly now. The bat had the knife. Tentacles tried to pull her back.

"I never saw the bat child. But I believe you. Was it the one who tried to steal from my tote just because it could?"

I nodded. Limply. Fighting is hard work.

"What's this?" Tess asked. She turned the jewelry over and over, examining the curved shapes by the light of the headlights from the pickups.

Most of the Sisters stumbled and limped over to their transport, packing up to go home and nurse their wounds now that the excitement was over.

"That looks like real gold," Sister Gayla said, peering over my babe's shoulder.

Of course it's real gold, *I snorted disdainfully.* Mum's garbage dump is high class. Not like the homes of some imps I know.

Ginkgo, Gayla's imp, took exception to that remark as well as my diminutive size.

I flashed my array of warts at her, and she subsided into a pout. I might be small, but I've now slain more demons than five of these so-called proper imps put together.

And I'll admit that the females don't interest me at all. Even the one going into heat. But the males now . . . Pine has a most interesting array of warts on his backside.

My babe found the loops on the back of the jewelry for either inserting a chain or attaching a brooch pin to the talisman. She hefted the weight of it and smiled.

"It looks a little like an abstract Goddess in the sky."

Did you notice how she capitalized the G in Goddess? She's beginning to believe. It's important to believe in something.

I puffed out my chest with pride.

"If that's the face of Kynthia, then these indentations must be places to set precious stones," *Gayla mused. She used the full name of the Goddess. I guess that means she believes more than my babe does.*

Jewels, right, *I added, wondering when and where I could find some fine diamonds in just the right size.*

"I count twelve settings," *my babe said.* "They feel rough, like stones have been ripped out."

"Oh, my Goddess!" *Sister Electra gasped. She'd wandered over to see why Gayla hadn't climbed into a truck with the rest of them.*

"What?" *Tess asked.*

"That's—that's—" She just pointed and gasped.

"That's what?"

"We need to get that back to Sister Gert. It's been missing for centuries."

Not on your life, Sister, I snarled. *I found it. I gave it. It stays with Tess.*

Arborvitae, Electra's imp, Ginkgo, and I got into a snapping match. I settled it, and they backed off. I guess we imps aren't meant to get along outside of the Citadel. That's how we survive in the wild. We earn our warts and seniority.

"But that is the talisman of the senior Sister. She gets to put a precious stone in it for every battle she survives." Electra tried taking it from Tess.

Tess snatched it away and held it close to her heart. "Tell Sister Gert to come get it herself. The Goddess chose me for a reason. She helped Scrap find this for me for a reason. Sister Gert and I will settle this between us."

I whipped out a cigar, lit it, and blew the smoke into Electra's face. Then I passed some gas. She backed off, coughing and fanning the air.

Take that, Sisters. My babe is gonna be top dog some day, and there's nothing you can do about it.

And I'm gay!

"I don't see why I have to go to school," Cynthia whined.

"You go to school because the state says you have to," I tried to soothe her.

We'd retired to the Mowath Lodge, slept, showered, and eaten. Now it was time to settle some things.

"But all I'm going to do all day is weave the blanket," she continued her litany of grief, all the while rubbing Sapa's ears.

The big, ugly dog licked her hand and settled back into a light doze. He hadn't done much but sleep and eat since the final battle with the Sasquatch. But he was healing fast and had found a girlfriend, an English mastiff, in town.

I suspected there'd be new puppies in about two months, an heir to Sapa's duties among them.

"You will not just be weaving the blanket," a tall and absolutely gorgeous Aboriginal woman informed us as she entered my suite, followed by a google-eyed Gollum and an openly drooling Donovan.

Some men have no loyalty whatsoever.

"You will have to learn to weave it properly and conserve it for future generations. Those fibers will not last long in an open and unstable environment," the woman announced. Pronounced. Assumed authority anyway.

"Excuse me?" I took a defensive stance between Cynthia and this stranger. Somehow, I'd come to think of Cynthia as mine. I'd even toyed with the idea of moving to Half Moon Lake so I could adopt her and keep her, and therefore the blanket, close to the demon portal.

But then, what would I do with Mom?

I didn't trust her living on her own without supervision. I didn't trust any of the motley crew I called family alone without supervision.

Except maybe my brother. And he'd decamped ages ago, as soon as he graduated from Harvard.

"Tess, I'd like to introduce you to Keisha Stalking Moon," Donovan said, never taking his eyes off the woman's finely honed features, full lips, and liquid chocolate eyes. Not to mention a more-than-adequate bosom beneath her crisp red wool business suit. The tight skirt was slit halfway up her thigh, revealing legs that seemed to go on forever.

She should have been a model.

Then her name struck me.

"Stalking Moon?" I think my heart forgot to beat.

"Yes, I'm Leonard Stalking Moon's eldest daughter, and Cynthia's new guardian." She appraised me with the same scrutiny I'd given her.

I had the feeling I came up short in more than just height. My faded jeans, threadbare cable knit sweater, and dirty running shoes just didn't cut the fashion mustard anymore. Let alone my rather tangled curls and lack of makeup.

Obviously, Scrap was missing again, or I'd have dressed better. He needed mold more than I needed a fashion assistant. The beer and OJ I left out for him had disappeared about an hour ago.

I scooped my hair into a twist and inserted the comb.

The world brightened, but nothing about this woman changed. She was still gorgeous, sexy, smart, and an alpha bitch—meant as a compliment if you know dogs.

"Dr. Stalking Moon is also going to be the curator of the new museum," Vern Abrams said, joining us with a sheaf of papers beneath his arm. "Keisha has an impressive array of degrees that qualify her for the job."

"Museum?" I'd only slept a night and a day, yet I felt as if I'd missed some major world events.

"The land beneath the casino still has value, but I think a less ambitious project is more in line than Donovan's original," Vern said, settling at *my* table with his papers.

"We are starting over with a spa, small hotel—only a dozen rooms in keeping with the water table requirements—and a museum. We'll pipe lake water up into hot tubs right over . . . right over . . ." Donovan trailed off, not knowing quite how to phrase the words "demon portal" in mixed company.

"We are also bringing in a consortium of tribes to run the place. This will no longer be a one-man operation or financial burden," Vern added. "Now I need some signatures, Donovan. And witnesses." He held out an expensive looking fountain pen.

I wondered if the ink was really Donovan's blood.

"What about the lake water?" I asked, remembering the complaints of the locals. "The lake levels are already too low . . ."

"But rising," Myrna Abrams said from the doorway. The suite was large but getting *way* too crowded. "Last night's rain broke a three-year drought, which accounted for part of the lower levels. I wonder if the open portal had something to do with that. Anyway, the portal was draining water out of the lake. That's why you smelled lake water every time the demons came and went. And the owner of the golf course was hoarding his share of water from irrigation, getting ready to sell it back to the ranchers at a profit. We've put a stop to that."

"We estimate the water table should be back to normal by spring if we have decent rainfall this winter," Vern continued brandishing his papers at the assemblage.

I wanted Scrap there to clear the room with his cigar smoke and a judicious fart or two.

Then I spotted him beneath the armchair teasing Gollum's cat with a feather stolen from Cynthia. Scrap, wearing something like a surgical mask, twitched the feather. Gandalf the cat swatted it and earned a smack across the nose for his efforts. He jumped back and hissed. Scrap waved the feather again, and the stupid cat tried to grab it, earning another swat.

Sometimes cats are victims of their own hunting instincts. Or just plain stupid. I hadn't figured out which.

Donovan grimaced as he signed in about fifteen places. The ink was black. But that didn't mean it wasn't his blood.

When I'd added my own name to appropriate places as witness, and so had Gollum, I looked around at the polished log walls, the burl wood tables, and the people who crowded around me.

"I guess there is nothing left for me to do but go home," I sighed.

"Until the next time," Gollum whispered.

"Tess, I'll call you the next time I'm on the East Coast," Donovan said. His warm brown eyes pleaded with me.

My knees wanted to melt. I scanned him for any sign of demonic genetics. Only that strange golden light with coppery overtones and the black braid writhing in the light.

"We'll see." I shrugged. "You'll keep in touch, Cynthia? I want to know how things go with you and Sapa. I need to know that you are safe. Thriving."

"Of course!" She hugged me tightly. "You're the best, Tess. I love you." She pulled another feather out of her pocket, along with a wildflower I didn't recognize.

I took them from her with shaking hands and blurring eyes.

"Don't let yourself get too lonely," she said quietly.

"Not anymore. I don't think I'll ever be truly lonely again."

"SOMEWHERE ON THE HIGH desert plateau, between here and there, yesterday and tomorrow, a walled fortress houses the Sisters of the Stars; devoted followers of a Goddess who holds the world in balance between good and evil. When a waxing moon caresses the Milky Way just so, the Goddess shows her face in the heavens. The Sisters know then that trouble is brewing." I read the opening lines of my newest book to a group of gathered fans, Gollum among them.

But Donovan was missing from this gathering of fans at a con. I wasn't sure yet if I truly missed him or not.

Only a few weeks after leaving Half Moon Lake, I found myself at yet another con on the West Coast. This one in Portland.

Donovan had sent me a couple of emails reporting on the good progress of the new spa and how well the town cooperated with the new building plans. He'd also sent a dozen red roses to my room here at the con hotel. Cynthia emailed me every day and we chatted on the phone at least once a week.

Other than that, my life had returned to normal.

Nice job, Scrap said from the region of my shoulder.

I'd persuaded him to leave his cigar behind. This con frowned deeply on any smoking inside the hotel. If Scrap wanted to smoke, he had to go outside, just like everyone else. He'd learned at least a few manners in the past months.

A round of applause erupted when I finished the prologue and closed the book.

As a group, the fans and I made our way from the small reading room down the hall to a larger meeting room. I still checked the walls for signs of shadows that didn't belong there. In this crowd I should be safe.

And Scrap was back, bigger and uglier than ever. And openly wearing his favorite pink feather boa.

I twitched the dangling end of the pink fluff. *About time you acknowledge the obvious, buddy.*

He almost purred as he rubbed my cheek with his own.

A larger group of people greeted us at the party already well underway. A lot of Bob Brown's friends had gathered to hold a wake for him in true con fashion. I couldn't think of a better way to finally say a proper good-bye to my best friend.

Gollum handed me a glass of single malt scotch. I climbed up onto the small dais and held my glass aloft.

"To Bob, may we always remember him with the love, the respect, the liquor, and the puns he deserves!" I toasted my best friend.

The crowd grew hushed as we downed Bob's drink of choice.

Gollum handed me a live microphone. Just like we'd planned.

I gulped and swallowed with uncertainty. Then the words in my heart made their way to my mouth.

"I knew Bob for a long time. We shared many things in common, including a love of filking. Which we will get to in a moment. But first, when Bob was dying in my arms, he asked that I sing at his funeral. I'd know which hymn."

I had to gulp back a spate of tears before I could continue.

"I couldn't bring myself to sing at the funeral." Just as I had not sung at Dill's funeral or his wake. Now I had to do it for both of the men I loved in very different ways. Maybe once I'd sung for them, as they both requested, I'd be able to say good-bye and move on with my life.

"Knowing Bob, and how much he loved a good con, I think this is the better place to celebrate his life with a hymn that meant a lot to him."

I opened my mouth and the beloved words of "Ave Maria" flowed from my soul. For both of the men I loved. For every person I had lost.

My voice soared, my heart swelled, and my tears fell.

Everyone in the room joined me in the last chorus.

After several long moments of grieving silence, someone in the back of the room, maybe Gollum, maybe someone who'd known Bob longer, struck up a rousing chorus of a folk song on a guitar. A flute and drum joined him.

Then we all burst into the best filk song ever written.

There's a bimbo on the cover of my book.
There's a bimbo on the cover of the book.
She is blonde and she is sexy;
She is nowhere in the text. She
Is a bimbo on the cover of the book.

There's black leather on the bimbo in my book.
There's black leather on the bimbo in my book,
While I'm sure she's lot's of fun,
My heroine's a nun
Who wears black leather on the cover of my book.

There's a white male on the cover of the book.
There's a white male on the cover of the book.
Though the hero-INE is black
With Art that cuts no slack. So
There's a white male on the cover of the book.

There's a dragon on the cover of the book.
There's a dragon on the cover of the book.
He is long and green and scaly,
But he's nowhere in the tale. He
Is a dragon on the cover of the book.

There's a rocket on the cover of the book.
There's a rocket on the cover of the book.
It's a phallic and a stout one,
But my novel was without one.
There's a rocket on the cover of my book.

There's a castle on the cover of the book.
There's a castle on the cover of the book.
Every knight is fit for battle,
But the action's in Seattle.
There's a castle on the cover of the book.

There's a blurb on the backside of the book.
There's a blurb on the backside of the book.
There's one story on the cover;
Inside the book's another.
There's a blurb on the backside of the book.

And my name is on the cover of my book.
Yes, my name is on the cover of my book.
Although I hate to tell it,
The publisher misspelled it,
But my name is on the cover of my book.

They reviewed my book in Locus magazine.
They reviewed my book in Locus magazine.
The way Mark Kelly synopsized it,
I barely recognized it,
But they reviewed my book in Locus magazine.

Well, my book won the Nebula Award.
Yes, my book won the Nebula Award.
Still it ended in remainders,
Ripped and torn by perfect strangers,
But my book won the Nebula Award.

So put that bimbo on the cover of my book.
Put a bimbo on the cover of my book.
I don't care what gets drawn
If you'll just leave the cover on.
(Don't remainder me!)
So put that bimbo, dragon, castle, rocket, vampire, elf,
or magic locket—
Please put a bimbo on the cover of my book!

Epilogue

Gollum and I flew to Seattle together the next afternoon. He stayed there. I flew on to Providence. As the plane circled Mount Rainier, the setting sun caught the folds of the uppermost glacier in a peculiar light.

"Is that what I think it is, Scrap?"

Might be. Y' never know, dahling.

"Can you sense anything?" I checked him for signs of solidifying and transforming. He remained a translucent pink.

The plane's in the way.

And then we were past the strange phenomenon.

The moment the captain cleared us to use the built-in phones, I dialed Gollum's cell, heedless of the hideous price they charged per minute.

"Gollum, have you ever noticed that the glacier on top of Mount Rainier looks an awful lot like Cthulhu, the alien god in Lovecraft's novels?" Cthulhu had become a cult figure, and most dealers at cons featured stuffed animals shaped like the multilimbed squid-faced embodiment of evil. "Do you suppose that Cthulhu is alive and well on top of that mountain?"

"Of course he is," Gollum replied nonchalantly. "The mountain claimed the lives of fifteen climbers and three skiers already this year. Can you think of a better explanation?"

Read a sample of *Moon in the Mirror*

In African folklore, trickster Hare was sent by Moon to first people with the message: "Just as the moon dies and rises so shall you." But Hare confused the words and said: "Just as the moon dies and perishes so shall you." Thus trickster Hare cost humankind its immortality.

THE WIND CIRCLED AND howled. It wailed with the pathos of an errant spirit trapped between heaven and earth with no hope. No end to its torment. It rattled the window latches and whistled down the chimney, seeking haven inside my old house.

My benign resident ghosts retreated, leaving me utterly alone.

That was all I needed. Another storm to knock the power out and trap me indoors with feet of snow blocking the doors. I saved the latest draft of my novel to a flash drive and switched to my laptop.

Finished or not I had to email it to my publisher first thing in the morning. If I had power and phone lines. Maybe I should do it now before the storm robbed me of access to the world outside. I had a reputation for punctuality to maintain. I also had a reputation for meticulous editing before I allowed Tess Noncoiré to appear on the cover.

I sent the email, with the promise to polish the last four chapters and resend them as soon as I was sure of power.

The wind increased its tortured moans.

I shivered in the preternatural cold. "Old houses are drafty," I reassured myself. If this kept up, I'd start believing my own prose.

Unconsciously I edged my chair closer to the huge hearth opposite my antique rolltop desk. My eyes strayed to the book on the plank floor, propped open with two other books. A research text on the folklore, monsters, and demons of the New World.

Research.

"Wendigo," I read and shivered. I'd encountered a mated pair of real Wendigo last autumn. Once human, they became one with the frigid northern wind, reclusive until they needed to hunt. Then they turned cannibal. They craved the blood of other humans, ever seeking to replace the souls they'd lost.

The book went on to theorize that the myth developed as an explanation for people of the north woods having to resort to cannibalism to survive especially harsh winters. If a monster bit them and they lost their souls, then humans hadn't done the unthinkable. Replace internal demons with external monsters.

Yeah. Right. The author hadn't ever encountered a Wendigo. I had. And I didn't want to do it again.

Ever. I'd come *this* close to becoming freeze-dried coffee grounds. All from a single touch of a shadow.

What the research book didn't say, but I'd learned on my own, was the Wendigo always hunted in pairs. To propagate they had to bite a victim and leave him living. He in turn had to bite a lover from his former life to create a pair.

Last autumn I'd killed one Wendigo. His mate still hunted me.

Was she the ravening wind that sought entrance to my home?

Did she seek a new mate, or was she bent on stalking me until one or both of us died? I didn't know.

"Damn it, go away," I shouted into the big empty house.

Not even my resident ghosts replied. I think they decamped to warmer climes along with my mother. After the third month when the temperature on Cape Cod didn't break freezing, Mom suddenly found a third cousin twice removed she hadn't seen since childhood who just happened to live in Florida.

Stay inside, Tessie babe. Demons can't violate the sanctity of a home.

Scrap, my otherworldly companion and weapon, whispered to me across the dimensions. From very far away. Too far away to come help me fight off a Wendigo.

Goddess only knew what Scrap was up to. Or where.

I'm stuck in the chat room. Big nasties trying to separate us permanently.

"Take care, buddy."

A pang of loneliness stabbed my heart.

Coffee. I needed more coffee. Well maybe I should switch to decaf. My nerves were jittery enough with that wind preying on my sanity.

I wondered if the tension in my neck was the precursor to a migraine. Normally I didn't suffer from them like Mom did. The wind often triggered them in her. Something about changing air pressure.

This wind was more than changing air pressure.

I coaxed my shoulders into a more relaxed position. No way would I fall victim to my mother's ailments. I was just worried about finishing the book. And staying free of the Wendigo.

I applied myself to the keyboard once more. Just a couple more hours of work.

If the damn wind would shut up.

The window rattled again, sounding very much as if a human hand tried to open the latch.

"Stay inside. Keep the doors and windows locked. Wait for dawn. Wendigo can't survive daylight," I repeated to myself over and over.

I dashed to the window anyway and checked the aging latch. Still closed.

Who could I call for help? My aunt, MoonFeather, the Cape's resident witch, didn't answer her phone. Gollum—Guilford Van der Hoyden-Smythe, Ph.D.—knew a lot about magic and demons and he'd helped me defeat the Sasquatch last autumn. Last I'd heard he was still in Seattle teaching anthropology in some community college. Too far away to do anything but talk. He was good at talking and not much else.

Then there was Donovan Estevez. Handsome, sexy, a fantastic fencer, and knowledgeable about demons. Too knowledgeable, probably from firsthand experience. No. No way would I make myself vulnerable to him by asking for help.

Something crashed in the kitchen. I jumped. My heart lodged in my throat.

"Scrap?" Please, oh, please, let it be the mischievous brat returning from wherever.

No answer. I crept from my office through the long dining room and adjacent butler's pantry, keeping well away from the walls and any shadows that might lurk there. At the entrance to the modern kitchen and breakfast nook, I paused and peered out.

No pots and pans littered the floor. The curtains lay flat against the windows.

Bang!

I screamed and leaped back at least six feet. Freezing air whirled around me.

Bang.

"Scrap, where the hell are you? I need help."

Distant mumbling and grumbling in the back of my mind.

Creak, creak.

Was that someone twisting rubber soles on wet linoleum?

I grabbed a butcher knife from the utility drawer and inched forward again.

Creak, creak.

A quick glance through the narrow archway. The back doors, on both sides of the mudroom, swung in and out, in and out in the freezing wind.

I wrapped my arms around my shivering body and cowered there in indecision for several moments.

Opening! I heard the wind wail.

Not daring to wait any longer I ran with every bit of strength I could muster through the mudroom and slammed the outside door closed. I twisted the lock and the deadbolt for good measure, something I rarely bothered to do. Then I shoved the heavy boot box across it.

A wicked laugh. *Not enough to keep me out.* An almost face appeared through swirling snow and shadows in the glass top half of the door. Frigid air made the aging wood pull away from the fragile pane. Shadows cast from the streetlight across the yard played tricks on my senses.

I couldn't tell if the Wendigo pressed close or not. Didn't dare wait to figure it out.

I darted back into the kitchen and closed the inside door. A chair shoved beneath the latch held it.

The laugh came again, this time followed by a voice singing a ditty from my childhood. A song my best friend Allie and I had cherished since kindergarten.

"Playmate, come out and play with me,

And bring your dollies three
Climb up my apple tree,
Holler down my rain barrel
Slide down my cellar door
And we'll be jolly friends forever more."

Cellar door! Oh, my God, were the slanted doors attached to the outside foundation latched? They'd been covered with snow for so long I hadn't checked the padlock on the outside or the crossbar on the inside for months.

No way was I going down the dark, narrow cellar steps with only a single bare bulb down there to light my way. No way in hell.

I jammed another chair under that door handle. "No lock!" I yelled. Why wasn't there a lock on this door?

Because that would make it too easy to get locked in the cellar while doing laundry. Damn.

Six volumes of an ancient encyclopedia on the seat of the chair anchored it better.

I sang the alternate version of the childhood ditty to bolster my courage.

"Enemy, come out and fight with me.
And bring your bulldogs three,
Climb up my sticker tree.
Slide down my lightning
Into my dungeon door
And we'll be bitter foes forever more!"

It didn't work. I still trembled in fear.

Not enough! A really cold gust whooshed down the chimney. The flames died. Coals faded from glowing orange and red to black.

I whimpered and threw some kindling into the grate. A cascade of sparks shot up the chimney. I added a log of heavy maple. Bright flames leaped and licked at the new fuel.

An otherworldly screech of pain responded to the fire.

You murdered my mate, an almost feminine voice snarled into my mind. *I will have retribution. A little fire won't keep me away for long.*

"Scrap, get your sorry ass back here," I screamed into the night. If he'd just come back he could transform into the Celestial Blade and I could defend myself.

Ordinary blades might slow down a Wendigo. All my mundane weapons were locked in a special closet in the cellar. Only the Celestial Blade could kill a monster.

The lights flickered, faded, then came back on. I bit my lip, waiting.

A crashing boom outside.

Dark silence. Not even the comforting hum of the refrigerator.

The wind kicked up three notches into a hysterical laugh.

I dashed from room to room replenishing every fireplace. In the parlor I used the very last piece of pine in the stack. Soft evergreen. It wouldn't burn long. I didn't dare close the damper or I'd smother in the smoke.

Ruefully I looked around, assessing the burnability of every bit of furniture in the house. The dining room table would last all night if I could break it up, along with the twelve chairs. Fortunately, I had a hatchet beside the big hearth in the office, to splinter kindling if I needed.

I double-checked every window and door. Prowling the house all night. Never once relaxing my vigil.

Neither did the Wendigo.

About the Author

Irene Radford is a founding member of Book View Café[1]. You can find a number of her books, both reprints and original titles, at the café. She has been writing stories ever since she figured out what a pencil was for. Editing, as Phyllis Irene Radford, grew out of her love of the craft of writing. History has been a part of her life from earliest childhood and led to her BA from Lewis and Clark College.

Mostly she writes fantasy and historical fantasy including the best-selling Dragon Nimbus Series and the masterwork Merlin's Descendants series. Look for her writing new historical fantasy tales as Rachel Atwood, a different take on the Robin Hood mythology, in *Walk the Wild with Me*, from DAW Books and the sequel *Outcasts of the Wildwood*. In other lifetimes she writes urban fantasy as P.R. Frost or Phyllis Ames, and space opera as C.F. Bentley. Lately she ventured into Steampunk as Julia Verne St. John.

If you wish information on the latest releases from Ms Radford, under any of her pen names, you can follow her on Facebook as Phyllis Irene Radford.

---

1.   https://bookviewcafe.com/bookstore/v

Other Book View Café Books by Irene Radford

http://bookviewcafe.com/bookstore/bvc-author/phyllis-irene-radford/

Merlin's Descendants Series *by Irene Radford*

Guardian of the Balance
Guardian of the Trust
Guardian of the Vision
Guardian of the Promise
Guardian of the Freedom

Confederated Star System by: Irene Radford writing as C.F. Bentley

Harmony
Enigma
Mourner

Trance Dancer

Trickster's Dance

Artistic Demons

Confessions of a Ballroom Diva
Confessions of a Piano Demon
Confessions of a Siren Singer
Confessions of a Changeling Dancer

Pixie Chronicles

Thistle Down
Chicory Up
Dandelion Twist

WHISTLING RIVER LODGE MYSTERIES

Whistling Down the Wind
Whistle While You Plow
Whistling Bagpipes
Ghostly Whistles

THE DRAGON NIMBUS NOVELS

The Glass Dragon
The Perfect Princes
The Loneliest Magician

The Wizard's Treasure
THE DRAGON NIMBUS HISTORY NOVELS
The Dragon's Touchstone
The Last Battlemage
The Renegade Dragon
SHORT STORY COLLECTIONS by Irene Radford
Fantastical Ramblings
Speculative Journeys
Steampunk Voyages
Magical Meanderings
NON-FICTION
Magna Bloody Carta
Committing Novel

ABOUT BOOK VIEW CAFÉ

Book View Café LLC (BVC) is an author-owned cooperative of over twenty professional writers, publishing in a variety of genres including fantasy, romance, mystery, and science fiction. Since its debut in 2008, BVC has gained a reputation for producing high-quality ebooks. BVC's ebooks are DRM-free and are distributed around the world. The publishing company is now bringing that same quality to its print editions.

BVC authors include New York Times and USA Today bestsellers as well as winners and nominees of many prestigious awards, including:

Agatha Award
Campbell Award
Hugo Award
Lambda Award
Locus Award
Nebula Award
Nicholl Fellowship
PEN/Malamud Award
Philip K. Dick Award
RITA Award
World Fantasy Award
Writers of the Future Award

Book View Café
304 S. Jones Blvd. Ste 2906
Las Vegas, Nevada 89107
www.bookviewcafe.com[2]

---

2.   http://www.bookviewcafe.com

www.ingramcontent.com/pod-product-compliance
Lightning Source LLC
Chambersburg PA
CBHW051059030726

47504CB00006B/1692